# A TIME FOR JUSTICE

A NOVEL

# A TIME FOR JUSTICE

ANONYMOUS

Hodder & Stoughton

First published in 1997 by Hodder and Stoughton
A division of Hodder Headline PLC

10 9 8 7 6 5 4 3 2 1



This novel is about crime, the victims of crime – and our prevailing criminal justice system. But no character in *A Time for Justice* is modelled on any real person, and no character who fills a real job-description or who occupies a real position in public life is in any way a portrait of any actual holder of such office or position, past or present. The motivations, relationships and conduct of all characters in this book are entirely fictitious.

The author and publishers are grateful for permission to quote from *A Clockwork Orange* by Anthony Burgess, published by William Heinemann Ltd, and reprinted with kind permission of Reed Consumer Books.

A CIP catalogue record for this title is available from the British Library.

ISBN 0 340 69297 9

Typeset by Palimpsest Book Production Limited,
Polmont, Stirlingshire
Printed and bound in Great Britain by
Mackays of Chatham PLC, Chatham, Kent

Hodder and Stoughton
A division of Hodder Headline PLC
338 Euston Road
London NW1 3BH

# A TIME FOR JUSTICE

## MAIN CHARACTERS

MARCUS BYRON, Crown Court judge
LUCY BYRON, his teenage daughter
JILL HULL, Lucy's mother, a probation officer
NICK PAISLEY, Crown prosecutor and Jill's partner
LOUISE POINTER, QC, Marcus's wife
SANDRA GOLDING, QC, Marcus's former mistress

MAX VENABLES, MP, Shadow Home Secretary, Sandra's husband
BRIGID KYLE, a journalist
JOE O'NEILL, a young journalist
WENDY BERRY, a court clerk, Marcus's sister
PATRICK BERRY, JP, a lay magistrate, Wendy's husband

SIMON GALLOWAY, of Oundle Square
SUSAN GALLOWAY, his wife
TOM, their small son
NIGEL THOMPSON, 16, of Oundle Square

LADY [CECILIA] HARSENT, JP, a lay magistrate
SIR HENRY HARSENT, a Crown Court judge
JIMMY HALEY-WHITE, a probation officer
LEELA DESAI, a probation officer
ANGELA LOFTUS, a probation officer
HEATHER STUART, a probation officer

LIONEL LACEY, Director of Public Prosecutions
GEOFFREY VILLIERS, an Oxford criminologist

INSPECTOR HERBERT KNOWLES, British Transport Police, brother-in-law to Marcus and Wendy
DETECTIVE SERGEANT DOUG MCINTYRE, of Eden Manor police station
DETECTIVE CONSTABLE CLIFF JENKINS, of Eden Manor police station
INSPECTOR KEN CRABBE, Metropolitan Police

SID GRIFFIN and his sons:
MARK GRIFFIN, 16
JOSEPH GRIFFIN, 15
DARREN GRIFFIN, 14 ('Rat Boy')

PAUL RICHARDSON, 17
AMOS RICHARDSON, 16
DANIEL RICHARDSON, 15
TRISH RICHARDSON, 13

# Criminal Justice System Abbreviations

| | |
|---|---|
| ABH | actual bodily harm |
| ACO | Attendance Centre order |
| ACOP | Association of Chief Officers of Probation |
| BTP | British Transport Police |
| C3 | Crime 3 (Home Office department) |
| CBA | Criminal Bar Association |
| CD | conditional discharge |
| CID | Criminal Investigation Department |
| CJD | criminal justice system |
| CPS | Crown Prosecution Service |
| DPP | Director of Public Prosecutions |
| GBH | grievous bodily harm |
| ID | identification |
| IT | Intermediate treatment |
| MCC | Magistrates' Courts Committee |
| NFA | no fixed address |
| PACE | Police and Criminal Evidence Act |
| PC | police constable |
| PS | Probation Service |
| PSR | pre-sentence report |
| QC | Queen's Counsel |
| TDA | taking and driving away |
| TIC | taken into consideration |
| WPC | woman police constable |
| YJT | Youth Justice Team |

# *Prologue*

SIMON GALLOWAY LEAVES HIS office in the City shortly after six, buys a *Standard* and heads for Bank tube station, his progress impeded by the rush-hour crowds. It is a warm summer evening and he would enjoy the longer walk to St Paul's station, but conscience prevails.

'Tom hardly ever sees you during the week,' Susie has chided him – and it's true: by the time he arrives home little Tom is normally asleep, his rosebud lips lightly parted. A kiss on his two-year-old son's warm brow is Simon's closest approach to fatherhood, Monday through Friday.

But what is a good father? Simon is now the family's sole breadwinner. He alone is earning serious money, though not serious enough – hence the pages of job ads in his briefcase. After a year with a firm of chartered accountants, Simon is convinced that it's time to move on and up. But the recession is still biting deep in the City and the competition is fierce.

Central Line trains are notoriously unreliable and prey to 'power failures' announced, if announced at all, in unintelligible English to jam-packed platforms. Simon squeezes into the crowded, west-bound train – no hope of a seat until Holland Park or Shepherd's Bush. Planting his briefcase between his feet, and strap-hanging from his upraised left hand, Simon attempts to juggle his *Standard* in his right hand, but gives up. Each rush-hour journey is forty-five minutes stolen from his life.

By the time they reach Shepherd's Bush the congestion has

eased. Simon slips into a vacant seat, glancing guiltily at an old Sikh who seems content to stand and a black lady who has just boarded the train. First come, first served?

Simon opens his paper.

He becomes conscious of a loud noise. It's a familar sound to any Londoner, a sort of bellowing-barking-honking- braying. The sound of drunken yobs. The doors of the railway carriage keep closing, opening, closing. The three young lads, each carrying several cans of Foster's lager, are in no mood to allow the train to leave the station. They keep ramming their legs and butts between the closing slide-doors.

'Hey hey ooay yea ooay!'

Simon glances guardedly towards them: all three are in their teens, one in a T-shirt, heavily tattooed, two in bomber jackets, all skinheaded. Despite a slightly comforting wall of standing passengers between himself and the yobs, Simon can see enough of their repulsive, drink-driven features to detect a familial link: could be brothers.

The train is moving now.

Simon pretends to read his *Standard*. Everyone around him is pretending to read newspapers, magazines, thrillers, or to stare into their own small, private unobtrusive space. Faces disappear behind barriers of paper.

Empty beer cans smash into the metal doors, roll on the floor. The lads seem content with abusing each other for the moment, but Simon knows the timetable of aggression, he has been here before.

The eldest boy is cross-eyed, low-browed and slightly moronic in appearance. The handle of a large screwdriver (probably) protrudes from his donkey jacket. The other two appear to be kidding him and stoking him up.

'You never fuckin' shagged her!' Simon – and everyone else, from one end of the carriage to the other – has to listen.

'I fuckin' shagged that cunt!'

'Wanker! You fuckin' never!'

The youngest – Simon's sidelong glance registers fourteen at the most – has grown bored with this family gathering, this fraternal dialogue. An unlighted cigarette dangling from his mouth, he is pushing along the central gangway, demanding a light. He accosts the old Sikh gentleman and the black lady, who stare glassily into space.

'Any fucker got a burn?'

Simon observes heads and necks disappearing into shoulders all around him. The lady in the adjoining seat is staring rigidly at the small adverts above the seats. This is no longer a world where men intervene to protect women. A laid-back youth with long hair and one leg cocked across the other looks faintly amused. A middle-aged City-man, who had also boarded the train at Bank, is closely examining the pink, financial pages of his *Standard*.

Conversation has died. The yobs have the sound-space all to themselves – though the passengers carrying Walkmans pretend that their headphones seal them off from all knowledge of what is happening. Simon is poised now to rise from his seat and confront the pale, spotty, pinch-faced, junk-food cigarette boy:

– You don't smoke on the underground, Rat Face.

But Simon does not move. Only three more stops and he'll be out. The other two beer-belching youths are following the youngest, egging him on, shoving and prodding people. Three stops seems like a long way.

Rat Face is now individualising his quest for a light. That's the fun, confronting people, picking on them, making them cower, one after another. He is leaning, swaying, over the petrified woman sitting beside Simon.

'Got a light, you old cow? Nah? Well, shit you, cunt!'

Is this London 1996? It is. Simon Galloway was born in the mid-sixties, at a time – his proud parents later told him – of 'social liberation and boundless optimism'. Well, that's gone.

'Gi' us a kiss, sweetheart! Nah? How about a shag then? So what's wrong with me, then? Hey, sooty, got a light?'

The train stops at White City. Any hope the yobs might decide they live here and tumble out?

No luck.

They're back at their door-prevention duties now, yelling, yodelling, honking, throwing empty beer cans at passengers on the platform.

'Up your fuckin' arsehole, motherfucker!'

Simon again glances towards them surreptitiously, like (he thinks) a cowering rabbit. All his instincts, his self-belief, his schooling are urging and prompting him to intervene, to confront these verminous bullyboys who trade on fear, but –

– he thinks of Susie, thinks of Tom, thinks of getting home intact. Social shame inhibits him, too: he knows he has so much to lose (including his glasses), whereas these young barbarians have nothing to lose. Brawling in a £400 business suit is not attractive. And they won't step back or cringe if you confront them. They'll simply raise the stakes! They're longing, itching for a bit of life, a bit of courage, a bit of a comeback from some have-a-go-hero. That's when the real fun starts. Even the yobs have a bit of 'morality' – that's why they assault far more young men than women.

Simon has not felt the same man since he decided he was too short-sighted to face the world without glasses.

The train is moving again. Thank you very much, incredibly decent of you. Simon's buttocks clench tighter in shame and dishonour.

Two seats down an elderly Pakistani gentleman is now the object of Rat Face's attention. They're all hassling the trembling old man. They're laying hands on him, they're trying to make him drink from their beer cans. Doubtless they have heard that 'Pakis' don't drink alcohol.

'Kindly!' the old Pakistani cries out. 'Kindly.'

'So why don't yer gi' us yer seat, yer Paki bastard?'

Simon slides his glasses into an inside pocket, grips his briefcase, discards his *Standard*, stands up and pushes past the standing passengers.

Close-in, the rabble stink of beer and unwash.

'I've got a light,' he tells Rat Face. 'You wanted a smoke?'

All three of the lads are focusing on him now.

'Yeah,' Rat Face says slowly. 'Show me your burner, cunt-head.'

'How big's your prick, Rat Face?' Simon asks.

'A comedian!' yells the other boy, not the cross-eyed one with the low brow, but the youth with the steady, filled-out face of a prize-fighter. 'We 'ave a fuckin' joker askin' for it!'

But all this takes time, all this swaying and circling and eye-contacting, and the train is slowing now, easing into Broadway Station. Someone has taken a bit of courage from Simon and pushed the red alarm button – the system instantly triggers into a high-pitched scream the length of the train. The uniforms of the British Transport Police, perhaps already alerted by the driver, can be seen running along the platform.

And in they come. They seem to know exactly who they are looking for. The brawl spills out of the train, rapidly spreading all down the platform. Evidently a whole lot more youths are involved. Simon steps on to the platform and into bedlam. Someone hurtles straight into him, sending him staggering.

The Griffin gang has been waiting to receive the Griffin brothers, Mark, Joseph and Darren. It's on.

The first policeman to board the fourth carriage of the Central Line train at Broadway Station is BTP Inspector Herbert Knowles. Someone has pulled the alarm, what they used to call the 'communication cord' in the better days when Herbert had first arrived in London from Barbados.

Doug McIntyre, of Eden Manor CID, has tipped him off in advance. A riot is planned – the lads call it a 'rev'.

'The Griffins are going to break up Broadway, Herb. You could be dealing with a dozen.'

Herbert Knowles knows why. Scores to settle. It's personal. It goes back in time. He has been at war with the Griffins for more than a year. Yes, it goes back in time, this business of the Griffin boys. They regard Broadway as their patch, their station, their 'Rule OK' – but Herbert doesn't agree. Last time he broke an arm making his point.

Simon Galloway observes the systematic vandalisation of the station with amazement. Walls, kiosks and ticket machines have already been defaced with aerosol sprays; new plastic platform seats are being ripped up, smashed with hammers. Glass panels shatter. The young hooligans in their flash trainers are far more mobile than the solidly built, thick-waisted Transport Police – there's nothing they cannot leap over, swing from, abseil down, whooping, yelling, feet thrashing.

Simon stands utterly helpless, and ashamed all over again. He sees a thick-set, sweating black BTP officer who has lost his cap in the mêlée, fasten the thrashing rat-faced boy in a headlock.

'You fuckin' nig arsehole cunt!' the boy yells. 'I'll kill yer!'

The lad is finally led away, handcuffed, by two policemen Simon recognises, McIntyre and Jenkins of Eden Manor CID. Isolated scuffles continue all along the platform and up the steps to the ticket machines, like the residual blazes of a forest fire.

Simon offers the black chap his name and address. 'I'd like to be a witness.'

Exhausted, chest heaving, Herbert Knowles extracts his notebook.

'Now, sir, did you press the alarm on the train?'

Simon blinks. The question sounds almost accusatory.

'No.'

'Are you prepared to appear in court as a witness?'

'Certainly. Definitely. That's what I meant.'

'People change their minds,' Herbert Knowles says with a hint of bitterness. 'Two months later they don't remember seeing anything.'

'Two months?'

'That's fast.'

Herbert Knowles has another case involving a Griffin boy in mind; Joseph Griffin has pleaded Not Guilty to dropping a concrete block on to the driver's cab of an InterCity express as it passed through Broadway Station at 70 m.p.h. At Broadway you have in fact two adjacent stations, connected by a bridge. One is the local, the Central Line, the other carries the high-speed British Rail trains in and out of Paddington. It was on the bridge spanning the main line that Inspector Herbert Knowles had recently arrested Joseph Griffin.

Hardly a day passes but some youth sidles up to him, outside the staff office or on the platform, warning him not to give evidence in court against Joseph Griffin.

'We know where you live, nigger.'

But this flushed have-a-go-hero, this Mr Simon Galloway, can know nothing of the real world inhabited by Herbert Knowles. Cross-eyed, plain brutal or rat-faced – no Griffin ever forgets.

Mark Griffin, sixteen; Joseph Griffin, fifteen; Darren Griffin, fourteen, otherwise known as Rat Boy: all three crawl like monstrous maggots across Herbert Knowles's upright life, their separate faces merging into one gargoyle at the moment when waking and sleep, duty and dream, are joined.

'Listen,' Knowles addresses Simon, 'you'd be wiser not to have seen anything. I can tear this page out of my notebook.'

'I don't understand. You need witnesses, surely?'

'It's up to you. But I've warned you, sir.'

# *One*

AT 8 A.M. SIMON GALLOWAY runs down the steps of 16 Oundle Square and heads for Ron Tanner's garage in Brancaster Road. A year or so ago Simon used to take the front steps two at a time, without looking, but now, as befits the father of a young son, he is a shade more cautious. He looks before he leaps. The glasses he wears are also new: strain of work, the optician said – stress.

Ron Tanner's repair shop nestles beneath the railway arches of Brancaster Road. As he strides along, Simon nods shyly to a neighbour he recognises but does not know by name. Simon's wife Susan is the one whom residents of Oundle Square stop and chat to. She cheerfully takes the minutes at quarterly meetings of the Residents' Association (at which one topic invariably dominates the agenda: crime). Simon is known as nice but reserved. He tends to carry a faint frown; his gaze is somewhere else, a little bit forbidding.

At this hour of the morning the streets are peaceful; the gangs of idling youths have not yet climbed out of bed. Mornings and birdsong gently wipe away the violence, the honking yells, the breaking glass of the night before. Mornings are the time of innocence.

Simon turns down a narrow alley beside the railway line. Ron Tanner's boots protrude from beneath a battered van. Although fitted with one state-of-the-art security device after another, Simon's L-registration BMW has been broken into three times during the past year. Brancaster Road resembles the emergency ward of a hospital unable to cope with a flood of battered casualties. Vandalised vehicles are regularly revandalised overnight – the gangs come like grave robbers.

Ron Tanner is a shortish, stoutish man, with a mop of dark hair and a grim humour. Emerging from beneath the van, he relights a burnt stump of fag which he keeps tucked behind his ear.

'The job's done, Simon, but I had to fit a new alarm system. How are your insurance premiums?'

'Terrible. Years of no-claims bonuses have been wiped out.'

'Perhaps you should trade in this BMW for a donkey cart. Mind you, these thugs would cut the ears off the donkey.'

'How do they unload what they've stolen?'

'Easy. They know the dealers. There's a villain called Alan Sanderson who supplies the mini-cab companies for miles around. For a new-model stereo the boys can get fifty, eighty or even a one-er.'

'A what?'

'A hundred quid. Frankly, this country's in a mess. On average I'm wasting my time at the magistrates' court once a month. Ever been to a magistrates' court?'

'No.' Simon glances at his watch.

'You lose half a morning before they send you home. Normally the vandals haven't felt like turning up.'

'Why don't they issue an arrest warrant?'

'You have to be joking. As often as not the lads are in the care of Social Services. No one wants them to miss their beauty sleep or their breakfast. "Victims of society" – that's what they are.'

'I'm late, Ron. Can I settle up with you later?'

'You're asking me to break the rule of a lifetime. No problem, Simon.'

The key is still in the BMW. Simon tests the new alarm. Gliding into the rush-hour traffic, he punches the pre-set on his radio. By coincidence his neighbour in Oundle Square, Jill Hull, is talking about crime on the *Today* programme. Simon's wife Susie works for Jill Hull three mornings a week. Jill's daughter Lucy baby-sits for the Galloways on the rare occasions they go out – little Tom adores her. Yet Simon has never felt easy with Jill Hull – or her daughter.

On the radio, as in life, Jill's voice comes across as flat and inexpressive. Deputy Chief Probation Officer Hull is talking about crime as if it were bad weather – no one is to blame and no one should get too steamed up about it. Simon waits for Jill Hull to use the word 'fear' – the fear now experienced by all residents of Oundle Square – but she doesn't.

'Generally we find that the best way to prevent reoffending is through diversion of the youngster,' she explains.

Guiltily Simon flips his pre-set to Radio 5 and the prospects for the coming Test Match. The thought of cricket restores his ailing sense of community. We are one people with shared values, surely? We keep the peace and help old ladies to cross the road – surely? Before he became a father, Simon used to enjoy a Sunday's cricket, or a game of squash, but now domestic duties have taken over. You can't be young for ever.

The day after tomorrow will be Simon's birthday, his thirty-second. Little Tom has been making a big thing of the secret present for his Daddy he has hidden away. Susie will certainly bake a cake. Simon smiles.

Lucy Byron lives at 23 Oundle Square with her mother, Jill Hull, and her mother's partner, Nick Paisley. On school days Lucy wakes early and 'sleeps late' – which means she lies in bed half the morning, day-dreaming, scheming, listening to her Walkman, and pretending to be sound asleep if Jill attempts to rouse her. Pretending figures high in Lucy's armoury of life-skills.

This morning she can hear her mother rising early in the adjoining bedroom. Lucy vaguely remembers that Jill is due to broadcast to the nation while its jaws are still fastened in disgusting slices of burnt toast. She can hear Jill reminding Nick that she has to reach Broadcasting House by 7.50 – and will he make sure that Lucy gets off to school on time?

'I'd be really grateful, Nick,' she says defensively.

By the sound of things through the wall, Nick, a senior official in the Crown Prosecution Service, does not regard this as one of his duties.

'You know I've got to be in the Crown Court by 8.30. You know it, so why ask? She's your brat.'

Yeah, that's Nick all through. Lucy reckons there is little love lost between them: it's more 'a marriage of convenience' – a phrase Lucy has picked up from a novel by Susanne Kaye.

Lucy knows her mother is worried about her all round. A note from Mrs Nearcliffe, Headmistress of St Hilda's, has described

Lucy's absenteeism as 'appalling'. The previous evening Lucy had overheard Jill and Nick discussing the Lucy-situation in the kitchen. (Overhearing is another indispensable skill, alongside pretending.)

'Perhaps I should cancel the broadcast interview,' Jill had said.

'You've got to do it,' Nick had insisted. 'You've got to speak out. We're going to stop this backlash dead in its tracks. I only wish *I* could get behind a microphone with an audience of a million.'

Lucy understands Nick's frustration – he's always muttering and seething. His boss, the Director of Public Prosecutions, has recently issued a directive banning all interviews by CPS staff unless cleared by his office. The CPS, like the Probation Service, is now feeling the heat of public criticism. 'We are gagged,' Nick keeps shouting, as if the word fires him up. 'Gagged! It's political. And we all know who's behind it.'

Lucy knows who he means. He means Jill's former husband, Judge Marcus Byron.

Lucy's father.

Lucy hears the front door close: Jill. Fifteen minutes later it slams: Nick. She can hear him revving his filthy old Toyota in the street below. She reckons it chokes him that Marcus owns a Rolls with a flash registration plate, MB1.

Marcus Byron occupies a smart flat three miles from Oundle Square. He and his new wife Louise live in a *beau quartier*, very posh. Lucy used to spend weekends with her father but not recently, no way, not with that pretentious bitch Louise installed. Lucy hadn't minded Sandra so much, mainly because Sandra Golding was just another mistress, married to someone else, and usually not there when Lucy arrived with her small suitcase.

But Louise – no way! Anyway, Marcus couldn't care less whether he sees Lucy or not – this has become an article of faith with Lucy. Articles of faith figure not far behind pretending and overhearing.

Marcus Byron has always prided himself on sleeping like the proverbial log. He has never allowed the pressure of work to disturb his seven hours of slumber, but recently his sleep has turned shallow, plagued by nightmares and grotesque, misshapen figures out of medieval allegory. He now wakes in the middle of the night with sweat pouring from him and newspaper headlines screaming in his ears:

– A woman stabbed fifty times while walking her child on a common.

– An infant boy abducted and beaten to death beside a railway line by two ten-year-olds.

– The stamped-on, smashed faces of five pensioners assaulted in their homes by a seventeen-year-old crack addict.

– A convicted rapist who was allowed to bicycle – alone! – from prison to adult education classes through the same leafy lanes where he'd raped a woman jogger.

– An £8,000 'working holiday' in Africa for a youth convicted of three robberies. A new Probation Service programme for hardened offenders announced by Jill Hull: to include drama workshop, cross-Channel sailing, waterskiing, rock climbing, abseiling, plus £30 pocket money for a shopping trip to Dunkirk.

– A father accused of repeated sexual abuse of his daughter, yet granted bail by Marcus's Crown Court 'colleague', Sir Henry Harsent, after four years on the run.

– Two policemen shot during a robbery, one while lying on the ground in a crowded street – yet no witnesses had come forward. No one saw anything. No one wanted to know.

Louise does not stir throughout the night. Blonde and thin, she lies beside him as if embalmed, her chest undisturbed by the procedure known as breathing. Awake, he studies his second wife's noncommittal expression without the joy he'd felt when this elegant, icy woman had accepted his proposal of marriage. Marcus had married Louise Pointer, QC, because she'd made it plain he wasn't going to get her any other way.

His radio alarm-call sounds, automatically activating the *Today* programme on Radio 4. His first wife, Jill Hull, comes straight through to him in her dreary monotone. 'Prisons are schools for crime,' she tells the nation, 'and they are expensive. It really is time our politicians and the media took a stand against the current popular hysteria instead of whipping it up to win votes or make money.'

Louise stirs ill-temperedly. Too often her day starts with one or other of Marcus's previous women sounding off on the radio, or breakfast TV, or in the newspapers. If it's not Jill it's Sandra Golding or Brigid Kyle. Occasionally it's Louise herself.

Marcus turns Jill off, plants his large feet on the bedroom Wilton, stretches and heads for the bathroom.

He's shaving while battling with condensation on the bathroom mirror when he hears the phone ring. Louise takes it in the kitchen. 'For you,' she calls. 'It's that woman.'

'What woman?' he shouts.

Louise keeps her finger pressed on the S button. 'Your latest.'

Lathered in shaving cream, he picks up the receiver in his study. 'Marcus Byron,' he says.

'Marcus, good morning.' He recognises the cheery, faintly Irish voice of Brigid Kyle, Journalist of the Year.

'Good morning, Brigid. And what mischief will you be up to today?'

'Marcus, if that's meant to be an Irish accent, I advise a weekend in Dublin.'

He chuckles. 'Oh yes? Who with?' Brigid Kyle always makes him chuckle. (Is Louise listening on the kitchen extension?)

'I'm visiting Eden Manor this morning in the company of a local journalist, Joe O'Neill,' Brigid Kyle says.

'Better you than me.'

'What's wrong with Joe O'Neill?'

'Never heard of him. I meant Eden Manor.'

'Marcus, your daughter lives in the neighbourhood. Isn't Oundle Square close to Eden Manor?'

'Too close.'

'Do you mind if I talk to Lucy after school? She probably knows the local youth scene.'

'All too well. Brigid, the girl is studying for her GCSEs. Lucy is journalism-crazy as it is. I'd rather you left her alone until after the exams.'

'Well, that's why I asked.' But Brigid sounds disappointed, perhaps slightly resentful.

Marcus offers to tell her a story about an Irishman who loved golf.

'Not now, Marcus, I'm late.'

Louise calls from the kitchen. 'Breakfast is ready if you could stop flirting.'

Lucy Byron turns over in bed, embraces the pillow, closes her eyes and settles to imagine love-making with Dan Richardson. She hasn't so far persuaded him to use a condom. 'It's down to you what happens,' he says. Restless, Lucy places both feet on her threadbare, tea-stained rug and yawns – must start getting to bed before 2 a.m. Twenty minutes later, both elbows thrust down among the unwashed cups and plates on the kitchen table, Lucy is twisting her long, wiry hair into tortured strands as she listens to her mother on Radio 4. Everything Jill says sounds to Lucy like an attack on her father. Lucy can clearly recall when they all lived in the same house in Charlbury Road, the one with the tiny duck pond. Dad used to feed the wild ducks when he remembered. Mostly he wasn't there. Lucy fed them.

In the hallway Lucy pauses at the mirror to inspect both her warring parents in her own reflection: sixteen years old and milk chocolate brown. Her contact lenses make her eyes sore. They fall to the floor and get trodden on. Must she wear 'granny glasses' like her mother? Lucy's broad nose and wiry hair belong to her father: but why am I not super-beautiful like Judge Marcus Byron? Why do people find me pretty at a distance but less so as I come closer?

Upstairs in her room, clasping a mug of coffee loaded with three lumps of sugar – she will never be fat – she opens a notebook and begins to scribble in a large, irregular hand which crashes down the page at an increasingly demented angle. In this notebook she rehearses her 'Bad Lucy' column for the 'Teen Scene' page of *Hello!* magazine, the column for which she earns one hundred quid – or will do when they recognise true talent and stop sending her literary pearls back.

> It had to happen, the backlash against last year's chichi frippery and prissy sweetness. The law-abiding deb look is out, the Bad Girl snarl is what it's about. This means lived-in lipstick, smudgy eyes, torn tights and all-night drinking dens of dirty dancing. The Bad Girl looks as if she's just vomited up a pint of Krug over a millionaire's lap, before accepting an invitation to redesign the bedroom of his Caribbean yacht. You'll find her in a sweat-stained pink rubber T-shirt and vixen high heels, stinking of grass and cheap sherry. The in-colours, sluts, are screaming fuchsia, organza and rotten cherry. Remember, witches, laws are for breaking.

If *Hello!* won't buy her gems, she can try the local paper again. The *Post*'s cub reporter, Joe O'Neill, always blushes to the roots of his thatch whenever Lucy raids his squalid hutch in her mini-mini skirt and threatens to sit on his knee. With eczema like Joe's, anyone would blush.

Lucy pinches herself: want to be an outright bitch?

It's a lovely day, clear blue skies after the morning mist. Susan Galloway is making a picnic for herself and little Tom. The boy is playing with his favourite teddy bear on the kitchen floor and chortling. Then he breaks off to search for Daddy's birthday present, a ritual game, though he's too young to know what a 'biday' really is. After the morning's shopping, Susie and Tom will head for the One O'Clock Club in Century Park. Tom is already making friends there.

Susie is fascinated by the behaviour of two-year-olds. They seem totally absorbed and delighted by each other's company. Old enough to make friends, they are too young to make enemies. They don't even know what an enemy is.

Simon has a theory about it – he inclines to theories. 'Only when children reach the age of three, and can take standing up for granted, is a bit of pushing and shoving feasible. By the time they are four, they're getting good at it. At five, they've discovered who does well at shoving and who does badly. At six it's turning nasty; at seven you have a playground full of criminals. At eight they're breaking into my car.'

Among the mothers she knows, only Jill Hull seems to take no joy in the role. Her Lucy is difficult, of course. Teenagers can be difficult. Jill strikes Susie as patient, long-suffering – and slightly evasive. Susie always feels she's hiding something.

Since having Tom, Susie hasn't wanted to go back to full-time employment as a teacher – she hopes to have another baby. Three mornings a week secretarial work for Jill, who lives a few doors down from No. 16, is just fine. Susie is mainly engaged in typing out Jill's speeches and articles.

Jill's Lucy is very good with Tom, an ideal baby-sitter when she remembers to turn up. It's on Susie's conscience, to be asking a girl who's studying for nine subjects at GCSE, but Jill believes that Lucy gets more homework done when baby-sitting. Tom is usually asleep by seven in the evening and there are no distractions.

'In theory,' Simon adds sceptically. He has his doubts about Lucy.

The house does occasionally smell odd when the Galloways return from an evening out and they sometimes have the impression that there have been visitors. The clues have included a couple of unexplained beer cans, a syringe which had failed to flush down the toilet and, fallen beneath an armchair, a small object which Simon's repair man, Ron Tanner, identified as a 'red-handled hammer'. Ron told Simon that they are commonly used to break car windows.

Simon had showed signs of annoyance. 'I'm going to ask Miss Lucy a few questions.'

'Darling, don't upset her. She's the only baby-sitter Tom really likes. With the others we can never get out of the house.'

'I wouldn't say that. I thought young Nigel Thompson was quite a hit with Tom.'

'Nigel's certainly very nice. But he seemed rather nervous – I'm not sure what he'd do in an emergency.'

'He'd simply call his parents. They live right across the square – no problem.'

Eric Thompson, Nigel's father, is one of the few Oundle Square residents Simon can be seen chatting to at weekends. Eric is a freelance inventor and engineer who has never quite hit the jackpot. Simon reckons Eric has been too trusting with the companies he approaches: they regularly 'reject' his inventions, then steal them. The Thompsons are quiet people; Simon likes quiet people, particularly Nigel Thompson, a studious boy currently winning the physics prizes at the Chaucer School.

Simon would like Tom to go to the Chaucer School one day. Meanwhile, he and Susie remain in mild disagreement about Lucy Byron.

Joe O'Neill and Brigid Kyle have taken a table in the Rialto café. It had been her idea – she'd insisted. The Rialto reeks of fried bacon and underdone pork sausages.

'I want to get into Eden Manor,' Brigid Kyle says. 'Right inside.'

'I wouldn't advise it,' Joe O'Neill says warily. 'Frankly, it's a no-go zone for . . .'

His pale Ulster eyes are evasive. This woman is famous for her piercing scrutiny – he can feel her counting the pimples on his chin. Eczema – he'd never shaken it off.

'They're not friendly to outsiders in Eden Manor, Mrs Kyle.'

'But you must know *someone* who would put me up for the night.'

'The night!' ('Put you up or knock you up?' he wants to say, but daren't.)

'I'm told that most of the action in Eden Manor happens at night.'

Joe assesses the charming woman across the grubby, Formica-topped table smeared with cigarette ash glued into pools of spilt ketchup. It's not a table to lean on. The woman looks slightly older than the little passport portrait which stares out at him, twice a week, above her celebrated column in the *Sentinel*, but her face is softer, warmer, than the fierce scowl which prefaces her famous diatribes. She's quite attractive if you dare to think about it. Glorious auburn hair – you can tell she's proud of it. Joe cannot help feeling flattered that she has contacted him. There isn't a public figure in the land who doesn't pray that Brigid Kyle will overlook his stupidity, incompetence, hypocrisy – or extramarital affairs.

Joe is uncomfortably conscious of two men laying eyes on them from an adjoining table. One wears a T-shirt with a violent, chainsaw logo; his hair straggles in long, bleached strands around his earrings; a stud gleams from his left nostril. Joe knows Alan Sanderson by reputation – very nasty. He's the one who pays expertly faked banknotes and no questions asked to the youngsters who bring him car radios, video recorders, graphic equalizers – anything with wires trailing out of it. He lends them screwdrivers and red-handled hammers when they're short. The other man wears nothing at all above his shiny beach-shorts. His muscular arms are covered in tattoos, mostly Union Jacks. He could be fifty years old but his bare torso is loudly challenging anyone to say so. Only a week out of Brixton Prison, Sid Griffin wears his hair closely cropped above his low, frowning forehead.

Joe O'Neill has never seen Sid Griffin without the frown. He'd rather not see him at all. Sid, father of:

Mark Griffin, Joseph Griffin, Darren Griffin.

The legend goes that local funeral directors cheer up whenever the head of the Griffin family is due out of prison on parole. Even the Probation Service has ceased to classify Sid as a 'victim of society'. But his three delinquent sons still qualify. 'They need help,' one of Jill Hull's probation officers recently told the Youth

Court justices. 'Some of their most vicious actions are really a cry for help.'

'Move on?' Joe asks Brigid Kyle.

She glances at her very expensive watch. He shudders: never do that! 'OK,' she says lightly. 'I'm in your hands.'

'We can walk by the canal,' Joe says. 'Might fish out a body or two.'

He can feel two pairs of eyes burning holes in their backs as they leave the Rialto. Three, if you include Sid Griffin's Alsatian.

'Look at all these shops boarded up!' she exclaims as they walk down the High Street. 'It's like a war zone!'

'The owners have all fled to Sarajevo.'

She whips a notebook from her handbag. 'Can I quote that, Joe?'

Young Joe O'Neill heats up titbits of boring news for the local paper. Brigid Kyle makes the news. Her salvoes and direct hits spread all the way down two columns of the *Sentinel*, then reverberate through Westminster and Whitehall. Joe can only dream of the fame, the power – and the salary! – this woman enjoys. According to rumour she also enjoys an intimate relationship with Judge Marcus Byron. If asked, at this moment in time, to define 'news', Joe would unhesitatingly reply: 'Marcus Byron.'

Brigid Kyle walks with the innate grace that some women have. She has an engaging way of pressing her shoulder into his arm while making him laugh.

'Joe, would I be far out if I guessed you were unlucky enough to be born in the Shankill Road?' (Among the most belligerent of Belfast's Protestant streets.)

'But which number?' he snaps back. She laughs. When she laughs she's seriously attractive. 'I might add,' he says, emboldened, 'that normally I have nothing to do with Catholics from Dublin.'

She tosses her auburn hair defiantly. 'You're going to tell me we breed like rabbits? And name me a single Ulster-Prod poet worthy of the name.'

'Seamus Heaney, Nobel Prize.'

'My God! Why not try Philip Larkin?' Then she laughs again and touches his arm. (How lovely she smells.) 'Joe, any work you do with me or for me will be paid for. Agreed?'

'I'm expensive, Mrs Kyle. There's a château in Normandy I have my eye on.'

They pass a young mother wheeling a small boy in a pushchair. He's clutching a teddy bear, poking its glass eyes and chortling. 'Biday!' he says to them as they pass. Brigid Kyle smiles at him. Tom Galloway smiles back.

'I thought he was going to propose marriage to you,' Joe says.

Joe O'Neill cannot know that he will be writing about the unknown young mother and her little boy before the day is out. He will remember her face, suffused with sunlight.

Susie Galloway and Tom emerge from Safeway's supermarket in the shopping mall and walk happily up the High Street in warm sunshine. Susie is thinking about Jill Hull and Lucy. While typing a speech in Jill's house the previous morning she had answered the phone.

'Give me Nick Paisley,' a West Indian voice commanded.

'He's at work. I can let you have his office number.'

'Just tell him Livingstone called. OK? Just tell him I've got some more of the usual, OK?'

Susie had duly written a message for Nick Paisley (whom she scarcely knew and didn't at all like when she met him – his expression reminded her of a ferret's). She'd wondered where she should leave the message. On the table in the hall? She then became aware that Tom was no longer with her in Jill's work-room. A small pile of coloured building bricks lay scattered across the carpet – but not Tom. Alarmed, she went in pursuit, calling his name. Finally she found him upstairs – these two-year-olds! – in Lucy's bedroom. Tom was sitting happily on the floor, playing with a grimy little plastic bag containing some white powder. Susie snatched it from him just as he was about to dip his fingers.

A framed photograph of Lucy with her father hung from the wall above her unmade bed. It must have been taken ten years ago – Lucy didn't look more than six or seven. Marcus Byron was smiling, slim, youthful and apparently without a care in the world. Both father and daughter sat astride bicycles in pleasant countryside. The picture exuded a feeling of happiness which Susie found moving and sad. Looking more closely, she saw that the father's face had been cancelled by two, thick, savage strokes of a felt-tipped marker pen – and later restored by rubbing.

'My God,' Susie had murmured to herself.

Nothing will ever part her from Simon, leaving Tom without a father in the house.

# *Two*

MARCUS BYRON'S SISTER WENDY BERRY reaches her office in Benson Street Youth Court at 8.45 a.m. Deputy Chief Clerk to the court, Wendy leaves her car in reserved parking, under guard, and enters the building by a private rear entrance. The current entry-code is AD1864, followed by an anti-clockwise turn of the handle.

Passing the fortified Securicor van which has shipped its daily cargo of youths held in custody, she can hear the more aggressive prisoners yelling and banging the bars of their cells below ground. Her court list for the day will reveal who these angels are.

Outside the main entrance to Benson Street Youth Court not a soul is to be seen at 8.45 a.m. An hour later, the deadline for the first batch of morning cases, human activity remains minimal. Towards eleven, gangs of youths, offenders and their supporters' clubs, will begin to gather, putting off the moment when they must submit to search. At the main entrance Burns Security guards run metal detectors across truculently twisting limbs.

'Keep still, son.'

'You're fuckin' me up!'

Smart baseball jackets, jeans, gleaming trainers; some youths arrive big and muscular, comfortable with themselves, while others of more fragile build lurk apprehensively. The younger Burns guards sport smooth faces of unspoiled innocence; the veterans resemble hotel rooms which have been trashed once too often. Most of the uglier 'customers' will arrive late, towards the end of the morning, just in time to prevent the magistrates issuing arrest warrants. The Burns guards know the regulars – seventy per cent are regulars.

They now include girls. Wendy can remember the time when, juvenile prostitutes apart, a single encounter with the law used to be enough for most of the girls caught shoplifting. Now even the girls are beginning to commit violent crimes: they arrive shouting and stay shouting. Four weeks ago a gang of fourteen-year-old girls hurtled out into Benson Street during the lunchtime recess, mugged a woman in a phone booth round the corner, tossed away her handbag and ran back inside the courthouse loaded with cash and credit cards.

The interior corridors of Benson Street Court, reserved for clerks and magistrates, are now secured by a succession of 'water-tight' doors with coded locks. Wendy's husband Patrick, himself a magistrate, says the setup reminds him of the submarine in which he served as a Royal Navy reservist. A computer programmer by profession, Patrick Berry is at ease with codes, but few of the lay magistrates can remember them and regularly have to be rescued. Cecilia Harsent arrives gaily shrieking for help and attention.

Lady H. adores attention.

Having set the coffee machine in motion, Wendy removes the dust cover from her new IBM. Under Patrick's somewhat impatient guidance she has now mastered the software, the Microsoft 'Word for Windows' programme, but the technology does nothing to mitigate the human problems in her work. She checks the orderly row of legal reference books, starting with Archbold, which will slide expertly through her hands whenever the defence lawyers become fractious – or Lady Harsent, today's Chairman of the Bench, decides that she is a law unto herself.

Wendy groans at the prospect of another long day in the company of Lady H. Patting her lacquered beehive and reeking of perfume, she will spray mindless chatter at a cowed court. Her hostility to Wendy is an open secret. Lady H. and Wendy's husband are currently in contention for the Chair of the all-powerful Magistrates' Courts Committee, known to professionals as the MCC – but not to be confused with the famous Marylebone Cricket Club. This is a fight to the death, no holds barred.

'I see your dear brother has been whipping up popular hysteria on television again, Wendy.'

Lady H. loathes everything Marcus Byron stands for. Her

husband, Sir Henry Harsent, is Marcus's colleague on the Crown Court, another 'circuit judge'. Here again the loathing is mutual.

How many conditional discharges will Lady H. hand down today? She adores CDs, insisting that they send the offender away with 'something to think about'. A CD incurs no penalty unless you commit another offence within a stated period of time, usually one year. In Patrick's opinion, CDs send all but first-time minor offenders away guffawing – you can hear them celebrating outside the court room in the company of their supporters' clubs – then off they go to the next offence, often within a stone's throw of Benson Street if not bang outside the court.

Cecilia Harsent would put King Kong on a CD after he'd eaten an InterCity express.

Patrick's duties as a lay magistrate are not onerous: once a fortnight on average. Most of his energies are absorbed as director of a security firm currently on test-trial for a potentially lucrative Home Office contract. Under a new scheme habitual offenders will be offered a curfew under bail, monitored by electronic body-tagging, as the alternative to custody.

Speaking for the Probation Service, Jill Hull has publicly denounced the scheme as 'unnecessary, provocative and tantamount to treating human beings like farm animals'.

Marcus had laughed his laugh. 'Yeah. Why not?'

Patrick hadn't wanted to stand for the chairmanship of the MCC but Marcus had insisted.

'It's only one skirmish in a wider war, Patrick, but it has to be fought. We can't let that plum-pudding Cecilia Harsent take over.'

Whatever Marcus says is good enough for Patrick. Marcus has obligingly heaped on Wendy the duty of coordinating Patrick's election campaign, which means nonstop telephone lobbying.

'A court clerk can't phone up magistrates to tell them who to vote for!' she had yelled at her brother.

'Just say, "This is a message from Marcus Byron." OK?'

Men! All so busy and burdened. She knows, of course, that Marcus will be making his own phone calls on Patrick's behalf, day and night. Marcus uses telephones like postmen use rubber bands; he loses half a dozen mobiles in the course of an average year. Dressed in wig and purple robes, he's quite capable of ordering a hot pizza on a mobile before sending a villain 'down' for seven years.

'Yes, yes, mozzarella with peppers take him down.'

Wendy checks her watch. In five minutes she must enter the retiring room to run through the day's court list with Lady Harsent. A young list-caller pokes her head in to report on the latest state of play in the public waiting area. Solicitors without clients, clients without solicitors – usual story. Extracting her private address book, Wendy checks several phone numbers she will call during the lunch hour. Each is marked with a blob of lemon-yellow ink. She suffers a stab of guilt: both Patrick and Marcus have warned her not to carry this address book to court – or anywhere.

She replaces it beside the small, firm lemon which sits at the bottom of her bag, takes a deep breath, and marches down the corridor towards Lady Harsent.

Brigid Kyle and her flaming hair continue their royal progress along the High Street under the nervous guidance of Joe O'Neill. A group of black lads are lounging outside Patel's corner shop, drinking from gleaming red Coke cans. Their eyes swivel constantly with that special alertness of the street-wise.

Joe can guess they haven't paid for the Cokes. Like other shopkeepers, the Patels have learned the hard way. The Richardson boys and their signed-up friends lift whatever they want, taking their time, bantering loudly, before drifting casually out of the shop with that special Afro-Caribbean swagger.

Two of them are sitting astride gleaming mountain bikes, newly 'liberated' no doubt.

'Hey, Joe!' Paul Richardson calls. Paul is the largest, heavy jowled, his jaw layered in stubble. You could mistake him for twenty-five though the police records say he hasn't yet hit eighteen. Magistrates of the Youth Court blink when Paul strolls in, hands in pockets. He sits before them with his powerful legs spread wide, laces unfastened, then cocks one big white trainer up on his knee, the price tag visible on the sole. Price tags don't get removed unless you pay for the shoes.

Paul Richardson:

> Burglary × 3. Supervision Order 1 year and 60 days IT [Intermediate Treatment] concurrent
>
> Fail to surrender [to police]. Fine £10
>
> Taking Vehicle without Owner's Consent. Supervision Order 12 months

Handling Stolen Goods. Supervision Order 9 months & 30 days IT
Burglary. Fine £20
Fail to Attend [court]. Attendance Centre Order 12 hours
Breach Attendance Centre Order. Fine £15
Theft. CD [Conditional Discharge] 6 months
Aggravated Burglary. Supervision Order 18 months (alternative to Custody)
Assault, GBH [Grievous Bodily Harm], Robbery, Theft x 3. Juvenile Offenders Institution [Downton] 3 months
Possession of Class A Drugs. Supervision Order 1 year.

Magistrates regularly see this lengthening *curriculum vitae* when sentencing Paul or setting bail conditions. Many of Paul's Supervision Orders are running concurrently, causing him no extra vexation at all – they simply melt down into one.

'Morning, Paul.' Joe nods, slows.

'So who's your posh dame?'

Joe glances at Brigid Kyle. He can tell she's about to whip out her notebook, flashing diamond finger-rings, a gold bracelet, a lovely little Swiss watch.

'Brigid Kyle of the *Sentinel*,' she says, extending her hand to the big black boy.

She'd be lucky to get her hand back, let alone the rings and her mobile telephone, but Paul Richardson is on his best behaviour while he's thinking. It's provisional of course. When Paul's thinking he tends to flex his shoulders as if pumping blood up to his head. The Griffins and Richardsons have one thing in common, a strikingly physical approach to the business of thinking. But nothing else: a Griffin never encounters a Richardson without disrupting the local ambulance crew's tea-break.

'Are you lads local?' Brigid Kyle asks intently. 'I'm writing a piece.'

A piece? Writing? The 'lads', as she calls them, look her over. They look Joe over. Writing isn't Paul Richardson's thing. No school has seen him, except during ram-raids and break-ins, since he was eleven. When Paul takes the oath in the Youth Court the usher has to read it out to him – Lady Harsent regularly emits a long moan of guilt on behalf of a callous society.

'Looking for a story, are yer?'

'Exactly,' Brigid Kyle says. 'I want to know how you young men see the world.'

Joe O'Neill could tell her.

'You're mixing with bad company,' Paul Richardson informs her.

The lady isn't sure what he means. Is he referring to himself and his friends, a nice touch of irony, of street humour?

'Sorry?'

Paul has often heard that word. Usually people are on their knees before him, grovelling in their own blood and gore, when the word 'sorry' emerges through shattered teeth.

'This fella.' Paul nods towards Joe O'Neill. 'He's got a bad attitude. He writes diabolical lies about us. He sucks the pigs' bums – shithead.'

It's clear to Joe that Paul is soon going to forget about being on his best behaviour. The 'thinking' bit is drawing to a close. His companions wear that furrowed expression, like dogs whose twitching ears await the master's command to strike. Brigid Kyle is gaily scribbling in her shorthand notebook. It's lucky the 'lads' haven't finished their Cokes and crisps – Joe makes a habit of conducting his most extensive street interviews with the younger generation as they emerge from the local fried-fish shop. You're fairly safe when they're carrying two quid's worth of haddock and chips.

The Richardsons idly observe a young mother and her push-chair toddler pass up the street, heading for Century Park no doubt. Paul's brother Amos studies her intently beneath his reversed baseball cap. He knows her husband's BMW well: 16 Oundle Square. No reason why he shouldn't get to know the missus.

In Joe's view Amos is the most dangerous of the Richardsons.

'You'll be late for your appointment with the Prime Minister,' he tells Brigid.

In fact the top politician most recently interviewed by Brigid Kyle was not the Prime Minister but a leading member of the Opposition, the Shadow Home Secretary, Max Venables, MP. She had grilled him for an hour on the hottest topic in politics, law and order, otherwise known as crime and punishment.

Almost every question she put to Max Venables had the same razor-sharp cutting edge: did he or did he not agree with Marcus Byron? Yes or no, please. How many of Byron's policies was the Opposition really taking on board?

Max had wriggled like a trout in a net. She had spared him in only one respect – she asked no questions about his wife.

Now, arriving at the House of Commons in mid-morning – moments after Joe O'Neill decided to move Brigid and himself away from the Richardsons outside Patel's corner shop – Max Venables is wondering whether he can ever again survive breakfast with his wife. It's a familiar feeling. It will wear off as soon as Max and the Home Secretary, Jeremy Darling, begin to toss hand-grenades at one another across the floor of the House.

The Rt Hon. Max Venables, MP, has had enough of Sandra but he has had enough of her for so many years – and she of him – that neither would feel comfortable in a home not riven with conflict.

No sooner did Jill Hull come on Radio 4 than Sandra began to tear strips off Marcus's first wife. To listen to Sandra, you might imagine that Marcus had deserted Sandra for Jill six years ago, rather than Jill for Sandra, but Max has given up accounting for the logic of women. Yet it is her devastatingly logical mind which enables Sandra Golding, QC, to prevail in case after case – one of the most sought-after barristers in England.

'Why does Jill have to sound like a half-empty kettle?'

'I wouldn't say that,' Max murmured.

'Jill can never forgive Marcus! Just listen to her! Drone drone! Why doesn't she just forget him?'

Max noted the battery-powered flutter of Sandra's already decorated eyelashes, the menacing thrust of her lower lip (blood-red today). Some High Court judge would be eaten alive in the course of the morning.

And yet Jill's position on crime and punishment is virtually indistinguishable from Sandra's. Both are leading members of the Congress for Justice, an ultra-liberal pressure group confined to 'practitioners' within the criminal justice system and criminologists. Having had Marcus Byron in the flesh, both women now want his head pickled in an autopsy jar. Sandra, too, can never forgive or forget Marcus Byron.

Max was attempting an escape through the front door.

'You're eating out of Marcus's hand, Max! You and the Boy! Max, come back! I'm talking to you. Are you listening?'

'I'm attentive.'

'You're betraying every principle of justice you ever believed in, Max.'

'I may be trying to protect the public.'

'Max, you're talking to *me*, not the readers of the *Sun.*'

'I'm late, darling.'

'And how can you enlist Marcus as your chief adviser when his current wife, that car-boot sale of a woman, is fighting me every inch of the way?'

'Marcus isn't my "chief adviser". We occasionally meet and talk, that's all.'

'And when did you last reject any proposal he offered you?'

It was like being interviewed by Brigid Kyle, only in reverse. 'When did you last fully take on board any of Judge Byron's proposals?' Kyle had challenged him, tossing her lovely auburn hair. Was it true that Marcus had bedded her?

Trying to ease his way out of the door, Max noted that Sandra remained an attractive woman, never more so than when ablaze. Her contest with Marcus's second wife, Louise Pointer, QC, was setting the legal profession into two fiercely warring camps – just as magistrates (so Max heard) were bitterly divided by the contest between Cecilia Harsent and Patrick Berry.

'It all boils down to Marcus Byron,' Max had advised the leader of his party, the Boy.

When they meet, Max and Marcus never mention the contest between Sandra and Louise for the chairmanship of the Criminal Bar Association. For both women winning is now less important than not losing; each wants the other's scalp as much as the prestigious job: in Sandra's case, a dark, heavily permed scalp; in Louise's, something more lank and Scandinavian.

Max obviously hopes his own wife will win – or does he? If Louise takes over the CBA, and steers all those truculent, rich barristers towards a saner system of criminal justice, his own work will be easier: one less powerful lobby at his throat.

Observing Louise Pointer, otherwise Mrs Marcus Byron, being interviewed on breakfast television earlier in the week, Sandra had assumed an expression sharper than the Oxford marmalade on the table. 'I've seen that blue suit before,' she remarked. 'I first saw it ten years ago. Louise must have let out the seams.'

And this morning Max had squeezed three-quarters of himself out of the front door when Sandra's battery-powered eyelashes snatched him back.

'I see Marcus is spread all over page ten of today's *Sentinel,*' she said.

'I hadn't noticed.'

'Of course you noticed, Max. Marcus is playing to the gallery as usual. It's that Brigid Kyle bitch who's egging him on. She's a hanger-and-flogger at heart. She's a paid-up Lemon, I'm sure she is.'

Bustling into his office in the House of Commons, Max Venables, Opposition Spokesman on Home Affairs, is grabbed by his secretary. The Boy wants to see him. She doesn't say 'the Boy', of course; they all speak of the Party's new Leader in awed tones. The Boy is very young, new to the job, and in danger of sweeping the Opposition into power after many years in the wilderness – so many years that Max Venables has seen his neat, goatee beard grow grey under the strain of permanent exile. The Boy has more than once made passing allusions to the beard – evidently the Road to Power is to be a clean-shaven one. But Max wouldn't recognise himself without the beard, indeed he's not at ease with the Boy's 'kitchen cabinet' of clean-shaven whizzkids who, masters of media manipulation, stormers of the City of London, friends of Industry, chums of Capital, worship only one word: New.

Max Venables is not entirely happy with New. Surely some traditional values have survived? 'Absolutely.' The Boy always agrees with him – an affectionate hand on Max's shoulder – 'Absolutely!'

Max can guess why the Boy wants to see him urgently. The Boy's timetable is as meticulously organised, grafted, smoothed, as a French high-speed train; at the end of the line, the destination, is a general election whose precise date the Boy has already predicted, though the Prime Minister of the day is normally thought to have that one up his trembling sleeve. Max has been summoned by the Boy, he can guess, because the Government, in the generally despised shape of the Home Secretary, the Rt Hon. Jeremy Darling, MP, is about to unveil a new package of draconian anti-crime measures. This, all opinion polls confirm, is what the public cares about. Even taxation is playing second fiddle to crime; even education and health. The Boy will want from Max a counter-package even more draconian than Darling's, even more punitive, but nicely garnished in a left-of-centre version of populism. Max's job is to steal all of Darling's clothes and then pump up the Remembrance Day poppy into a red rosette. Each time the desperate Darling attempts to put 'clear water' between his own policies on crime and the Opposition's, Max is instructed by the Boy to bump Darling's boat.

'Get close to Marcus Byron and stay there,' the Boy has instructed Max. 'He's the most popular Crown Court judge in England.' A pause. The Boy is famous for his pregnant pauses. 'And he's black.'

With a sigh Max prepares to confront his leader with some rather disconcerting rumours concerning Marcus Byron. They have landed on Max's desk anonymously and under plain cover. He'd been poised to shred them with contempt when several details arrested his attention. Whoever had compiled these documents knew a great deal about Marcus Byron – and his daughter Lucy.

Lucy has decided to drift into St Hilda's after all. She usually does. She's sporting a nose-ring already banned by the Head, Mrs Nearcliffe, and she's wearing non-matching psychedelic socks (also banned) beneath carefully torn jeans. Lucy weighs less than eight stone; food is ridiculous, though she occasionally plunges into the fridge on a binge and sicks it all up. In the art-and-design room she lays out the pages for the school magazine she edits.

The shock-horror item in the next issue will be on Truancy. Dynamite! When he sees it, that pimply Ulsterman Joe O'Neill will be on his knees, grovelling for first serial rights. Lucy knows all about first serial rights, though she's not sure what they are.

> Statistics show that girls truant as much as boys. And why not, sisters? What's so great about our ugly, horrible £10.5 billion education system? Let them drag us to the School Attendance Panel – ever heard of it? – or the Family Court (tremble tremble).
>
> Yeah. Truancy is down to lesson dissatisfaction. The National Curriculum, soul-mates, means National Boredom. All my skool-skipping buddies say so. Me and my mate Anonymous launch ourselves into fieldwork.
>
> Our first port of call is Ma Griffin, who twitches the curtains, takes us for social workers, sets her pit bull alight, and yells at us to f—off: you can read her lips through the grimy glass. Do we look like socials? Finally Ma Griffin opens the door of her odorous council flat wearing a go-away expression and tight Lycra cycling shorts which fit her only because they'd fit anyone – even my ex-Dad, who's famous for his biking and everything else he does in front of the cameras. (Sorry, personal diversion.)

Ma's pit bull and husband Sid's Alsatian clearly aren't keen on 'niggers' (Ma apologetically explains). Ma asks my friend Anonymous whether he isn't one of the Richardson boys, in which case he's got ten seconds to be the other end of Eden Gardens or dog food. Anon says he ain't, though he is, and Ma says she could smell a Richardson in a sewer. So far so good, very cosy.

Inside the flat the TV is shouting. A mess of half-clothed kids are cheerily strangling each other. Are they Sid's or Ma's latest fancy man's? Sid's done twelve of the last twenty years inside so you have to wonder. Me and Anonymous, we come clean about our mission – to find Jessy Griffin, aged nine at the last count, who's been missing from skool since god knows. We are indeed social workers. Ma Griffin calls the Headmistress of Eden Manor Primary a stupid bitch you can't talk to. She claims that the stupid bitch called her daughter Jessy stupid.

Ancient letters from the Council are glued by jam to the kitchen table but Ma G. can't read or write.

Finally she relents and offers us each a biscuit from the bottom of a packet. Judging by the mildew, Jack the Ripper must have eaten the others.

We can now reveal that one-fifth of kids fail to show up at skool because of boredom, one-fifth because they hate the teachers, and three-fifths because, like me and Anonymous, they're out researching the problem in depth.

My famous Dad wants to prosecute delinquent parents like Ma Griffin. He'd impose strict bail conditions on her pit bull too. His big political pal, Rt Hon. Max Venables, whose brilliant wife serviced my Dad for six years of nonstop poke, and who grovels to the Boy, wants to prove that the Opposition is every bit as bone-headed and vote-winning as the Govt. Cheers. Lucy.

Oh by the way, Lucy can now reveal: her Dad wants to be Lord Chancellor in the next Govt. It's on offer, almost, from the Boy. Ssssh. Handsome Marcus won't make it, too many women and other dark secrets. I'm one of them. I'll keep you posted, watch this space.

Cheers again.

English is the one GCSE subject that Lucy could pass with flying colours in her sleep. She knows that Mrs Nearcliffe will not only censor the report, she'll also summon Jill for a berating. 'Really, Ms Hull, deliberate illiteracy!' Mrs N. loves to say 'Ms' to a divorced mother with a sneering hiss. Yeah. Lucy reckons she'll barge in on spotty Joe O'Neill with this gem and threaten to turn him into a clockwork orange if he doesn't print it.

Haw haw, Joe will snigger. He fancies her, she can tell. Always greasing for an excuse to examine her Niger-Delta earrings.

Lucy opens the tabloid section of the *Guardian* at page 5. The hatefully self-promoting actress Teresa Kent is pictured in the latest Jane Austen TV serial. Typical! Lucy dreams of raking her nails across Teresa Kent's flawless, million-dollar complexion. The bitch's gold-lined life is always 'so tragic' and she loves every minute of it so long as the cameras keep turning.

One night, long ago – Lucy knows exactly when – she had discovered Teresa Kent in her father's bed. The celebrated judge and the glamorous actress had both attended some posh celebrity do to raise corn for the victims of crime. Yeah. Lucy remembers that incident as if it happened yesterday.

Yeah, Milady Kent is asking for it. Asking to be a 'victim of crime'.

Simon Galloway's L-registration BMW is trapped in traffic on the Hilton Avenue flyover. Anxiously he examines the digital clock on his dashboard. This is one job interview he cannot afford to miss – an American firm of trouble-shooters is offering a big salary to 'the right Account Executive preferably in his early thirties and prepared to work whatever hours it takes'. Simon feels sure the pay would be big, although the ad merely teased, 'Salary by negotiation.'

Roadworks!

Simon rehearses yet again all the ways of selling himself. He runs out of ways. He sometimes wishes Susie would go back to work. A teacher's salary isn't much but it helps. Still, she's happy with Tom. Money isn't everything. He has a theory about that – several.

He tunes his new car radio – his fourth in a year – to Radio 4. A clutch of legal pundits are arguing about 'crime'. They don't seem to agree about anything, except that society is to blame for the crime wave. 'The system is failing our young people,' he hears an elderly man called Geoffrey Villiers insist. 'The schools are failing them, the family is failing them.'

This Villiers is apparently an eminent criminologist from Oxford. Marcus Byron was one of his pupils – you can tell he's very proud of that because he keeps mentioning it. Villiers sounds to Simon like a drag queen.

'As I always impressed upon my distinguished former pupil, Marcus Byron, you cannot suppress crime without suppressing the economic causes of crime. Unfortunately Marcus did not listen.'

'Balls!' Simon tells Villiers. In Simon's view the country needs more Byrons and fewer bleeding-hearts like Villiers.

The traffic inches forward along Hilton Avenue. Simon sees a flashing blue light through his rear mirror. The screaming police car passes him, weaving from lane to lane. You always wonder what's happened – and what is going to happen.

# *Three*

WIGGED AND GOWNED IN purple, Judge Byron peers down from his raised dais in Crown Court 3. As usual the lighting leaves much to be desired; the English seem to believe that justice is best achieved in funereal shadow. His face is virtually featureless to any stranger sitting in the well of the court. Only two large, questing eyes indicate an acute brain humming beneath the white wig.

The defendant has been ordered to rise by the usher. Marcus leans forward to blast the Home Office and the police:

'Here we have a young man who had previously been released with a mere caution after confessing to aggravated burglary of people's homes. Released, he promptly did it again. He was again cautioned by the police. Why? "Aggravated burglary" means terrorising householders and threatening them. The relevant police inspector has appeared before this court and attempted to excuse his conduct by citing a Home Office directive. I draw the Home Office's attention to the law of the land. The will of Parliament is quite clear in the Theft Act: aggravated burglary merits a maximum sentence of fourteen years.'

The black judge glowers at the defendant.

'You are now convicted of a third aggravated burglary. I cannot blame you if the supine conduct of the Home Office and police on the previous two occasions led you to believe that you were engaged in a lark deserving a mere caution.'

Marcus Byron pauses.

'Four years. Take him down. Next case.'

The next offender, charged with possession of an offensive weapon and 'going equipped', had elected Crown Court trial – then changed his plea to Guilty shortly before coming into court. Nineteen years old, Wayne George is from Eden Manor and closely associated with the Griffin gang. Marcus listens to a long plea of mitigation from the defending barrister, Edgar Averling, a fat, paunchy, sloppily dressed man with the air of a fraudster on parole. Averling is a leading light of the Congress for Justice. His heavy lower lip pursues a half-life of its own; Marcus suspects that Averling's jowls may have been carved out of puff pastry.

'Your Honour,' concludes Averling, 'will of course wish to call for a pre-sentence report.'

He slumps into his chair.

'No need,' Marcus snaps. 'Show me his previous.'

Averling adopts the outraged expression of a barrister who can expect no justice from this judge.

The usher brings Wayne George's list of previous convictions to the judge. Marcus's large eyes flash down it.

Now he stares at Wayne George. 'Stand up.'

He waits. The court is very quiet.

'So why did you not plead Guilty in the first place, saving the overloaded system time and money? I'll tell you why. This morning you realised that the prosecution was able to produce its witnesses. Your counsel has predictably asked this court to mitigate your sentence because you have pleaded guilty. But when? Thirty minutes ago. The police witnesses are already waiting outside, wasting the taxpayer's money. A full half-day has been set aside by this court in expectation of a trial.

'Given your record, you might have avoided a custodial sentence if you had pleaded guilty to the magistrates' court. I am giving you six months. Take him down.'

Wayne George is brandishing his fist at Marcus. 'Fuck you, nigger! You'll be sorry.'

At this juncture the convict's mother pulls a dead cat from a sack and hurls it across the court at Marcus. It doesn't quite carry and lands at the clerk's feet in a splosh of blood and gore. The ushers throw themselves on the mother but Marcus waves them off.

'Madam, if you do that again I shall have to take a serious view of it.'

'Black bastard!'

'Guilty on one count only,' he murmurs.

He rises and strides out, leaving it to his elderly clerk, Arthur Henderson, to try and bring some other business forward to fill the empty morning. Reaching his retiring room, he writes another memo to Max Venables.

'Pleas should come first in the magistrates' court, mode of trial and committal proceedings afterwards.'

He had traversed this ground with Venables on previous occasions. 'The Bar Association will fight it,' Max had warned.

'What won't they fight, Max? They'll fight anything which reduces their fees for making something out of nothing. The public pays. The victims of crime also pay in terms of protracted wear and tear on their nerves. Months after they were robbed or burgled, no verdict has been reached, no sentence passed.'

Marcus knows he is making enemies among the powerful vested interests of the criminal justice system like a toad spawns tadpoles. He has always been at ease with the Press – far too much at ease, in the opinion of colleagues who grumble in corridors and club rooms about 'the sensationalist media inflaming the fears of the ignorant public'. In a recent interview with Brigid Kyle, Marcus had raised the temperature.

'Everyone now believes in open government,' he told her, 'except when their own professions come under the searchlight. Then it's time for discretion, for not rocking the boat.'

Even at this moment Brigid may be getting herself into trouble in Eden Manor. The Irish are headstrong! Why does he catch himself so frequently thinking about that flow of auburn hair?

'They'll destroy you if they can, Marcus,' she had warned him. 'They'll stop at nothing.'

He knew what she meant. 'Nothing' is a girl called Lucy.

The day after Brigid's interview with Marcus appeared in the *Sentinel*, Geoffrey Villiers replied on behalf of the Congress. Evidently there was no 'crime epidemic'. It was a myth:

> Statistics expose the stale myth of the good old days when ordinary citizens could supposedly walk the streets in safety, or supposedly leave their front doors open to the world, as an Arcadian fantasy. There never was such a time. Crown Court judges who cynically perpetuate this myth should be called to account.

* * *

Good old Geoffrey. The signatures supporting his letter were predictable: Jill Hull (Probation Service), Nick Paisley (Crown Prosecution Service), Cecilia Harsent (magistrate), Sandra Golding, QC (barrister), Edgar Averling (solicitor-advocate), Jimmy Haley-White (Youth Justice) . . . and so on.

What do these bleeding hearts really care about? Not the pensioners and single women who now cower behind locked doors after dark, the travellers shying clear of the Underground after the pubs close, the pedestrians scuttling through graffiti-fouled underpasses, the parents who no longer dare allow even their bigger children to make their own way home from school.

School! Marcus's mind freezes on Lucy. Lucy! He is flooded with pain.

Yes, the Congress can make any case out of statistics. But fear is something you can smell. No doubt the tabloid press invents monsters, psychopaths, brutes, thugs, yobs, rapists and child-abusers – but that still leaves us with the real ones.

Returning to his chambers during the lunch break, Marcus finds a message on the answerphone. Max Venables, the Shadow Home Secretary and desperate to become the real one, wishes to meet him in the Bow Street Tavern tomorrow at 12.45 p.m. The Tavern is a stone's throw from the Royal Opera House and a favourite watering hole for the legal profession. Marcus had once been an amateur opera singer of some talent, a resonant if ill-trained baritone who dreamed – no harms in dreams – of singing Verdi's Othello at Covent Garden.

'You are now an Othello surrounded by Iagos,' Brigid has told him, reaching across the table for his hand.

He had been touched and not merely by her hand. 'My wife never says things like that.'

'I'm glad to hear it.'

Now, alone in his retiring room, he opens a law journal and unwraps a cheese sandwich made by Louise. As he'd feared it's cheddar; she can't abide the French garlic cheeses he prefers. He tries to imagine Brigid surviving Eden Manor, but can only see Louise's taut face as she says, 'It's that Brigid Kyle on the phone again.'

Joe O'Neill listens to the snappy click of Brigid Kyle's sensible high heels as they approach the vast, sprawling housing estate via

Brancaster Road and Century Park. He points out the high-rise tower blocks of Eden Manor poking above the summer foliage. His stride falters.

'I think we may be walking into something,' he murmurs.

'Good! Much as I enjoy your company, Joe, it's time things livened up.'

Joe has spotted Darren Griffin's gang leaning against the railings of Century Park. There are five of them, all lads of fourteen and fifteen years old, all wearing brand-new trainers unlaced, and guarded, street-wise expressions implanted on pale, half-formed faces. Darren is the palest. Their eyes are sunken-dead as they watch Joe approach with his provocatively smart lady.

Joe has published two articles about the notorious 'Rat Boy' – and Darren knows it, though he can scarcely read the football league tables. The Griffin family, like their deadly enemies, the Richardsons, take a keen interest in their own Press coverage; beating up hostile journalists is something you do before climbing out of bed.

'How old is Darren Griffin now?' Brigid Kyle asks.

'Still short of his fifteenth birthday and therefore immune from imprisonment. The joke goes that the local Chamber of Commerce, the police and the Fire Brigade are planning to buy him the largest fifteenth birthday card ever seen.'

Susie Galloway and Tom have reached Century Park.

Married for three years, and together for seven, Susie and Simon have recently bought a lease on a four-room maisonette in Oundle Square, with a pleasant view of its small, tree-fringed public garden. Susie had given up teaching in a primary school to have Tom. She is guiltily aware of the extra financial burden on Simon; aware, too, that it is no longer customary for young mothers to abandon their careers.

Her secretarial work for Jill Hull is pin-money, barely sufficient to pay for Tom's clothes and washing-machine powder (she prefers the new liquid solvents you pour into a plastic ball). Jill has entrusted her with a key to No. 23. She and Tom arrive promptly at 9.30 three days a week and she works to noon. Often Lucy joins them in mid-morning and wants to play with Tom.

'But, Lucy, you should be in school!'

'Not today. We've got a reading period.'

'Then go and read, Lucy!'

Susie doesn't believe this 'reading period' pretence – Lucy strikes her as a fundamentally nice girl whose sense of discipline has been eaten away from inside. She smells odd, too. Susie knows little about the teenage drugs scene but Simon is convinced Lucy is addicted. When Susie once plucked up courage to mention Lucy's chronic absenteeism to Jill, the response was disconcerting:

'Oh, Lucy's a girl who has to find her own way. Adult censure is counter-productive. You will discover that when Tom grows older.'

Her work for Jill leaves Susie in no doubt that Jill is perfectly adept at censure when high principle requires it. Susie spends her mornings typing out one biting polemic after another. The target is invariably the same: Judge Marcus Byron and what Jill calls 'the new school of diehard floggers'.

Having heard the judge on TV and read his interview with Brigid Kyle in the *Sentinel*, Susie would not describe him as either 'diehard' or a 'flogger'. She has heard him make the best case against capital punishment she has ever encountered. Equally painful was Jill's phrase, 'Byron is despised as an Uncle Tom in the black community.' Evidently the judge had called for 'a calm debate' about the high proportion of muggings and aggravated burglaries committed in inner London by young black males. Jill had piled on her desk a sheaf of newspaper cuttings quoting angry rebuttals from black community leaders, politicians, probation officers and social workers.

> Byron's aim is to destroy ten years of progress [Susie was forced to type]. He has welcomed the Home Secretary's plan to build special prisons for children under fifteen.

Susie and Tom have reached the friendly little wooden gate of the One O'Clock Club. Tom leaps at the sight of his friends – those peace-loving two-year-olds! Susie crosses her fingers for Simon's job interview: better him than me!

Roadworks!

Should he call the American trouble-shooters from his car phone to explain that he'll be late for the interview? To make excuses? Is that the way to start? They say that first impressions are decisive. Yes, Mr Galloway, the traffic is always very heavy along Hilton Avenue. The other fifty candidates for the job all arrived an hour ago.

He fiddles with the bands on his radio, irritated by the queenly old don called Villiers and his fellow-criminologists. Villiers has been tenderly interviewing a fellow called Pete who has been in and out of probation centres, attendance centres, bail hostels and prisons.

'Do you regret what you did, Pete?'

'Nah. They didn't send me to Downton that time. It was just a squeeze. Nothing else matters so long as you don't get put into Downton or Brixton. They treat you like an animal in Brixton.'

The job interview is slipping away and with it the 'salary by negotiation'. Simon's thoughts slide despondently to Susie and Tom – his dependants. Where are they now? At the One O'Clock Club?

Back in wig and gown after consuming Louise's cheddar-cheese sandwich, Marcus Byron studies the afternoon list – one trial scheduled for two hours. Charge of street robbery and assaulting police. Two defendants. By a miracle all the witnesses, prosecution and defence, have arrived. The jurors are in place, looking eager to exercise their civic responsibilities now that they are in court at last, after the tedious hours of sitting around, waiting, being sent home.

Marcus explains their responsibilities to them. They must listen to the facts and the facts alone. The defendants are innocent until proven guilty.

'The burden of proof is on the prosecution. If in reasonable doubt, you will acquit. I warn you against the "I bet he done it" state of mind. "I bet he done it, what a pity they can't pin it on him" is no good. If they can't pin it on him by the rules of evidence, ladies and gentleman of the jury, he did not do it. As for the rules of evidence, you will listen to me and only to me. Is that understood?'

The prosecutor drones through the facts of the case. Marcus listens and doesn't listen. It's rather like driving. You can wake up from a long reverie, when your mind has drifted far away from the road, the traffic, and marvel that you didn't have an accident. Your driving consciousness was suppressed but nevertheless operational.

'Objection, your Honour.' Defence counsel is up.

Marcus nods. 'Objection sustained. Hearsay.'

But was it? Hearsay is one of the most complex branches of the rules of evidence. Decisions in the Appeal Courts constantly add a new twist. Geoffrey Villiers is the acknowledged authority on the subject but – as he recently told Marcus – 'I have to run to keep up.' Dear old Geoffrey. His most recent public attack on Marcus had been painful, but the price is worth paying. While intoning, 'Objection sustained. Hearsay,' Marcus is wishing he could chat to Geoffrey.

Geoffrey, of course, had founded the Congress for Justice. How many years ago? Marcus can't remember – yes, he can.

Villiers had been Marcus's law tutor at Oxford, the occupant of a splendid suite of rooms in a famous quadrangle graced by extravagant gargoyles. Marcus had heard about the notorious Villiers while still at school, but was still taken aback, on arrival, by the shoulder-length hair, the velvet jacket, the embroidered silk waistcoat, the cravat flopping at the neck – and the camp voice extended in permanent self-mockery.

Emboldened, defence counsel is objecting again.

'Don't overdo it, Mr Danbury,' Marcus murmurs. 'Continue.'

'My dear boy,' Villiers had greeted him, twenty-five years ago, when an awed young black face nervously poked round his door. 'You must not regard yourself as an outsider here. Oh dear me no. You are the Establishment's dream-scholar. You assuage our conscience. Heavens! Born into a family of six, raised in an East End council flat by your mother alone, you survived the roughest of comprehensive schools and went on to win an open scholarship. Oh very good.'

'Yes, sir,' Marcus had mumbled.

'Well, it all goes to show that Socialists like myself who moan about poverty and deprivation are despicable defeatists. Mix natural talent with ambition and the sky's the limit. Sherry?'

It was Marcus Byron's first taste of sherry and it went straight to his head.

'You don't sound as if you mean what you say, sir,' he ventured boldly. (He'd heard that you are allowed to say anything at Oxford.)

'You must call me Geoffrey. But a word of warning, dear boy: never tell any of your tutors round here what they mean. There is no more sensitive subject in Oxford than the meaning of meaning – if you follow me.'

Marcus had nodded shyly, though he didn't quite follow.

'Now tell me, dear boy, why you want to study law.'

Marcus had hesitated. 'To make money.'

'Oh, that's very good! I like that! Usually they tell me they want to serve the cause of justice or some such twaddle. What are your politics – if any?'

'I'm a member of the Young Socialists.'

'Oh, you'll soon grow out of that,' Villiers remarked sardonically. His suede shoes fascinated Marcus, who had never seen anything like them before. During his second year he stretched his scholarship grant to buy a pair at Dobbin & Son, in the Turl, but they always looked vulgarly new compared to Villiers's.

The prosecution has called its second witness, a police constable. He asks permission to read from his notes.

'When were they taken?' Marcus asks.

'Approximately one hour after the incident, your Honour.'

'Everything was still fresh in your memory?'

'Yes, your Honour.'

'Very well.'

*Just imagine him saying, 'No, your Honour, I couldn't remember a damn thing, I was pissed out of my mind, I made it all up.'*

Dear Villiers, the 'Dame' as his adoring undergraduates called him, had remained a friend for life – for more than twenty-five years. And more than a friend.

Marcus's thoughts swivel back to Brigid Kyle. She should never have gone into Eden Manor.

Brigid and Joe O'Neill stop short of Darren Griffin's gang as they lounge against the railings of Century Park.

'Morning, Darren. I'd like you to meet my friend, Mrs Kyle. She's a famous journalist come to interview you.'

Darren Griffin is known to the police, local shopkeepers, and finally to the community at large, as Rat Boy. This tag stuck after Joe O'Neill reported that the gang's latest hoard of loot had been found in a builder's tip close by the Binding Street entrance to the sewerage system.

At the age of fourteen Darren Griffin is too young to be put away in a Juvenile Offenders' Institution and too young to be named in the Press. And he knows it. Fines and Attendance Centre Orders have failed to deter him. He doesn't 'attend'. Saturday afternoons are for playing the hooligan on the terraces of the local Premier Division football club, not for taking shit from Ken Crabbe, the notorious disciplinarian who runs the Attendance Centre. As for fines, Darren doesn't pay them. Who does? When bailed on strict conditions, he immediately breaks the conditions – he will steal from a shop at 9 p.m. despite a curfew confining him at home after 6 p.m. Denied bail and put in Local Authority Care, he quickly proved himself too hot to handle. Ignoring curfews and the rules of the hostels in which he was accommodated, he was brought back to court again and again, and sat slouched, legs apart, sneering at helpless magistrates. After he set fire to a hostel kitchen he was convicted of arson, allowed to live at home again with Ma Griffin and given a year's Supervision Order. He never turned up.

This fact was not, however, reported by Social Services to the Youth Court. When a magistrates' Bench chaired by Patrick Berry interrogated the leader of the Youth Justice Team, Jimmy Haley-White, they were merely told that Darren's attendance had been 'patchy'.

'"Patchy"? What does that mean, Mr Haley-White?'

'We have to be sensitive to Darren's dislike of the criminal justice system, sir. Before we can address the reasons for his offending, we have to explore the reasons for his failure to cooperate with his case manager.'

Jimmy is a black Ghanaian and a charmer. Lady Harsent adores him and even the more punitive magistrates, such as Berry and the redoubtable Miss Swearwell, find him beguiling. A product of the Probation Service and a protégé of Jill Hull, he remains her most devoted disciple. With Jimmy at the helm, she maintains an iron grip on the policies of the Youth Justice Team.

Meanwhile, the computers of the criminal justice system race to keep pace with Darren Griffin, Rat Boy.

Criminal Damage, Burglary, Arson. Supervision Order, 1 year
Going Equipped, Burglary. Fail to surrender. Supervision Order, 1 year
Breach Supervision Order, Threatening Words & Behaviour,

Burglary, Handling. Attendance Centre Order, 24 hours (12 × 2 hours), Supervision Order, 2 years

Breach Attendance Centre Order, Offensive weapon. Actual Bodily Harm, Malicious Wounding. Compensation order £25

Burglary × 4. 143 TICs [similar offences taken into consideration]. Supervision Order, 3 years. Thirty days night restriction, 7 p.m. – 5 a.m. Compensation Order £205

Affray, Theft, Burglary. Supervision Order 2 years + IT. Attendance Centre Order 12 hours

Walking towards Century Park from the High Street, Joe has been explaining to Brigid Kyle that the only way Darren Griffin could be put out of commission is Secure Accommodation – but the Youth Court is not empowered to order Secure Accommodation. The Local Authority must apply for it, and fails (in fact refuses) to do so on the ground that Darren's crimes have been 'non-violent'. It's expensive, too.

Joe O'Neill's most recent report on Rat Boy in the *Post* – 'By Our Crime Reporter' – had caught the famous Brigid Kyle's attention and prompted her to seek him out.

> So Rat Boy and his gang continue to rampage down the High Street, and round the Broadway, and every street you could name, roaming ever further afield, thieving, robbing, burgling, threatening, revenging, and terrorising neighbourhoods in stolen cars and motorcycles. Shops are permanently boarded up. One florist suffered broken windows five times in two years before leaving the district. Rat Boy rides round on stolen mountain bikes taunting shopkeepers, particularly those from the Indian sub-continent: like others of his ilk, he hates 'Pakis'. Britain for the Brits.

Darren Griffin remembers who wrote that. Someone had read it out to him since he's not much into reading himself. The Griffins have warned Joe O'Neill. But Darren remains in ignorance of Brigid Kyle's follow-up piece in the *Sentinel.* Surely, she had argued, we do need secure detention centres for the most dangerous boys aged twelve to fourteen. She quoted Judge Marcus Byron:

> 'This issue will not go away,' he says. 'A very small proportion of very young boys are responsible for a very high proportion of

serious crimes. All remedial, cautionary and diversionary action has failed with these boys. They are in effect beyond the reach of the criminal justice system. Yet they are criminals.'

Now Brigid Kyle stands a few feet from Darren's gang as they lounge against the railings of Century Park, their jaws slowly rotating.

'Morning, Darren!' she says cheerfully, her gold earrings and gold watch glittering in the bright midday sun.

The gum-chewing youths are sizing her up. They've never seen this 'cunt' before – all females are 'cunts' unless beyond the age of sexual attraction. It's not even an insult.

'Not in school today, Darren?' Brigid asks.

No response.

'Do you believe that crime pays, Darren?' she presses.

'What else does?'

'How many brothers and sisters do you have, Darren?'

Darren smirks. 'Ask my mum.'

Even Joe has to suppress a smile, though smiling doesn't come easily when within mugging distance of a Griffin.

'Darren, would you take me to meet your mother?' Brigid earnestly presses the boy.

Joe shudders. For the past week or two he's had a hunch (from his police sources) that Darren's elder brother Mark is back on the scene. Mark Griffin is habitually on the run but occasionally surfaces around Eden Manor before vanishing into his hole. Darren's violence has hitherto been non-psychopathic but Mark is a different kettle of fish. Detective Sergeant McIntyre and Detective Constable Jenkins, of Eden Manor police station, are agreed about that.

'If Darren wants something,' McIntyre has told Joe, 'he'll do what he has to do to get it. Joseph is more prey to self-pity and blind rage. As for Mark, he should be in a secure hospital.'

McIntyre is sure that when Mark is 'on the scene' he goes home to be fed by his mum: he's very fond of food. Joe O'Neill is sweating. Brigid Kyle doesn't know what she's letting herself in for: Sid and his Alsatian, the illegal pit-bull terrier, and maybe Mark in amorous mood . . .

Mark Griffin's first indecent assault on a girl from a neighbouring flat in Eden Manor had occurred when he was nine, and therefore below the age of legal responsibility. Ma Griffin claimed that 'my Mark' had been teased and baited by other children until he didn't know what he was doing. He was put in Local Authority Care but later came home. At eleven he attacked a six-year-old girl in the boiler room beneath the flats. This case was proceeding slowly when he raped the same girl in a car parked across the road from where her mother was having her hair cut.

Mark was put in Local Authority accommodation for his own protection as well as the girl's, and the public's, pending trial. The Griffins' family lawyer, Edgar Averling, produced a psychiatrist who opined that Mark had a mental age of six, and virtually nil sense of responsibility when sexually aroused.

'In your opinion, does Mark know right from wrong?' Averling had asked the psychiatrist.

'Most probably not at the time of the offence. Guilt may surface later under severe pressure. We call this the Post-Event Syndrome.'

Cross-examining, a keen young prosecutor called Derek Jardine had asked the psychiatrist why, if he had virtually nil sense of responsibility, Mark had run away after each alleged offence and hidden himself.

Had the Griffins not been the Griffins, they would have had to leave Eden Manor, such was the high temperature of indignation and fear throughout the neighbourhood. It so happened that Sid Griffin was out of prison at the time; getting his retaliation in first, he assaulted the raped girl's father, accusing his daughter of being 'a fucking liar' and 'a tart who goes around asking for it'. Sid threatened to burn out their flat. The family left Eden Manor.

Mark had been in a number of Special Needs homes but had rapidly been expelled from each after assaults on staff. It cost £1,700 a week to keep him in Secure Accommodation at Nelson House, where the furniture is bolted to the floor, beds are welded into concrete plinths, windows are made of unbreakable glass, and no boy leaves his room except under the surveillance of two social workers, at least one of whom must never take his eyes off him. But Mark's assaults finally took their toll; the young murderers and rapists of Nelson House were as terrified as the staff of his sudden mood-swings.

Mark was released and disappeared. Frequently sighted but never caught. There was cunning in his madness.

Joe O'Neill had taken up the case:

> This boy, who cannot be named for legal reasons, is known by name to every resident of Eden Manor. No school in the country will admit him. No children's home can contain him. His father is currently in prison. The boy's mother told this reporter to 'Piss off!' As he retreated down the stairwell under a hail of invective, he gathered that the boy had been victimised by school teachers, by the police, by social workers, by quack doctors, by evil neighbours and by 'young sluts' who made false claims which they hoped to sell to the newspapers.

Joe reckons that Brigid's present 'interview' with Darren Griffin, which has so far yielded about five words from the boy, has lasted long enough. Her jewellery has become the main topic of attention.

'Let's walk on,' Joe suggests, 'or you'll be late for your interview with the Prime Minister.'

The attractive woman at his side accords him a look of polite contempt. 'The Prime Minister can wait,' she says. 'I always keep him waiting.'

Little Tom Galloway is playing happily in the One O'Clock Club sandpit. Susie and the mums have been gossiping and drinking tea. Tom has just poured a bucket of sand over another boy who rubs his eyes tearfully but shows no sign of anger. The mum leaps to stop him rubbing sand into his eyes.

'Oh, I'm sorry!' Susie says.

Peace is restored. Two-year-olds have no enemies. Everyone will need a big bath tonight but that's fun. With luck Simon will be home from his job interview in time for Tom's bath.

Then Susie sees him. It's a double-take: she looks, then looks again. A youth is leaning on the fence of the One O'Clock Club, staring at the toddlers intently. He might be fifteen, he might be seventeen. Low-browed and cross-eyed, he reminds Susie of the traditional village idiot. His dark hair is glued to his skull, matted with sweat and mud. Different calculations, even sensations, seem to take place behind each eye.

Susie scoops up Tom then runs towards the Supervisor's hut. Ruth Tanner is today's Supervisor. A local councillor and Chair of the Eden Manor Tenants' Association, she works for the

Borough's Leisure & Rec. department. Ruth is nice, fat and fortyish.

'There's an odd-looking boy over there,' Susie says.

Ruth Tanner peers through her small window towards the fence. Then she picks up the receiver of her telephone (newly installed by the Borough after a series of incidents, including one attempted abduction of a toddler).

'Can I speak to Doug?' she says softly, as if the cross-eyed youth staring over the fence might hear her. 'It's you, Cliff? Ruth here. I think we've got Mark Griffin about to join the One O'Clock Club. Get on your bike, lad, the one with four wheels.'

Ruth Tanner steps out of her hut and swiftly passes from one mum to the next. 'Don't leave this area,' she murmurs urgently to each. '*Do not* leave.'

'Who's Mark Griffin?' Susie asks, pathetically trailing after her and averting her gaze from the boy leaning on the fence.

'Mark's life has been a series of blown fuses, of trip-switches which failed to trip. One of the psychiatrists who treated him concluded that Mark no sooner wants something than he anticipates inevitable failure, the outcome being an ungovernable anger directed at whatever stands in his way. At whatever he cannot get.'

Susie glances – she cannot help herself – towards the cross-eyed youth.

'He's gone,' she says.

'He may not have gone far,' Ruth says. 'Mark Griffin can turn himself into a tree.'

'Do you know him?' Susie asks timidly. 'I mean, personally?'

'Boy! Don't I know each and every Griffin!'

# *Four*

MARCUS BYRON'S AFTERNOON DRAGS on. The charge is aggravated burglary. The two defendants have pleaded Not Guilty.

Marcus has been paying attention to the evidence while not listening. What he pays attention to is the technical status of the evidence. He can guess what's coming from the defence counsel. Ever since the right of silence was eroded, defence lawyers have been trying to get trials thrown out moments before they have to decide whether to call the defendants as witnesses.

'Your Honour, I wish at this stage to make a submission. I submit that there is no case to answer . . .'

No case to answer because the prosecution has failed to make a case requiring rebuttal. No case to answer because the charge has been wrongly worded under the relevant section of the Act. No case to answer because the crucial identification evidence is 'unsafe' – for example, the victim had later identified his assailant when the man was surrounded by uniformed police officers.

Anything, in short, to sever the trial before the jury could draw conclusions from the defendant's failure to testify or – if he opted for the devil in preference to the deep-blue sea – from his shifty, unconvincing performance under oath.

Almost invariably Marcus can predict the upcoming submission from the defence. Keeping awake until it arrives is the problem. He often wishes he had followed Geoffrey Villiers's advice and become a don, a criminologist, heading for the exciting frontier where law and ethics collide.

Marcus glances at his twelve jurors. Anyone awake? Of course, they're riveted. It's all new to them and the power of decision is theirs – unless, of course, Marcus throws it out, no case to answer, leaving them faintly aggrieved.

Marcus recalls his several confrontations with Max Venables after it became clear that the Government intended to erode the ancient and sacred right of silence. The Shadow Home Secretary is programmed to resist and denounce anything proposed by the Rt Hon. Jeremy Darling. Max had almost choked on his Australian lager when Marcus insisted that Darling, for once, had got it right.

'You want me to stand up and agree with that bastard, Marcus? I'd rather be seen on television eating a baby in Parliament Square.'

Marcus had laughed deeply. 'Just accuse Darling of botching a golden opportunity to reform the entire system – then abstain.'

Max had tugged nervously at his beard. 'The whole legal profession will be down on me like—'

'Then you'll know you are right.'

'You're not an easy fellow, Marcus. But I admit the opinion polls are on your side.'

'The public regards the untrammelled right of silence as a crooks' charter. So do I.'

Privately Louise agreed with Marcus, but she had begged him to keep his trap shut in public until she had won her fight against Sandra for the chairmanship of the Criminal Bar Association. For the Bar a defendant's undiluted right to silence – which means that no inference can be drawn from it – is the most sacred of cows.

Marcus promised her nothing.

The afternoon drags on in Crown Court 3. The usher approaches Judge Byron, inclines his head and hands him a sealed envelope. Only the most urgent messages are passed to him in court.

Is it Lucy again? Or has Brigid Kyle been murdered in Eden Manor? His mind constantly leaps across London to the flame-haired journalist. Was he wise to have told her, over a long dinner at Chez Victor, the whole story of his childhood, his Oxford years, his marriage to Jill – and Lucy's distressing decline into delinquency? He had never before confided so fully to anyone. Can any journalist be trusted?

* * *

Marcus and Jill Hull had fallen in love in an Oxford punt, drifting down the Cherwell past the gardens of Magdalen on a summer day. Love? Had they both mistaken gratitude for love? Each was captive to loneliness and insecurity. When he invited other girls into punts they brought a friend; Jill came alone, an intense, idealistic girl reading Politics and already set on a career in the Probation Service. It was Jill who inducted him into the National Council for Civil Liberties and the Howard League for Penal Reform. He failed to notice that she was also depositing him in her emotional savings account.

When they married four years later, she was the breadwinner and he still a struggling 'junior' in chambers. When they divorced in the middle of a messy custody battle over Lucy, Marcus was one of the youngest 'silks' (Queen's Counsel) in the country and effortlessly earning six figures for easing hardened, big-time, can-pay criminals out of the jaws of justice. He could make the slightest infraction of a defendant's right to silence sound like a disembowelling in Count Dracula's dungeons. The fees he received enabled him to donate his services virtually free to victims of police racism, authors prosecuted for obscenity, country footpath 'trespassers', nuclear protesters and an idealist civil servant charged under the Official Secrets Act.

In short, the clients sent to him by Geoffrey Villiers.

If Marcus was a Cavalier by temperament, Jill was a Roundhead. She saw less and less of him; news of his philanderings, his conquests, filtered back to her. Lucy scarcely knew him. His attention-span with the child was minimal. He forgot to feed the wild ducks. On the rare occasions Marcus was at home, he listened to opera records, dandling the devoted girl on his knee and smoking pot.

Brigid Kyle and Joe O'Neill are still engaged in edgy dialogue with Darren Griffin and his gang. Brigid does most of the talking, occasionally eliciting monosyllabic grunts from the slouching lads. No one has called her a 'cunt' to her face yet, but Joe reckons it's only a matter of time. Her watch and earrings both dazzle and provoke the Robin Hoods of Eden Manor.

One skinny boy is thawing out. He's quite keen on talking to the posh lady. His name is Jeff. Brigid extracts a miniature tape-recorder from her bag and holds it close to Jeff's mouth – now what would the main neighbourhood dealer,

Alan Sanderson, pay for a miniature tape-recorder, a real neat Japanese job?

'So you mean to stay on drugs, Jeff?' Brigid asks.

'It's not always the same drug, I mean you'd get bored. When I was less than five foot off the ground I was into Tippex thinner and lighter fuel. Later I rolled on from grass and hash to speed, but speed keeps you awake all night and you can't eat nothing without spilling it straight up. But I reckon the best trip is acid, just brilliant, know what I mean?'

'But you have to steal to pay for it,' Brigid says. 'That could land you in trouble.'

'I haven't been in no trouble,' Jeff says. 'I'm a fast mover.'

'And the future, Jeff? Your future?'

'The future takes care of itself, don't it?'

Darren is growing jealous. He's supposed to be the famous one here, the leader of the gang, the subject of miles of newsprint. Now he pushes Jeff aside and grabs Brigid's tape-recorder. But she holds on to it firmly.

'The reporter holds the mike, Darren. Now tell me, would you steal from anybody?'

'If I had to.'

'From your own mum, even?'

'I wouldn't steal from my mum but I might borrow something out of her benefit money if I was skint. Then I might forget to pay it back, because I couldn't, then we'd have a fight over it and she'd throw me out. I kicked a panel out of the front door, that brought our neighbours out, there was this fellow about fortyish waving a hammer, calling me a hooligan and everything, so I lost my temper and gave him one. That's how they got me for ABH but it was really self-defence so the police stitched me up, they're all sods.'

'You sound as if you feel sorry for yourself, Darren?'

'Who says?'

'What about your elder brothers, Mark and Joseph?'

'What about them?' Darren's aggression is rising. This cunt's jewellery is a fucking insult, it's a liberty, and she's still wearing all of it. Joe O'Neill can read Darren's thoughts, if that's the word. He wishes Mrs Kyle would call it a day.

'I'd like to meet your family, Darren,' she presses.

Suddenly his gaze shifts into long-shot. He laughs. 'Yeah. Here's one of 'em. Hey, Mark!'

Joe's attention follows Darren's: a cross-eyed youth is bearing down on them, grinning broadly, a hysterical little girl tucked under one arm. Her underpants are already down her legs; Mark Griffin is probing her privates with filthy fingers and guffawing. Drool drips from his chin. Joe sees a group of screaming mothers led by Ruth Tanner running in pursuit.

Joe moves to block Mark Griffin's passage. 'I'll take her,' he says.

Rage fills Mark's lopsided features. 'Fuck off! I'll kill yer!' The words rise thickly from a tortured throat; his Adam's apple is pumping.

Brigid Kyle steps forward. 'Hullo, Mark,' she says cheerfully. 'I've come to see you. I heard you're a very attractive young man to women.'

Mark stares. Grins. 'Yeah.'

'Surely a woman is better than a tiny child,' Brigid says. 'Don't you agree, Mark?'

'Yeah.'

'I have a little daughter just that age. Her name's Beth. I wonder what this little girl's name is. Why don't you ask her, Mark?'

Spittle is dripping off Mark Griffin's chin. The little girl slithers from his grasp into Brigid's arms. The wailing mother grabs her and runs.

Mark looks about him. He looks up at the high sycamores and beech trees as if listening to the birds. Now he studies his hands as if they were foreigners. He sees they are empty. Rage again pumps up through his twisting neck. He lurches towards Brigid Kyle, arms rigidly extended, fingers wide, as if to throttle her. Joe's fist thuds into his jaw. His hand yells in pain as the bones splinter. Mark staggers, stunned, but he's still on his feet. Joe kicks him in the groin; Mark howls, doubles up. Mucus drips out of his open mouth.

Rat Boy and his lads are watching all this with apparent detachment. Seconds later they have spirited Mark Griffin away. It's sewer time.

Marcus is about to open the sealed envelope handed to him by the usher when one of the jurors apparently suffers a heart attack. An elderly gentleman with a florid countenance who (Marcus noticed) had listened to most of the evidence with closed eyes, has suddenly keeled over.

'The court will adjourn.' Marcus rises. 'Make sure his family is informed at once,' he instructs the clerk as the court staff set about pumping the man's flagging heart.

Marcus carries the sealed envelope along a carpeted corridor to his retiring room. He is reluctant to open the envelope. It must be Lucy.

Brigid had been fascinated, nibbling at her poached salmon in Chez Victor, by one particular story he'd recounted about Lucy. Two summers ago Marcus, Louise, Lucy and her schoolfriend Amelia Harsent had embarked on a camping holiday in the Dordogne. He described Lucy sitting cross-legged outside her tent, reading by the light of the gas lamps gently flaring on the fold-up camping table. Skinny little Lucy in elaborately torn designer jeans, waiting for her hips to broaden, sucking the massive psychedelic bow which fastened her long plait of wiry hair. Lucy had begun to demand from Marcus those special hair creams for black women – as if to remind him.

Lucy squatting under the cloudless night sky of the Dordogne, absorbed in Anthony Burgess's *A Clockwork Orange*. Geoffrey Villiers had sent the book to his goddaughter as a fourteenth birthday present. (Many years earlier Marcus had noticed a copy lying on his tutor's table in college.)

Lucy had brought her friend Amelia to the Dordogne. Lady Harsent's daughter caused friction from the word go. Expensively dressed and quite incapable of lighting a gas burner without setting her long blonde hair on fire, Amelia made it plain that camping was an uncomfortable bore. She complained of the heat and mosquitoes all night long. Petulantly, with an expressive groan, she evaded Louise's educative attempts to persuade her to do her share of the washing up. Her dirty clothes she left where they lay. Louise fumed. On top of her spoilt, slovenly nonchalance, Amelia displayed a precocious interest in what went on in the tent shared by Marcus and Louise. She constantly dropped snide little remarks beyond her years. Marcus had no time for Lady Harsent, but the girl had recently adopted Lucy in school and Lucy thought she was the bee's knees (as Louise drily commented to Marcus).

The two girls went everywhere together, manically repeating phrases from *A Clockwork Orange*:

'Now for the other vesch, Bog help us all!'

'So he did the strong man on the devotchka, who was still

creech creech creeching away in very horrorshow four-in-a-bar . . .'

Lucy grinned impishly at Marcus. 'Do you know what "bar" means, Marcus?' (Lucy always addressed her father by name.)

'What does it mean?' (He hadn't disclosed that he knew the book.)

'You think "bar" means a place where adults buy alcohol, don't you? In fact it's all about music. Alex is high on music.'

'Really? Who's Alex?'

'The young hero of the story. You know that perfectly well.'

'"Hero", you say? From what I hear of him, he should be behind another kind of bars.'

'You would think that! You're the cobwebbed Establishment. Anyway, that's what *they* do to Alex when they catch him. Only it's not an ordinary prison, but a place where they give you a new drug and subject you to every kind of torture, I mean scientific experiments, that sort of thing, until you come out quite different.'

'Good idea.'

'You would say that!'

Furiously the book was thrown down, and off they would go, Lucy and Amelia, away and out of sight.

'Marcus, you shouldn't provoke her,' Louise murmured.

'She wants a father. She's got one. She needs to bang her wilful head against a firm super-ego. She'd hate me for humouring her. She doesn't want to see "Fuck the World" on my T-shirt.'

'I hope you're right.'

Marcus sighed. 'So do I.'

'Marcus, there's something I should have told you. Lucy says she keeps a list of the people you've sent to prison. She calls it her black notebook.'

'She doesn't know who I've sent to prison.'

Louise hesitated. 'Lucy says Jill and Nick keep her informed.'

Marcus fell silent for a moment. 'Should we believe her?'

'She showed me the black notebook.'

'Jesus.'

'You're mad to let the girls go off into the night, alone.'

'I can hardly put two fourteen-year-olds in shackles.'

One morning Marcus drove up the steep, winding track to the camp site from a shopping expedition in the village. As he parked, carefully reversing between the two tents, Louise was folding freshly washed clothes with unusually irritable motions. He assumed that she was about to complain that the girls treated her 'like a skivvy'. But her lowered voice made it clear that something more serious had happened.

'The police were here, asking questions about the girls.'

'Questions?'

'Apparently there was a break-in last night at a house in the village. The intruders got into some kind of outhouse – I wish my French were better. The owners were in bed, an elderly couple. They smelt smoke. They swear they saw two "youngsters" running away. One of them had long, blond hair.'

'Hm. Blond or blonde, I wonder.'

'The gendarmes are investigating a string of local break-ins, a succession of fires, all of them during the past week. They wanted to know when we'd arrived here.'

Marcus's face clouded. 'Where are the girls?'

'God knows. I think it's time to decamp, Marcus. I really do.'

He put an arm round her shoulders. 'Take it easy. Kids have to work things out for themselves.'

'We really must search the girls' tent and rucksacks – or you must. I'm merely "Dad's other woman".'

'But—'

'Marcus, I've really had enough of this so-called holiday. I've had that supercilious little Amelia bitch up to here!'

'I'll speak to the girls when they get back.'

'Like all fathers who feel guilt about a broken marriage, you'd go to any length to avoid your child's displeasure. And if you search their tent you're afraid of what you may find, isn't that it?'

'I'm not a snooper.'

Louise's expression tightened further. 'Marcus, those gendarmes advised us to leave. They know who you are. They spoke of you as "Monsieur le Juge". They said they'd prefer to avoid what they called "a diplomatic incident". You realise that you're responsible for whatever the girls have been up to? Arson is serious.'

'We're not due to leave until Friday. I don't want Lucy to think I run away from the consequences of what she does.'

The girls trailed in an hour later, hungry, Lucy sprightly and Amelia straggling behind, her long hair in a mess, complaining of blisters, flies, thirst, the heat.

'What's for lunch?' Lucy asked Marcus, although it was clearly Louise who was preparing it.

'Ask Louise,' Marcus replied.

'Not disgusting sausages again!' cried Amelia.

Louise didn't look up from the gas burners. Marcus could see she was trembling with anger. And so, finally, was he. He walked once round the girls' tent, bent to remove the pegs from the fly-sheet in a series of quick, decisive motions, then did the same for the main tent, lifted the frame, the uprights and the ridge pole, dismantled them into their components, then rolled the tents into their bags. But as he did so his hand encountered a number of objects hidden at the bottom of the bags.

A dozen boxes of matches. A packet of firelighters. A piece of firm, slender plastic evidently designed for springing locks. A pocket-size screwdriver. A tin of rolled cannabis with cigarette papers.

An assortment of stolen objects including a small, prettily gilded, mantelpiece clock '*produit de France*'.

The two girls were watching Marcus as if hypnotised. Carefully he loaded the stolen goods into his own canvas grip.

'Get in the car,' he told the girls.

'But, Dad—'

'Get in. We're going to visit the police. Then we will apologise to each of the local residents you have abused.'

An artificial smile was now fastened on to Amelia's flushed, sugar-plum features.

'That wouldn't be at all wise, Marcus. A Crown Court judge doesn't want a scandal, does he? I ought to know! Daddy's a Crown Court judge! Mummy's a magistrate! And when I telephoned Mummy to report that you and Louise are sharing a tent, she was very shocked, when you're not even married. "What a thing to do in front of Lucy," is what Mummy said. And I told Mummy that I could smell you smoking cannabis after you thought we were asleep.'

Surprise and distress were etched into Lucy's smooth young features. Tears were welling in her soft brown eyes. Marcus could guess that Amelia had put her up to the break-ins, the fires, the thefts – but Lucy was biting her tongue, loyal to her friend. They decamped without visiting the police station.

By the time Marcus finished this story in Chez Victor he was destroying a huge slice of chocolate gateau layered in cream while Brigid played with a crème caramel.

'And do you still believe, Marcus, that it was Amelia who put Lucy up to it?'

He shrugged grumpily. 'Louise shares your view.'

'But I didn't express a view! I only asked!'

As Marcus opens the sealed envelope in the retiring room of Crown Court 3 there is a knock on his door. It's old Arthur Henderson.

'The afflicted juror has miraculously recovered, your Honour. We are ready to resume.'

Marcus nods distractedly. 'Diabetic, is he? Give me two minutes.'

The door closes softly. Marcus reaches into the envelope.

Simon Galloway's L-registration BMW is still trapped in traffic on Hilton Avenue. He has abandoned all hope of making it to the interview on time – or at all. Each time he tries to get through to the office of the American trouble-shooters, the line is engaged. Are all the other candidates similarly jammed up?

A slender, rather shy-looking black youth is walking slowly down the line of stationary cars, offering to squeegee windscreens. At least he asks! At least he doesn't just bore in and lather the glass in filthy soap! Touched by this rare display of consideration, Simon finds twenty-five pence and nods at the black boy. He's in favour of a bit of enterprise.

So is Lucy's friend Daniel Richardson. Daniel has recognised the BMW of the bloke who lives at 16 Oundle Square. He'd kept watch each of the three times his elder brother Paul had done the car. A new radio and cassette deck on each occasion, twenty quid from Alan Sanderson, no problem. Daniel even knows the inside of the Galloways' house. Lucy had invited him in for a cuddle and a snort – or was it a jab? – when she was baby-sitting. Daniel is fond of Lucy, though Paul says she's just a cunt like any other cunt. She treats him nicely. She gives him books from her school library which never get returned. Lucy says she's black though her mum isn't. Sometimes she talks about her dad, a famous judge, in a funny way. If Daniel had a famous dad, or any dad, who took an interest and bought him things, he wouldn't slag him off – probably he wouldn't – but Lucy can't forgive her dad for jumping ship years ago. In Daniel's experience they all jump ship.

The boy begins to apply soapy water to Simon's windscreen. Simon studies his intense, thoughtful expression – almost studious – until it disappears behind the soap.

Simon hears the front passenger door open.

The note in Marcus's hand isn't about Lucy. It's from the Lord Chief Justice of England.

> Dear Marcus, I am frankly disturbed by your most recent exchange with the Congress. Your close association with the Shadow Home Secretary is also causing widespread adverse comment. I have spoken to the Lord Chancellor about it. He is not the least bit pleased. This is something we should discuss without delay. I suggest dinner at the Fitzroy. Would either Monday or Thursday of next week be convenient?
>
> Yours, as ever . . .

'The court will stand!'

Returning to his raised chair, Marcus's mind is squarely on Lord Chief Justice Theodore Bowers. This is it; Louise had warned him; Villiers had warned him; Wendy had warned him, though she and Patrick were one hundred per cent behind him; damn it, even Max Venables had warned him.

'Those whose heads rise highest above the parapet, Marcus, fall soonest!'

And that from a politician! Everyone had warned him.

He jerks his attention back to Crown Court 3. Not entirely to his surprise, the defence now submits that there is no case to answer. The essential identification evidence is 'unsafe'.

He nods. It is. Unsafe his whole life has been. He cuts defence counsel short, in mid-sentence.

'I can save you the trouble, Mr Nixon.'

'Thank you, your Honour.'

'The case is dismissed.' He turns to the clerk. 'Was it legally aided? No? In that case full costs are awarded against the Crown.'

He would like, as usual, to throw four words at the 'innocent' defendants: 'Don't do it again.' But that's not allowed. He rises and strides out, the Chief's note burning a hole in his pocket beneath his purple robe.

Vividly he recalls their first meeting at the Fitzroy Club in Pall Mall, shortly before Marcus's appointment as a recorder

– an 'apprentice' judge – of the Crown Court. A genial man at heart, Theodore Bowers is adept at disguising it. His bushy eyebrows seem to belong to a children's comic until they settle into a long, forbidding frown.

The Chief hadn't waited for the food before firing his first shots.

'They say we need more black judges,' he began. 'Personally I couldn't care less what colour a man is.'

If this was an invitation to an argument, Marcus readily accepted. 'Don't you think we need more black policemen, sir? To send a message?'

'It's a point of view. Pupil of Villiers, were you?'

'Yes.'

'What do you think of him?'

'His legal brain is second to none.'

'His legal brain doesn't seem to steer him clear of compromising situations in and around public toilets.'

Marcus sat silent on that. The Chief then began what was clearly a *viva voce*:

'A perfectly respectable man is involved in a minor traffic accident. Fearing that he is about to lose his licence, which is essential to his work, he later claims that his wife was driving. She goes along with it. What would you do?'

'That's a hard one.'

'You can't sit on the bloody bench, scratch your wig and say "This is a hard one."'

'Six months' Community Service for the wife, three months inside for the man.'

'Hm. I don't think much of this Beaujolais, do you?'

'It's very pleasant.'

'A young man takes a young lady out for the evening. He spends forty or fifty quid on the meal. Afterwards, the worse for wear, he misses his train, perhaps deliberately. She offers him her spare bed. They begin to kiss and cuddle in her bedroom. She allows him to remove her clothes without protest – that's agreed by both parties. When he then attempts intercourse with her, she says "No" several times. By the time he penetrates her by force she is crying. He does not claim that when she said "No" she meant "Yes"; he argues that her conduct had been so sexually provocative that flesh and blood would not allow him to hold back. As you can tell from my account, both parties display a high standard of probity as to the facts. The man is of previous good character. By the by, he's a solicitor. A rape conviction would finish his career. How would you guide the jury?'

Marcus had been sure that the Chief had chosen this one because of Sandra. Marcus remembered the case; it had come to trial at the height of his affair with S. Golding, QC. The solicitor accused of rape had been shrewd enough to ask for her services and she had refused. Her refusal had caused a storm in the profession; Marcus himself had berated her; Louise had promptly agreed to defend the man. Marcus had married Louise.

The Chief and his bushy eyebrows are waiting impatiently for Marcus's verdict.

'Well, sir, I would advise the jury to consider whether the woman's conduct had been such as to lead a reasonable man to believe that she was inviting intercourse. And whether she had then given him due notice that she was not.'

'What's "due notice"?'

'I'm not the jury.'

'If that's your guidance, wouldn't it simply depend on whether there were more men or women on the jury?'

'Yes, it often does.'

'Very well, Byron, the jury has found the bugger guilty. What are you going to give him?'

Marcus shrugged. 'On appeal one year was increased to eighteen months.'

'But what would *you* have given him as trial judge?'

'A Community Sentence. Hugely mitigating factors. Career ruined.'

The Chief smiled for the first time. 'I shall recommend your appointment to the Lord Chancellor.'

It didn't seem to occur to the Chief that Marcus might not wish to exchange a six-figure income for £60,000 a year – although that sacrifice would be deferred until Marcus Byron Esq., one of 440 circuit recorders, had graduated to his Honour Judge Byron, one of 246 circuit judges.

His windscreen lathered in soap, Simon hears his passenger door open – but how? Hadn't he locked the system? He sees another, larger black youth snatch his mobile telephone and run off through the stationary traffic. He's gone. Simon jumps out of the driver's door only to catch sight of the 'squeegee boy' also haring away. His wallet is missing from the inside pocket of his jacket, which has been hanging from a hook behind the driver's seat.

Other drivers are hooting at him to get a move on. No one offers to help.

Bastards! Quite apart from the loss of probably two hundred quid from his wallet, his precious time is stolen. He will have to look up his All Risks insurance policy to determine whether he's covered and there will be tedious phone calls to credit card companies, his bank, the AA, never mind his driving licence, his motor insurance certificate and his various memberships.

Merging with his rage is a sense of personal humiliation. Is he a dupe, a gullible softie, to allow this to happen? Fancy falling for the oldest two-handed trick in the world!

Simon is unaware that a motorcyclist has observed the whole operation and set off in pursuit. Detective Sergeant Douglas McIntyre had been patrolling Hilton Avenue in plain clothes, waiting to pounce following forty car-robberies during the past month, always at traffic jams; usually it was women's handbags and Rolex watches – any lone woman driving a BMW or a Merc is asking for it. But now the boys are growing bolder.

What a f—day! Simon Galloway heads for home.

Joe O'Neill and Brigid Kyle are passengers in Detective Constable Cliff Jenkins's red Metro – very cramped. Joe is nursing his broken hand.

'Stop wimpering, Joe.'

'He was a hero,' Brigid rebukes Jenkins. 'Of course,' she chatters gaily, 'we probably survived because I insistently addressed both Darren and Mark Griffin by name.'

'Oh really?' Jenkins says, turning the car into the casualty entrance of St Luke's Hospital.

'Yes. Few people will kill you if you address them by name. The reason is psychologically complicated. Basically, we all of us hide from ourselves when we are about to behave badly.'

'Really? Fancy that.'

'Oh yes, definitely. We hide behind the group, we hide behind anonymity.'

'And Mark Griffin is at this moment hiding behind a tree,' Jenkins says. 'Very fond of trees, Mark. Someone's for it unless we find him before dark.'

The 'very fond' sounds very Welsh. Jenkins helps Joe out of the Metro, places a comforting arm under his elbow, then leads him inside the casualty ward through glass doors which fail to open automatically. Alone in the police car, Brigid Kyle is already dictating by mobile phone a perfectly composed report for the *Sentinel.*

A mile away, Susan Galloway and Tom start their journey home through Century Park. The plastic carrier bags containing the morning's non-perishable shopping swing a bit awkwardly from the curved handles of Tom's pushchair. Susan is still trembling: she will never forget the moment when that cross-eyed brute called Mark Griffin pounced on the little girl. The police said he got away even though that brave young man knocked him down and hurt his hand. 'Walk home carefully, ladies,' Cliff Jenkins warned.

The park seems very large and very quiet. Susie glances at her watch: it's just after half-past two. Time for Tom's afternoon nap.

Three hours later Simon Galloway steps into an empty house.

# *Five*

'THE COURT WILL STAND!'

At 10 a.m. sharp Marcus Byron mounts the raised dais of Crown Court 3 in his purple gown, bows to the court, sits. The morning list will begin with the sentencing of two men, Knight and Green, convicted of cleaning out £150,000 of computer equipment from a technical college, inflicting grievous bodily harm on a security guard in the process.

A medical report in front of Marcus indicates that the victim might never work again.

Knight and Green are both residents of Eden Manor – or were until they took off and went to ground, living off stolen social security cards from a series of NFAs – no fixed address. Knight and Green belong to the criminal ring whose presiding baron was Sid Griffin, until Judge Byron put him inside.

Marcus's thoughts slide briefly across town to Benson Street Youth Court. His brother-in-law Herbert Knowles, Inspector of the British Transport Police and married to Marcus's elder sister Marcia, will be giving evidence this morning against Sid Griffin's beautiful son, Joseph. Wendy has warned Herb that Lady Harsent will be chairing the Bench. As Deputy Chief Clerk she knows the rota.

'Well, change it!' Marcus had roared at her over the telephone. 'Put Patrick on instead! The Griffins have to be nailed!'

'I can't, Marco, you know I can't! It's not in my power!'

Patrick had come on the line, taking the receiver from Marcus's simmering sister.

'It's just not on, Marcus. I'm standing against that Harsent bitch for the chairmanship of the Magistrates' Court Committee, but that doesn't mean I can kick her off the Bench every time a Griffin or a Richardson is due in court.'

'OK. Say sorry for me to Wendy.'

'That's a message I'm conveying to her rather too often, Marcus.'

Recalling the justified rebuke from a protective husband, Marcus glances down at Knight and Green. It's true that he has been short-tempered with Wendy lately. He believes it's due to frustration. In his view the national Press is unduly obsessed by the tiny minority of cases that reach the Crown Courts. Benson Street Youth Court is *the* battleground against today's crime and tomorrow's.

'That's where you should be looking,' he had told the flame-haired Brigid Kyle, star columnist of the *Sentinel.*

'But the Press isn't allowed inside, Marcus!' Brigid had said.

'Yeah.'

Yeah. But Louise believes his short temper with Wendy has a great deal to do with his sister's constant chidings and warnings about Lucy.

'I can handle my own daughter!' he had roared at Wendy.

'Marco, talk to Doug McIntyre and Cliff Jenkins! They're always warning me during the lunch break. Lucy is in with the Richardsons and the Richardsons are worse news than the Griffins!'

'I know all about the Richardsons.'

'Yeah, so do the Galloways.'

'Who?'

'A couple who live in Oundle Square. Lucy baby-sits for them. I'm telling you it's no coincidence they were both done over by Richardson boys in separate incidents on the same day!'

'What happened?'

Wendy told him. His anger rose like mercury in a boiling thermometer as he heard what had befallen the Galloway woman.

'That's nothing to do with Lucy,' he growled. 'Lucy wouldn't bring harm to anyone.'

'Except you?'

'You can leave me out of this.'

'Yeah. How long do you think "England's most popular judge" is going to be wearing his wig unless we do something about his daughter?'

Marcus again glances at Knight and Green as defence counsel embarks on his predictable pleas for mitigation. Marcus both listens and switches to his inner track.

The war for the sanity of England – it extends this morning from Benson Street Youth Court to the Court of Appeal, where Sandra Golding, QC, is no doubt explaining to their lordships why Marcus Byron is incompetent, biased and unfit to judge a turnip competition at a village fête. Yeah. Darling Sandra. Heavily made up beneath her little barrister's wig, she stands at this very minute before three justices of the Appeal Court, beautifully turned out in her famous, ground-breaking trouser-suit. Reporters and TV cameramen will have gathered on the pavement outside, in the Strand, to await the outcome of the appeal.

The case is listed as *Regina* vs *Dean*. To Sandra it's Golding vs Byron. Without exception, media editors have interpreted the Donna Dean case as an episode in the formidable lady's ongoing vendetta against her former lover, Marcus Byron. They cannot say so, outright, but they can hint.

Donna Dean is thirty-four years old. Marcus sent her to prison 'for life' after a jury convicted her of murdering her partner. She had stabbed him twenty-eight times as he slept. Sandra had argued 'provocation' and 'self-defence'. The dead man, she explained, had been violent for years, forcing Donna Dean to watch pornographic videos and to take part in degrading sexual practices. She had wanted to leave him but he had threatened to track her down – that was Donna Dean's story, and that was the basis of Sandra Golding's defence.

Was Donna Dean to be believed? The dead man, of course, was not in court to give his side of the story. The dead are inclined to silence (as Marcus reminded the jury in his summing up). The prosecution had offered evidence that Donna Dean had once secured a mortgage payment by fraud; she had also been found guilty of making a false income-support claim. So why believe her about the amount of abuse she had suffered from the man she had killed?

Women's groups had demonstrated outside the court during the trial. Justice for Women expressed 'outrage' at the woman's conviction, blaming Judge Byron for 'grossly misdirecting' the jury. Justice for Women is virtually Sandra's creation.

For murder a life sentence is mandatory – the judge enjoys no discretion.

Sandra took the case to appeal. Judge Byron, she is arguing before their lordships, including the Lord Chief Justice, at this very moment, had erred in ruling out 'long-term provocation' as a notion unknown to the law. Judge Byron had 'wrongly' directed the jury that a murder charge could be taken down to mere manslaughter only when severe provocation had *immediately* preceded the crime.

But Donna Dean had killed her man while he slept.

In Crown Court 3 Marcus has been listening carefully to defence counsel's pleas on behalf of Knight and Green – but he has so far 'heard' nothing. By 'hear' Marcus means something he didn't know already.

At the lunch adjournment the reporters will be waiting outside the Court of Appeal for the most famous female QC in England.

'Miss Golding, is it a coincidence that the trial judge in the Donna Dean case was Marcus Byron?'

Sandra will smile brilliantly. 'You know perfectly well that counsel is not permitted to discuss a current case. Besides, I never remember judges' names.'

'But', they will press her, 'what about your contest with Judge Byron's wife, Louise Pointer, for the chairmanship of the Criminal Bar Association?'

'Let's say that Louise Pointer would have some difficulty taking on Donna Dean's case. Mrs Byron has never been very strong on women's issues. She recently defended a leading medical man, a consultant, accused of sexually harassing a woman patient and two nurses. She reduced the women to tears during cross-examination. "Hell hath no fury like a woman scorned!" – she actually quoted that hideous epithet.'

Will Sandra go that far? Probably not. But Louise thinks she will. 'She'll stop at nothing to destroy us both.' The previous evening Marcus and Louise had shared their drawing room in constrained silence. Both were working but each was aware that work had become an alibi for non-contact. Marcus has observed tiny crow's feet nibbling beneath the curve of Louise's almond eyes, the patches of fatigue surfacing through her morning smile.

When they'd first met, he couldn't believe she was forty, but now he could.

'Marcus.' Louise laid her papers aside.

'A drink, darling?'

'I wanted to ask – and do forgive me – whether you really must – just at this juncture of my contest with Sandra – attack the prevailing system of legal fees.'

'Did I?'

'Your remarks were quoted in yesterday's Brigid Kyle column.'

'The legal profession is insatiably greedy, Louise. You've said as much yourself.'

'I may have said so in private.'

'Barristers demand huge "brief fees" in advance, they bring an army of solicitors or solicitors' clerks into court when it's quite unnecessary, passing the bill to the client. They place separate lawyers to represent each party even when they all want the same outcome from a case. They string out cases on points of procedure, totting up the "refresher" fees for each day and—'

'Marcus Byron, QC, was exorbitantly expensive if I recall. And I'm pretty expensive.'

He had shrugged. 'I'm not saying lawyers should earn four pounds an hour. I'm saying they should *earn* it.'

'With your help,' Louise said, 'a polecat could beat me for the chairmanship of the Criminal Bar Association – let alone a genuine fluffy pussycat like Sandra.'

The telephone rang. Louise took it then resignedly handed the receiver to Marcus. 'It's your favourite journalist again.'

He accepted the receiver. 'Good evening, Brigid. How was Eden Manor?'

'Lively. I interviewed the notorious "Rat Boy", Darren Griffin, then saw a child snatched by his maniac brother Mark. Joe O'Neill went to the rescue and broke his hand.'

'He's obviously not a professional.'

'And what does that mean?'

'Journalists are supposed to report rapes, not prevent them.'

'Thank you, Marcus. If I'd known that I would not have offered myself to Mark Griffin if he would spare the little girl.'

'You what!'

'Did you hear about the Susan Galloway case?'

Marcus remembered Wendy's painful warnings about Lucy and the Richardsons. 'Yes,' he said.

'An innocent young mother wheeling her toddler home!'

'It happens every day.'

'Apparently Susan Galloway works part-time for Jill.'

Marcus fell silent, reluctant to admit Brigid to the darkest of his most private premonitions.

'Brigid, did you hear the one about the Irishman who loved golf?'

'I presume it's a thoroughly obscene story?'

'He's very keen on golf, you see, this Irishman, and he's getting on in years, so he goes to his priest and puts a question: "Father, are there golf courses in Heaven?" The priest replies that he'll need to consult his superiors, and invites the Irishman to come back in a week's time. Which he duly does. "Well, Father, what did you find out?" the Irishman asks eagerly. "My son," replies the priest, "there's good news and bad news. The good news is that Heaven is a golfer's paradise." He pauses. "So what's the bad news, Father?" "The bad news, my son, is that you're due on the first tee at 7.30 tomorrow morning."'

That was yesterday. Emerging from his reverie in Crown Court 3 without having missed a word about the saintly potential of Knight and Green, Marcus bends his ear to defence counsel's concluding plea:

'Both men, your Honour, deeply regret their actions and the injuries suffered, though unintentionally, by the victim. I need hardly remind your Honour that both defendants are family men, with children to support, two in the case of Knight, four in the case of Green. Your Honour will perhaps agree that the children are invariably the ultimate victims of long custodial sentences.'

Marcus nods. 'Thank you, Mr Stainforth.'

His eye runs swiftly down the lists of previous convictions, then fastens on Knight and Green.

'Stand up, both of you.'

They barely can, such is this black bastard's reputation.

'Five years for Knight,' he says, 'seven years for Green. Take them down.'

'Everyone stand!' calls the usher in Benson Street Youth Court.

Beaming her 'Good morning!', Cecilia Harsent bustles into a crowded court room flanked by her two 'wingers'. Lady H. (who is simultaneously a member of the Adult Court, the Youth Court and the Family Panel) is a woman of inexhaustible energy. She knows how to fill her life. Cecilia Harsent belongs to that breed of upper-middle-class women who are accustomed to serve as full-time wives and mothers (despite the maids and nannies), until the passage of the years notifies them that there is no one left to mother. They then plunge into the magistracy.

In the retiring room, Lady H. habitually imposes two 'social' topics of conversation on her colleagues: her five grown-up children and her 'other place' in Yorkshire.

'We have this other place, you know.'

There is also her youngest, Amelia, 'who arrived late'. She is a pupil of St Hilda's School, in the same class as Lucy Byron. 'They used to be friends,' Lady H. explains to her colleagues, 'but poor Amelia finally gave up. The less said about Lucy Byron the better.' Cecilia Harsent can talk for fifteen minutes on why 'the less said the better'.

The Griffins also have 'other places', other residences – but not in Yorkshire. Joseph Griffin has been on the run and is now held in a cell below the court room.

Fifteen years old, and the second of the Griffin boys – younger than daft, cross-eyed Mark, older than 'Rat Boy' Darren – Joseph has repeated his name, age and date of birth in court many times. On occasion, when first arrested, he offers alternative names, addresses, ages. The spitting image of his father, Sid, deathly pale, skinheaded, he is covered in tattoos. If Mark does it for sex, and Darren for money or loot, Joseph often does it for kicks. In his estimation, every year his dad has spent in prison is worth a Victoria Cross.

Joseph is now an expert on Victoria Crosses because he stole one from a pensioner's flat, at knifepoint, without knowing what it was. The silly old geezer had put up a struggle and been sorry. Aggravated burglary – the case should have been committed to the Crown Court, but a bench chaired by Lady Harsent had retained jurisdiction, despite protests from the prosecutor, Derek Jardine, and Lady H. had later refused to send Joseph to Downton Juvenile Offenders' Institution: in short, to prison.

A pre-sentence report from Jimmy Haley-White's Youth Justice Team had recommended yet another supervision order for Joseph, and that was that. Lady H. never overrules a PSR. She pats her beehive hairdo and beams compassion and understanding.

Four weeks have passed since Joseph's trial on quite a different matter – even experienced court clerks have difficulty keeping up with which offence is at which stage of the judicial process. Today Joseph appears for sentencing. Deputy Chief Clerk Wendy Berry remembers in total detail what had transpired, a month ago, when Joseph pleaded Not Guilty to a charge of dropping a lump of concrete from a railway bridge at Broadway Station straight through the cab-window of an oncoming InterCity train.

For the prosecution, Derek Jardine swiftly outlined the case then called his witnesses: two civilian bystanders who had observed the event, and British Transport Police Inspector Herbert Knowles, who had been called to the scene.

This being a case involving the Griffin clan, special precautions had been taken. The witnesses were accommodated in a reserved room during their two-hour wait for the trial to begin; and when they stepped up to give evidence Wendy invited them to write their addresses on a slip of paper which the usher then handed to her.

Joseph's counsel, Edgar Averling, had objected to this procedure; the addresses might reveal that the witnesses were neighbours of the Griffins, or bore a grievance, real or imaginary, against Joseph. (Many people did.)

Wendy Berry had intervened firmly, addressing Lady Harsent.

'Madam, I can tell the court that no one about to testify lives within half a mile of Eden Manor. Madam, witnesses appear in court today on condition that their addresses will be protected.'

Lady H. nodded. 'Very well.'

For the better part of half an hour Edgar Averling had cross-examined the two civilian witnesses, both of them passengers who had been waiting for a Central Line train on the day in question. Averling did not challenge their good faith, merely their eyesight.

'I put it to you that Joseph could easily be mistaken for any one of a hundred other boys of similar age and physique. I put it to you that Joseph was innocent of the deed but merely ran to the scene after hearing a dramatic crash.'

But the witnesses were stubborn. They had seen Joseph drop the concrete block on the speeding train.

Averling smiled sceptically. 'And what boy would not want to have a look, madam?' he asked Lady Harsent.

Next to be called was Inspector Herbert Knowles, of the British Transport Police. Wendy always avoided eye-contact with her brother-in-law when he appeared in court. Good old Herb resembled the walnut you cannot crush after Christmas dinner. They – Wendy and Marcus – normally had Christmas dinner with Herb and Marcia, who was the best cook in the Byron family, though Marcus's attendance depended on whom he was married to at the time. In Jill's time he had always turned up with his wife and little Lucy. In Sandra's time – not that he was married to her – he came alone, unless spending Christmas in Cannes or St Tropez. As for Louise, her own family obligations had so far prevailed.

No one found the frosty Louise easy. Marcus told his family she was 'shy'.

The little usher was timidly asking Herbert his religion before he took the oath.

'Baptist,' he replied huskily.

That threw her. She was new to the job. A new religion. In vain she fumbled through the pile of Bibles, Korans and Torahs beside the witness stand.

'The Christian book will do,' he told her, barely suppressing a chortle and a Hallelujah.

Herbert then described how the concrete block had lodged in the window of the driver's cab as the train passed through Broadway station at 70 m.p.h., nearly killing the driver (who had been off work ever since) and putting at risk the lives of two hundred passengers.

'Were you present when the offence took place, Inspector Knowles?' the prosecutor, Derek Jardine, asked.

'No, but I was on the scene within two minutes.'

'Where was Joseph Griffin when you arrived?'

'He was standing on the bridge from which the concrete block was thrown. He was looking two hundred yards down the track towards the stationary express train. He was grinning. Even as I approached him he laughed. "Spot on," was what he said.'

'Did you caution him?'

'I did.'

'What did he say?'

'I am a Christian and do not like to repeat his exact words.'

'You may use the word "expletive".'

'He said, "Expletive off, you expletive nig."'

'Was the expletive a four-letter word beginning with f?'

'It was.'

'Did you arrest him?'

'I did.'

'Did he resist arrest?'

'He did. I was kicked in the shin. I handcuffed him after a struggle.'

The obese Edgar Averling, who had recently qualified as one of the new solicitor-advocates, with entitlement to appear in the Crown Court, rose heavily to cross-examine. Averling nowadays confined his personal appearances in the magistrates' courts to serious cases only – and the Griffins, like their Eden Manor neighbours the Richardsons, were excellent, long-term clients. The legal-aid fees flowed and flowed.

'Inspector Knowles, you did not see Joseph Griffin commit any unlawful act, did you?'

'No.'

'You did not see Joseph drop a concrete block on the train, did you?'

'No.'

'Would it be true to say that you have personally been involved in confrontations with Joseph and other members of his family both before and after the time of this incident?'

'That's true.'

'Did you take part in the arrest of Mark, Joseph and Darren Griffin at Broadway Station on the fourth of this month?'

'I did.'

'Did you say to them, "I'll nail you this time, you bastards"?'

'I did not.'

'Were you hurt during that incident?'

'Several minor bruises.'

'So you are biased against the Griffins, are you not?'

'No, sir. I see what I see.'

'You have taken upon yourself a personal mission, a crusade, to "nail" Joseph Griffin, have you not?'

'Only for what he has done.'

The defence called no witnesses. Joseph chose not to give evidence. The Griffins never did.

The Bench retired. The verdict came swiftly. Even Lady H. could not gainsay the overwhelming evidence.

She called for a pre-sentence report from Jimmy Haley-White's Youth Justice Team.

'Serious enough to merit a community sentence,' she added quickly. Wendy could sense from their expressions that Lady H. had consulted neither of her colleagues, both of whom would have insisted on 'So serious as not to exclude a custodial sentence.' But Lady H. was adept at the rapid, irreversible decision – the Bench could hardly stage a blazing row in front of the court.

Wendy Berry was seething. She could imagine the feelings of Herbert, seated at the back of the court. She had discussed the case at home with Patrick. Both were agreed that Joseph Griffin should originally have been committed to the Crown Court, since a sentence of six months' imprisonment – the maximum available to a Youth Court – was totally inadequate. But Lady H. had been sitting on the day when the Youth Court resisted the prosecution submission and accepted jurisdiction.

And now she was ruling out a custodial sentence!

Wendy glanced at the prosecutor Derek Jardine. He should be up on his feet, lodging notice of appeal against a non-custodial sentence – but young Jardine's boss within the Crown Prosecution Service was Nick Paisley, who did not believe in sending youngsters to prison. Or anyone.

Six weeks have passed.

Joseph Griffin has been on the run, or 'hop'. He has skipped the date set for his sentencing on the small matter of dropping a concrete block on to the driver's cab of an InterCity express. It has taken a warrant-without-bail (issued by Patrick Berry) and several policemen to bring him in to Benson Street Youth Court. Surrounded by Securicor guards, Joseph enters the court room with something between a slouch and a swagger, Sid Griffin's heir apparent.

Wendy knows what prevails in Edgar Averling's thoughts: Lady Harsent is again chairing the Bench. Joseph will not be going to jail. Nothing else counts; no alternative sentence will make a dent on Joseph's life-style. Downton Juvenile Offenders' Institution is the only sentence he fears.

Wendy Berry addresses the Bench. 'Madam, the first matter is Joseph's breach of bail and failure to attend on the date set.'

Edgar Averling rises heavily. 'Madam, the date slipped Joseph's mind entirely and his mother tells me that she was at fault for not reminding him. She was confused by several different court appearances involving her children.'

Lady Harsent nods. 'But it was Joseph's responsibility.'

'Yes, madam, and he deeply regrets any inconvenience caused. He realises that in the event of a similar mistake in the future the court will not be so lenient.'

So lenient! Averling has the cheek to anticipate the Bench's decision! To Wendy's disgust, Lady H. does not even 'put' the formal charge to Joseph, she merely waives the episode with a dismissive motion of her jewelled hand. Patrick or Miss Swearwell would have gone straight for a £20 fine, to sharpen the Griffin memory.

Lady H. has the Youth Justice Team's pre-sentence report on Joseph and a list of his previous convictions before her. Wendy has made sure that there are three copies available; when only one is photocopied, Lady H.'s two colleagues on the Bench don't get to see much.

Robbery, Assault. Conditional Discharge, 1 year

Attempted Robbery, Criminal Damage, Assault. Attendance Centre, 24 hours

Robbery, Attendance Centre, 12 hours

Robbery. Conditional Discharge, 1 year

Offensive Weapon, CD, 2 years

Theft. Fine, £30

Criminal Damage, Assault With Intent to Resist Arrest, Common Assault. Conditional Discharge, 2 years

Resisting Police Officer, Breach of CD × 2. Attendance Centre, 24 hours

Breach of Bail. Fine, £5

Fail to Attend. Attendance Centre Order, 12 hours

Public Order Act (Sect. 5). Fine, £6.40p

Interfere with Motor Vehicle × 2. Attendance Centre Order, 18 hours × 2 (concurrent) & £10 costs

Breach Attendance Centre Order × 2. ACO Revoked. Fine £15 on each matter

Burglary × 5. Attendance Centre Order, 18 hours

The floor belongs to Edgar Averling. Joseph having been found guilty of dropping a concrete block on to an InterCity express, Averling can no longer argue that he didn't do it. He pleads that Joseph never understood that his 'foolish but spontaneous and unpremeditated action' might endanger lives.

'Madam, Joseph feels he was unjustly accused of fare-evasion recently, and so bears a grudge against transport staff in general. In retrospect he is repentant, indeed horrified by the folly of his behaviour – madam.'

Lady H. addresses Joseph, who sits with his legs wide apart, hands in pockets, a blob of chewing gum perched on the tip of his tongue. Wendy seethes: make the bastard stand up!

'To you it was just a prank, Joseph?'

'Yeah.'

'And you would never do anything so silly and dangerous again, would you?'

'Nah.'

'The pre-sentence report before us stresses the need to persuade you to address your offending behaviour, Joseph. Are you prepared to do that?'

'Yeah.'

'Your social workers will help you to manage your anger. You will fully cooperate with them, won't you?'

'Yeah.'

'You promise me?'

'Yeah.'

'You realise that a Supervision Order is an alternative, in this case, to Downton?'

'Yeah.'

'Your record is appalling, isn't it?'

Silence.

'Well, isn't it?'

A grunt.

'Very well. A Supervision Order for one year with IT.'

At the back of the court Doug McIntyre and Cliff Jenkins wear their stoniest faces. It happens so often that they may turn into statues. At the prosecutor's table Derek Jardine looks up from his notes and glances at Wendy. She has redone her hair today, fluffed it up – for tearing. Her face is expressionless as she writes another page into the file of Joseph Griffin.

British Transport Police Inspector Herbert Knowles, who had arrested Joseph on a bridge overlooking the railway line, is not in court. As a mere witness he has no right to return to the Youth Court to attend the sentencing.

He is waiting outside, on the street, fending off questions from Joe O'Neill – who has no right to print Joseph Griffin's name.

Herbert knows Joe well and trusts him, but with the Broadway Station affray and vandalism case against all three Griffin boys still in the pipeline, Herbert isn't saying anything. Above all he isn't saying that he is going to need the evidence of a mild-mannered young gentleman called Simon Galloway.

Will Galloway turn up on the day? Few of them do. They get all fired up at the time and then they cool. They remember they have jobs to attend to. They remember how busy they are. They hear rumours that giving evidence against a Griffin catches up with you. Always.

'Give me a break, Herbert,' Joe is pleading. 'We're off the record.'

'Yeah?' Herbert chuckles grimly. 'Well, I'll tell you what Judge Byron would say.'

'You've met him?'

'He was at my place for lunch last Sunday,' Herbert says proudly. 'Now ask me why.'

'Why?'

'Because he's family.' Herbert lets this sink in. 'Marcus is family. And Wendy. They reckon my Marcia is the best cook in the family.'

Joe absorbs this. 'What's Marcus Byron really like?'

Herbert Knowles's walnut-countenance solidifies. 'Marcus is the best. My brother Marcus Byron is a great Englishman.'

Entering the waiting taxi, arguably the best-dressed man in London, Marcus Byron is immediately recognised by the driver.

'Saw you on the telly the other night, Guv.'

'Aha? I hope you didn't miss *EastEnders*. I'm an East Ender myself.'

'But you got off the bus at Oxford. You made it.'

'True.'

'Strawberries and cream?'

'Not exactly.'

'To be perfectly frank with you, Guv, what most of these young villains need is a short, sharp shock.'

'Aha? How short?'

'Good question! I'd put them away for life and when I say "life" I mean life.'

'Not so short, then?' Marcus shoots his crisp white cuffs (the last of the starch addicts) down the sleeves of his Bentley Bros worsted suit. A fob-watch chain flamboyantly dangles from his waistcoat pocket.

Marcus is on his way to the Bow Street Tavern for his 'secret' rendezvous with the Rt Hon. Max Venables, MP. In an age of endemic – Max says 'epidemic' – leaks, both Government and Opposition fear hostile leaks to the Press. Cautious by nature, Max Venables is wary of the rising hostility of his traditional friends. His 'unelected kitchen cabinet' is under fierce attack from certain quarters. The civil libertarians have gathered their forces within the Congress for Justice. Every opinion poll shows that crime heads the list of public concerns. With a general election imminent, the stakes are high.

Max's wife Sandra is quite blunt about it. 'Get rid of Marcus Byron, Max, or we get rid of you.'

Max has reported this remark to Marcus, who remembered his own final, bitter quarrel with Sandra when he finally handed in his notice and married Louise:

'I will destroy you, Marcus.'

No need to tell Sandra's husband about that. Marcus has always laughed at Max's caution and coded messages. 'Max, we have nothing to fear but fear itself.' But now, with the Lord Chief Justice's summons in his pocket, he remembers Rudyard Kipling's tale, 'How Fear Came'. If the Chief and his colleagues on the Court of Appeal sustain Sandra's appeal, if they condemn Marcus's directions to the Donna Dean jury, it will be a clear signal not only to Marcus himself but also to Max Venables.

And more. Marcus's friends are beginning to warn him. Wendy has spelled it out painfully: unless Lucy's headlong rush into drugs and delinquency is checked, unless he brings his daughter under control, Marcus will not merely be rebuffed by his superiors: he will fall. He will have to go.

The name Galloway, previously unknown to Marcus, continually circles his head; was Lucy involved in what happened to that young mother as she wheeled her toddler home?

No! Lucy is a tender, gentle soul. She has suffered and she is crying out for attention.

The taxi driver is persistent. 'What do you think of the Guildford Four, Guv? The day they walked free I couldn't eat my dinner and that's a fact. If that's justice, I'm Marlon Brando. I mean, someone in the IRA blew up that pub, didn't they?'

'Someone certainly did. The question is: Who? Certainly not

those who were wrongly convicted on the basis of false confessions.'

That terminates the conversation: the famous judge is a black bastard after all. (They're all the same.)

Marcus reaches a decision: he will not mention to Max the Lord Chief Justice's note, particularly one cutting sentence: 'Your close association with the Shadow Home Secretary is also causing widespread adverse comment. I have spoken to the Lord Chancellor about it . . .' Max would panic.

Reaching the Bow Street Tavern, Marcus is observed by a man in a leather jacket standing beneath the portals of the Royal Opera House with a telephoto lens.

Max has taken what he imagines to be a discreet corner table. Marcus orders a double whisky, Max a half of pale shandy. (Sandra has told him to cut down: 'Jeremy Darling doesn't carry a paunch.') Max is tugging nervously at his small goatee beard. The Boy wants him to cut it off, but the beard seems like Max's only claim to his own past, the CND marches, banning the Bomb, keeping out of the Common Market, nationalising every industry in sight, comprehensive education, a world fit for social workers.

Gloomily Max produces a pair of half-lens reading glasses, which seem to add ten years to his age as they perch on the end of his nose. He is holding a draft policy document from Marcus, which he keeps in a locked cabinet.

'I'm afraid this has leaked. I left it lying on my bedside table while I took a bath. Sandra's friends are hopping mad.'

'Showers are quicker,' Marcus says.

'But not as quick as Sandra.'

Max Venables is a highly intelligent, wide-angled politician, but when it comes to private life – his wife – he's a simpleton. Max managed never to know, or want to know, about Sandra's affair with Marcus, even though it lasted six years. The joke had gone round Westminster that when Max returned from an overnight trip to find Marcus with Sandra at his own breakfast table, he merely said, 'You're just the man I want to talk to. I hope I haven't kept you waiting.'

Marcus is filling his pipe. Louise doesn't care for his smoking; Sandra had hated it; Jill had meekly accepted it – in those days a man was entitled to smoke.

'Max, what we need urgently are tough new measures to deal

with persistent anti-social neighbours. You've heard what's been happening in Eden Manor? This country of ours is littered with Eden Manors.'

Max nods reluctantly. 'I like the working title of your document – "A Quiet Life: Tough Action on Criminal Neighbours". But the Bar Association won't buy it, Marcus, the Law Society won't like it, the Probation Service will hate it. As for the Congress, Nick Paisley has already warned me: their opposition is total. Nick told me you should be working for Jeremy Darling.'

'Darling's a turd. I'm an East End boy. You can't beat crime while you've got underfunded schools, overcrowded classrooms, demoralised teachers and thirty per cent unemployment in the inner cities. I detest this callous Government.'

'Our black and Asian MPs are now accusing me of selling out to the police and the crime-control lobby.' Max sighs. 'That's you, Marcus.'

'Forget the politics.'

'Forget the politics!' Max tugs at his beard, aghast.

The man in the leather jacket has entered the tap room. A wide-angled 38mm lens has replaced the telephoto.

'We are proposing a decisive step forward,' Marcus says. 'A new court injunction, called a Community Safety Order, allowing courts to impose curfews and exclusions from an area, as well as new powers to curb witness intimidation. Police will be able to report complaints without naming the complainants.'

'And you're really proposing that a breach of this Community Safety Order will carry up to a seven-year jail sentence? Seven years!'

'That's negotiable,' Marcus says. 'Face the facts, Max. The system is currently not coping with chronic crime committed over a period of months. The criminal justice system is dealing in snapshots. What we have to tackle is the continuous film. Gangs of youths, joy riders, local drug pedlars – families like the Griffins and Richardsons of Eden Manor.'

'I don't know them.'

'You're lucky. You should talk to Brigid Kyle about what she witnessed recently.'

'The social workers won't like any of this,' Max objects, slapping Marcus's policy document.

'We also need a new charter for victims.'

'The CPS won't wear it, Marcus.'

'The DPP will. I've spoken to Lionel.'

'Lionel Lacey resembles the captain of a ship locked into his cabin by his own crew.'

'And Nick Paisley's what the Royal Navy calls his "Number One".'

Max lowers his voice to a whisper. 'I hear on the grapevine that Lionel Lacey is in some kind of personal trouble.'

Marcus shrugs but Max presses his inquiry.

'They say he has a . . . a weakness. A vice.'

'Who doesn't? Yours is politics.'

Max Venables looks even gloomier. 'And you really expect me to go along with Jeremy Darling's new prisons for boys aged twelve to fourteen – his so-called Secure Training Units?'

'Did you ever hear of Darren Griffin, of Eden Manor?'

'No.'

'The notorious "Rat Boy"?'

'Ah. Ah yes, perhaps I did. But—'

'All you have to do, Max, in the House of Commons is to quarrel with the details of Darling's scheme – then abstain.'

'The Congress would slaughter me.'

'You should talk to my sister Wendy and her husband Patrick. They know the youth court scene from the inside. Under the present Section 23, certain offences, however persistently repeated, are not serious enough to send the culprit into custody. You have a new generation of street-wise kids, the Griffins and Richardsons of Eden Manor, who know the law better than the lawyers. They hear the adults arguing about it in court – magistrates, lawyers, social workers, housing officers, all tearing their hair in frustration.'

'Social workers and probation officers are dead against imprisoning youngsters.'

'Or anybody.' Marcus drains his glass and smiles. 'How many votes do they have? Do you remember what Stalin said about the Pope? "How many battalions?"'

'Stalin?' Max quivers. 'The Boy – our leader – is in agreement with you. But he wouldn't want to be quoted. I mean—'

'You mean every good idea has to be his own idea. Fine by me. I'm not running for office.'

'He wonders whether you'd consider a seat in the Lords.'

'Why?'

'We'll need a Lord Chancellor who can bang heads.'

'I'm content with the Crown Court.'

'You haven't heard from the Lord Chief Justice, by any chance? We hear he's . . . not happy.'

'That's just propaganda put out by Jeremy Darling's spin doctors.'

'The Congress is powerful, Marcus. It must be painful for you to be denounced by your own law tutor, Geoffrey Villiers . . .'

'Senile.'

'How's your Lucy?' Max asks.

'Lucy? She's busy with her GCSEs. She now wears two studs in her nose instead of one. Nice of you to inquire, Max,' he adds sharply.

Max averts his gaze. (The Boy has instructed him to probe the rumours. 'I'm not losing this election because of an obscure delinquent schoolgirl, Max – is that quite clear?')

'Why did you ask?' Marcus presses.

'Oh, we're all very fond of Lucy. Sandra was asking after her only the other day. "A pity we don't see more of Lucy," she said.'

The man in the leather jacket has departed. He'd found Judge Byron's habit of glancing around and waving a hand of greeting to friends at neighbouring tables very helpful. An averted all-black face at a corner table is a difficult subject without a flash, even at 1/60 and f2.9.

Wendy Berry leaves Benson Street Youth Court seething – it's normal when Lady Harsent has been chairing the Bench. She buys an evening paper and rapidly scans the report of Sandra Golding's impassioned denunciation of Marcus before the Court of Appeal in the Donna Dean case. The court's ruling, of course, will come later.

Wendy's blood boils all over again. Having witnessed her Herb's crushed expression as Lady Harsent blew kisses at Joseph Griffin, she is filled with rage by Sandra Golding's specious arguments. Wendy is a hot-tempered woman – it runs in the Byron family. She is also a feminist who believes that battered women are due a fair deal: but to repeatedly stab a man as he sleeps!

If Patrick beat her up, she'd damn well kill him while he knew about it!

No, she wouldn't. She'd seek refuge with Marcus. Marcus!

Why does she love that conceited chauvinist Big Brother so much? Look at the way he treats women! Look at his only child, Lucy! Oh God, when will he wake up to what's happening to that girl, the torment in her heart, the screaming sense of desertion? Wendy has an awful premonition of what is going to happen.

She and Patrick are visiting Marcus tonight. Very well, gloves off – she will have it out with him. But will she? His vast, baffled, stifled pain about Lucy always clamps Wendy's mouth.

Patrick, of course, won't say a thing about Lucy. Marcus is his best friend and that's that. Men! As she negotiates the rush-hour traffic, her thoughts float back a couple of years to her first lunch with the young lay magistrate, Patrick Berry. Blond, breezy and blue-eyed, he had brazenly picked her up in the street as she left the staff entrance to pursue her lunch-hour shopping.

'Lunch, Ms Byron? I know an Italian place which does a passable tagliatelle.'

Patrick Berry walked with a muscular swagger which she, a keen sportswoman herself, found attractive. He seemed to be shaking invisible dust from his broad shoulders. He'd even reserved a table for two: had someone else stood him up or was this sheer cheek? Once seated, he lost no time in asking whether she was related to the famous Marcus Byron.

'My brother.'

'Really? Do you approve of him?'

Patrick's bright, boyish gaze was instantly disarming. He leaned across the table with the intensity of a gardener sniffing a prize rose, but Wendy declined to be drawn about Marcus.

'What do you think of Lady Harsent?' Patrick asked.

'Is this off the record?'

He laughed. 'How do we get rid of her?'

'You tell me.'

'So where does the Byron family come from?'

'We were all born in the East End. My parents . . . my mother was from Barbados.'

'Ah – planters?'

'Slaves. So what about you?'

'I can be boring about that.'

'Be boring.'

'Very well, you asked for it. The electronic monitoring of curfew orders was first mooted in the Criminal Justice Act of 1991. As you well know, a curfew is a provision of conditional bail, confining the accused to a particular place, normally his residence, between specified hours.'

Wendy nodded. 'Schedule 9, paragraph 39, of the Criminal Justice and Public Order Act, 1994, provides for trial of electronic monitoring in selected areas of the country.'

Patrick was studying her admiringly.

'My firm is one of several bidding for the Home Office contract. The device is about the size of a diver's watch, and is attached to the ankle or wrist. The tag emits a signal which is picked up by a receiver resembling an answering machine and attached to a telephone socket. The device merely records whether the individual has remained within range of the receiver.'

'But there's a lot of opposition to it.'

'Oh certainly. The Congress has denounced it. Lady H., Villiers, Jill Hull, Nick Paisley, Sandra Golding and Averling have issued dire warnings: electronic tagging is totalitarian and contrary to basic human dignity.'

'Yes, I remember. Jill Hull even predicted that the next step will be to attach an electric shock which is activated every time the man strays beyond his zone. After that the shock will be strengthened, to stun him.'

'Quite right.' Patrick smiled gaily. 'We are planning to treat human beings like farm animals.' He paused. 'However, electronic tagging requires the offender's consent. If he prefers custody, it's his choice.'

'But is that really a choice, Mr Berry?'

'Yes, it is. Please call me Patrick.'

Wendy smiled. 'But not in court?'

'Er . . . perhaps not. You could always address me as "Sir Patrick".' He threw her a sly look. 'By the way, did you know that the ineffable Lady Harsent's home was burgled recently?'

'Really? Great!'

'Someone knew – evidently knew – precisely when she and her husband had tickets for the theatre. Apparently the burglars left a lemon on her pillow.'

'A lemon?'

'I was the burglar.' He winked. 'But don't quote me.'

They finished their lunch without Patrick revealing that he knew Marcus and was a member of the same cycling club, the Gadabouts. When Patrick finally proposed marriage to her he confessed that Marcus had threatened to 'veto the union' unless Patrick promised never to take the law into his own hands again.

'He told me I was a juvenile idiot. He told me I was an arrogant bastard. He told me I should be in Wormwood Scrubs. He told me that I would marry his sister over his dead body.'

'Did he, indeed! Who the hell does he think he is?'

Patrick had folded her in his arms. 'Your big brother, darling, is the last best hope of all decent Englishmen.'

'And what about the women?'

Two years have passed since she married Patrick. He has been as good as his word and given up 'noble cause burglary'. Lady H. had remained unconverted – she still blew kisses to Griffins as they staggered into court with their loot.

Towards eight in the evening, Wendy and Patrick press the bell of Marcus's comfortable – he gets ratty if you use the word 'luxury' – apartment in South Kensington.

'Lemons!' Patrick barks into the intercom.

'Never say that!' Wendy punches him hard in the back.

Reaching the second floor, they find Marcus in jeans and a cowboy shirt, a glass of whisky in his hand. His expression is uncharacteristically grave – it carries some kind of immediate warning. There is no sign (as Wendy has predicted to Patrick) of Louise, but Marcus is not alone.

A pallid, gaunt gentleman is standing stiffly beside the unlit fireplace, a gin and tonic in (Wendy notes) a slightly unsteady hand. At a glance he is pure Establishment and distressingly English; his thinning hair is brushed back thirty years; his blue suit is expensive but frayed and ill fitting, his collar a size too large, his drab tie a gesture of allegiance to a forgotten era of rectitude.

Neither Wendy nor Patrick knows him or particularly wants to. Normally a late visit to the Byron apartment is a ticket to the Pleasure Dome – or was until Marcus married the forbidding Louise. Marcus's natural pals are actors, opera singers, writers, media faces, theatre directors, flash lawyers and the more disreputable type of politician. In the era before Louise, the visitor was likely to walk straight into the handshake of the Academician whose version of Marcus now hangs on the ground floor of the National Portrait Gallery.

Sandra was at ease with such people, and they with her. Sandra could effortlessly play brilliant hostess for two men, her husband

and her lover, without embarrassment. The joke went that you thanked Sandra at the door, drove straight from Max's party to Marcus's party – and were greeted by Sandra wearing a different outfit and new eyelashes. To top it, you'd find Max and Marcus at both parties.

The gaunt, pallid man does not offer his hand to the Berrys – evidently he belongs to that generation: handshaking begins at Calais. 'Yes, well,' he murmurs, 'I'd better be going.'

'Finish your drink, Lionel, then have another,' Marcus says.

'What? Oh yes – no, no, I'm driving.' He yields an awkward half-smile and is gone.

'That man is terrified!' Wendy says, sinking into a white leather sofa and crossing her long legs, no longer encumbered by courtroom hemlines.

'Lionel has good reason to be terrified,' Marcus says.

'He's one of us?' Patrick asks.

Marcus nods. 'Wendy, there's a prosecutor working in your court called Derek Jardine. How well do you know him?'

'Derek's all right,' she replies guardedly. What is Marcus up to this time?

'Jardine's problem is his boss, Nick Paisley,' Patrick says.

'Recruit him,' Marcus says to Wendy, sinking down with a large whisky. Wendy is hungry – ravenous – but her brother notoriously loses interest in food when a full bottle of golden-brown fluid stands on the Chippendale table beside him. (Louise swears it's a fake, along with much of his furniture and many of his friends.)

'I've never recruited anyone,' Wendy says.

'We need someone inside the Crown Prosecution Service to monitor Paisley's activities.'

'I'll talk to Jardine,' Patrick says.

'How's your telephone canvassing for Patrick going?' Marcus asks Wendy imperiously. 'Have you explained to every magistrate in London that Cecilia Harsent is the darling of the Eden Manor criminals?'

'I prefer to stress Patrick's virtues . . . when I can invent some.'

Marcus tosses a large, hard lemon into her lap. She catches it deftly.

'Paisley is the dynamo of the Congress. They're scared stiff that the next Government's policies on crime will be masterminded by the Lemons. Their aim is to knock us off one by one – and they're in a hurry. The DPP is their first target.'

'The Director of Public Prosecutions, Lionel Lacey?'

'Exactly. The man you just met – almost.'

'Wow!' Wendy cries. 'God, he looked a wreck!'

'Lionel now stands between the Congress and total control of the CPS. Paisley has patiently built up a network of acolytes seeking to control two thousand staff handling one and a half million criminal cases a year.'

'And the next step is to get your friend Lacey out?' Patrick asks.

'Precisely. Lionel wants new guidelines and new legislation to put an end to the extravagant powers now enjoyed by defence lawyers.'

'Good for him,' Patrick says. 'We need to curb the amount of evidence and paperwork the prosecution must disclose in advance to the defence.'

Marcus nods. 'Defence lawyers representing the big criminal consortiums are constantly embarking on fishing expeditions which threaten to uncover confidential information about an informant or sworn witness. As a result the CPS drops the case and the thugs spend the evening celebrating at the Windmill.'

'The Windmill closed its doors long ago,' Wendy says.

Marcus winks at Patrick. 'Marriage must have reformed me.'

'So where's Louise tonight?' Wendy asks.

Marcus sighs. 'She's running for the chairmanship of the Criminal Bar Association. That means not entertaining the Director of Public Prosecutions.'

'Your activities must be tricky for her,' Wendy says politely.

'An understatement.'

Both brother and sister are aware that Louise is ill at ease with the Byron clan. They are altogether too vulgar and boisterous for her taste. Wendy is too flash for Marcus's new wife, too East End. When Marcus was courting Louise – if that's the right word for the love life of a caveman – he had taken Louise and the Berrys to dine at Annabel's. Louise hadn't liked the place. 'So brash,' she murmured to Marcus. Very drunk, Wendy had invited Louise to arm-wrestle across the table. 'If you win, you get my brother. That's our custom in Barbados.'

Louise had almost broken it off with Marcus there and then.

Patrick takes the conversation back to the DPP.

'How does Paisley expect to get him out of his job?'

Marcus adopts his gravest air. 'This is strictly between ourselves.'

'Haw haw,' Wendy says. 'You mean between ourselves and your glamorous friend Brigid Kyle?'

Marcus turns to Patrick. 'You see what I've had to put up with for thirty years. When you married her, I told you: beat her regularly, it's the only way.'

Wendy bridles. 'You should drive the taxis you ride around in, Marco.'

'Cut it out,' Patrick says, 'or I'll tag you both for curfew.'

Marcus nods. 'Lionel Lacey is in the grip of a vice he cannot shake off. He knows he must and he knows he can't. It's an absolute compulsion – he confessed as much to me.'

'Drink?' Patrick asks.

'No.'

'Drugs?' Wendy asks.

'No.'

'Kerb-crawling?'

'No.'

'I've run out of sins.'

'Lionel's a baby-snatcher. It hits him every Friday night.'

'What does?' Wendy always bridles when her brother is about to talk dirty.

'He has to smell nappies every Friday night. The excitement builds up all week. "I need a blow-job from an unclean urchin or a ragged little *misérable.*" Those were his words. He leaves his office at eight p.m., climbs into his old Daimler, and heads for Les Enfants du Paradis.'

'That's a movie?' Wendy asks. She hates to ask Marcus anything.

'It's a paedophile club in Wardour Street – regularly busted by the Vice Squad.'

'But only on Thursdays?' Patrick says cynically.

Marcus shrugs. 'Nick Paisley hinted to Lionel only yesterday that they're on to his nasty little habit. It seems that a child prostitute facing a drugs charge – a serious "supplying" charge – told her probation officer that she'd seen rent-boys regularly unzipping the DPP Friday nights.'

'She couldn't possibly know who he was,' Wendy objects.

'Lionel tells his unclean urchins and ragged *misérables* exactly who he is.'

'He tells them!'

'That's part of the shame and degradation Lionel craves.'

'Presumably the child prostitute was looking for a trade-off on her drugs charge?' Patrick says.

'And she got one,' Marcus says, 'after the good news reached my former wife.'

Wendy groans. 'And Jill lives with Nick Paisley.'

'You're there. Paisley is the most powerfully placed opponent within the CPS of the DPP's proposed reforms. The Congress is backing the Bar Council. They claim that such reforms are driven by the demands of the police, who want convictions, not by the demands of justice. They claim that such reforms would undermine the essential presumption of innocence. Paisley is now murmuring in Lionel Lacey's ear: "Go before there's a scandal."'

'Why warn him?' Patrick objects. 'A front-page scandal would be just up the Congress's street.'

Marcus refills his and Patrick's glasses, Wendy declining.

'Patrick, you're driving,' she says severely.

'This is only my second.'

'Your second double-triple, Marcus pours it in like milk. Lady Harsent would just love you to get done for drink-driving.'

Marcus nods. 'You'll take a taxi home tonight.'

'I'll drive,' Wendy says. 'The female, as always, saves the day.'

'Is your distinguished baby-snatcher prepared to mend his ways?' Patrick asks Marcus.

'Lionel hates their guts, loathes Paisley and is determined to stay. He has evidence that Paisley is currently going easy on several indictments of the drugs baron, Livingstone Lord.'

'And Lord,' adds Wendy with deliberate cruelty, 'happens to be the fancy man, off and on, of Ma Richardson, who gave the world Paul, Amos – and Lucy's friend Daniel.'

Marcus is silent. Wendy had come determined to raise the whole issue of Lucy, but now the distress on her brother's face silences her – as she had known it would.

By now everyone is too tired to go out and find a meal. Wendy lifts the phone and calls in hot pizzas from Pizza Palace. It's a new firm, very efficient – remarkable how rapidly it has closed down all the local competition. As she gives the order, Wendy observes Marcus refilling Patrick's glass.

'We should do a job on Paisley,' Patrick says, his speech now slightly slurred. 'The house must be stuffed with incriminating documents.'

'No. Enough burglaries.'

'These bleeding hearts can never imagine it happening to them,' Patrick growls.

'We don't fight criminality by signing on as criminals,' Marcus says.

Patrick is far from sober. 'Got t' do so'thing.'

'He thinks he's the bloody Scarlet Pimpernel,' Wendy says, dropping back into the white leather and laying her legs across Patrick's.

The downstairs buzzer sounds. Marcus moves swiftly from his chair to the intercom – drink never seems to have the slightest effect on him.

'Pizzas,' he hears.

He presses the lock-release button. 'Come up, flat four.' He opens the door and waits. Presently a slender black youth in a clean white linen coat surfaces with a broad smile and three large pizza boxes.

Marcus tips the boy generously, closes the door and takes the boxes into the kitchen. Wendy follows. Slumped in his chair, Patrick hears their banter abruptly fall into silence. He doesn't feel like moving.

Lying across the hot pizzas in the boxes are two blown-up photographs of the Director of Public Prosecutions standing with his back to a grimy brick wall while a shadowy little creature in rags kneels before him, its head thrust into his loins. Each box contains the same message neatly printed with a felt-tipped pen:

'Lemons Go Bad.'

Had either Wendy or Patrick caught sight of the slender black delivery boy at the door they could have told Marcus exactly who he was – Daniel, the youngest of the surviving Richardson boys.

# *Six*

DOUG McINTYRE AND CLIFF JENKINS call at 16 Oundle Square bearing a small gift, out of their own pockets, to mark Simon Galloway's birthday. It's a large box of Smarties, along with a Get Well card for Susan signed by all the PCs and WPCs of Eden Manor police station.

They find Simon at home, though it's a weekday. He stares at them, or through them, into a void within his head. Unshaven and red-eyed, he looks shattered. McIntyre identifies the classic symptoms of trauma. Little Tom is sheltering behind his father's legs.

'It's for Tom to give you,' McIntyre explains. 'Hullo, Tom! It's Daddy's birthday today, isn't it.' He offers the small parcel to the child, but Tom shrinks back.

'Very kind, you shouldn't have bothered,' Simon says, taking the parcel in a trembling hand. His hair is uncombed; his shirt is grimy at the collar; behind his new glasses his eyes refuse to focus. Tom stares up at the strangers with the glassy gaze of terror. He has tried to stop his father answering the door.

'My wife's cooking you a cake,' McIntyre tells Simon. 'She's hard at it, she'll be round later in the day. How many candles, she instructed me to ask you.'

'Sorry?'

'How many candles, Simon?'

'Oh – thirty-two. No, no, three would do. You can blow out three candles for me, can't you, Tom?'

The little boy staring.

'As a matter of fact,' Simon murmurs, 'your gift is just the thing. Tom has hidden something for me but now he can't find it.'

The policemen understand: it would take Susan to find it. Susan is still in St Luke's Hospital.

'The lady from Victim Support will be with you about noon,' Jenkins tells Simon.

'Really? It's not necessary.'

'It's always a good idea,' McIntyre says. (He doesn't add that the Support ladies sometimes pick up vital details which the police still lack.)

'We'll see you later, Simon.'

'Yes.'

'Bye, Tom! Don't let Daddy eat all those Smarties at once!'

'Bye, Tom!' Jenkins waves.

The boy almost smiles. Will he ever smile again?

The sun is shining on Oundle Square. The leaves are in full bloom, the birds in good heart. A black cat slinks out from beneath the police Metro as McIntyre and Jenkins open the doors.

'That bloke has plenty of trouble ahead of him,' McIntyre says. 'It's not many people who'd fancy giving evidence against two Richardsons followed by three Griffins.'

'How's that, then?'

'Paul and Daniel Richardson robbed him in his BMW. Then there's the Broadway station affray involving the Griffin shitheads. Simon Galloway is Herb Knowles's main witness.'

'He'll probably back out of that.'

'He doesn't strike me as likely to back out of anything.'

'Hm. This could be Simon Galloway's last birthday.'

'That's no kind of joke, Cliff.'

Lucy Byron is not at school. From behind half-drawn curtains she observes the conversation on the front doorstep of No. 16, her small face burning a hole in the glass. What are the pigs saying to Simon Galloway?

Jill has told her that it happened right there, on the front doorstep where the two policemen are now standing. Lucy has crept across at night, to look for blood, for tears, probing the iron railings for their hidden knowledge.

She watches the two uniformed wankers, the agents of the System, as they retreat down the front steps. She can see them waving to a small, half-hidden figure cringing behind Simon's legs. Lucy hopes they will come straight to her own door at No. 23. Last time they came, two nights ago, asking questions, Jill was at home, then Nick turned up, no fun at all. Lucy would like to receive the sheep-shaggers McIntyre and Jenkins alone – have them all to herself.

Dan knows where Amos is hiding. But he wouldn't tell her where.

The pigs had released Dan on police bail, charged with robbing Simon Galloway in his car on Hilton Avenue. Lucy had asked Dan what Amos had done.

'Dunno. He rang my Mum and said it was an accident.'

'What was?'

'Dunno. The woman across the Square.'

'*What was*, Dan?' Lucy caught the imperiousness in her voice, the echo of her dad. She didn't want to be a *bourgeoise*. It was a word she had picked up in France, in the Dordogne, from that snob bitch Amelia Harsent, who regularly won all the French prizes at St Hilda's.

Dan had sounded a bit shaky on the phone. Apparently the bastard cop McIntyre had given chase on his motorbike and spiked Dan in full flight. They got Paul later. Dan was asking, rather incoherently, for help from 'your Mum and your step'.

'How, Dan?'

'They're both bent, ain't they?'

This had shocked Lucy. 'Bent? My mum?'

'Well, Paisley is. Tell him if he don't look after Amos we'll shop him straight to the pigs.'

'Why should we help Amos, why not you?'

'Stupid cunt! Amos is really in it, ain't he? Paul and me, we just took the bloke's wallet, never laid a hand on 'im.'

'What do you want Nick to do, Dan?'

'Downgrade the charge against Amos to handlin'.'

'I don't understand.'

'From robbery and grievous to handlin', cunt! Are you stupid or somethin'?'

'You want me to talk to Nick?'

'Yeah. Remind him what we've got on 'im. Otherwise you'll all be in it.'

'I thought you were my friend, Dan.'

'Yeah, you're supposed to be mine, eh?'

Later, after Nick came home, Lucy had tried to explain. Nick listened in silence. Then he took a soft little package from his pocket and slipped it to her.

'Have you mentioned Daniel's message to your mother?'

'Of course not.'

'Well, don't.'

'OK. OK! I'm used to *that*, aren't I?'

Lucy wipes her breath from her bedroom window. The red police Metro vanishes round the corner into Brancaster Road. She doesn't fancy school. Sitting at her table, she composes a letter from the Headmistress, Mrs Nearcliffe, to Marcus. 'Dear Judge Byron, I very much regret to inform you . . .'

Yeah.

Tenderly she probes Nick's soft package. Good enough to snort, high quality, no needles, no bruises.

She runs down the stairs, out of the house, along the street to No. 16. She presses the bell, waits. Finally the man opens the door.

'I've come to play with Tom,' she says. 'You could go to work! Honestly! I could look after him all day, give him his dinner, take him to the park . . .'

Simon Galloway looks at her, then closes the door on her, without a word.

Lucy will not forget that look, nor forgive.

The ghost in Marcus Byron's machine is his first wife, Jill Hull. For years he has pushed her to the farthest frontiers of his consciousness. But no longer. She haunts his sleep, that small, quiet, plain, powerful ex-wife, as he lies beside Louise. Whatever is happening to Lucy, Jill knows all about it. Allows it. Whatever Nick Paisley is up to, Jill condones. She shares with other members of the Congress for Justice a bitter, implacable opposition to everything Marcus stands for. But for Jill it's from the heart as well as the head. This is a woman who has always masked her emotions, whereas with Sandra you can hear them a mile away, rattling around the Court of Appeal in a cloud of perfumed oratory and media-beckoning fuck-me shoes. Jill goes flat-heeled and unobtrusive; she has bided her time.

Wendy has warned him: 'Jill is using your daughter to destroy you, Marco.' Louise reluctantly agrees, although she has not disliked Jill on the rare occasions when their paths have crossed.

As for Brigid, having interviewed Jill in her office, she had nothing good to say about her. 'She's a chilly customer, Marcus. Don't trust her an inch.'

Deputy Chief Probation Officer Jill Hull reaches her office on the fifth floor of Probation House shortly before 9 a.m. Plain, earnest and very bright, Jill is wearing an oatmeal trouser-suit and a jade necklace – a present from Lucy – and a slight frown; her pale eyes are guarded behind large, oval glasses. Today her normal, single-minded concentration on her work is frayed by what has happened to her neighbour and part-time secretary Susan Galloway.

Amos Richardson, elder brother of Lucy's friend Daniel, is on the run. The question racking Jill is whether Susan Galloway had been a victim chosen at random or whether Amos had been tipped off about her routine on the days when she was not working for Jill.

Jill has squeezed a confession out of Lucy: she had twice invited Daniel into the Galloways' home at No. 16 when she baby-sat for them. Should Jill believe Lucy's passionate profession of innocence? She saw not a flicker of guilt in the girl's eye when Detective Sergeant McIntyre and Detective Constable Jenkins called at the house 'in connection with our inquiries'.

'Why ask us, Doug?' Jill had protested.

McIntyre had kept his gaze firmly on Lucy. 'We're looking for Amos Richardson. Lucy knows Daniel. We are asking ourselves why all three Richardson boys were involved in crimes against Susan and Simon Galloway on the same afternoon.'

Lucy had shrugged her slender shoulders. 'No idea.'

Nick had arrived home while the CID men were still probing.

'It was a ghastly business,' Nick told McIntyre. 'But what makes you think Amos Richardson did it?'

'That we can't disclose – even to the Crown Prosecution Service.'

The sardonic sting in this remark brought home to Jill the hostility the Eden Manor police force felt for Nick.

So Jill has nothing on her conscience, but she had felt ill at ease when she called on Simon Galloway to offer sympathy. The look he gave her was not friendly. She had hurried away after a few words of routine commiseration on the doorstep. What still haunts her is little Tom's fearful gaze as he clung to his father's legs.

Entering her fifth-floor office, with its expansive view of Westminster and Whitehall, London's square mile of power, Jill drops a herbal teabag into a paper cup, then riffles through her mail and a pile of internal memos.

Jill Hull presides over a vast province of Probation. A brave new, glass-fronted, high-rise building has replaced the old ramshackle Victorian headquarters with their soot-stained red-brick walls, yellowing net curtains and wilting aspidistras.

Deputy Chief Probation Officer Hull, who has in her time been involved in liaison with the Crown Prosecution Service, liaison with the Juvenile Courts and what is hopefully called 'Crime Reduction', has recently been delegating many of her nominal responsibilities to her immediate subordinate, Senior Probation Officer Angela Loftus, while throwing her own energies into the rapid expansion of the Public Relations and Communications Department. The Probation Service's new brochure, mailed to all MPs, judges, magistrates and the media, proves that probation is a more reliable, and much cheaper, form of rehabilitation than prison.

> Whereas 55 per cent of former prisoners reoffend within two years, the comparable figure for former clients of the Probation Service is only 39 per cent.

No one has yet disputed these statistics. They are hard. They are a fact.

'But surely', Brigid Kyle had asked her during a recent interview, 'you are not comparing like with like. A man gets sent to prison because of the gravity of his offence or his long record. Your "clients", as you call them, are by definition the softer cases.'

'We have had overwhelming success with former prisoners,' Jill replied. 'You surely know that many of our clients have already seen the inside of a prison, Mrs Kyle.'

Jill had been reluctant to grant the interview. Kyle's jolly, jaunty personal manner hid a stiletto pen, but the prominent casualties who littered her columns did not include Marcus. Another conquest, no doubt – or so the gossip went. Nick had advised Jill to refuse an interview but she, more adept at public relations, knew the downside of a straight rebuff.

'What Does the Probation Service Have to Hide?' – Jill could write the headline.

When Brigid Kyle bounced in, beaming, a rather glamorous,

flame-haired creature, Jill experienced the lurch in her stomach she felt whenever she encountered one of Marcus's mistresses.

'Kind of you to see me, Ms Hull.'

'That's my job.'

'May I use a tape-recorder?'

'As you wish.'

'Good. Can we start with Probation Service policy on the broad issue of crime and punishment?'

Jill nodded.

'You have called prisons "overcrowded colleges of crime"?'

'Yes. More than once.'

'Because young offenders are thrown together with hardened criminals?'

'Exactly.'

'Does not the same apply to your special probation courses at Hillhouse?'

'At Hillhouse we encourage offenders to confront their own behaviour. They also learn from the mistakes of others.'

'Yet many of them join forces to commit new crimes, even while the ten-week course is in progress?'

Brigid had then challenged the Service's official statistics on reoffending. At one stage in the altercation she even asked, bluntly, whether they had been 'doctored'. The temperature between the two women descended from cool to icy.

'You are a leading member of the Congress for Justice, Ms Hull?'

'An active member. It's important to bring practitioners from the different sectors of the criminal justice system together. But I think we are straying beyond the agreed parameters of our interview.'

'Would you agree that the hidden agenda of the Congress is to get rid of the present DPP, Lionel Lacey?'

'Kindly switch off your tape-recorder.'

Brigid Kyle had complied. 'As you wish.'

'Your outlook bears an uncanny resemblance to Marcus Byron's.'

'That earns a zero rating, does it?'

Rising behind her desk, Jill had handed her a glossy brochure packed with pictures of smiling offenders at work on computers and video cameras.

'Here are the facts,' Jill said acidly.

It was a dismissal. Kyle has not yet published a word about the

Probation Service. Jill is in no doubt that it will come. The woman is holding her fire.

Lying on Jill's desk, one document, four pages long, commands her attention: Leela Desai's pre-sentence report on Alan Sanderson. And Angela Loftus's attached comments.

Jill reaches the section called 'Recommendations'. Her small jaw tightens.

Marcus had been the trial judge in the Sanderson case; he will be sentencing. Anyone (like Sanderson) connected with the Griffins of Eden Manor is a prime target for Judge Byron – look at the savage sentences he has just handed down to Knight and Green. And Marcus's greatest fan in Probation House is Angela Loftus.

Jill knows more about her subordinate's clandestine activities than Angela realises. There have been at least two secret, out-of-London meetings between Angela and Marcus. Jill's source – one of Angela's trusted aides – is convinced that confidential PS documents have passed hands.

Nick wants Angela out. Out of her job, out of the Probation Service. But the PS is tenderly protective of its staff; the PS, after all, is a 'caring' organisation. Even a senior executive in Jill's position cannot simply point to the door and say, 'Out!' Evidence of misconduct is required, codes of practice deliberately flouted.

'Then manufacture the evidence.' That was Nick's view.

The file on Angela Loftus in Jill's locked desk drawer is expanding rapidly.

The phone rings.

'Jill Hull.'

She hears Nick's voice – he never introduces himself.

'Just to confirm that the DPP visited Byron last night – as anticipated. The Berrys were there, too. They're obviously aware of the situation. We need a mole in there. Angela Loftus may be the answer.'

'Angela?'

'Think laterally, Jill, and remember Byron's weakness for hemlines. Talk to Heather.'

He rings off.

Jill walks to the window, gathers her thoughts, then presses her intercom.

'Angela, do you have a moment?'

* * *

Angela Loftus has been biting her fingernails ragged – you must kick that spinsterly habit, Angela! – in anticipation of Jill Hull's summons, that deceptively polite 'Do you have a moment?' When nervous – and the very thought of little Jill gives her the shakes – Angela tends to get through three or four cream buns instead of two. Marcus says she should cut down. He also slaps her very broad bottom, despite remonstrances from her trombone throat.

Marcus! She hasn't set eyes on him for months – except on TV. Must remember that. But Angela is a rotten liar.

Judge Byron had called for a pre-sentence report on Alan Sanderson after a Crown Court jury had convicted him of handling stolen goods, conspiracy to commit burglary (Sanderson uses underlings like the Griffin boys) and conspiracy to pervert the course of justice (intimidation of witnesses and victims). Judge Byron had instructed the Probation Service to produce a PSR, adding that the crimes, in the light of Sanderson's criminal record, were 'so serious' that a custodial sentence could not be ruled out.

The probation officer in court that day had been a tiny lady in a sari, Leela Desai. The task was hers. Returning to Probation House, Leela had lost no time in tremulously consulting Senior Probation Officer Angela Loftus.

'Jill Hull never allows a PSR to recommend custody, isn't that the case, Miss Loftus?'

They all call Angela 'Miss Loftus'. She is that sort of lady, a forty-four-year-old spinster, rather posh, the daughter of the late Rt Reverend Charles Loftus, and cheerfully overweight – no cream bun or chocolate cake survives her glance. Leela Desai has great respect for Miss Loftus but fears her rather uncomfortable sense of humour as much as the sudden flashes of temper that illuminate her fleshy countenance like a red light-bulb switched on.

'And Ms Hull', added Leela Desai nervously, 'was once married to Judge Byron . . . I'm told.'

'So?'

'Well, I . . . Frankly, this is a tricky one.'

'My dear Leela, the judge's comment merely obliges you to consider custody in your report. Your job is to interview Alan Sanderson, to take a wide view of his background, his criminal record and his professed attitudes – then say what you think. What *you* think.'

'But what do *you* think, Miss Loftus?'

'I'll tell you when I've read your report.'

'Sanderson's list of previous convictions is appalling! He's served four terms of probation! Nothing seems to stop him!'

'And he's the main handler for the Griffins.'

'Yes.'

'Was Sanderson ever in prison?'

'No.'

'Draw your own conclusions.'

'But Ms Hull will also see my report?'

Angela chuckled grimly (she's an artist at that). 'You bet!'

'I'm sure she—'

'It's called "gate-keeping", isn't it, Leela? Jill is a very keen gate-keeper, dear. No PSR must "discriminate" against the "client" on account of his gender, race, sexual orientation, disability, religion or tendency to resist "anger management".'

'But we agree with that . . . don't we?'

'Oh we do, Leela, we do! It's only when we learn that we mustn't "discriminate" against our "client" on account of his crimes that some of us may begin to ask awkward questions. Have a cream bun?'

'No, thank you.'

'Do you Hindu wallahs ever eat anything but lentils, Leela?'

That was three weeks ago. Sanderson, meanwhile, remains free on bail. Marcus – Judge Byron – had indulged in this uncharacteristic leniency because . . . Angela shouldn't know why, so she doesn't. By the time she reaches Jill's fifth-floor office she mustn't know anything she shouldn't know.

Angela has to make the ascent from the third floor. She's not keen on the stairs: squeezing into a crowded lift, she vows to do something about her weight and follow a strict regime – but she has never been over-burdened by her own good intentions. Flushed for battle, she eases her broad beam into the ridiculously small visitors' chair beside Jill Hull's desk. The petite Jill, who would never touch a cream cake, seems almost lost in the wide leather swivel-chair she occupies.

Angela places her large, floppy handbag beside her feet. Notices throughout Probation House warn of the risk of theft – 'Jacket? Wallet? Handbag? Always Take It With You! Better Safe Than Sorry!'

Angela had once remarked, during a clandestine meeting with Marcus Byron and Patrick Berry, that it wasn't clear whether the warning was primarily directed against visiting criminals or other probation officers.

Marcus had guffawed. 'Set a thief to catch a thief.'

Now, as Angela's handbag flops to the floor, a large, bright lemon rolls out of it and across Jill Hull's line of vision. Angela turns scarlet as she scrambles to retrieve it.

'It's for my tea.'

'I thought you were a coffee addict, Angela.'

'Bad for my heart. Doc said give up or else.'

'Well, you should stop smoking, too, Angela.'

'I should probably just stop, period.'

Behind the hearty laugh there is little geniality; Jill and Angela are virtually contemporaries and both are aware that Angela might be sitting in Jill's chair if the Service's current policies were reversed.

'I wanted a word with you about this Alan Sanderson PSR,' Jill says.

'Ah yes – thought you might.'

Angela believes in looking people in the eye but somehow she never can with Jill. Her superior's placid gaze behind the glinting glasses always carries a latent threat.

'I daresay you want my guts for garters,' Angela adds.

'What a horrible expression.'

'Oh well, fire away.'

'Did you persuade Leela to alter her own recommendation from Community Service to custody?'

'Leela's interview with this man Sanderson left her shaken. An outright Griffin thug. No sign of genuine repentance, just cynicism. He told Leela that he could "stitch up" any little "cunt" from the PS.'

'That's the way they talk, isn't it? You can't expect a lifelong victim of the prevailing macho culture to show overt respect for a woman.'

'Did you say "victim"? Did you say "overt"? You mean there's latent respect for women shyly waiting to poke its head out?'

'It's our job to instil that respect. Do you have Leela's original PSR with you – the one she wrote before you persuaded her to change her recommendation from Community Service to custody?'

'It's here.' Angela pushes it across the desk, still flushed from the disaster of the itinerant lemon.

Jill skims the original report with a fast, impatient eye.

'I see that Leela gives four reasons why Sanderson would respond positively to a Combination Order. She specifically says that he is ready to confront his own anti-social behaviour.'

'That's policy, isn't it? No one goes to prison except murderers and rapists.'

Jill is studying her intently. 'You're not happy in your work, are you, Angela?'

'Happy? Is one supposed to be happy when dealing with society's most obnoxious specimens?'

'I do find your choice of language disturbing.'

'Not PC, hm?'

'Perhaps you need a rest? A break. I'm sure Heather could fill in for you.'

Angela heaves indignantly. 'Heather Stuart is *my* assistant. She works for *me*.'

'We all work for the Service.'

'You won't turn Heather against me, if that's what you're after!'

'Does she drink lemon tea, too?'

Angela pushes her way back into the crowded lift – Going down! you can say that again! – her eyes popping with rage, her cheeks burning. Her heart is hammering dangerously. The doc has warned her about high blood pressure. He should work for little Jill!

Back at her desk, Angela calms down. Marcus will send Sanderson inside whatever the PSR recommends. In fact he'll bloody well enjoy trashing the PSR in front of a crowded court and the Press.

Marcus is the kind of chap you have to support – to help – unless you want to watch your once-proud country going to the dogs. Going to the Griffins.

She scribbes a note to Marcus: 'Their fangs are out. You're too trusting, Marcus. The Congress means to have your guts for garters.'

'Operation Lucy', Angela Loftus had called it. The phrase has stuck in Marcus's mind. He has great respect and affection for that gallant lady – and she is one of his few female friends he cannot be suspected of impropriety with. At least not *that* sort of impropriety.

These thoughts surface on the morning Marcus receives a summons from Mrs Nearcliffe, Headmistress of St Hilda's. A fine teacher and a strict disciplinarian, Mrs Nearcliffe had once sent admiring reports about Lucy's intelligence and creative gifts, but in recent times the sauce has soured. At their last meeting the Headmistress had been blunt:

'Lucy has sadly become the most ill-mannered, uncooperative, disruptive influence in the school.'

Marcus takes a taxi to St Hilda's. What did Angela mean by 'Operation Lucy'? The big black gent in the rear of the cab is brooding, remembering, trying to fend off the taxi driver's usual chat without seeming impolite. The driver has recognised him and is vigorously recommending the birch.

'They still use it on the Isle of Man, Guv. And what's the result? – no crime.'

'Aha.' Marcus is sometimes alarmed by his own 'constituency', by the great public which would elevate him to Lord Chief Justice if judicial appointments were elective.

Lucy! Louise had spared no effort to make herself acceptable to the girl. She strove gallantly to be a good stepmother, to win Lucy's affection. For Christmas she gave the girl a handsome cheque and a huge packet of large, Friends of the Earth brown envelopes made of recycled paper. But Lucy had boycotted their register-office wedding and the grandiose reception in Lincoln's Inn.

'Flash' was Lucy's word for it. 'We're not flash enough for you, me and Mum, so don't pretend,' Lucy had scribbled across a violent 'Clockwork Orange' postcard she had designed herself.

One of Louise's large brown envelopes soon came back, through the letterbox. 'Your wedding present,' Lucy had scrawled. It contained a video-cassette tape showing Lucy in bed, naked, legs spread, feeling herself with one hand while holding Anthony Burgess's *A Clockwork Orange* in the other.

Marcus and Louise stared at their television screen in a state of shock.

Lucy read aloud her chosen passages with venom, stretching her vowels in the style of London's young, a crazed smile on her vulnerable little pale-brown face.

> Our pockets were full of deng, so there was no need from the point of view of crasting any more pretty polly to tolchock some old vek

> in an alley and viddy him swim in his blood while we counted the takings and divided by four, nor to do the ultra-violent on some shivering, starry grey-haired ptitsa in a shop and go smecking off with the till's guts. But, as they say, money isn't everything.

'Jill must see this!' Marcus had exploded, jumping towards the telephone as soon as Lucy's tape ended with a terrible two-fingered gesture up from the genitals and straight into her father's eyes.

'Wait,' Louise said. 'Let's think.'

'I want custody of that girl!'

'Sit down, darling. Have a whisky. Have a double. Let's think this through.'

'She's not your daughter!'

'You should have thought about that when you ran off with Sandra.'

'I did not "run off"! Jill kicked me out.'

'Who wouldn't have kicked you out? Marcus, how can you be so lucid in court, or on television, or in debate, and so blind stupid about your own daughter?'

He had sunk back into a deep leather chair and stuffed the neck of the whisky bottle into his mouth.

'You're married to a coon,' he said. 'We coons all desert our children.'

'Lucy is very clever as well as deeply disturbed. She wants nothing more than for you to seize the phone and start yelling at Jill, demanding custody.'

During the days that followed, Marcus had re-read *A Clockwork Orange*.

A character called F. Alexander, an author by trade and the kind of liberal, cloud-cuckoo dupe whose heart bleeds for young criminals, is battered in his home by Alex's gang, who then proceed to rape his wife. She dies of it. Yet F. Alexander clings to his insanely progressive views about crime and punishment. Only later, when he befriends the reconditioned Alex, and recognition begins to dawn, does he exclaim:

'*Yes. For by Christ, if he were I'd tear him, I'd split him, by God, yes yes, so I would.*'

Marcus had visited his old tutor, Geoffrey Villiers, to consult him about the moral of the story (he didn't mention the video tape of Lucy's genitals). Villiers shared Marcus's concern. Whenever they met Marcus felt that Villiers, the 'Dame', was the only friend he could always trust.

'Lucy, of course, knows that you once defended the nastiest criminals, Marcus, and preached the kind of progressive tenderness represented by Anthony Burgess's dupe.'

Marcus's hands were deep in his pockets as they prowled the quadrangle. 'And still preached by Lucy's mother? Is that it?'

'No, no, Marcus, it's you she's getting at. Lucy is telling you that your own conversion was as shabby as F. Alexander's.'

'In other words I jettisoned Jill and my progressive philosophy in a single motion of opportunism?'

'The moral is surely obvious, Marcus. Lucy admires the young anarchist hoodlum Alex, the gang leader, because he rejects parental control and practises crime as an art form. Need I add that Lucy is very young and—'

'I'm still baffled, Geoffrey. That book is almost thirty years old now. The young criminals you and I encounter today have little in common with Alex and his gang, who wrought havoc for the fun of it, for kicks. Our "customers" are in it strictly for the money – or the drugs.'

'I wouldn't be so sure. Don't forget the modern boys who "rev" council estates like Eden Manor all night long in stolen cars and motorbikes.'

Returning to London, Marcus had composed a long, loving letter to Lucy, ignoring the obscene tape and asking her to believe that he was not a reactionary.

> I don't believe in hanging, darling, and I don't believe in flogging, and I don't support the Rt Honourable Jeremy Darling's new Public Order Act which may yet stuff our jails with ravers, New Age Travellers and the more lively opponents of blood sports. Haven't I called, time and again, for massively funded educational and vocational programmes in the prisons and the inner cities beset by vandalism, mugging, joy-riding, arson? All I have ever said for prisons is that they put cynical, hardened, recidivist criminals out of the way.

Posting the letter, he realised with despair that he was now pleading his case with Lucy as if she were an impartial adult. Louise would have told him he was wasting his time. 'If she wants to quarrel with you, she'll find one pretext or another. She'll twist anything you say in order to sustain the torture.'

It was time to see Clive Wellings.

They met in the Sea Breeze Fish Restaurant in Pont Street. A forensic wizard working for the Drug Squad, Wellings was excessively fond of fish fried in batter, a man who had learned to turn a blind eye to his waistline. At a glance Clive could be mistaken for a bloated haddock.

'Did you ever hear of Livingstone Lord?' Marcus asked.

'The Jamaican drugs baron?'

'He's out on bail at the moment, having shopped enough of his kith and kin to ensure his early demise. The CPS did a trade-off with him.'

'So?'

'I want you to ask your Drugs Squad chums whether they can pin down any narcotics traffic between Lord and Nick Paisley. The Richardson family of Eden Manor could be the couriers.'

Wellings shook his head. 'They never disclose surveillance at that level. There are too many corpses hanging on the end of a loose word.'

Marcus was staring at his friend. Of all the Lemons he knew, Clive Wellings was the most timorous, a man terrified of his own shadow. Yet sheer disgust at the failings of the criminal justice system, and total admiration for Marcus Byron, had induced him to sign on.

'Clive, kindly examine this cassette for me.'

Wellings had been beckoning to the waitress for the ketchup.

'Ta, love.' Stuffing a hunk of fish in his mouth, he nodded at Marcus. 'Understood. Whatever you say, Boss.'

'Clive, I want to know the exact specification of the video camera they used.'

'I'll do my best.'

Marcus cleared his throat, acutely embarrassed. 'Clive, would you have to play the tape on to a screen to determine the camera used?'

'You'd prefer I didn't view it? Understood.'

'Thanks. I'm grateful.'

'How's your daughter Lucy these days?'

'You seem to be running short of lemon on that fish, Clive. Have one of mine.'

Marcus produced a beauty from his pocket then, making his excuses, hurried out of the Sea Breeze Fish Restaurant and back to his chambers.

The taxi is ticking over outside St Hilda's. Marcus's tip, as usual, is handsome – he and the driver between them have reintroduced the birch, hanging, the stocks and hand-chopping on the Saudi Arabian model. The driver has assured him that crime is a thing of the past in Saudi Arabia.

'Almost as good as the Isle of Man, eh?'

'You got it, Guv.'

Whenever he is shown into Mrs Nearcliffe's office, Marcus feels like a small boy in short trousers. Whenever he visits a friend in hospital, he becomes convinced that he himself will be slammed on to an operating table. He remembers standing over his brother-in-law Herb Knowles in St Luke's after Herb broke an arm, a year ago, arresting a gang of Griffins at Broadway Station. Marcus immediately felt the pain in his own arm. To make sure it wasn't fractured Marcus put it round Marcia's shoulders.

'How are we going to keep your Herb out of trouble, sister?'

Marcia had smuggled a dish of Herb's favourite salmon cakes to his bedside, and was now spooning them into the greedy bugger's wide-open maw.

'You tell me, Marco,' Marcia said solemnly.

Wendy had always been the clever girl of the family, Marcia the second mother to her five siblings.

'I'll tell you!' Herbert announced between mouthfuls, in the stentorian voice of a Baptist lay-preacher. 'I'll tell you how Herbert Knowles can stay out of trouble! He just swops jobs with his Honour here!'

Marcus had chuckled. 'Someone threatened to "do a Ku Klux Klan" on me in court the other day, Herb.'

'At your salary I wouldn't complain, brother.'

'Now none of that,' Marcia chided Herbert. 'You know Marco took a big drop in pay when he gave up getting villains off.'

Marcus shakes these warm memories out of his head. He is in St Hilda's School for Girls and a secretary is conducting him into Mrs Nearcliffe's office, or 'study' as the Headmistress prefers to call it. Marcus notices the peculiar blend of the feminine and masculine in the decor, a token, he assumes, of women's struggle for educational equality.

Mrs Nearcliffe is wearing her ice-box expression. He feels ten years old.

'Judge Byron, Lucy is sitting nine GCSEs.'

'Yes, how is she coping?'

'Frankly, she's not. No lack of ability but her recent record of absenteeism is appalling. If she *does* turn up at the start of the day, which is rare, she's more than likely to drift out whenever she feels like it. Even in the middle of a class, right under her teacher's nose.'

'May I ask whether Lucy's mother has been informed?'

'Of course. Regularly. Am I to infer, Judge Byron, that you are totally unaware of what we have been telling Ms Hull? Frankly, it doesn't make our work easier when parents behave like children.'

'I shall speak to her.' He clears his throat. 'To Lucy, I mean.'

'And not before time, Judge Byron. But I'm afraid that's not the end of it. Lucy has repeatedly been sighted in a variety of local pubs, consuming what's called TNC liquid dynamite – that's packaged cider—'

'Yes, I know what it is.'

'Plus Thunderbirds, Snakebites and Blastaways – in short, the lot.'

Mrs Nearcliffe is studying the large, twisting hands of the father seated opposite her. His handsome face is a lino-cut of guilt. Her tone softens.

'I'm an admirer of yours, Judge Byron. You are a man of courage.'

'Thank you, Mrs Nearcliffe. I'd like to be a good father but I may not be cut out for it.' He hesitates, shrugs. 'I never had one myself. Just my good Uncle Jeremiah.'

But Mrs Nearcliffe is not to be diverted down Memory Lane into the Old Kent Road.

'Frankly, Lucy may be getting back at you – has that ever occurred to you?'

'It occurs to me all the time.'

'Lucy's problems are even more serious, I fear. She's been seen in the Mirage Club with the youngest of the Richardson boys, Daniel. I have made it abundantly clear to every girl in the school that the Mirage Club is strictly out of bounds. It's a dangerous place. Teenagers have collapsed and died there after tanking up on wine then swallowing ecstasy tablets. They become hyperactive, they over-heat during hours of frantic dancing, they boil to death with body temperatures up to 41 centigrade. Pupils dilate, the jaw tightens, blood pressure rises. The Richardsons are notorious suppliers – their 100mg tablets carry dove-shaped markings and cost £12 each. But Lucy is never short of money, isn't that the case?'

'I do my best. If I cut down on her pocket money she would only—'

'It wouldn't make any difference, Judge Byron. Doug McIntyre, our local CID man, is convinced that the Richardsons are supplying Lucy free of charge – through an intermediary.'

'I – I see.'

'Now why would they do that?'

'I really have no idea. We need to get Lucy to professional counselling,' Marcus adds lamely.

'I've said as much to Ms Hull. I asked her whether Lucy had been experiencing any of the standard symptoms of addiction: anxiety, insomnia, psychosis, hallucinations – at the very least heavier, irregular menstrual periods or none at all.'

Marcus does not want to ask but has to: 'What did Jill say?'

'Ms Hull said Lucy sometimes has difficulty waking up in the morning and getting to school – nothing more serious than that.'

Mrs Nearcliffe is wearing an expression of dramatic scepticism.

'Did you believe her?' Marcus asks, realising too late that this is the tone he employs from his raised chair in court.

'Actually, I was far from convinced.'

He nods. 'Jill is covering up.'

'But why? Most mothers—'

'Most mothers, Mrs Nearcliffe, don't have to worry about retaining custody of their child.'

'That's still an issue between you, is it?'

'And Lucy knows it, Mrs Nearcliffe.'

As he reaches the door the Headmistress offers him a word of consolation.

'Lucy is showing a remarkable talent for tennis.'

He smiles gratefully. 'I bought her one of these new, big-headed graphite rackets.'

'You'll be pleased to hear she has been chosen to play for the school. She seemed quite delighted – I was pleasantly surprised.'

Driving away from St Hilda's, deeply depressed, Marcus asks himself whether custody is really still the issue. Would Louise put up with Lucy or Lucy with Louise under the same roof? Would custody be an issue but for the presence of Nick Paisley in Lucy's home? Whichever way he turns, Marcus sees Nick Paisley. If the Richardson boys are supplying Lucy free – free! and she's a 'rich' girl! – why?

Joe O'Neill's hand is still in plaster, nothing serious, though the smell is terrible on hot days when he's been sweating at his desk. He hopes Brigid doesn't notice the odour and mark down Ulstermen as soapless barbarians. He's pleased to find himself in a taxi, moonlighting again for Brigid Kyle, but less pleased to be taking her back to Eden Manor. Fixing her a visit to Ruth Tanner had been his bright idea, but he just wishes Mrs Kyle had dressed for the occasion a little less conspicuously. The kids of the estate may not have much use for her crocodile-skin shoes, but the jewellery is a diabolical provocation.

A missionary approaching a cannibal's camp fire couldn't feel less relaxed than Joe does. She's asking for it!

Still, the money is good and Brigid pays promptly. Besides, it's an honour to work for her – they say she's an intimate of Marcus Byron, for whom Joe's admiration is unreserved. But what does 'intimate' mean?

Ruth Tanner had been tickled pink by the idea of giving this famous journalist a bed under her roof. Ruth remembers the cool way Brigid Kyle had taken the abducted child from the groping paws of Mark Griffin. Ruth had been one of the party of distressed women running in pursuit that dreadful day.

Ruth Tanner is the wife of garage-owner and ace repair man Ron, but you'd never guess. Ron is squarely of this earth whereas Ruth, though fat and fortyish, can affect a voice posh enough to slice a French baguette. She's a local councillor, too, and Chair of the Eden Manor Tenants' Association – and permanently at war with the Griffins and Richardsons. She regularly reports their truant kids to the schools (who don't want to know), she has a buzz-alarm wired to Eden Manor police station, she openly fraternises with the cops, offers McIntyre and Jenkins cups of tea in broad daylight – and yet no one has ever laid a hand on her or hurled her window boxes through the glass into her sitting room, or put lighted papers through her letter box, or heaped all her furniture on a bonfire – incredible.

Perhaps it's because they all know the personal tragedy she and Ron have suffered – but she will not be talking about that to Brigid

Kyle or any stranger. Joe O'Neill knows but has decided not to mention it to Brigid.

Not that Ruth escapes verbal abuse. The females of the Griffin and Richardson tribes (which include several allied families) don't take it well when she remonstrates with them about litter, filth, dogs, drunkenness.

'Ruth, you're a fucking bitch! If yer don't fuck off I'll come down and smash yer face!'

But they call her Ruth.

'So long as they call me Ruth,' she warmly greets Brigid Kyle and Joe, 'it really doesn't matter what they say.'

Brigid passes admiring remarks about the interior decoration of Ruth's small council flat.

Ruth smiles at her guest. 'What did you expect?'

'Well, I—'

Brigid Kyle is already writing in her head. The sharp phrases will pass straight from her laptop computer to the *Sentinel*'s waiting screens on the Isle of Dogs.

> I have been privileged to meet a remarkable woman, the kind of British citizen we would all, regardless of sex, like to be. I mean the kind of brave, principled person who keeps our civilisation afloat.

'Well,' says Joe, rising from the sofa, 'I'll be off then.'

It's as much a question as a statement, but neither woman puts any obstacle in his way.

'Keep out of mischief, Joe,' Ruth Tanner calls.

He hesitates at the door. 'In case of trouble—'

'Goodbye, Joe,' Brigid waves cheerily. 'And don't punch anyone's jaw on your way out.'

He's gone. 'The younger Griffin kids will probably empty a chamber pot on to his head,' Ruth chuckles. 'Par for the course.'

'I want to ask you about Lucy Byron.'

'Oh.' Ruth's eyes widen. 'There's no shortage of rumours about that one. I've heard that parents at St Hilda's are threatening to withdraw their girls unless Mrs Nearcliffe gets rid of her.'

'Why?'

'She's considered a disruptive influence – but that's only the half of it. Girls from St Hilda's simply do not consort with Richardsons in druggy clubs and on street corners – and frankly, I dread to think what is going to happen next.'

'To Lucy?'

'Ha! Well, you might put it that way! Talk to Doug McIntyre and Cliff Jenkins, Brigid – may I call you Brigid? Of course, they'd have to be careful, speaking to a famous journalist.'

'Ruth, I should tell you something. I'm not interested in Lucy as a journalist. Her father is a friend of mine . . .'

'Well, no offence, but he hasn't done very well as a dad, has he?'

'But he cares.'

'Tea? Milk? Sugar? To speak perfectly frankly, Doug, Cliff and Ken—'

'Who's Ken?'

'Ken Crabbe. Inspector Crabbe. He runs the local Attendance Centre at Mason Lodge. His Saturday-afternoon "clients" include a regular run of Richardson and Griffin boys who Lady Harsent wants to keep out of Downton. Ken keeps his ear to the ground.'

Ruth Tanner bustles into the kitchen and emerges with tea and biscuits on a tray. Brigid helps her make space on the sitting-room table.

'You were going to tell me what all these police officers think, Ruth.'

'I don't want to be indiscreet. This is between ourselves?'

'Of course.'

'Doug, Cliff and Ken all believe Lucy Byron is heading for the courts. And she knows it – very bright, that girl, despite the drugs.'

'She's courting trouble?'

'And someone's pushing her. No sugar, did you say?'

'No, thank you. Ruth, I'd like to talk to this Inspector Ken Crabbe – might that be possible?'

'I'll see what I can do but I can't promise anything.' She drops two lumps of sugar into her cup and stirs it thoughtfully. 'Our Ken is a changed man in my opinion.'

'Changed you say?'

Ruth nods. 'Scared. If you want my guess, they've got to him.'

'They?'

'Yes, dear. They.'

# *Seven*

THEY HAVE BROUGHT PAUL RICHARDSON in, on a charge of robbing Simon Galloway. Having been granted police bail, Paul has failed to attend, been arrested under warrant and held in the cells overnight.

His younger brother Daniel had turned up on schedule and been granted bail by Patrick Berry on condition that he did not approach the victim, Simon Galloway – or any member of his family.

'That's understood, Daniel?'

'Yeah.'

'And you are forbidden to enter Oundle Square and Brancaster Road. Understood?'

'Yeah.'

'And if you do not turn up here, at this court, on the date given, in two weeks' time, you will have committed a separate offence. Understood?'

'Yeah.'

Today Lady Harsent is sitting. Wendy takes Paul Richardson through his all-too-familiar details: name, residence, date of birth. Tall, broad-shouldered, heavy-jowled, his jaw layered in growth, his hair sculpted flat on his head, Paul is only seventeen but could be mistaken for twenty-five. Four security men stand guard.

Wendy remembers Paul's last visit, only ten days ago. He had been convicted of possessing Class A drugs, mainly cocaine, with a street value of £650. He'd been carrying an offensive weapon when arrested and had assaulted PC Cliff Jenkins.

Paul's criminal record filled two pages.

Five minutes after the Bench retired to consider sentence Wendy had been summoned to the retiring room by two thrusts on her buzzer. On arrival, she heard a new magistrate, a 'wingman', Rodney Parker by name, vehemently insisting on custody.

Patrick had already struck up a friendship with Rodney Parker. 'He's a potential Lemon,' Patrick had confided to Wendy.

'Every alternative punishment has failed in the past,' Parker was protesting. 'Just look at his record. Appalling.'

Lady Harsent wore the serene smile of experience.

'I have been around a long time, Rodney. I know this young man. Paul Richardson is a victim first and last – sexually abused as a child and out of school since he was eleven. Appearances can be deceptive. You will learn that when you have been around as long as I have.'

'No school would tolerate him for more than a week. The PSR admits as much.'

'Blame the system – it's never a child's fault.'

'He hasn't paid a penny of his previous fines.'

'Paul has no money, of course – the Richardson family are destitute, apart from Income Support.'

'And Housing Benefit. The lad was carrying over a thousand pounds when arrested, not to mention the value of the drugs!'

The magistrates had fallen silent. They should not be arguing vehemently in front of the justices' clerk.

'Ah, Wendy,' drawled Lady H., casting an evil eye on the faintly frivolous collar in floppy silk caressing the lapels of Wendy's severe dark suit. A diamond brooch shaped like a palm tree, a wedding present from her brother Marcus, hinted at a better life elsewhere.

Wendy waited to be addressed.

'My colleague Mr Parker believes that we cannot avoid custody in this case,' Lady H. said, opening her compact mirror and repainting her mouth. 'Kindly explain to Mr Parker that we enjoy absolute freedom of decision.'

Wendy had no need to consult the Archbold law manual she carried.

'You have to bear in mind that Paul is charged with two separate offences. Possession of Class A drugs normally incurs a custodial sentence and—'

'But Jimmy – Mr Hayley-White – says in his excellent pre-sentence report that imprisonment in Downton will merely foster criminal attitudes in Paul.'

'He doesn't seem short of criminal attitudes,' Parker remarked.

Wendy kept her eye fixed on Lady H. 'I am merely advising that the prosecution could appeal against a non-custodial sentence.'

'Derek Jardine, you mean? I must say, I don't care for that young man at all. Over-zealous.'

Wendy had not said 'madam'. She would address the no-nonsense Miss Swearwell as 'madam' even in the Ladies', but with Lady H. the grudging courtesy was reserved for the open court. The point was not lost on Lady H., who divided the clerks between those who 'madam-ed' her in private and those who did not. This young Berry woman was also the wife of Patrick Berry, Lady H.'s impudent rival for the chairmanship of the Magistrates' Courts Committee.

And, worst of all, Marcus Byron's sister.

Wendy glanced at the third magistrate, old Mr Dickenson, who had been nodding off throughout the fierce exchanges. She could predict that when Lady Harsent finally turned to him with a 'Don't you agree, Albert?' he would murmur abjectly, 'Oh yes, Cecilia, entirely.'

It was all stitched up, the two-to-one majority. Young Rodney Parker would learn the hard way.

'Very well.' Lady H. nodded dismissively to Wendy.

Wendy returned to her desk in the court room, evading an interrogatory grimace from Derek Jardine. Five minutes later, the usher commanded everyone to stand as Lady H. swept in ahead of her two male colleagues, one docile, the other livid.

'A Supervision Order for one year. Now stand up, Paul. Yes, stand up. Kindly take your hands out of your pockets. Let me tell you, Paul, that you were within a whisker of Downton. We have given you one last chance – take it.'

Paul's hands remained deep in his pockets. He already had a one-year SO, so what was new? The two sentences would virtually run concurrently.

Wendy could guess how dearly Derek Jardine would like to appeal against this decision but his immediate superior was Nick Paisley. No Richardson boy went to Downton if Paisley could help it.

So now Paul is back before Lady H., under heavy Securicor

guard, having committed a robbery on Simon Galloway within days of receiving a Supervision Order on the Class A drugs charge. Marcus had raged when Wendy gave him the bare details, faxing them on to the Shadow Home Secretary, Max Venables, with a stinging message: 'It's time the politicians knew what the public is not allowed to know.'

Paul is as cool as ever, and Lady H. serene. The issue is bail. Representing Paul, Edgar Averling points out that the charge will probably be downgraded from robbery to theft, since the stolen goods had not been taken from Simon Galloway's person, merely from his car, and no force or intimidation was alleged.

'Well, that's a very good point,' Lady H. smiles.

Derek Jardine is up. 'The charge, madam, is robbery, and I oppose bail on the following grounds. One, likelihood of further offences. Two, the offence was committed while Paul was on bail on other charges. Three, the high probability of attempted witness intimidation.'

Jimmy Haley-White, who has been in protracted conference with Averling, offers Local Authority accommodation for Paul.

'A bed and breakfast?' Lady H. asks.

'Yes, madam. You can of course attach further conditions.'

Averling again: 'Yes indeed, madam.'

Derek Jardine is seething but helpless. 'Madam, regarding the high probability of witness intimidation—'

'Yes, Mr Jardine?'

'Madam, I would point out that the victim's wife, Mrs Galloway, remains in hospital after being robbed and subjected to grievous bodily harm. The suspect the police are looking for is Paul Richardson's brother, Amos. Madam, I ask you to consider the wider picture when considering the Crown's application for a remand in custody.'

Averling objects. 'Madam, my friend knows perfectly well that two cases cannot be run together, particularly when no one has yet been charged with the alleged robbery of Mrs Galloway.'

Lady H. turns to her clerk. 'Can you give us any advice on that, Mrs Berry?'

'Madam, under the law as it now stands Paul has no right to bail, having been charged with an offence while on bail. Madam, this being so, the court may feel its first duty is to protect the public and the victims.'

Averling is up. 'Madam, your learned clerk's first sentence

is correct, as a matter of law, but her second sentence is a recommendation which usurps the role of the Bench.'

Wendy chokes. 'Madam, I have to agree with that submission and I therefore withdraw my advice.'

Paul swaggers out, no longer in custody, remanded to a bed and breakfast in which he does not intend to spend a single night.

Darren Griffin comes next, pale, sallow, chewing gum. Edgar Averling remains in his chair: another client.

Rat Boy has been found guilty of two car thefts, known as TDAs, plus driving without a licence or insurance. Darren sits with his gleaming trainers thrust out, the laces untied, and an expression of weary contempt as he awaits sentence.

The principal witness had been the garage-owner Ron Tanner, husband of the redoubtable heroine of Eden Manor, Ruth. Darren Griffin's happy hunting ground is Brancaster Road, where Ron parks the cars brought in by Simon Galloway and other clients for repair. At a previous, pre-trial hearing, Ron had confronted five youths, including Joseph and Darren Griffin, each represented at public expense by his own lawyer.

Each lawyer had given Ron Tanner a hard time in cross-examination: *which* boy had done *what* and precisely *when*? Ron found it impossible to remember every detail – but he was certain they'd all been in it together. It was bloody obvious! But Ron discovered – not for the first time – that there is no such thing as 'them' in a court – only individuals. And there is no such thing as bloody obvious.

'You're not a credible witness, are you?' Edgar Averling had puffed at him.

A Bench chaired by Patrick Berry had reluctantly eliminated four of the boys from the case; Darren Griffin, the obvious ring-leader, remained the only defendant to stand trial.

So now, four weeks later, Lady Harsent addresses Darren.

'You have been very naughty again, but your case worker reports that you have made some progress. Isn't that so, Mr Haley-White?'

The head of the Youth Justice Team jumps up, his dreadlocks leaping like playful snakes.

'Yes, madam. Darren's case worker believes Darren is finally confronting his own patterns of offending.'

'And the distress to his victims, I hope.'

'Definitely, madam.'

Wendy glances at Rodney Parker, slumped in his chair, his expression a study in simmering rage. Derek Jardine is scribbling in his notebook. All three are joined by a common thought: the public pays Senior Probation Officer Jimmy Haley-White £23,481 a year – including thirty-six days' leave – to unprotect it.

Lady H. is patting her beehive, a motion which brings her bosom into prominent play.

'Well, Darren, you have clearly begun to confront your own selfish behaviour, and I'm going to treat this new offence as a lapse. I don't want it repeated, do you understand? I don't want to see you back here again.'

'Yeah.'

'Very well, twenty-four hours' Attendance Centre, two hours a week, every Saturday. Will that be at Mason Lodge, Mr Haley-White?'

'Yes, madam.' Jimmy is not very interested. Attendance Centres are not run by probation officers and social workers, which is why the pre-sentence reports from Jimmy's Youth Justice Team rarely recommend them.

Not for the first time, Darren Griffin will be running rings round Inspector Ken Crabbe at Mason Lodge.

That night a brick smashes through the Galloways' sitting-room window. Tom wakes up screaming. Stumbling out of bed, Simon hurries down to inspect the damage, calls the police, then goes back up to comfort his still-motherless little boy.

Cliff Jenkins is on night duty. He reaches 16 Oundle Square three minutes after receiving the call. He examines the brick.

'It's a message, Simon.'

'Who from?'

'That's the problem. You're taking on both the Richardsons and the Griffins. Frankly, and I never said this to you, Simon, I'd advise you to drop out of the railway vandalism case – though Herb Knowles and Doug would kill me for saying it.'

Lucy Byron stands in her darkened bedroom, observing No. 16 through drawn curtains, her eyes alight.

Councillor Ruth Tanner parks her Ford Escort – lovingly serviced by husband Ron – half a mile from Mason Lodge.

'Anything closer and you're asking for it,' she tells her passenger, Brigid Kyle, with a fat-and-fortyish wink. 'The Attendance Centre lads will do over a car faster than a snake takes a mouse.'

'I must remember to hang on to my handbag.'

The two women begin to walk briskly up Orchard Avenue, a sleepy street of Victorian semis more or less dominated by dustbins and black plastic refuse sacks from which rivulets of pee meander across the cracked paving stones.

'Stuff your purse and credit cards in your bra,' Ruth advises. Yells, honking and braying up the street indicate that a few of the Attendance Centre's customers have turned up early. Brigid notices a flash car parked bang outside the entrance to Mason Lodge.

'Crime evidently pays!' Ruth chuckles.

'That's Marcus's Rolls.'

Hearing from Brigid that Ruth had negotiated the visit with Inspector Ken Crabbe, Marcus had promptly invited himself. 'Ken's an old friend.'

Drawing closer, Brigid sees that Marcus and his gleaming Rolls – registration plate MB1 – are surrounded by a dozen youths, all engaged in a lively debate as to whether it is legal to park on a single yellow line at 1.45 on a Saturday afternoon.

'It's legal!' Marcus declares. 'Would I break the law, lads?'

'So that's your famous friend,' Ruth says. 'I've seen him on telly often enough. I hadn't realised he's so big.'

'Yes, Marcus enjoys being tall.'

'And those shoulders! I admire your taste.'

'Thank you, Ruth.'

'What does his wife think?'

'Oh, I'm sure she admires my taste, too.'

'Now, you fellows', Marcus is shouting, 'would have been deported to Australia a hundred years ago. After a good birching. Many of you would have died on the voyage. Good idea, eh?'

'They don't seem to mind,' Brigid murmurs nervously to Ruth.

'Oh they're lapping it up. Except Darren Griffin – he's the one sulking and skulking against the railings, with his mini-mafia.'

'You don't have to tell me who Darren Griffin is, Ruth.'

'I forgot your little encounter with him. He's just been given twenty-four hours for two TDAs. Perhaps he thinks he should turn up once, for ten minutes.'

Marcus greets Brigid and shakes hands with Ruth. 'I've heard all about you,' he says.

'I've never heard of you.'

'Well, I'm a shy fellow, low profile.' He turns back to his audience of reluctantly admiring young offenders. 'Now listen to me, boys. How about two years' national service for every eighteen-year-old, like we used to have? Defend your country instead of robbing it, eh? Did you ever hear of Winston Churchill?'

Most of the lads are peering through the smoked windows of the Rolls, drooling.

'That's Daniel Richardson over there,' Ruth murmurs to Brigid, 'the very young-looking black boy.'

'He's the one I want to talk to.'

'Well, go ahead, now's your chance, before Ken Crabbe calls them inside.'

Brigid notes that Ruth has not offered to accompany her. She crosses the road and approaches three black youths, who have set themselves apart. 'Daniel?' she says with a cheery smile, 'Daniel Richardson?'

'Yeah.'

She offers her hand. 'I'm Brigid Kyle, a friend of Lucy's dad.'

Reluctantly, as if her hand might bite, he token-touches it.

'How's Lucy?' she asks. 'I hope she's working hard for her GCSEs.'

Daniel is shy, guarded. He shrugs. 'Yeah.'

Across the street, Marcus is bellowing. 'Now, lads, I'm parking this car of mine right here. It's full of top stereo equipment, graphic equalisers, mobile phones, all that kind of stuff. When I come out, I want to find it as I left it.'

'Are you very fond of Lucy?' Brigid is asking Daniel. 'I know she's very close to you.'

Another shrug. 'Dunno.'

'Daniel, if you're fond of her, you'd want to keep her out of trouble, wouldn't you?'

'Yeah. Got to move.' Daniel and his friends drift away from her, towards the entrance, although no one is going in yet. Brigid rejoins Ruth.

'No luck?'

'He's very shy.'

Marcus is leading the ladies inside as if he owned the place.

'Every Griffin boy, and every Richardson,' he announces in his loud baritone, 'has seen the inside of this derelict Victorian boys' club.' He conducts them into a fusty little office at the rear of the building, piled with cardboard boxes.

'Afternoon, Ken.' Marcus gestures at the boxes. 'We've come to charge you with handling stolen goods.'

Inspector Ken Crabbe rises wearily. 'Afternoon, Ruth.'

'This is Brigid Kyle, Ken.'

'I read your columns, Mrs Kyle.'

Marcus takes Brigid on a conducted tour. 'Ken has run the place for ten years, three Saturdays a month, forty Saturdays a year, pretending to do some good to lads ordered by the courts to turn up for a couple of hours at 1.45 p.m.'

The boys are pouring in now, recording their names in the register and then seating themselves at long trestle tables, waiting for the first written exercise, which may be about the quickest of four alternative routes from A to D, or which men from a list are married, employed and live in Ipswich. Brigid has positioned herself behind Daniel Richardson, leaning over his shoulder. She sees a printed list of common surnames running down the page:

Brown is single
Jones lives in Ipswich
Sinclair is employed
Brown lives in Ipswich
Jones is married
Sinclair lives in London
Jones is unemployed
(and so on . . .)

'Easy?' she asks Daniel.

'Yeah.' His pencil flicks down the list, eliminating every name with one or more defect: single, unemployed and not living in Ipswich. He instantly puts a cross against 'Brown lives in Ipswich' because Brown is already out of the reckoning – an indication of intelligence.

'Will you be taking GCSEs, Daniel?'

'Yeah, English, maths . . . maybe physics.'

'You've got a bright future ahead of you, then.'

Brigid notices that Darren Griffin – who is seated at another table, black boys steer clear of Griffins – is staring at the list of printed names in frustration and rising anger. Marcus is standing over him.

'Good afternoon, Darren. The secret of this exercise is elimination. Anyone who does not possess all three desired qualities goes out. Yes?'

The pale, sallow face remains sullen. His pencil stays on the table.

'You sent my dad down,' Darren says.

'The laws of England, Darren, the laws of England.'

'Yeah, run by nigs.'

Ken Crabbe has been observing this exchange from the Supervisor's desk. 'Show respect for his Honour, Darren.'

Marcus has wisely moved on, fists clenched in his trousers pockets. Brigid and Ruth follow.

'I've lobbied the Home Office for additional funding. Through no fault of Ken's, the regime here is broken-backed, under-staffed and of course ineffective. The boys spend half their time lounging around in the street, smoking and eyeing likely vehicles for a snatch. Wispy ten-year-olds are bunged in with strapping seventeen-year-olds – a scandal. Now the Home Office – the Rt Hon. Jeremy Darling – plans to throw girls in as well.'

Ken Crabbe has joined them. 'If that happens, I quit.'

Some of the lads cheer derisively.

A grim smile creases Crabbe's craggy features as he leads his visitors to the model kitchen, where three keen lads are whipping up scones, and then to the gymnasium upstairs, where a few youths are kicking a ball around under the lazy eye of Crabbe's elderly colleague 'Old George'.

'Frankly,' Marcus says, 'this is no kind of punishment. What's needed here is half an hour of a strict, boot-camp regime.'

'Then fund me the staff,' Crabbe says. Brigid senses that Crabbe is not at ease with his 'old friend' Marcus Byron.

'No one's blaming you, Ken.'

'Ten years you've done this, Inspector Crabbe?' Brigid asks. 'In your free time?'

'Ten years, yes. When I first took over I hoped to offer boys who usually lack male role models something closer to their real needs than the feminising mouthwash of the Probation Service and the Youth Justice teams – and no disrespect to you ladies.'

He excuses himself and rapidly assembles a group of lads to learn the rudiments of first-aid. He instructs one of them to lie doggo on the ground. Then he turns to the sullen Darren Griffin.

'Right, Darren! This lad has just been hit by a car. You're walking past. What's the first thing you do?'

Darren shrugs. 'Go through his pockets.'

Brigid turns away, stifling a laugh, but Marcus doesn't see the joke. In his view there is nothing funny about Darren Griffin.

'The regime here is crap,' he mutters. 'Nobody gets sent to Mason Lodge unless he's a hardened reoffender. Burglary, robbery, TDAs, you name it. Look at Old George over there, broken-backed, cynical, shuffling about drinking one cup of tea after another. Two or three months ago Joseph and Darren Griffin spray-gunned the newly redecorated toilet. Old George turned two blind eyes. When Ken came down from the gymnasium, Old George hadn't seen a thing.'

Brigid notices that Ken Crabbe has gone rigid and very pale. He moves away.

'Marcus, I think we ought to get you out of here,' Brigid says. 'It's not good for your blood pressure.'

'Nonsense. I'm here. I stay.'

Ruth takes Brigid by the arm, drawing her back towards the kitchen. 'It was that remark by Darren about nigs,' she murmurs. 'It must be hard not to drag the brat outside by the scruff of the neck.' She lowers her voice to a whisper. 'Which is what Ken did after the spray-gunning incident – with fatal consequences.'

'Fatal?'

'I say no more.'

Crabbe dismisses the boys early. He's clearly fed up. Brigid divines that the Police Inspector rather resents Marcus's caustic criticisms. There's an uneasiness between them just below the surface. She remembers Ruth's comment: 'They've got to him.' What did she mean? What did she mean by 'fatal consequences'? What can she 'say no more' about?

Crabbe takes his visitors back into his office. 'No one has laid a finger on your car – yet,' he tells Marcus. 'But Darren Griffin and his gang are hanging about across the street.'

'Plucking up courage,' Marcus chuckles.

'Perhaps you should take a look, Marcus,' Brigid suggests.

'No way.'

Crabbe is eager to unburden himself to Brigid. She soon gathers the extent of his contempt for the C (Criminal) Department officials of the Home Office.

'Total neglect. They couldn't care less provided we avoid bad publicity. I have to leave every external door wide open in case these tender little babes, who'd mug you as soon as see you, all fry to death. What's the result? I begin with thirty lads at 1.45 – or call it 2.00, or call it 2.15 – and by 3.15 I'm lucky if I've still got ten of them. So I say to old George, "George," I say, "we'd better count who's here and who's not here." "Don't bother," says George, "what you don't see you don't know."'

A crash of splintering glass from outside. Marcus and Ken race for the street door. Brigid makes to follow but Ruth catches her arm.

'Stay. Women who play spectators to violence only raise the stakes.'

'Yes but—'

'But nothing. I see that staying with me in Eden Manor hasn't taught you as much I thought.'

Brigid flushes. Just occasionally, beneath her flaming thatch, her fast Dublin blood can be sent spiralling beyond her control.

'Shall I tell you a story about Ken?' Ruth consoles her.

'Oh please do.'

'The Youth Court – Lady Harsent was sitting that day – sent Ken a lad he could tell at once was a psycho. The boy had a record of robbing old people. He should have been straight inside but Lady Harsent thought it wouldn't "redeem" him if he fell among criminals! He was the hardest to handle Ken ever had. Then he started stomping on the face of the eighty-year-old widows he'd robbed in their homes. Old Bailey trial, full publicity, a life sentence. A reporter came round, tracking the young villain's passage through the criminal justice system. Ken was indiscreet about Lady Harsent and the Youth Court. He was promptly summoned to Home Office C3 in Queen Anne's Gate. They read him the Official Secrets Act.'

Brigid sighs sympathetically. 'It's a familiar story, of course. If the truth is awkward, suppress it.'

Marcus returns, fuming, followed by Ken Crabbe. 'That little bastard!'

No one dares speak, such is his wrath.

'What did he do?' Brigid whispers.

'Bastard!'

'Now, Judge,' Ruth says, 'you listen to me. Did Darren Griffin just rape your wife? Did he just batter you senseless because you refused to hand over the day's takings? Did he steal your Victoria

Cross before hospitalising you? He didn't? He monkeyed with your £60,000 car, is that it?'

Marcus subsides. 'Brigid says you're a fine woman, Ruth.'

Brigid lays a hand on Marcus's. 'I'm going to bite the bullet, Marcus.' She turns to Ken. 'Inspector Crabbe, what can you candidly tells us about Marcus's Lucy?'

The impact of this question on the rhino-hard Police Inspector is remarkable. Brigid knew from Ruth that Crabbe had learned his trade in a city suburb where even the most law-abiding motorist will jump a red light to avoid the perils of being trapped in a stationary car. He had spent ten years on the beat in Leeds's notorious Chapeltown district, where the druggies regularly batter pensioners as they leave the post office, scattering pathetic plastic bags of groceries in pools of motor oil and blood. Yet if a man could turn himself into pure vapour – Ken Crabbe now would.

'Can't help you,' he mutters.

'But surely,' Brigid presses him, 'you know Daniel Richardson pretty well, and he's close to Lucy.'

'They don't talk,' Crabbe says. 'That's their first rule.' Abruptly he changes the subject. 'Frankly, I'll tell you what gets me – they're brainwashing us into fucking social workers! Pardon my French, ladies.'

Brigid looks to Ruth for support but Ruth is embarrassed. She doesn't know Judge Byron. Marcus, too, seems to be relieved not to be discussing Lucy.

'Too many cautions?' he asks Ken Crabbe.

'Marcus, I've seen custody officers in the police stations blandly handing out cautions to thugs previously prosecuted and convicted.'

'We know the dismal statistics,' Marcus sighs. 'One-third of police cautions are offered to offenders previously cautioned or even convicted. That's got to stop.'

'Put that in your paper,' Crabbe addresses Brigid. He rises, takes a broom, and begins to sweep the cigarette ends and paper wrappings from the ground floor of Mason Lodge.

Amos Richardson had been cornered in one of Livingstone Lord's retreats – a cockroach-infested cold-water apartment stinking of dope and uncleared garbage. McIntyre took four men in. If high on crack cocaine, Amos was the most dangerous of the

Richardsons. They had to batter down the door on a warrant signed by Patrick Berry. Most magistrates (McIntyre commented to Jenkins) were careful to scribble their initials indecipherably across search warrants, but Patrick Berry takes pride in a legible signature.

In the event Amos was found alone and fast asleep across an old sofa and covered in filthy blankets. It took ten minutes to bring him into the world. During those ten minutes McIntyre's men found Susan Galloway's Rolex watch, her necklace, her cheque book and several credit cards. But, even after ransacking the apartment, no knife.

Amos, whose Rasta dreadlocks had gone, swore his name was Mason Stanley and swore he didn't live here – 'Just bunkin' for the night' – and swore he knew nothing about the stolen goods, and swore he couldn't remember who did live here.

'Just visitin'.'

'Who are you kidding, Amos?'

McIntyre took the tall, loose-limbed, rag-doll Amos in to Eden Manor police station, along with his red baseball cap.

'Cut your hair recently, Amos?'

'You 'aven't fuckin' cautioned me, 'ave yer?'

'Yes, we did.'

They flung him in a cell and offered him a solicitor from the rota list, but Amos would deal only with Edgar Averling or his sidekick, Simmonds.

Amos's previous cautions and convictions – some of them – spilled off the National Police Computer.

Attempted Burglary. Conditional Discharge, 6 months
Burglary. CD 1 year
Burglary, Criminal Damage. CD 1 year
Assault, Breach of CD × 4. Fined £5 × 4
Taking Vehicle Without Consent, No Insurance, Criminal Damage, Handle Stolen Goods. CD 1 year
Theft. Attendance Centre Order 18 hours. Compensation £75
Theft, Fail to Appear, Breach of CD × 5. Supervision Order 12 months
Attempted Robbery. Supervision Order 6 months
Breach ACO. Attendance Centre Order 24 hours
Theft, Theft, Breach of Bail. £24 Fine

McIntyre noted that Amos had served a three-month custodial sentence in respect of thirteen offences committed during one calendar year. (Miss Swearwell or Patrick Berry must have been chairing the Bench that day.) In June of the following year he had been returned to Downton for nine further offences.

Cautioned again by the Custody Sergeant, Amos was charged with (a) robbing Susan Galloway, (b) causing her grievous bodily harm and (c) possession of her stolen belongings.

Simmonds eventually showed up. After a conference in the cells, Amos refused to answer any questions when formally interviewed.

McIntyre vehemently opposed police bail and insisted Amos be held in custody until he appeared in court. But the Custody Sergeant shrugged. A social worker from the Borough turned up to represent Amos's interests, insisting that the youth be put in Local Authority accommodation for seventy-two hours until he appeared in court.

'Amos is a juvenile,' she declared. 'You cannot hold a juvenile in the cells for seventy-two hours.'

McIntyre refused to bend. 'Now that he knows the charges, he represents an immediate danger to the victim, who left hospital yesterday. He knows where she lives. He robbed her on her own doorstep.'

But the police no longer enjoyed the luxury of following their own judgment. The matter was referred to the local Multi Agency Juvenile Offenders Panel, chaired by Jimmy Haley-White. Sitting in on the discussion, McIntyre ground his teeth. His view was identical to that of his friend, Inspector Ken Crabbe: the Police Youth and Community Section had finally succumbed to the hegemonic social-work philosophy and was now resigned to remanding even the most dangerous youths into the care of little women weighing 130 pounds.

Four hours after Amos was brought in, he stepped out into the street with his red baseball cap jauntily reversed, a female social worker half his height, a broad grin and a clenched fist raised.

No blood had been found on Amos's clothing, and no knife.

'It's going to be hard to make the robbery charge stick,' McIntyre told Jenkins.

'If Nick Paisley has anything to do with it, there won't be a robbery charge. The CPS will drop it.'

'It all depends whether Susan Galloway nails him at the identification parade.'

'I'll be surprised if she can face the ordeal, frankly.'

'She'll remember that scar on his cheek. I only wish I'd inflicted it myself.'

'That honour belongs to Joseph Griffin – the battle of Century Park.'

'I'm going to make sure Ken Crabbe is in charge of the ID parade on the day. A lot of traumatised victims have seen straight under Ken's guidance.'

Jenkins laughed. 'Don't say "guidance", boyo – that would breach the sacred PACE.'

Both CID men shared the general police hostility to the Police and Criminal Evidence Act. Jenkins called it a 'villains' charter drafted by defence barristers'.

McIntyre jingled his car keys. 'While there's Ken, there's hope. Meanwhile, I might go up to have a word with the Galloways.'

'Give Susan my respects, Doug.'

Slotting his damaged Rolls into reserved residential parking – Darren Griffin had not only smashed a window but, more deadly, left two trademark knife-scratches across all four doors – Marcus hears a bleep on a horn beckoning him. The bleep is discreet and feminine. A black Fiat Punto is parked across the road, its diesel engine chugging.

A ravishing honey-blonde has him squarely in the sights of her mirrored sunglasses. He thrusts his head through the open window of the Fiat. She lifts her glasses to reveal greenish cat's eyes. The roots of her hair are not honey-blonde.

'Amazing,' he murmurs.

She might be smiling, he can't be sure. The young woman wears a 'might be' expression.

'What is "amazing"?'

'You uncannily resemble . . . someone I knew.'

'Three out of ten for originality.' She hands him a package without comment. Her diesel engine revs for departure. His eye has come to rest on a pair of very fine legs in black stockings.

'They make a filthy noise, these diesels,' he says. 'Lousy emission, too.'

'Not all of us can afford an MB1 registration plate.'

'You need to meet the right man, then.'

'Oh!' The cat's eyes slither angrily. 'Angela warned me I'd be meeting the world's MCP1.'

'Does the messenger have a name?'

'Heather Stuart.' She takes the large black hand extended through her window with a very light touch.

'You're Angela's trusted assistant? he asks.

'I hope so.'

'You work in Probation House, then?'

'I specialise in Juvenile – that's the Youth Courts.'

'That puts you above or below Jimmy Haley-White?'

If Heather Stuart notices the sexual innuendo, she ignores it.

'Jimmy is Jill Hull's protégé. There's no one "above" him except Jill. I'm merely the Head Office coordinator – under Angela.'

'You know Jimmy?'

'I've met him.'

'I may run out of questions before you come up for a drink.'

'I really can't, I'm—'

Marcus reaches across the black-stockinged legs and gently turns the ignition key. The diesel engine stutters, dies.

'Angela would be upset if you didn't – wouldn't she?'

The Fiat's window hums closed. Marcus opens the door for Heather Stuart. The young woman more than confirms her promise when displayed upright: her gleaming, doctored hair lies lightly on two gently curving shoulders; a thin black sweater is pulled tight over a challenging bosom beneath a Jaipur jacket of Indian cotton; a white pleated skirt teases perfect legs as she follows him across the street and into the lift.

'I always use the lift,' he tells her, 'though I live only one floor up.'

The lift is mirrored, wall-to-wall. Its maximum load is four but even two is tight if you're feeling tight.

'You're lazy, then?' she asks.

'No. But on the stairs there might be someone waiting to cut my throat.'

'Who would want to do that?'

'Ever heard of the Congress for Justice?'

'No.'

He flourishes a large set of keys, then steps back to allow her to enter Flat 4 ahead of him.

'My wife will be disappointed not to have met you,' he says.

'Louise is attending a meeting of the Northern Bar Association in Manchester. She's fighting Sandra Golding for the chairmanship.'

'Yes, I'd heard. It must keep her very busy.'

'Would you like a glass of orange juice – or something stronger?'

'I prefer lemon.' She smiles – or does she? 'I have one with me if you're short.'

He examines her up and down, undressing her with his large, mischievous eyes, while she parades around the sitting room, examining the paintings.

'Did Angela recruit you?'

'Yes.' She sinks down in the white leather sofa and folds her black legs.

'Good old Angela,' he says, opening the package she has given him. 'This may be a plum-pudding with brandy butter.' He winks.

'It's mainly the Sanderson case.'

The package contains (1) Leela Desai's first PSR on Alan Sanderson: Community Service; (2) Leela's second PSR, revised at Angela's behest: custody; (3) Leela's final PSR, following Jill Hull's intervention: Community Service; (4) Angela's notes on her most recent clash with Jill (though nothing about her lemon shamefully rolling across the floor – Marcus could be unforgiving).

'I hope Angela hasn't been using her officer copier.'

'No, she remembers what you told her about that.'

'What did I tell her?'

'That each copier carries its own "signature" so that leaks can be traced. I always take documents to a commercial agency during my lunch hour.'

'Good.'

'Do you know Angela well?' Heather Stuart asks.

'Very. Officially – not at all.'

She nods. 'I'm afraid for Angela. I think her days are numbered.'

'How will Jill dispose of her – an overdose of cream cake?'

He throws off his jacket and sits beside her on the sofa, tamping Virginia tobacco into his Sherlock Holmes pipe.

'You don't look like a probation officer,' he says.

'Oh? How do probation officers look?'

'Tell me something, Heather. What did your criminal clients make of you when you were doing case work? The male ones.'

'What do you mean?'

He lights his pipe, drawing strongly. 'You don't mind the smoke?'

'It smells very nice.'

'When Jill and I were married she once told me a story. A felon with a string of convictions laid a complaint against one of her more attractive female colleagues. "How about", he said, "a dress code to go along with No Racism, No Violence, No Discrimination, No Sexism, etc., etc. – the usual Probation Service wallpaper."'

'A dress code?'

'For female probation officers who swing beautiful legs in front of their clients, well knowing that if the man puts a hand wrong he goes straight back to court and into Wormwood Scrubs.'

Heather Stuart is bridling. 'Some men do find femininity a challenge to their male chauvinism. I agree it can be a problem.'

'Would you expect a policewoman, or a prison warder, or a nurse to display herself like our modern probation officers do?'

'But the whole ethos is different! We're very deliberately not in uniform.'

'That doesn't prevent you being in something. You exercise authority over your male "clients", don't you? And if they stay in bed, or play the fruit machines, or steal a few cars, when they should be attending on you – what happens?'

'I can't see what my clothes have to do with it.'

'What your clothes say to most of your male clients is, "Fuck me – but don't you dare."'

Heather Stuart is on her feet now, tossing her long honey-hair. 'I must go.' The cat's eyes swivel fiercely.

'So what do you make of Jimmy-Haley White?'

'I think you've already asked me that.'

'I merely asked you whether you knew him.'

Her pretty chin lifts defiantly. 'I don't agree with Jimmy's attitudes on crime, but he shows respect for women.'

'And I don't?'

'No, your Honour.'

'And what are your own "attitudes" on crime?'

Heather is at the door now. She shrugs her graceful shoulders. 'The same as Angela's.'

'Heather, come back and sit down, I'm going to tell you something.'

She doesn't move. Her graceful body is carved into defiance.

'You're a Lemon, Heather. No Lemon refuses when another asks her to sit down.'

Heather sits down again – but not beside him on the white-leather sofa.

'Do you know where the name Lemon came from?' he asks.

'No.'

'From a law tutor's fruit bowl.' He draws on his pipe. 'We are clockwork lemons.'

'As in *A Clockwork Orange*?'

'Precisely. Have you read it?'

'Of course.'

He rises. 'What are your hobbies?' he asks, standing over her imposingly, a very powerfully built man famous for his marathon bike rides.

'Well . . . I ski when I can. I play tennis and squash.'

'My sister Wendy is a keen athlete.'

'Really? I believe I may have seen her when visiting the Benson Street Youth Court. She's very beautiful.'

'It runs in the family – haven't you noticed?'

'Angela warned me that you are incredibly conceited.'

'No jokes allowed in the Probation Service?'

'Does your sister use the Riverview Sports Club? She does? I may have seen her in the gym.'

'You work out?'

'Yes.'

'You've given me an idea, though it may not be a good one. In fact it may be the silliest idea ever to have lodged in the head of a Crown Court judge.'

'Though the competition is stiff.'

'Heather, a very important man – not me! – is in desperate trouble. He's one of us. Would you help if you could?'

'How?'

'I mean you and Wendy together.'

'Yes, but how?'

'What are you doing next Friday night?'

'I was going to a friend's party. But I'm free on Tuesday and Thursday.'

'It has to be Friday. This "very important man" needs help on

Fridays. He has to be diverted – to use an expression beloved to your profession, Miss Stuart – from his normal disastrous habits. On Fridays.'

'OK, I'll skip the party.'

'Good. Wendy will be in touch with you.' He looks at her. 'The resemblance is amazing,' he says.

'Who to?'

'You don't know?'

'No idea.'

Left alone, Marcus sinks back into melancholy, ashamed of his unstoppable pitching for pretty women, his loss of gravitas. It always feels as if an automatic pilot has been switched on, and the voice he hears is not quite his own, insistently pressing its claims out of the echo-chamber of past conquests, past fiascos. Lust is depressing. Even lust gratified heralds sadness, depletion, betrayal.

Isn't Brigid enough for you? Have you ever known a nicer woman, and one graced by the wit you prize and so rarely find in the opposite sex?

These morose thoughts carry him away from sexual desire and back to its most bereft product, Lucy, the ultimate fiasco in his life. His day has been clouded by the message he received from her by the breakfast post. One of the dreaded Friends of the Earth brown envelopes lay on the mat beneath the letter flap. Lucy always used them, if only to mock Louise's efforts to please her. A small newspaper cutting, from the *Post*, had been enclosed.

It was a report written by Brigid's henchman, Joe O'Neill. Marcus stood rigid beside the front door as he read it, his heart thumping painfully.

> PENSIONER DEVASTATED. A heartbroken local pensioner has spoken out after three schoolgirls snatched an irreplaceable keepsake belonging to her late husband. The watch was grabbed from Ethel Ramsden, who is 77 years old, along with her handbag, as she walked through Century Park on her way to a doctor's appointment last Monday morning. Mrs Ramsden has cataracts in both eyes which blur her vision, and knows only that the girls were between 13 and 16 years old, two 'Coloured' and the other 'Black'. Detective Constable Cliff Jenkins said: 'This was a cowardly attack on a defenceless and vulnerable old lady.'

Lucy had enclosed no message. Marcus was overcome by a

sickening premonition. This time Eden Manor police would surely take her in. Or was it a hoax? Had the coincidence of the girls' ages and skin colours proved irresistible to her?

He had dialled the number at 23 Oundle Square. No answer. Reaching his chambers, he tried Jill's extension in Probation House. Her secretary answered.

'This is Marcus Byron for Jill Hull. It's urgent.'

'She's in a meeting.'

'It concerns our daughter.'

Jill came on the line. 'Yes?'

'Jill, Lucy has just sent me a cutting describing the robbery of a pensioner by three girls. There was no message. Do you know anything about it?'

'First I've heard of it.'

'For Christ's sake, who is she mixing with?'

'I suppose this is the first salvo in a new bid for custody?'

'It's nothing of the sort. Is she in trouble with the police?'

'No.' The phone went down. Marcus grabbed the Business Directory and dialled the *Post*.

'Put me through to Joe O'Neill, please.'

An Ulster voice came on the line. 'Joe O'Neill.'

'This is Marcus Byron speaking. You know who I am and we have a mutual friend in Brigid Kyle. I've just seen your report of the robbery of a pensioner, a Mrs Ramsden, by three teenage girls in Century Park.'

'Yes, I remember. How did you see my report?'

Marcus ignored the question. 'Are there any suspects?'

A moment's hesitation at the other end. 'I've not been notified of any arrests, sir. But I gather the police are active on the case.'

'Nothing you can tell me, Mr O'Neill?'

'You're putting me in a difficult situation, sir. Whatever I'm told is in strict confidence. I suggest you try DC Cliff Jenkins at Eden Manor.'

'OK. Thanks.'

By luck, he was able to get straight through to Brigid at her desk at the *Sentinel* – he hated the static on mobile phones.

'I'll speak to Joe,' she said. 'Call you back. When are you in court?'

'In fifteen minutes.'

Brigid came back to him in less than a minute. 'It's bad news, Marcus. Apparently Lucy has been "running", as they say, with

Daniel Richardson's sister Trish and a girl called Debbie O'Grady. Both girls have long records extending well beyond cautions.'

'Jesus! That bitch Jill! She must know!'

'Yes, Marcus,' Brigid said gently. 'She must.'

'Did O'Neill tell you anything else?'

Brigid spoke tenderly, as if walking on his heart. 'Lucy was taken out of school yesterday for questioning.'

'Out of school! Jesus! Who told O'Neill? The police?'

'The informant was Amelia Harsent.'

'Then Harsent knows. So Jill knows. She knows! That bitch!'

Marcus now had three minutes before he was due in court (as his elderly clerk, Arthur Henderson, discreetly reminded him). Marcus got through to Eden Manor police station.

'Give me Detective Sergeant McIntyre, please.'

'He's out on duty, sir.'

'Is the Custody Sergeant available?'

'Who's calling, sir?'

'Judge Marcus Byron.'

'I'll try to connect you, sir.'

The clock hands on Marcus's wall now pointed to ten.

Arthur Henderson was clearing this throat respectfully. 'The court is ready, your Honour.'

The Custody Sergeant came on the phone. 'Yes, sir?'

'Good morning, Sergeant. I have just learned that my daughter Lucy Byron was questioned yesterday.'

'I can confirm that.'

'Was she legally represented?'

'Yes, sir, by Mr Simmonds.'

'Simmonds! Averling's man?'

'That was her request, sir. She knew Mr Averling's number by heart.'

Marcus's own heart was hammering with alarm, rage, frustration. Averling! The crook who represented all the Griffins and all the Richardsons! 'Say Nothing' Averling, a key figure in the Congress for Justice! 'Right of Silence' Simmonds, his abject sidekick!

'What is the charge against Lucy, Sergeant?'

'No charge as yet, sir.'

'"As yet"?'

'Investigations are continuing, sir. I see that Doug McIntyre has just come into the station. Would you care to speak to him, sir?'

'Yes. Thank you.'

Old Arthur Henderson is hovering with that strange, bitter-sweet smile of his, like an illustration from a children's edition of Dickens.

'Your Honour . . . You have a crowded list this morning and—'

'They can wait!'

A familiar voice came on the line. 'Doug McIntyre speaking, your Honour.'

'What's it all about, Doug? Why wasn't I informed?'

'We have been advised by Lucy's mother, sir, that she has full legal custody of your daughter and that we should communicate with Ms Hull alone.'

'Doug, you're a father.'

'Strictly I shouldn't be telling you this, Marcus, but there were no witnesses to the robbery other than the victim. Mrs Ramsden suffers from trachoma. Her chances at an identification parade are slim and even if she nailed . . . excuse me, even if she—'

'The defence could challenge her evidence on medical grounds?'

'Aye.'

'Thanks, Doug.'

Two minutes later Judge Byron strode into Crown Court 3 in wig and purple gown.

'The court will stand!'

He bowed, sat down. 'My apologies.'

Now, alone at home pondering his best course of action, Marcus pours himself a double whisky. Louise will soon ring him from Manchester, she never fails to remind him that husbands and wives should keep in touch. His thoughts drift back to the gorgeous creature who was sitting on this sofa only ten minutes ago, then spiral away to the women's prisons he has visited – the constant slamming of metal gates, the claustrophobia, the neat little cells decorated with pin-ups and woolly mascots, the tiny, barred windows, the high walls topped by barbed wire, the frisking of visitors, the drugs smuggled in by swallowing plastic bags, the fights and punishment cells, the mounting depression as lives slip away, the running battle against suicide – the shocking helplessness of captivity.

Lucy!

Joe O'Neill takes the phone. He spends his life answering the phone. He has been day-dreaming about Brigid Kyle. What would his family say if they knew he was planning to marry a Catholic ten years his senior and already married? More to the point, what would Brigid say? She'd called him a Puritan. 'You Apprentice Boys are such puritans,' she'd said. 'No wonder you people have so few children. No wonder the fate of Ulster will finally be settled in the maternity wards.'

He adores her insults. He's head-over-heels.

'Joe O'Neill, the *Post*,' he says.

The female voice he hears is semi-coherent and clearly high as a kite. Heavy rock music and partying yells in the background don't make things easier. Joe checks his watch, then the sky: yes, it really is mid-morning.

'Lemons,' she giggles, 'they're all Clockwork Lemons.'

'Who are?' Joe activates his telephone recorder.

More giggling. The telephone at the other end is being banged about.

'Ask Daddy.'

'Daddy?'

'All Daddy's friends, the shitheads of the Establishment, they're all Lemons.'

Joe sits up (he's already sitting up) and fingers his eczema with his free hand.

'What's a lemon?' he asks.

A yelp of laughter at the other end. More giggling, banging, yells . . .

'Daddy's on drugs,' the girl drawls. 'Hard stuff. But the great public mustn't know, must it?'

'Can you please tell me who you are?'

'Fuck off, Joe. You never printed anything of mine, did you, though I've got more talent in my little finger than you've got spots.'

The phone goes down (to the floor by the sound of it). Joe has recorded the conversation. The law says you must ask the caller's consent but the law is a reporter's ass. Joe plays back the recording several times. Brigid will beg him for a copy of this! The battle of the maternity wards is on!

A mile away, maybe two, maybe a zillion, Daniel Richardson lies on the floor in Lucy's arms, the unhooked receiver in his limp hand. He's happy and high with Lucy. She's great, she has class. The party has gone on since the dawn of time, they're all here,

Paul and his three girlfriends, Amos and his chicks, Livingstone Lord surrounded by skirt, plenty of booze, loads of stuff.

'A Chinese planet's crashing into us,' Lucy murmurs.

'Yeah. I know.'

The Youth Court can stuff its curfews, its bail conditions, its remands into Local Authority accommodation. A Richardson is a free man if he's not in Downton. The court is shit.

And the sound! The big Chelsea Wharf warehouse which serves as headquarters for Livingstone's Pizza Palaces, rocks, shakes, thunders all night long and into the day.

'Joe's a prick,' Lucy says.

'Yeah.'

Daniel is small and slender with large, thoughtful eyes, a boy capable (Lucy says) of eloquence. Dan's really into the English language himself, poetry even. The youngest of the surviving Richardson brothers, he can't really remember little Wesley, who had died of a fractured skull at the age of three after a smart young drug dealer called Livingstone Lord moved in with their mother. Lord had decamped that night, disappeared, and Diane Richardson had insisted the boy died from a fall.

By the time he was eight, Daniel had picked up from his brothers Paul and Amos a basic rule of street crime – work as a team. This meant: *you* get caught, *we* weren't there. Daniel was instructed how to snatch a purse, a wallet, a bag, then vanish into the crowd while the bigger boys acted as decoys. How to change clothes as you run. Daniel was nabbed several times but the courts couldn't touch a child under the age of legal responsibility, and social workers learned to steer clear of the Richardson household, which they rated as being one of the two most dangerous in Eden Manor, alongside the Griffins'.

Bullied as a matter of routine by his brothers, Daniel displayed a disturbing inclination to get on with his own life and with the world. He even enjoyed school (which his brothers regarded as close to treason). Exceptionally bright for his age, with surprising verbal skills and a head for maths, but slightly built, he was marked down for bullying.

One day Paul and Amos dragged him by his ears to Oxford Street and inducted him into bag-snatching. While Amos scanned the street for fuzz, Paul would mark out a likely victim – usually female, or elderly – then vanish into the shadows while Daniel pounced. But he didn't pounce, he couldn't do it. Despite periodic beatings from Paul in the side-streets, the weeping Daniel failed every time to make the snatch. Finally he ran into a large department store, vanished, and was not seen at home for a week.

It was the same with vehicle crime. Paul and Amos forced Daniel to test the doors and boots of cars parked by Ron Tanner's repair garage in Brancaster Road while they kept watch from a distance. To the disappointment of his teachers, Daniel began to skip school; Paul and Amos said they'd cut him up if he didn't. They said he'd die like Wesley and no one would want to know. His duties had now been enlarged from testing car doors to smashing the side windows with a red-handled hammer when a radio-cassette or a car telephone was visible.

Daniel Richardson:

Interfere with Motor Vehicle, CD 1 year
Criminal Damage. CD 1 year & £15 compensation
Criminal Damage. CD 1 year & £50 compensation
Theft, CD 1 year (concurrent)

On Monday Dan will be before the Youth Court again, for sentencing. His case worker has assured him that his part in the robbery of Simon Galloway on Hilton Avenue hasn't been proved yet and won't count.

Jimmy Haley-White has promised him Lady Harsent, rather than Patrick Berry or Miss Swearwell, so that's all right.

The pre-sentence report is all stitched up: another conditional discharge for Daniel, since his family cannot afford to pay fines. The PSR advises the magistrates that Mason Lodge Attendance Centre (which is run by Inspector Ken Crabbe rather than social workers) only brings vulnerable boys like Daniel into contact with criminals (like his brothers), and a Supervision Order would exceed the offence.

So it's all OK.

Doped to the gills, Lucy rolls over in Dan's lap.

'Who shall we phone now?' she murmurs. 'How about Daddy?'

# *Eight*

SIMON GALLOWAY HAS NEVER before been inside Benson Street Youth Court. He didn't even know where it was and had to look it up in his *A to Z.* Confined to the witnesses' waiting room for two hours, he tries to fend off his mounting impatience – this is how they reward public-spirited members of the public! – by scanning the jobs pages. Susie had wanted to be with him, to hold his hand, but Tom continued to cling to one or the other like a limpet, and in any case Susie's nervous system was still in tatters. Her forthcoming ID parade would be enough of an ordeal.

Simon hears continuous bellowing and honking from many coarse voices in the corridor outside. Whenever the door opens, a thick cloud of cigarette smoke stinks the room. Each voice seems to have a megaphone attached. Simon had vaguely imagined court houses to be places of subdued decorum, like hospitals – not a bit of it.

He opens today's *Sentinel* at Brigid Kyle's column, which he has been reading regularly of late. She is describing life in Eden Manor:

> The obscenities all night long are not inventive, merely repetitive. Whatever drink may do for poets, there are few in Eden Manor. These are human beings driven by alcohol and drugs to a state of degeneration unknown to animals. Young mothers and elderly pensioners drag their beds away from the windows to escape

> bricks and flying glass. Some mornings the estate resembles a war zone. There's a grim joke in Eden Manor: residents are leaving to seek sanctuary in Sarajevo.

Simon's eyes widen. Brigid Kyle moves on to report the attack on Mrs Susan Galloway.

> A boy has been charged. But will the final charge be robbery or merely 'handling stolen goods'? This downgrading of the appropriate charge is happening time and again. The police of Eden Manor feel they are constantly let down by the Crown Prosecution Service. The Director of Public Prosecutions is a man of the highest integrity but he now faces determined opposition – indeed sabotage – from a self-elected mafia within the CPS. They will not rest content until they have Lionel Lacey's head on a plate – by one means or another.

Simon ponders these extraordinary allegations. He knows very little about the CPS, except that one of his neighbours, Jill Hull's partner Nick Paisley, occupies a senior position in it. How senior, Simon is not sure. Paisley has always struck him as an unpleasant character, rather like a ferret. Rarely seen, he plays no part in the communal life of Oundle Square.

Simon remains in the witnesses' waiting room while Joseph and Darren Griffin are brought into court (Mark is now on the run). A witness must hear nothing before he testifies. Two female custody officers wearing the green uniforms of Securicor sit between the boys, while four male officers remain standing, alertly rocking on their feet.

Lady Harsent is in the chair, fanning sky-blue feathers. The court room is packed. Although no member of the public can be admitted to a Youth Court, the Griffin brothers seem to have produced enough 'parents' to sink a lifeboat. Derek Jardine's summary of the 'facts', for the prosecution, is constantly interrupted by snarls, growls and expletives.

'You have to be joking, mate!' is the politest.

'Stuff it up your arse, son,' is standard.

Both Griffins have pleaded not guilty to the charges: (1) causing £150,000 worth of damage to Broadway Underground Station (criminal damage); (2) knocking over and causing terror to staff and passengers (affray under the Public Order Act).

In the witnesses' waiting room Simon's nervous reverie is abruptly interrupted by an usher.

'Mr Simon Galloway, please.'

Simon jumps up, his heart pounding. 'Yes? Ready, are we? Shall I—?'

'Bring everything with you.'

Entering the court room, which is much smaller than he had imagined from TV trials, he immediately hears the words 'Wanker!' and 'Cunt!' directed at him from the massed ranks of the Griffins. Yet nobody rebukes them.

The black lady clerk invites him to write down his address.

'We know where he fuckin' lives,' Simon hears.

The prosecutor immediately invites Lady Harsent to intervene. 'Clear witness intimidation, madam.' But she waves him down.

'I have full control of this court, Mr Jardine.'

Derek Jardine takes Simon through his experience on the Central Line train from the time the Griffin boys boarded it at Shepherd's Bush Station.

'Mr Galloway, did Joseph and Darren Griffin appear to be drunk?'

Simon finds himself trembling uncontrollably. His first word lodges in his throat. He clears it and tries again.

'Yes. They all carried beer cans, belched loudly, shouted obscenities and behaved like young drunks. They regularly impeded the closing of the carriage doors at stations.'

'Reg-oo-lah-ly,' someone mocks his accent.

'Did they accost other passengers?'

'The youngest, the boy I now know to be Darren Griffin, had an unlighted cigarette in his mouth. He demanded a light from several passengers and was fairly abusive about it.'

'That's a load of shit!' yells Darren's father, Sid Griffin, now back in prison on remand, who has been 'vanned up' for the day to protect the good name of his progeny.

'You say Darren was abusive?' Derek Jardine presses Simon.

'Females who failed to produce a light were offered a "shag". Black people were called "nigs". An elderly Pakistani gentleman was told to stand up and yield his seat.'

'Did the passengers appear intimidated?'

'Totally. I remember thinking, it's lucky the Wehrmacht isn't on its way.'

'The what?' Sid Griffin shouts. 'Are we speaking English, your Honour?'

Wendy Berry glances at Lady H. She doesn't terribly mind being addressed as 'your Honour' – Sid always does it.

'The Wehrmacht being Hitler's army?' Jardine asks Simon.

'Yes. Exactly. The British generation of 1940 would have known how to deal with that rabble.'

A stout man whom Simon assumes is the Griffins' lawyer objects. 'Irrelevant and pejorative speculation, madam.'

Lady H. concurs. 'Stick to the questions, Mr Galloway.'

Simon looks her over. A fruit-cake, three-quarters icing. He notices that his hands are no longer shaking as they rest on the witness stand.

'You finally intervened?' Jardine asks Simon.

'Yes. I left my seat and pushed up the carriage to where the Griffin boys had surrounded the Pakistani gentleman.'

'What did you say?'

'I don't remember exactly. My thought was to distract their attention from the Pakistani gentleman until we reached Broadway Station.'

'Did you succeed?'

'Yes. In fact someone else pressed the alarm button.'

'Who?'

'I didn't see. I just heard the alarm ringing. There were men in uniform running along the platform. They came straight into our carriage.'

Derek Jardine then invites Simon to describe the ensuing riot along the station platform and the vandalism he witnessed.

'Did you see either Joseph or Darren taking part in the destruction?'

'Certainly. Both.'

'Fuckin' liar!' yells Sid Griffin. 'Arsehole!'

Jardine again objccts to Lady Harsent, but more severely this time.

'Madam, I submit that this witness should not continue his testimony until the court has been cleared.'

'Now, Mr Griffin,' Lady Harsent says, 'you pipe down, understood? Continue, Mr Jardine.'

But Jardine has no more questions of his own. The obese Edgar Averling slowly heaves himself up for cross-examination.

'Come now, Mr Galloway, what did you really say to the defendants inside the Central Line train?'

'I don't remember.'

A new outbreak of derisive hoots from the Griffins.

'The gist of it, then, Mr Galloway. Your memory seems to achieve total recall on everything else. Did you tell Darren Griffin that you had a light?'

'Yes, I may have done. I believe I did. And he replied, "Show me your burner, cunt-head."'

'Did you then say, "How big's your prick, Rat Face?"?'

'No.'

'Given your previous amnesia, how can you be so sure?'

Simon is sweating. 'It's not my kind of language.'

Howls from the Griffins. 'Liar!' yells Darren.

Derek Jardine is up again. 'Madam, I ask for a short adjournment while the court is cleared. No witness can be expected to testify in these circumstances.'

'Pipe down,' Lady H. repeats herself to the Griffins. 'Not another word, is that understood?'

Averling resumes. 'The fact is, Mr Galloway, that neither Joseph nor Darren had laid a hand on anyone before you intervened.'

'They shoved their way up the crowded carriage.'

'But not a hand laid?'

'They barged people aside.'

'And you chose to provoke them into what ensued on the station platform?'

'That's nonsense.'

'Are you a snob, Mr Galloway?'

'A snob?'

'Do you despise boys like the Griffins as "common", "ill-bred", not your "class"?'

'Merely their behaviour. I judge people by their actions.'

'Thank you. No further questions.'

'You may leave the court, Mr Galloway,' Lady H. says imperiously. 'And don't hang about. We don't want any friction outside.'

A moment later Simon is out on Benson Street and heading for Broadway Station, his heart and head hammering with rage and indignation. And with shame, too – he had told a lie, having sworn to tell nothing but the truth.

Back in court, Derek Jardine calls his next witness. Inspector Herbert Knowles has been put in a different waiting room from Simon Galloway at the request of the defence, which claims to fear collusion.

Herbert Knowles mounts the witness stand with his gaze fixed rigidly on his sister-in-law. A few feet away, the entire Griffin clan is snarling at him. Expletives like 'nig!' and 'black shithead' ricochet off the walls. The red lights above the two exit doors blink constantly, signalling that the security staff are not happy with the situation.

The Griffins revel in the blinking red lights.

Derek Jardine invites Herbert to explain the annual cost of graffiti to the railways. Averling immediately objects to this question but Lady Harsent's two colleagues on the Bench lean into her with such unanimity that she is forced to disallow the objection.

'Graffiti', says Herbert, 'cost the railways three million pounds annually, not counting the loss of passengers who object to graffiti as indicating uncontrolled crime. Graffiti are the messengers of racism, of hatred. Vandals put at risk not only themselves but trains, staff and passengers.'

Jardine then takes Herbert through the sequence of events at Broadway Station. Yes, the trouble, the vandalism, had involved other youths and had begun before the Griffin boys were pulled from the Central Line train.

'The lads seemed to be waiting for their arrival,' Herbert adds.

Averling objects. 'Speculation.'

Jardine goes at this point again. 'What led you to believe the other youths were waiting for the Griffins?'

'They were chanting, "We are the Griffins!"'

'Thank you, Inspector Knowles, no more questions.'

Edgar Averling cross-examines. His line is clear from the first question:

'You have a personal vendetta against the Griffin boys – have you not? Your aim is to be revenged upon them – is it not?'

Fury chokes Herbert. It may be true. He prays to God for guidance.

'My evidence is the truth and nothing but the truth.'

'But you do *feel* you have a personal grievance against these boys, Joseph and Darren?'

'I am telling what happened, that's all.'

'You are not answering my question, Mr Knowles.'

'I do my duty. Nothing personal.'

Edgar Averling calls neither Joseph nor Darren as a witness.

He accuses the station staff and British Transport Police of having caused the affray by over-reacting to the spray-painting. Unidentified staff had hurled insults at the boys, calling them 'scum' and, worse, 'fucking Griffins'.

'Madam, Joseph and Darren have legitimate grievances against staff who constantly harass them and accuse them of evading their fares when, in fact, they have merely lost their tickets.'

'And that's the truth!' shouts Sid Griffin.

'Oh, heavens,' Averling appeals to Lady Harsent, 'we were all young once. It was merely graffiti! When we are young we all want to tell the adult world something.'

Lady H. beams and nods. She is a great believer in self-expression. 'We all know what it is to be young, Mr Averling.'

But at this juncture her much hated winger, Rodney Parker, leans into her ear in a harsh whisper:

'Consult your colleagues before you speak. And what about the physical destruction on the platform?'

Lady H. has always suspected that Parker is one of Patrick Berry's clones, but the young black magistrate Conde Jackson, a newcomer to the Bench, also leans into her ear. He, too, has been incensed by her blatant refusal to control the court during the barrage of insults from the Griffins.

Herbert Knowles glances at Deputy Chief Clerk Wendy Berry. His sister-in-law's handsome features are resolutely set in an expression of professional neutrality.

Determined to crush the rebellion taking place on either wing of the Bench, Lady H. announces a short recess.

'The court will stand!' cries the usher.

Sid Griffin leaps up in a flamboyant display of respect for Lady H. – though not for the 'nig' on the Bench, of course.

In the magistrates' retiring room the atmosphere is nuclear. Drawing herself up, and snapping open her make-up compact, Lady H. has scarcely launched into her reprimand when Rodney Parker cuts her short:

'Guilty. Agreed?'

'Agreed.' Conde Jackson nods.

Rodney Parker immediately anticipates another typical Harsent move.

'And when we call for PSRs, we will classify the crime as "so serious" as to justify custody for Joseph and secure accommodation for Darren. Agreed?'

'Agreed.' Conde Jackson nods again. 'And if I may say so, Cecilia, your handling of the court today was an affront to justice.'

Lady H. is ablaze. 'When you have served as long as I have, Conde, you will understand that—'

'It's no good, Cecilia,' Parker snaps. 'The public must be protected.'

'Then we are not in agreement, Rodney.'

'We're in agreement two-to-one.'

Five minutes later the Securicor custody officers are instructed to lead Joseph and Darren back to the cells. Immediately there is a scuffling uproar as the Griffins, led by Sid (himself in custody and under guard), demand the 'right' to comfort Joseph and Darren in the cells.

Securicor aren't having it. The company is under contract to the Home Office to maintain prison regulations on 'access' while their charges are in transit from prison to court and back again. Securicor assesses every situation. The Griffins out in full force is not a good situation.

'Yes, yes, of course Joseph and Darren must see their parents.' Lady H. waves a bejewelled hand indulgently.

Wendy Berry quickly intervenes. 'Madam, strictly speaking—'

'I am in charge of this court,' Lady H. snaps at her.

'Madam, nothing outside the court room itself lies within the Bench's province.'

'Correct,' Rodney Parker says loudly.

Lady H. knows as much. She knows she should always listen to the professional advice of her clerk. But the Berry woman is no ordinary clerk.

Leaving the court, Herbert Knowles is abused and jostled by members of the extended Griffin family and their friends.

'Fuckin' black bastard! Fuckin' nigger!'

Doug McIntyre and Cliff Jenkins have been waiting for Herbert in a CID Renault Clio. In fact they had been keeping an eye open on Simon Galloway's behalf, too, but he had made his exit before the court emptied like a jug of overnight slops. They watched him stride away, gripping his briefcase, and apparently muttering to himself, as if giving his evidence all over again.

The two Eden Manor cops are out and among the mob before Herbert receives the first kicks and blows. Jenkins guns the Renault away into the traffic, expecting a brick through the rear window.

'Smile for the cameras, Herbert,' McIntyre says.

'Neither of you fellows could open a Bible the right way up,' Herbert fumes.

McIntyre and Jenkins buy Herbert a cup of tea in the workmen's café round the corner from Divisional HQ. Three lemons sit on the table between them.

'It's our treat, Herbert,' Jenkins announces, 'so long as you pay.'

'So what sentence will those Griffin boys get?' Herbert asks. 'That woman Harsent is a disgrace!'

'We've had enough of Supervision Orders for Griffins and Richardsons,' McIntyre says. 'What's needed is a whopping financial Compensation Order, and a parental Bind Over in the sum of £5,000.'

'The Griffins haven't a bean between them,' Jenkins says sarcastically. 'You have to feel sorry for them. They can't even find a coin for the meter when they park their latest stolen BMW or Merc outside the supermarket. They trolley out of Safeways with ten bottles of French wine and fifty cans of beer, but they haven't a penny to their name.'

'Bastards,' mutters Herbert Knowles.

McIntyre bites into a bacon sandwich. 'And tell me, Cliff, what fines, Attendance Centres and Downton all have in common.'

'No fucking social workers involved.'

'Which is why Lady H. doesn't like fines or Downton.'

'No swearing, boys,' Herbert says. 'I'm a Christian.'

'Herb,' McIntyre says, 'we want to talk to you about a young female relative of yours.'

Herbert drops his gaze.

'Only an old lady's trachoma saved Lucy from a robbery charge, Herb. She's out of control. It's time you spoke frankly to Judge Byron. They're setting him up, Herb.'

'For the fall,' Jenkins adds.

'"They"?' Herbert's tone is wary, defensive. He knows from Marcia that she and Wendy are worried sick.

'The Congress,' McIntyre says. 'More specifically, Lucy's mother and Nick Paisley.'

'Jill? Nonsense. I know the woman. She's a good mother. Why should she harm her own child? You tell me that.'

* * *

Spread across Jill Hull's desk in Probation House is Brigid Kyle's report on life in Eden Manor. A few nights under Ruth Tanner's roof seem to have shaken the woman to the core. Jill has drawn a textliner across one particular phrase:

> These are human beings driven by alcohol and drugs to a state of degeneration unknown to animals.

This phrase will whip round the estate; Kyle can never step inside Eden Manor again and Ruth Tanner will get the stick. Nick is running a rival against Ruth Tanner in the forthcoming Local Council election.

But even more demanding of Jill's textliner is Kyle's account of the attack on Susan Galloway.

> The police of Eden Manor feel they are constantly let down by the Crown Prosecution Service. The Director of Public Prosecutions is a man of the highest integrity but . . .

What does Kyle know? Jill looks out of her fifth-floor window and reflects on Kyle's relationship with Marcus. Another conquest, another feather in his cap. What does Louise think about it? Jill scarcely knows Marcus's frosty new wife. Does Louise Pointer, QC, privately support his vendetta against the Probation Service and progressive values?

It has been bonanza-time for the Service: during the past seven years its resources have doubled to meet the demands of new legislation. Two key civil servants in the Home Office had fended off Darling's reactionary instincts, but both have now retired – or been retired. The PS now faces a freeze: worse, an ideological backlash. And her ex-husband is in the vanguard of it, flashing those teeth of his, shooting his starched cuffs, chuckling into television cameras.

Max Venables is now in Marcus's pocket. 'Max's ear is dripping with lemon juice,' Sandra Golding has told her. 'The Boy's, too.'

Sandra! Jill bitterly remembers the year when the society pages of the Press began to bring her photo-reports of her husband dining with the glamorous barrister Sandra Golding in smart restaurants and nightclubs, not to mention their forays to the opera. Jill had concluded that she could dispense with a husband so much at ease with infidelity.

'Destroy him, Mum,' Lucy said.

The Director of Public Prosecutions has invited Marcus and Max Venables to lunch at the Reform Club in Pall Mall. Members and guests gather under the High Rotunda to drink sherry and to bark. Marcus accepts his sherry reluctantly – the sweet brown piss of a hundred Spanish cats.

Lionel Lacey surveys the company with pale, watery eyes that the great public never sees. Unlike Marcus Byron, the DPP takes care to retain an invisible profile. Once a distinguished QC, he admits to possessing the soul of a civil servant.

'Civil servants don't have souls,' Max Venables tells him. Then flinches. His arch-enemy, the Rt Hon. Jeremy Darling, has just swept in, attended by an ill-disguised 'minder' and his Parliamentary Private Secretary, Hector Coombe, MP.

Marcus and Lionel Lacey exchange flickering glances. Coombe is the Lemons' deepest mole within the government. He will not greet them; he will not even know who they are.

'Darling must be Stanhope's guest,' Lacey murmurs. And indeed the Home Secretary is being effusively greeted by the roastbeef figure of Sir Lawton Stanhope, MP, Chairman of the Commons Select Committee on Home Affairs.

Max Venables tugs nervously at his beard. 'They're here to spy on us,' he mutters.

Marcus slaps him on the back. 'We must be doing well, then.'

Max Venables is now convinced that Marcus Byron faces imminent disgrace. If he were regularly battered and heckled across the floor of the Commons, Marcus might shed some of his arrogance. If Max knows the state of play at Eden Manor police station regarding Lucy Byron, then Lord Chief Justice Bowers knows it, too.

Admittedly the Appeal Court has dismissed Sandra's appeal in the Donna Dean case: Marcus's view that 'long-term provocation' is not a legal concept, unless Parliament legislates, and is not a valid reason for downgrading murder to manslaughter, has been upheld. But, listening in to his wife's breakfast-time telephone conversation this morning, Max saw Marcus heading straight into the eye of a worse judicial storm.

Sandra had received an urgent call from a charity called Women

Inside, of which she is founder-member. Judge Marcus Byron had given advance notice that he intended to impose a four-year jail sentence on Liz Hargreaves, a twenty-one-year-old mother with a baby son only six months old.

Max had observed Sandra brimming with joy.

The judge has taken the unusual – and hazardous – step of communicating the sentence in advance to the woman's counsel so that provision could be made for the child if Hargreaves chose not to take him with her to the notorious Holloway prison, a rat-infested slum where women are kept in shackles before and after giving birth by order of the Rt Hon. Jeremy Darling.

(Darling had hotly denied it when challenged by Max in the House of Commons. 'I have no operational responsibility. That properly belongs to the Director of Prisons.')

Peeping from behind his *Sentinel* at the breakfast table, Max had observed Sandra studying the state of her purple fingernails as she listened to the agitated solicitor from Women Inside. An urgent appeal was required. Could she please help?

'I'll be in my chambers in half an hour.'

Max noted that Brigid Kyle's report on life in Eden Manor was cleverly designed to support Marcus's line on social crime.

> Hordes of youngsters swarm around on summer evenings, loud-mouthed and foul-tongued. A boy earns respect only by trashing everything within reach. They hunt in packs, snapping car aerials, smashing car windows, ripping out radios. Eden Manor is a factory for the manufacture of yobs. Long-term truancy in the local comprehensive school runs at 20 per cent, but the number of youngsters skipping whole days, or some classes, is far higher. The school suppresses the real figures; any pupil who signs on in the morning is recorded as having spent the whole day in school.

Sandra was hurriedly gathering her papers. 'Your pal Marcus is about to jail a young mother for four years,' she called.

'What are the facts?'

'The facts are bloody awful. An utterly stupid young woman called Liz Hargreaves was out joy-riding with her boyfriend, when she accelerated her car straight at a pedestrian. She was three times over the alcohol limit. She hit the bloke at high speed and drove on without stopping. The man died from multiple injuries.'

'If the boyfriend had been driving, he'd have got eight to ten years,' Max muttered.

'Max, you're impossible! It was a one-off.'

'A what? You mean the drunken Liz Hargreaves had never mowed down a man in cold blood before? You mean that she's never likely to do it again?'

'Imprisonment will cause irreparable damage to her relationship with her child. It is the child who will suffer.'

'So women should never go to prison?'

'I have never said that.'

'No, Sandra, you are too clever to say that.'

Max's thoughts return to where he is, the Reform Club. The flock of men in grey suits begin to shuffle out of the Rotunda, moving in straggling procession into the long, tall-windowed dining room, where they take their places at reserved tables. Sir Lawton and his distinguished guest are seated well beyond spitting distance from Lacey's table – though a rock-hard bun would travel. The High Steward of the Reform does not make mistakes.

Even so, little Max Venables keeps tugging at his goatee beard irritably.

'Max, you have paranoia like dogs have fleas,' Marcus tells him. 'We're here to talk about Nick Paisley, who most certainly is not in this room.'

'Local claret acceptable?' Lacey asks his guests. He smiles bleakly. 'Who's driving? Nobody? Good.' Marcus notes that you do not gesture to the waiters here, you wait.

Five tables down the room, Her Majesty's Secretary of State for Home Affairs is in gloomy conclave with Hector Coombe and Sir Lawton Stanhope.

'Take a look – Venables is with Byron again,' he observes. 'We've got to put a stop to it.'

The morning papers have brought Jeremy Darling their usual crop of hostile, even derisive, headlines.

DARLING ACCUSED BY VENABLES OF 'YOB CREATION'
DARLING ROASTED BY APPEAL COURT JUDGES
LOCAL AUTHORITIES GIVE THE BOOT TO DARLING'S BOOT CAMPS
BYRON BLASTS UNDERFUNDING OF CJS

'What are we going to do about Byron?' Darling says.

Sir Lawton is sanguine. 'Bobby will suspend "Sambo" from his duties if Teddy gives the go-ahead.'

Like much else Sir Lawton says, this requires deciphering. Bobby is Lord Chancellor Robert Burns: Lord Burns of Loch Ness. Teddy is Lord Chief Justice Theodore Bowers: Lord Bowers of Granchester.

'I thought Bowers had already summoned Byron for the chop,' Darling sulks.

'I gather Bowers had second thoughts,' Coombe says smoothly. 'He postponed their meeting.'

'That's good news not bad news, Jeremy,' Sir Lawton says. 'Bowers has got wind of something even more serious coming up against Sambo.'

'What?'

'Something personal. The *coup de grâce*.'

Five tables away, Marcus notices that Lionel Lacey's eyes are capable of switching on and off like light bulbs. Friends passing his table receive a variable wattage.

'I gather Paisley has been at you again?' Marcus addresses Max Venables.

'He's persistent.'

'Desperate,' Lacey says.

'Whenever I hear Paisley's name I smell the dubious odour of a Pacific Islands pizza,' Marcus growls. 'Livingstone Lord now runs the new delivery firm, Pizza Palace, on the principle that a long look through the door of a well-appointed home can yield dividends.'

'Did that happen after I visited you the other night?' Lacey asks.

'It did. There was a message inside the box: "Lemons go bad." Lord has hired the Richardson boys to close down the local competition.'

'Paisley is the kind of ferret who never puts on weight,' Max says. 'He tells me he and the Congress are determined to reverse my "opportunistic lurch towards nineteenth-century crime control".'

'That's me,' Marcus says.

'I wish I knew more about Paisley's past,' Lacey says. 'Is there dirt in the box?'

A pale sun barely penetrates the high panes of glass, as if (Marcus reflects) timidly applying for membership. He is the only black man in the room. Everyone recognises him but no one looks. You don't look, here. It's not the 'form'. After all, everyone here is somebody.

'I know Nick well,' Max says. 'After graduating from Law College, he was articled in a legal-aid firm specialising in criminal and family cases.'

'Averling & Simmonds?' Lacey asks.

'Correct. At that time, as I recall, Nick favoured string ties, worse-for-wear drainpipe trousers, scuffed shoes and a lapel loaded with good-cause badges – until warned by the Senior Partner to smarten up. The ragged sideburns were also banished.'

Marcus nods. 'Paisley became an expert on the right of silence, police interrogation procedures and bail applications. He learned the ropes. Get to court early, soon after nine, and constantly harass the Crown Prosecutor to find out what kind of bail application he has in mind.'

Lacey cuts in: 'Our prosecutors normally have to reach a decision on two dozen files within thirty minutes, working from seriously deficient information.'

Marcus winks at Venables. 'Take note, Max. The Police National Computer doesn't list appearances pending or failures to appear in court when on bail. Even better for the Averlings and Paisleys, large numbers of microfiches are withdrawn at any one time for updating. The liveliest criminal clients are therefore the most likely to carry invisible life histories.'

'How did Paisley find his way into the CPS?' Lacey asks.

'There was some scandal,' Marcus replies. 'It was hushed up. He applied for partnerships in other firms but no one would touch him. The CPS was struggling into existence, short of staff, and not asking too many questions.'

'And the scandal you mention?' Lacey asks.

'He was representing Livingstone Lord. Paisley got himself involved in witness intimidation.'

'And how did this fervent civil libertarian justify joining the oppressive System?' Lacey asks Venables. 'It was before my time.'

'Nick's a cool customer. When friends and political colleagues raised an eyebrow, or made jokes about poachers and gamekeepers, he had a ready answer, solemnly delivered: "The best defence counsel is a prosecutor."'

'He's been as good as his word on that!' Marcus chortles.

Lacey nods. 'He climbed the CPS hierarchy remarkably rapidly. Everyone was new to it and quite a few recruits departed, disenchanted by the prevailing chaos and poor pay.'

'That was when he first met Jill,' Marcus says. 'A woman disgustingly ill used by an arrogant, self-loving barrister called Marcus Byron, who flamboyantly donated half his earnings to private legal-aid schemes for poor people, mainly blacks and immigrants.'

'Thanks for the commercial, Marcus,' Max says drily.

'Soon after my arrival,' Lacey recalls, 'Paisley moved up to become one of eighty-six Branch Prosecutors. I rewarded him for his diligence, his ability to sum up the evidence in a case, and the options, with lightning rapidity. He was duly promoted again, becoming one of the CPS's thirteen Area Chief Prosecutors, before I gave him a Grade 3 job in Headquarters. Too late I realised what he was up to.'

Marcus nods. 'By that time Paisley had built a state within the state.'

Max has been thinking about Lucy Byron. 'Does Jill love Nick, Marcus?'

Marcus shrugs. 'She's had a spasmodic affair with Jimmy Haley-White for several years. Her deep, puritanical guilt about desiring a younger man keeps her usefully subservient to Nick.'

'And Lucy?'

'What about Lucy?' Marcus snaps back.

Five tables down, Jeremy Darling is pulling a cutting out of his pocket. He glowers at Stanhope and Coombe.

'Listen to this drivel. "The law is now in total confusion," says Wendy Berry, a spokeswoman for the Justices' Clerks Association. "No one knows what the law is on any particular day."'

'The Berry woman can be discounted,' Sir Lawton says. 'She's Byron's sister. Almost certainly a Lemon.'

'A what?' Darling asks.

Sir Lawton and Coombe exchange glances. If sheer ignorance made a great Home Secretary, Darling's portrait would already be above the mantelpiece of his Whitehall office instead of Disraeli's.

The world is stitching Jeremy Darling up. Only a year ago his star was high in the sky – rapturous applause when he presented his twenty-seven-point law-and-order crackdown to the annual

Party Conference. A standing ovation. Downhill ever since. Violent crime figures up. The Boy grinning from ear to ear while Max Venables shines his shoes.

Darling is now delivering his set speech to his two companions.

'I came into office to make a difference. I intend to make a difference. There are many out there determined to frustrate me. I shall not be deflected.'

'Jolly good,' Coombe says. Hector Coombe bears a remarkable physical resemblance to an actor who made the nation laugh in the TV series, *Yes, Minister.*

'The Prime Minister is hopping mad,' Darling announces. 'He thinks the Boy has run off with the law-and-order issue. He wants me to bring Judge Byron on-side.'

'How?'

'Well, think of something! We're trailing 25–30 per cent in the opinion polls, month after month. We've been virtually wiped out in the Euro-election and two successive local council elections. The Party hasn't won a parliamentary by-election since the Norman Conquest.'

'Even the City expects the Boy to win,' Coombe adds smugly. Darling has never quite trusted Coombe, though he's not sure why.

Down the vast dining room, at Lionel Lacey's table, Max Venables wipes his mouth on a crisp napkin.

'I had a visit from Nick Paisley the other day.'

Lacey's face is a study in thunder. 'I expressly instructed him to avoid all politicians.'

'That might be construed as an infringement of his civil liberties, Lionel.'

'Balls. I had him into my office. I reminded him he was a public servant. I reminded him that it was my job to make public statements about CPS policy. I told him to shut his trap.'

'I don't suppose he lay down under that,' Marcus laughs.

'He was wearing that ferrety expression. He reminded me that he's a candidate for Parliament.'

'Only because he managed to avoid one of those all-women short-lists he and Jill so approve of.'

'They've now been declared illegal,' Max says defensively.

'I told Paisley to stop shooting his mouth off to the Press,'

Lacey says. 'Then he turned ugly. He said, "Perhaps we should go baby-snatching together, you and I, next Friday night."'

Lionel Lacey emits a disturbing giggle.

Marcus holds his fire while the waiter clears the course.

'Lionel, I want you to tell Max about your . . . affliction.'

The smears which pass for eyebrows on Lionel Lacey lift a fraction. 'Venables knows.'

'Lionel insists on telling everyone,' Max says. 'It's all part of the fun, isn't it, Lionel?'

'Oh, definitely.' Another giggle.

Marcus resignedly lets his signet ring flap on the tablecloth. 'It's got to stop, Lionel.'

'Why? I've been doing it for years. It keeps me alive.'

Marcus glances down the long room, with its steady murmur of reasoned discourse. He studies his host. Lionel's collars have always looked a bit desperate. Marcus has never met 'Mrs Lionel', but imagines her as a keen gardener who long ago lost interest in a husband determined to toss his career to the wind every Friday night in Les Enfants du Paradis.

Max sighs. 'The CPS urgently needs a new strategy, Lionel.'

'You're changing the subject, Max,' Marcus chides him.

'Yes, I am.'

'What point in discussing CPS strategy with a DPP who's going to be out of his job next Saturday morning?'

'They'd never dare,' Lacey snaps.

'Paisley will dare.'

Max brushes this awful topic aside. 'Lionel, the CPS is dropping too many cases which ought to go forward. There have been awkward questions in Parliament. I asked a few myself.'

'I won't achieve that until I get rid of Paisley and his clique,' Lacey says.

'Paisley told me that the CPS should never proceed with a case unless ninety-five per cent sure of a conviction. Downgrading charges, he said, is the best way to keep the public happy.'

Marcus is heaving with rage. 'During the past year, the CPS has "discontinued" 168,707 cases – twelve and a half per cent of prosecutions. That's unacceptable, Lionel.'

'I agree. But I cannot personally supervise the one and a half million cases we service every year.'

Max plops a grape into his mouth. 'Nick told me that his agenda for the immediate future is to discontinue 25 per cent of cases. He claimed that only the CPS is capable of understanding the "public interest" and the arcane mysteries of "diversion".'

Marcus snorts. 'Cases are then invisibly diverted to social services without involving the courts. But always invisibly.'

Max nods. 'That's precisely what Nick wants. He told me that a population inflamed by scare stories in the Press is incapable of understanding that trained probation officers and social workers can effectively divert many victims of poverty and joblessness – people ***driven*** to crime – into voluntary rehabilitation schemes.'

Lacey smiles sardonically. 'People are driven to crime?'

Five tables along, Jeremy Darling is glowering at the cheese-board as if it were a chamber of High Court judges pouring scorn on his new batch of mandatory life sentences. He takes a slice of English mousetrap with the air of a man who has been deceived long enough by foreign concoctions.

'Take a discreet look at Byron,' Coombe murmurs. 'He wears an expression worthy of Othello after Iago put the idea in his head.'

'What idea?' Darling asks.

Coombe sighs. 'Iago led Othello to believe that his wife had been unfaithful.'

'You mean Byron's wife has—'

'No, Jeremy. Forget it.'

'"Sambo" Byron is worth millions of votes, white as well as black,' Sir Lawton says. 'He has the best TV smile currently on offer. Those neat pearly teeth, that winning guffaw, that habit of agreeing with his opponents before politely slaughtering them. Frankly, we have to break him and break him fast.'

'What do you have in mind?' Darling demands.

Sir Lawton winks. 'Smear him. We've already got his pal, the DPP, in the bag. Friday night.'

'What bag?' Jeremy Darling asks.

'Lionel Lacey is a baby-snatcher.'

'He's a what!'

'A confirmed urchin-abuser. He prefers his meat under-done.'

Darling has turned very pale. 'But I appointed him!'

'No, you didn't, Jeremy. The Attorney General appointed him.'

'But a scandal is bound to hit the Government! Everything does!'

'It will be the beginning of the end for the Lemons,' Sir Lawton reassures him.

'Wait a minute. Why are we against these Lemons? I thought you said they are good on law and order?'

'Yes, but they don't think we are,' Coombe says. 'Which is why they have lunch with Max Venables.'

Darling stares gloomily down the room. 'Ah.'

Sir Stanhope has produced a typed-up list of names. 'Look at this, Jeremy.'

'All confirmed baby-snatchers?'

'All confirmed Lemons. Lacey's the only Friday-night maniac. You find them in key positions in every department, and at every level, of the criminal justice system. Police commissioners, prison governors, judges, magistrates, detective sergeants, court clerks, prosecutors, even a few in the Probation Service.'

'Why the hell do they call themselves Lemons? What does it all mean? What do they want?'

Coombe smiles his *Yes, Minister* smile. 'Justice, Secretary of State.'

'I've told you never to use that word in my presence, Jeremy. They have Ministries of Justice in Europe.'

'We are in Europe.'

'No, we are not!'

Five tables up, or down, Max Venables may be in Europe but not enjoying it.

'Nick Paisley told me I am losing friends fast,' he says.

'One loses some, one gains others,' Marcus says.

'He said it was his "duty" to warn me about Marcus Byron. He said you may come across as "Mr Clean" but there are cockroaches under the floorboards.'

'Aha?'

'No point in beating about the bush, Marcus. He claims that your Lucy has a tragic drug problem. Apparently Jill is worried out of her mind. Your girl is being drawn deeper into petty crime.'

'What else?'

'He alleges that you yourself are the source of Lucy's drugs problem.'

'That's original.'

'You smoke grass, don't you?' Max shoots at him.

Marcus laughs. 'We call it ganja.'

'What's so funny? It's illegal. You're a judge.'

Lionel Lacey wheezes sardonically. 'I'm not listening. I might have to prosecute. Coffee, gentlemen?'

But Max is relentlessly boring into Marcus: 'Paisley told me "in confidence" that Lucy's trouble started after she returned from a camping holiday in France with you and Louise. There seemed to be two Lucys suspended from the same head, was how Nick put it. "We found her rucksack stuffed with pills and poppers," he said.'

'And he told you to drop me from your circle of advisers before the scandal hits the headlines?'

'Marcus: what is the truth of all this?'

Five tables along, Sir Lawton Stanhope has been thinking. With Darling in the top job, somebody has to.

'We need a two-point strategy, gentlemen. One! We smear the Lemons, hound 'em out. Two! In desperation the Boy and Venables turn back to their traditional, soft-pinko libertarian allies, Nick Paisley and the Congress for Justice. Three—'

'You said a two-point strategy,' Coombe reminds him.

'Three! Muggers, burglars, druggies, hooligans, yobs, joy-riders, ravers, hunt saboteurs and New Age Travellers parade through the steets hailing Max Venables and the Boy. Four! We win the general election.'

'Hm.' Jeremy Darling is impressed. 'In other words, the softies, pinkos and bleeding hearts are our allies – for the time being?'

'Not allies, Jeremy. Our pawns.'

'Well, that's what I've been saying all along,' Darling says.

'My dear Jeremy, this entire strategy is yours! I was merely summarising your own thoughts! Coffee?'

'What about this scandal hanging over Byron?'

'It's imminent.'

An unlit Havana cigar already rests lightly in Sir Lawton's hand as they pass Lionel Lacey's table, eyes rigidly averted – you never fraternise with the Enemy less than five hundred days before a general election.

Max Venables's nervous eye settles on Marcus. 'Sandra means to have your balls on this Liz Hargreaves case.'

'She's welcome to them, Max. She was always welcome.'

'Does Louise agree about that?'

* * *

Louise Pointer is giving up her lunch hour to be interviewed by Brigid Kyle. She had always admired Kyle's columns until Marcus began to take such a close interest in the woman behind them. Kyle clearly detests Sandra Golding and Louise is determined to stay the course in her battle with Sandra for the chairmanship of the Criminal Bar Association.

'I wouldn't mind losing to *anyone else*,' she told Marcus.

Shortly before lunch Louise opens the *Sentinel* and reads Kyle's report from Eden Manor with grudging admiration.

> Ambulance crews refuse to come to Eden Manor during the hours of darkness. Firemen will turn out only under police protection. Social workers no longer venture here at any hour, night or day. Terrified residents, peering out behind drawn curtains from darkened rooms, dare not talk to the police. As soon as it becomes known that you are listed as a witness against a member of the G— family, or the R— family, your life is not worth living. You may as well leave. Many have.

A knock on her door. Louise offers her cool hand to Brigid Kyle.

'Please sit down. Congratulations on your article on Eden Manor. I admire your courage.'

'Oh, thank you! Quite a place!'

Each woman is pretending not to be looking the other one, and her clothes, over; each is asking herself what Marcus sees in the other; each knows this; each would like to help Marcus in his wars but not at the price of giving an inch to the other.

'So how shall we arrange ourselves?' Louise asks. 'Do you use a tape-recorder?'

'Actually I have a photographer waiting outside. He's a young fellow I want to give a leg up' – she smiles – 'though not a leg over.'

Louise is astonished by such sexual brashness. Of course that's exactly what Marcus likes, exactly what he got from Sandra!

'Well, bring your photographer in.'

'I thought we might walk around King's Bench Walk while we chatted.'

'Oh. If you wish. Does every word register accurately in your head?'

'It does!'

Joe O'Neill is waiting for them outside. He can handle a camera, of course, though he's not a member of the NUJ's Freelance Branch and shouldn't, strictly, be 'scabbing'. Brigid introduces him to Louise Pointer as 'the hero who saved me from a fate worse than being saved by an Ulsterman'.

The joke passes Louise by. To Joe's eye she looks stiff, frigid even – clearly nervous. There may be something going on between these two ladies – you're a brilliant lad, O'Neill. By now he's head-over-heels for Brigid and would eat his Orange Order bowler hat to kiss her shining Irish eyes. And she keeps paying him!

'So may I fire away?' Brigid asks cheerily as the two women walk sedately around King's Bench Walk, Joe leaping about them like a circus seal with eczema.

'Yes, please do.'

'It's unusual, is it not, to have two women candidates contesting the chairmanship of the Criminal Bar Association – and no men?'

'It's unique. There has never been a woman in the post before. Barristers are conservative animals, greatly attached to tradition. On the other hand, twenty-three per cent of members of the Bar are now women compared with eight per cent twenty years ago. Last year forty per cent of those called to the Bar were women – progress!'

'You have been praised for your extraordinary calm in court, even when faced with blatantly chauvinist judges.'

'I don't flap much.'

'And your husband – it can't be easy for a QC to be married to a Crown Court judge?'

'I have never appeared before Marcus and never shall. I have only once had to drop out of a case when it became clear it was heading for his court. I waived the whole of my fee.'

'Your rival, Sandra Golding—'

'She is my opponent, not my "rival". We remain friends.'

'Friends?'

'Well, let's say she is "my learned friend".'

Brigid laughs and Louise warms to her. But not for long.

'Sandra Golding has said that it is not appropriate for the wife of a Crown Court judge to head the Criminal Bar Association.'

'Frankly, I couldn't quite follow Sandra's line of reasoning on that. She's a famously rational person, so that's rather unusual.'

'You and she differ on recent legislation? She has opposed it all, whereas you—'

'The present Government has been throwing new legislation at us like a drunken wedding guest hurling confetti. Every morning you go into court with something new caught in your hair.'

'Sandra Golding has criticised you for taking on poll-tax cases. It is said you sought to have one defaulter returned to jail even though you conceded that he had no means of paying.'

'We have what we call the "cab-rank rule". This obliges barristers to take any case offered within their competence.'

They walk on. Joe is taking huge, wonderful pictures, mainly of Brigid.

'Actually,' Louise adds after a reflective pause, 'you might say Sandra broke the cab-rank rule when she refused to defend a man charged with rape.'

'I remember the case. What are your views on the clothes women can wear in court?'

'Women were first admitted to the Bar in 1922, when a woman in trousers would have been regarded as bizarre. But to insist on skirts in the 1990s is equally bizarre.'

'Well, thank you, an excellent interview.'

'When will it appear?'

'Quite soon, I hope.' She breaks off. 'Joe,' she calls, 'take your dreadful pics straight to the *Sentinel* then sit down on the floor outside my office like a cringing Prod dog, and wait cowering until I've seen them. OK?'

'Yes, Boss.'

'And be asking yourself why a grand lady like myself, descended from O'Connell, W. B. Yeats and James Joyce, should be throwing crumbs to an Apprentice Boy.'

Louise is appalled by such flippancy. She can't imagine why the spotty young man is grinning with delight. Louise rather distrusts Catholics and thinks everyone should. And suddenly all her fury against this flame-haired woman surfaces.

'Do you believe in birth control?'

Brigid goes very broad. 'Don't worry, I won't get your husband pregnant.'

Marcus has pencilled the date into his diary. St Hilda's are playing tennis this afternoon, a home match against Belvedere Grange, of Hertfordshire. He has a free afternoon. Lucy will be pleasantly surprised (Louise says) if he shows up.

'And go alone, Marcus.'

'Of course! – what do you mean?'

He knows he should go alone – being a father should be a full-time occupation. But he also recognises one of the many flaws in his nature; hyper-active, and bored in prospect by sub-standard tennis, he cannot resist a couple of phone calls.

Keen and competitive cyclist though he is, Marcus has never gone in for 'games'. Glumly surveying the sparkling-white tennis dresses scurrying about the courts, he remembers why, in his own time, black boys never visited Upton Park to watch the legendary heroes of West Ham United – Bobby Moore, Martin Peters, Geoff Hurst. In those days there were few black faces in the stands or on the pitch. Football belonged to *them*.

'Which is your daughter?' Clive Wellings asks. Clive had been the first of his phone calls.

'Lucy? Wiry hair, milk chocolate skin and always as far from the ball as possible.' He chuckles. 'Lucy's mother and I were dead against sending her to a private school, of course, but I decided my child came before my principles. I expect you've heard that one before.'

'I'd do the same if I could afford it.'

Marcus is studying Lucy's movements on the tennis court. Not since he arrived has she acknowledged his presence by the smallest gesture. He feels empty and lost among all these smart 'Hullo–hullo' parents with their picnic hampers and glass-cutting voices.

Clive Wellings is also observing Lucy Byron intently. Years of voluntary work in a drugs rehabilitation centre have endowed him with an unerring eye for the phased-out movements of a stoned youngster.

'You're sure she's well?' he murmurs.

'She's play-acting for my benefit.'

Wellings slips him a package. 'I've checked the tape. You'll find the specification of the camera enclosed with the cassette.'

'Thanks, Clive. Did you have to view the tape?'

'It wasn't necessary.'

'I'm grateful.'

'Marcus, your daughter has been on hard drugs within the last twenty-four hours.'

'Hm.'

'They're setting you up.'

'I know.'

'Things are getting hot my end, too. I've been tipped off that my name's on a list. I have to think of my family.'

'Clive, all we have to fear is fear itself.'

He sees Heather Stuart walking rapidly towards them across the finely mown grass – his second phone call.

Wellings takes a couple of paces. 'I'll be off.'

Marcus grabs his arm. 'Clive, a frightened Lemon is a rotten Lemon.'

Heather Stuart pauses a tactful distance from the two men and studies the tennis courts with the expert eye of a sportswoman. Wellings scampers away, followed by Marcus's troubled gaze.

Heather draws closer. 'Did you know I'm an alumna of St Hilda's, captain of hockey in my time and centre-forward for Middlesex Juniors?'

'Is this classified information?'

The green eyes swivel. 'Which is your daughter?'

'You tell me.'

'Is it the girl who combines your nose with Jill Hull's chin?'

'It's the one who's never where the ball is.'

Marcus notices that Heather has forsaken the short skirt and tight sweater which had provoked him to lecture her at their first meeting. She wears a light suede coat over a full cotton skirt and flat-heeled shoes. Her blonde hair is tied up today. The greenish eyes are the same.

Lust and guilt engulf him in a sudden fireball of middle-aged misery. Does she know how he burns for her? Those eyes are stacked with erotic knowledge. What the hell is she doing in the Probation Service? She should be slinking round the Sacher Hotel in Vienna, or the Ritz in Paris, employed by an international merchant bank to tease out the actuarial risks on supermodels getting kidnapped by Islamic fundamentalists.

Something like that.

'I'm glad you came,' he says.

'So am I.'

'I thought I was an MCP who believes every woman is a carrier for my spare rib.'

'You said you needed my help.'

'Riverview Sports Club, Friday evening, sevenish. Wendy will meet up with you.'

'Fine.'

'It's . . . it's to do with a very important man. He's in deep trouble.'

'So you said last time. Your daughter's watching us. Bye.'

Heather Stuart is walking rapidly away from him.

The tennis players on Lucy's court are shaking hands. Marcus waits. This is the part he dreads most, when she walks straight past him, without a glance. But Marcus has observed the expression of fury worn by the St Hilda's games mistress throughout the match. As she moves to grab Lucy, the girl raises her arms to her father in extravagant greeting and trots into his arms.

'Hullo, Lucy.'

He notices that contact lenses leave her eyes sore and watery. 'You need new lenses,' he says.

'You've had a lot of visitors,' she says.

'Just a chap I know who's wondering whether to send his daughter here.'

'Yeah? What about the dish?'

'Dish?'

'The gorgeous bird you couldn't take your eyes off. Is she your latest hit? Does Louise know? Does Brigid know?'

'Lucy, dear, there is nothing to know.'

'Yeah! Know who your new dish reminds me of?'

'No.'

'The famous bitch-actress Teresa Kent. Remember her?'

'No, Lucy, I don't.'

'Liar. Did you read that interview with her in yesterday's *Standard*?'

'No.'

'Bet you did. Poor thing! She has just been offered a rich-for-ever slush part in a Hollywood movie – Kent calls it "very challenging" – but that would mean abandoning plans to play a battered single mother at the Bush Theatre in a "tremendously significant play about the awful plight of abandoned women". Gosh, gosh, guess which she'll choose! Oh, that gorgeous white complexion – just like your new friend's.'

'Come to tea with me, Lucy?'

'You mean straight into a methodone clinic, yeah? What do you care, anyway?'

'Why am I here then?'

'Greasing your conscience.'

'Glad to hear I've got one. How's yours, Lucy?'

'Fine. I mean terrible. I'm letting his Honour dahn, ahnt Ah?'

'Maybe you're letting yourself down. Come and have tea with your father.'

'What abaht the operah?'

'That would be great, Lucy. I'm busy tonight but—'

'You've been "busy tonight" since the day I was born.'

'Come with me tonight, then. I'll cancel everything. We'll get standbys at the Coliseum.'

'Oh yeah. Yah.'

Lucy is walking away from him, twiddling her new graphite racket frenetically. The games mistress seizes the opportunity to confront him.

'Judge Byron, this is very serious. I shall have to report it to Mrs Nearcliffe. Your daughter desperately needs help.'

'Thank you. I know. As I explained to Mrs Nearcliffe, I don't have custody of Lucy. That's my problem.'

'She has been in trouble with the police, you know. Mrs Nearcliffe spoke to Lucy's mother about it. This is not for me to say, Judge Byron, but we simply do not know how much longer we can keep Lucy at St Hilda's. We have to consider the other girls and—'

'And their parents?'

'There have been representations made.'

'Well, thank you for putting her in the tennis team.'

'Oh, this is the last time, I assure you.'

Marcus walks to his car feeling like a twig broken from a fatally diseased elm.

Lying beside Louise Pointer, QC, in the plain, sensible John Lewis double bed she had purchased after their marriage – she had insisted on selling Marcus's own, a flamboyant four-poster, genuine-imitation Elizabethan, along with its attendant fragrance of Sandra – Marcus slips into a troubled sleep. He is determined not to dream about Lucy, who haunts him night after night.

But dream he does.

Marcus finds himself peeping through a half-open door built of very grand, inlaid timbers, no doubt imported from the colonies and hewn by slaves. At the far end of the huge room a small man is bent over his desk – the Chief. Lord Chief Justice Theodore Bowers.

Lucy is standing beside the Chief, shuffling his papers like cards, mixing them all up, one case with another. He doesn't seem to notice. She whispers in his ear.

'Really?' he says. 'Thank you for telling me!'

They both know that he, Marcus, is peeping at them. He feels shame, chagrin: some flunkey will grab him by the collar, from behind, any moment. 'Gotcha!'

'Marcus!' Louise remonstrates.

'Er? Wha'? What? No, no, I—'

'Marcus, you're keeping me awake with all this shouting.'

'I had a bit of a dream.'

'Did Brigid Kyle come into it?'

'Who?'

'Marcus, I have to be up at six-thirty tomorrow.'

'Sorry, darling.'

'Well, at least you know the word.'

'Louise.'

'*Yes?*'

'You're my baby.' He reaches for his wife.

'For God's sake, I've got my period. Go to back to sleep!'

# *Nine*

'WALK ALONG THE LINE, Mrs Galloway, look carefully at each one, then walk back again. Then repeat the procedure. Take your time.'

Susie nods, mute.

'There's always a temptation,' Inspector Ken Crabbe continues placidly, 'to snatch. Suppose you feel sure. "That's the one! That's him!" So why bother with the others? However sure, you feel, Mrs Galloway, you should look at each boy very carefully, four times. Going up the line, going down, going up again, going down.'

'Yes, I understand.'

'It's a bit of an ordeal, isn't it?'

'There's one thing I've wanted to ask: where do the others come from?'

'The others in the line? Some are boys we've just recruited down at the local Social Services hostel plus a few straight off the street – five quid an hour and they leap at it. What you have to remember is that the genuine suspect may not be in the first batch we show you. If you don't make a positive identification on the first round, we'll set up a second lot. But that takes a bit of time. We have to fit them up.'

'Fit them up?'

Ken Crabbe hoists his bushy eyebrows in a friendly manner.

'The rules about identification now prevailing, Mrs Galloway, God bless the Home Office, are somewhat baffling. For instance, you have told us that your lad was tall.'

'Yes, he seemed quite tall. Very.'

'So all the lads we show you will be seated.'

'But why?'

'Because, Mrs Galloway, any little lady – and I hope I don't sound patronising or "sexist" or anything not "politically correct" – any small person like yourself who gets set upon is liable to see her attacker as taller than he is. So if we had them all standing up you might, out of the goodness of your mind's eye, just go for the tallest.'

'Oh. I see.'

'On the other hand, if you tell us your assailant was male, and black, brown or white, or Asian, we have to believe you. So all your boys will be black.'

'Yes.'

'And there again, you described your one as "loose-limbed, moving a bit like a rag doll". Correct?'

Susan shudders. 'Yes, I remember that.'

'But we can't ask seven innocent boys to move about like rag-dolls for your inspection, can we? The real one is going to move about like a toy soldier, isn't he?'

'Yes, I suppose so.'

'So they don't move. And there again, clothing. You told us he was wearing a red baseball cap back-to-front.'

'Yes, I'm quite sure of that.'

'So we could have all eight wearing identical red baseball caps back-to-front. But the Home Office isn't into that – expensive. Besides, an innocent lad might be wearing the cap more the way you remember it. You end up accusing a baseball cap of violent robbery.'

'But—'

'I understand your feelings, Mrs Galloway. We have discussions among ourselves, particularly about scars and dreadlocks.'

'Yes, he had a scar on his right cheek – no, his left, I . . .'

'We do have a scar or two among this batch but you won't see them. Each boy will wear an identical plaster on his right cheek.'

'But that's ridiculous!' Susan is close to tears.

'Mrs Galloway, if we bring innocent boys off the street are we to limit ourselves to those bearing scars on their right cheek?'

'Well, why not? I saw it! Just as I saw the dreadlocks.'

'As for dreadlocks, Mrs Galloway, the first thing a boy on the run does is cut them off. So let's forget the hair, shall we? Each boy will be wearing a white skull cap.'

Susan looks deeply crestfallen.

'Mrs Galloway, I know what you've been through, and three nights in hospital, so I'll tell you something I shouldn't. The lad we've arrested, our prime suspect, was no longer wearing dreadlocks.'

'What about his voice? I remember his voice when he asked me the time? "Got the time?" he said. I remember thinking, why can't he say "please"?'

'Yes. You can ask to hear the voice of the lad if you have correctly identified him as the suspect.'

'You mean the one you found in possession of my watch, my necklace and my credit cards!'

'Now, Mrs Galloway, calm yourself. I know how you feel. Members of the public, victims like yourself, always think it's obvious. But possession of stolen goods doesn't of itself prove robbery. These things get passed around, sometimes within minutes.'

'Yes, I suppose so.'

'I know so, Mrs Galloway. On the other hand,' Inspector Ken Crabbe smiles gently, 'we may be lucky. Let's hope so. I'll call you in just a jiff. Must make sure everything's hunky-dory.'

This long and exhausting conversation has taken place in the waiting room of an identification centre half-way across London from Oundle Square. It has taken Susan an hour to get here, by tube then bus, and finally on foot, and every minute of that hour was replete with terror each time she saw a black youth. She kept telling herself that she had lived for twenty-eight years without ever having been assaulted, and in all that time she must have passed or sat next to literally thousands of black youths without the slightest problem. What Susan could not grasp, in her pain and fear at being at large in the brash, noisy, jostling city, was that she had subconsciously been expecting it to happen for years.

That was the 'fear' Marcus Byron spoke of.

Susie wishes she could meet Jill's former husband. But she never will.

Anyway, she's not going near Jill Hull again. Doug McIntyre has warned Simon that Lucy Byron knows one of the Richardson boys who robbed him on Hilton Avenue. Susie remembers the strange smells and syringes she and Simon used to find after Lucy had been baby-sitting. McIntyre reckons the Richardsons had probably done all of the 'jobs' on Simon's BMW. It was certainly very bizarre to think that Lucy, a famous judge's daughter, should keep such company. McIntyre had informed Simon that Jill Hull's household was involved in 'more than meets the eye'.

'The police clearly know more than they're letting on,' Simon had told Susie when he and Tom collected her from the hospital. He hadn't wanted to bring Tom but really had no alternative because Tom wouldn't let him out of his sight. If Simon even moved across the kitchen, Tom desperately scampered after him.

It's not every day a two-year-old sees his mother with a knife at her throat and then thrown to the ground. Sees terror on his mother's face. But what did he see? Tom's still too young for proper language. All Susie can remember is the tall, rag-doll youth with the scar, the dreadlocks and the reversed baseball cap asking her the time – 'Got the time?' – as she and Tom were leaving Century Park (and very glad to leave, too, what with that cross-eyed boy, who'd snatched and sexually assaulted a little girl, still at large and pretending to be a tree – Mark Griffin, his name comes back).

Apparently you should never show your watch, particularly a gold Rolex – it had been a wedding present from Simon. The rag-doll youth hadn't said 'thank you' or 'cheers' or anything. No manners nowadays, she'd thought, then chided herself: you're getting old. She and Tom had walked on along Brancaster Road, passing the busted cars outside Ron Tanner's workshop, all those smashed windows and coils of wire hanging out like guts from a slashed stomach. Fifty yards on she'd faltered; a group of black youths were systematically peering into parked cars, then leaning their backs against the doors and testing the locks. In broad daylight! What's the use of Neighbourhood Watch if you have youngsters who don't give a damn who's watching!

She and Tom had crossed the road. Her heart was in her mouth. She remembers Tom chattering away nonstop, not real words but his own: everything he saw he wanted to name – cats, cars, car thieves. The plastic bags from the supermarket continued to swing awkwardly from the curved handles of his pushchair.

'Mrs Galloway!'

She jumps. Her heart pounds. The Inspector is beckoning. She hadn't wanted to come today but she and Simon agreed she must. Simon is normally slow to anger but she'd never seen him possessed by such rage.

Susan finds herself staring through one-way glass – so that's how they do it – at eight peas in a pod. Each black youth wears a white, close-fitting cap down to his ears. She's reminded of the surgeons bending over her just before they gave her the general anaesthetic to sew up her arm. She keeps walking, the Inspector at her side, and she finds herself longing to ask him, 'Which one is it?'

She comes back down the line, trying to concentrate, to remember.

'Take your time,' she hears.

They had turned into Oundle Square, she and Tom, heading for his routine hour of sleep, after which he'd shout 'Tea!' – one word he really does know. Getting Tom and his pushchair up the steps of No. 16 backwards always requires care and a bit of effort – she remembers removing the shopping bags and laying them on the ground and then . . . then . . .

'No luck?' the Inspector says. 'Like to try a second time?'

'Please tell me if he's one of this lot!'

'I'm not allowed to say, Mrs Galloway.'

Then a scorching on the skin of her wrist as her watch was ripped off and then that tall black youth in the reversed baseball cap was going for her throat, her necklace, the pushchair slipped from her hands, she felt it roll down the steps, heard Tom scream, she wanted to scream herself but was totally paralysed, as if her throat was filled with choking glue. She must have kicked out, fought, because suddenly the knife was at her throat and she saw the eyes of her assailant, livid, like an animal at bay. Her arm went up to protect herself, she felt a tearing in her arm and then she was on the ground, her head smashed on the steps . . .

She walks up the line again.

The pushchair had turned over. Someone was picking Tom off the pavement. She later learned it was young Nigel Thompson returning home from school. Then she fainted (they told her in the ambulance).

The police had passed the hospital doctor's report on to the Crown Prosecution Service: 'Multiple small contusions and lacerations to the extensor aspects of the left wrist and four large scratch marks to the volar aspect' (in plain language, the palm side). Her left arm had required twelve stitches along the knife wound – she wonders whether the scar will ever disappear.

She walks down the line again. All those pairs of eyes beneath those white plastic caps seem so docile, passive, defeated, nothing like what she saw in—

'I don't know,' she tells the Inspector. 'I'm rather tired. I'm not very well. Sorry.'

Thirty minutes later she drags herself through a second identity parade. She is utterly exhausted. Finally, in desperation, she 'identifies' the wrong boy.

She only wants to get away, no more blank black faces, wants to get home, but the thought of the journey terrifies her.

'Can you call me a taxi?' she asks Inspector Crabbe.

'It could cost you fifteen quid, Mrs Galloway.'

'Never mind.'

Inspector Crabbe hands her fifteen pounds. 'We have a fund from Victim Support . . . for deserving cases.'

'But this means he'll never be convicted! I've failed!'

She cannot know how Ken Crabbe feels. As Saturday-afternoon Supervisor at Mason Lodge Attendance Centre, he knows Amos Richardson all too well. Each time this woman had walked past Amos in the line he'd wanted to pinch her ear. But the 'other' Ken Crabbe had made sure that she did walk past Amos.

Inspector Crabbe was the first Lemon they had succeeded in bending.

Trish Richardson, younger sister of Paul, Amos and Daniel, arrives late in Benson Street Youth Court. Her social worker has been unable to find her. Daniel has skipped school to track her down and bring her in. 'You only make things worse if you flip out.'

Even Lucy had deferred to him. She has skipped school, too.

Daniel and Lucy wait for Trish in the street outside. Paul and Amos would barge in there, cursing the Burns Security guards during the compulsory body-search, but Daniel hates the atmosphere inside, the aggro, the echo of heavy metal doors closing in the cells below, the oppression.

Lucy has recently moved into Trish's street-gang. She enjoys the adrenaline and the violence. Only thirteen years old, Trish is big for her age and believes she rules the High Street. She and her mate Debbie O'Grady have marked out their territory with graffiti and spit, then fought other girl-gangs to protect it. Lucy remembers her first time out. Trish had pointed to a grubby phone box in the High, opposite the Co-op.

'That's our private line, OK? We don't let anyone else use it.

Mates can call us any time and we order spliff and tabs on it. Nobody messes with us. Got it?'

Lucy has been accepted by the gang only on sufferance, as a hanger-on. She doesn't really belong. She's half-posh, though she tries to hide it. She goes to school. She does exams. Her dad's a judge or something. Lucy has no street cred, Trish Richardson says. No one argues with Trish.

Trish belongs to a drug-running family but they keep her short of the hard stuff because she's a girl and just a kid. Lucy produces free joints – never asks for money. Hard to turn her away when you're aching for cannabis or B&H. But it's Lucy's super-mature relationship with Trish's brother Dan which gives her real status.

'We smashed up two birds who called us slags,' Trish proudly informs Lucy. 'We beat ten tons of shit out of the pair.'

Lucy enjoys the aggro when the girls link arms and fill the width of the pavement and everyone else has to jump for it. They know how to frighten adults by sheer noise.

With other gangs, more than noise is needed. Trish and Debbie carry tyre levers, chisels, hammers, screwdrivers – which they hide in various 'safe' spots, knowing all about 'possession' and how that leads on to drugs found under your Lycra skintights or up your holes.

They also recognise the various female screws who operate in plain clothes around the High Street and the Broadway. Some of these sows fancy themselves in minis.

'Nowadays you have to get your retaliation in first,' Trish says. 'You get girls slagging you off. You're not going to stand there like a plum.'

'Or a pudding,' Lucy adds helpfully, but Trish doesn't get it. Her brow tends to disappear when she doesn't get it.

Debbie O'Grady is Trish's closest mate. They style themselves the 'Kray Sisters', after the famous East End gangsters, though they aren't sisters at all. Both girls carry a long list of cautions and convictions for assault and affray. Trish will 'do' any female seen talking too long to any boy she fancies, or fancies she fancies. A girl from the Longhorn Estate needed hospital treatment for burns to her face and bruises to her back and head after she'd been locked up by the 'Kray Sisters' in a bedroom, beaten with a metal bar and tortured with lit cigarettes.

The police got nowhere on that one – the victim wouldn't talk.

Debbie's elder brother and uncle are both in prison. They are heroes. Debbie's father was black and died from drink in his mid-thirties. Her Irish mother lives in Donegal with a bookie. Debbie started drinking at twelve and claims to down half a bottle of vodka when she goes out. 'I have a filthy wicked temper with my drink,' she warns Lucy and everybody.

Debbie hates 'Pakis', foreigners and 'Yids'. She may never have met a 'Yid' but she knows they disguise themselves as 'Christians' who knock on your door with messages of Love and Hope, to make you feel bad. The trick is to trap them in the public toilets in Broadway and take their stuff, after beating them up. Unfortunately few foreigners or 'Yids' visit Broadway, and the 'Paki' girls have learned to come in numbers.

Trish and Debbie are thirteen touching fourteen and there's really nowhere the courts can send them. But Lucy, because of her age, is taking real risks. She wants trouble. Her dad needs trouble. Her dad needs to come to court and stand in front of 'Auntie Wendy' and the blue-eyed Sir Patrick, down on his knees and humbly offering up one thousand quid as a surety for his delinquent daughter.

Lucy keeps a list of adults who need trouble, apart from his Honour. Those wankers Wendy and Patrick, for example. And maybe she is adding Simon Galloway to her list – the way he looks at her. And Teresa Kent.

The robbery of Teresa Kent will be the perfect robbery. Lucy claims to know where the actress lives but isn't saying.

'She's ex-directory,' Lucy explains mysteriously. 'She's a classic. She's a real-life soap. She shags judges. Her crotch smells. Men stow their tackle in her every night of the week. She's a complete scam. She has designer labels on her bum. She's in need of a gang-bang. OK?'

Lucy's mental landscape is beyond them. She has dreams of her own, trips you can't follow. She knows that the great patriarch Marcus got the hots for Teresa Kent after he met the famous star at a super-posh charity do and thought Lucy wouldn't wake up while he bonked the actress in the next room. But Lucy had stayed awake, waiting.

Which bird of paradise are you poking tonight, with your famous dick and hairy-backed balls, your Honour?

Shortly after Lucy joined them, the gang had terrified a bakery manageress at knifepoint before making off with ninety quid. Trish had threatened to 'slice her loaf' if the woman reported it.

The big trick is to get a woman with a handbag somewhere quiet. Then you surround her and scare the shit out of her until you get the bag. Trish is into bag snatches. She knows all the tricks. They'd lifted a nice load from that old bird in Century Park, the one who turned out to be called Mrs Ramsden and seventy something – she'd come straight from the post office. It's the only way to pay for the nice things you see in shops surrounded by store detectives. There are two or three store detectives marked down by Trish for slaughter.

Lucy is growing bored standing about waiting for Trish outside the court.

'Hell, she can find her own way home, Dan!'

'Nah. They might take her back into care.'

Lucy tosses away her Marlboro stub and tries again, coaxing Dan into an adventure far from London, a life of freedom and joy among the Tree People in Wiltshire.

He looks apprehensive. 'Sounds like a lot of fuckin' sky,' he says.

Inside the court Wendy Berry observes Trish Richardson slouching in sulkily, dragging her feet and chewing gum. The charges are shoplifting and assault. Trish had entered the ladies' department of C & A and begun to fiddle with tags and labels. When a store detective challenged her, she punched the cunt in the face.

Patrick Berry and his colleagues study Trish's record of previous convictions – two pages of them. The system has run out of options. The girl is too young to be remanded in custody. Her social workers have given up. She doesn't behave like a 'girl'.

Patrick looks to Jimmy Haley-White, leader of the Youth Justice team.

'So it's either bail to live at home or Secure Accommodation?'

'There is no Secure Accommodation, sir.'

Taken down to the Care Room, Trish continues to warn the world that she will go back and kill that 'fucking bitch' of a store detective.

Time passes. Outside, in Benson Street, Lucy is holding Daniel's hand. They are happy to be together. Lucy isn't bothered about not working for her GCSEs. Her head is pleasantly fuzzed by dope. Time is merely a magical dimension of space – you make your own time.

So what's this? Three phantoms in blue from the Chinese astrologers' charts or three turkeys who imagine that Benson Street is Christmas? Two male, closely resembling McIntyre and Jenkins, one female, and the female in her neat chequered hat is already prodding Lucy up against the wall while the cocks do over Dan.

'Yeah, I'm loaded,' Lucy smiles as the WPC extracts pills and packets from her clothing. 'It's all Class A. Have some.'

'I'm arresting you.'

'Yeah. My dad sent it me. Have a free ride to fame.'

Lucy has seen many pairs of handcuffs but never fastened round her own skinny wrists. However, these cuffs keep floating free, like blow-bubbles at a kids' party, and Lucy keeps floating after them, abseiling to nirvana, sending the WPC, who's a proper piglet, into paroxysms (Lucy is hazy on the spelling, and everything) of frustration and mindless violence.

'Aren't they beautiful,' Lucy giggles, 'these Iron Age bracelets.'

'Now come along, Lucy.' It's McIntyre. 'We're taking you in.'

'I recognise your voice, Doug, but where's your face?'

She hears Dan protesting that he wants to come with her but they've found nothing on Dan. Lucy had made him empty his pockets before they danced into Benson Street.

She's in the back of the police panda now, still chained to the WPC with the hat. They're soon floating above that beautiful arc-shaped, shiplike building designed by Lucy's favourite Swedish architect, Sjornsomething. Lucy has written to Marcus in a Friends of the Earth envelope: 'I'm going to be an architect designing prisons. OK?'

'Hey, Doug.'

McIntyre is driving. He glances at her in the mirror. 'Yes, Lucy?'

'Do you fancy me?'

'Shut it,' the WPC says.

Lucy giggles. 'Daughter of famous judge beaten up in panda by wound-up WPC suffering from *coitus interruptus* with Welsh dynamo Jenkins the Boot.'

'Shut it!'

'Go on,' Lucy whispers into her ear, 'smash me up. Do it! You're longing to, all that suppressed violence which keeps the sties full, grunt grunt.'

'Be a good girl, Lucy,' McIntyre says gently.

'I want my dad!' Lucy giggles.

'The court will stand!' bellows the usher.

Marcus Byron is about to send a young mother to jail for four years, but first his court has other business. Before him on his bench lies Leela Desai's final pre-sentence report on Alan Sanderson, cousin to Sid Griffin, 'handler' for Joseph and Darren. In Marcus's head resides the complete documentation he received, clandestinely, from Angela Loftus by the hand of the beautiful Heather Stuart.

Sanderson has been found guilty of ABH while engaged in robbing an off-licence. According to Leela Desai's PSR, Sanderson comes from a chaotic family background, was abused by his father (who spent much of his life in prison) and was beaten by two of his mother's temporary partners. The PSR evades Marcus's earlier advice that the offence was 'so serious' as to warrant a custodial sentence. Sanderson 'deeply repents' his offence and needs to be urgently persuaded to 'confront his own masculinity and lack of self-esteem', concludes Leela Desai's PSR – or Jill Hull's.

Marcus believes that PSRs should be written by a new corps of probation officers and social workers directly employed by the court, not by the Probation Service or the local authority. They should carry a status analogous to that of court clerks. The idea had been Wendy's and Marcus had conveyed it to Max Venables, MP.

Max's sad eyes had listed wearily. 'More wars with Jill and the Probation Service?'

'Tell me about a worthier war, Max.'

And what would Community Service for Alan Sanderson be likely to involve in practice? Turning out once a week to shore up the banks of the Long Water in Kensington Gardens? Erecting a low oak retaining fence a metre from the bank, then infilling and planting to prevent erosion and to protect trees, plants, wildlife? Saturdays only. Works stops for the duck- and goose-breeding season.

Having listened to pleas from Edgar Averling, representing Sanderson, Judge Byron instructs Sanderson to stand. The man before him wears a T-shirt with a violent, chainsaw logo, his hair straggles in long, bleached strands, a stud gleams in his left nostril.

'Alan Sanderson, I do not accept the recommendation of the PSR. For many years your behaviour has been criminal, sometimes viciously criminal, and you have shown no regard or respect for the rights of others. Your behaviour is a menace to society. Every type of remedy short of custody has been tried and failed. I do not know whether prison will reform you but I do know that the long-suffering public deserves to have you out of the way.

'Five years. Take him down.'

Averling immediately gives notice of appeal – and asks that Sanderson be released on bail. Judge Byron has hitherto allowed bail to Sanderson, despite grave misgivings, but now he refuses.

'It's always time for common sense,' he says. 'Next case.'

The Press benches are filling up. Word is out that Marcus is about to send the mother of a six-month-old child to jail for four years. Word is also out that Sandra Golding has taken over the defence of Liz Hargreaves.

An hour later Brigid Kyle's notebook is full. She has underlined two key declarations. The first was Sandra Golding's.

'Your Honour, here is a young mother who has never offended before, and who has always been highly regarded by family, friends and employers. She made one mistake. Deserted by the father of her child, she attempted to drown her despair in drink. We all know the tragic consequences, a death she did not intend and which has affected her deeply. The question before your Honour is whether her innocent child is to suffer a double bereavement: the disappearance of his father followed by forcible separation from the one human being who can guarantee him love and security – his mother. Your Honour, let justice be tempered with mercy, and let compassion be a component of justice.'

And, later, Marcus's, as Liz Hargreaves stood quaking before him.

'The law properly punishes intentional crimes more severely than unintentional. The vast majority of deaths caused by reckless use of a motor vehicle are not intentional. The victim is nevertheless as dead as if he had been deliberately assaulted. There are no degrees of death. Society has warned us not to drink beyond a stated limit before we drive. To do so is a criminal act. You did it. You killed a man. You did not stop.

You attempted to avoid detection. You denied involvement when first questioned.

'This is a crime where sentence must put a high premium on deterrence. I am not entitled to send a reassuring message to others who may be tempted to climb behind the wheel of a car when three times over the limit.

'I have listened to your learned counsel most carefully. I am not insensible to the human factors pertaining to a young mother who is also a single parent. I am giving you a sentence far below the norm and my powers under the law.

'Four years. Take her down.'

Hissed by the women gathered in the public gallery, Marcus slowly gathers his papers then walks from the court. Outside in the street, Brigid is immediately recognised by an angry knot of incensed women who rush towards her. One spits in her face.

'He's finished, your big black dick!'

Hailing a taxi, Brigid wipes the spittle from her face with a tissue and directs the driver to Probation House. Jill Hull's major press conference has been rescheduled for late afternoon and everyone knows why. Marcus's anticipated verdict in the Liz Hargreaves case is manna from heaven.

The gathering is officially sponsored by the Association of Chief Officers of Probation (ACOP), but it makes no difference. Waiting in the overspilling conference room, Brigid flips through several printed handouts. One of them informs her that during the past year sixty per cent of custodial sentences were imposed by judges and magistrates despite alternative proposals from the Probation Service.

Short and stocky, Jill Hull bustles on to the platform, her glasses glinting in the bright lights. She goes straight into the attack yet sounds defensive, even plaintive. She keeps referring sardonically to 'What we all read in the Press.'

Brigid opens a fresh shorthand notebook.

'You might be excused for believing that every offender in the care of the Probation Service is sent to sunbathe in Bermuda. You might be excused for believing that probation officers regularly do the weekly shopping for their clients, just in case they don't have enough time to commit more offences. You might be excused for believing that we all graduated from the Faculty of Soggy Compassion.'

Brigid scribbles a note in the margin. 'Does she know that Lucy is on the edge? Does she care?'

'Are prisons expensive? Yes, they are far the most expensive form of deterrence yet devised by human society. But do prisons deter? Not on the evidence. Fifty-five per cent of ex-prisoners reoffend within two years. I find that a truly frightening statistic.'

Another scribbled note. 'Poor Marcus. My poor darling.'

'When we send a man or woman to prison, we in effect wash our hands of them. We put them "out of the way", unseen and unheard. We deprive children of fathers and mothers – the children, as always, are the ultimate victims.'

Jill pauses. Brigid doodles. 'Here it comes.'

'I daresay most of you have just heard about the atrocious sentence handed down this afternoon in the Crown Court. A small baby has been deprived of his mother for four years.'

Brigid cannot bear it. She lifts a hand. 'Two years after remission, surely?'

Jill's glasses glint angrily as she identifies the source of the interruption.

'There will be time for questions later.'

'It wasn't a question. It was a point of fact.'

Jill resumes dismissively. 'We have heard a lot lately about the feelings of the victims of crime. We are now told by Judge Byron that the victims should play a role in the courts. Courts will have to take into account not only what they have suffered, but how they would dispose of the offender. Hang him? Flog him? Lock him away for life? This is nothing but a charter for crude vengeance.

'Must our criminal justice system now be handed over to blind prejudice, blind ignorance? Are we to throw away everything we have learned about crime and punishment during the past two hundred years?'

Brigid scribbles another note. 'She is without personal vanity. She merely serves a cause. It is Marcus who has chosen to make that cause dependent on his own destruction.'

Brigid does not stay for the questions. She has already interviewed Jill Hull and knows the answers and non-answers. Only the 'Marcus factor' has induced her to come today. And the one question she would like to ask is out of bounds:

Is Jill Hull willing to sacrifice her daughter in order to bring down Marcus? People rarely confront themselves candidly; the greatest force in human affairs is self-deception.

Brigid telephones Marcus soon after seven.

'He's out,' Louise answers coldly, 'and, to anticipate your next question, no, I don't know where he is.'

The Riverview Sports Club boasts three gymnasia, a sauna, a solarium, a dozen squash courts, twenty indoor tennis courts and a lavish brasserie–bar designed to restore any weight which has been lost. You pay £1,500 a year to belong to this super-modern, super-gloss palace of pleasure; the waiting list now stretches to eighteen months and rising.

Patrick had been a member long before he bought Wendy a subscription as a wedding present. Marcus calls the Riverview 'a pleasure dome for Yuppies', which does not trouble Patrick but incenses Wendy. Wendy is not entirely at ease with the knowledge that Patrick's quick killing on privatised water-company shares guarantees her a life-style which her poor mother could only have dreamed of.

'I'm not taking any shit from you, Marco! Anyway, you spend way over the Riverview annual subscription on replacing wrecked mountain bikes.'

'In the mountains you find yetis not yuppies.'

'Oh yeah? Did I mention your flash Rolls, MB1?'

Patrick is more indulgent. He regards Marcus's 'socialism' as a quaint foible, a hangover from the immigrant culture of the East End. What interests Patrick is tomorrow, not yesterday – for example, the new computer hookup his company is selling to police authorities and Neighbourhood Watch schemes. He has urged Marcus to invest.

'As news of crimes is received, the information is automatically disseminated by e-mail or fax to designated local coordinators, who then distribute reports on carbonised paper to their neighbours. It's a guaranteed winner.'

Marcus usually laughs down his brother-in-law's 'guaranteed winners'.

'Sounds to me more like a victory for community spirit than for hi-tech, Patrick. Anyway, judges should avoid a financial interest in law enforcement.'

Wendy has always been vulnerable to Marcus's jibes. His power to sting her goes back to childhood, to the Old Kent Road. Marcus was the apple of their mother's eye, the one destined by the heavens to 'make it'. The rest – four out of six went to university – crept along in his shadow, telling him he was a greater singer than Gigli (which was how Pavarotti then spelled his name).

Hitting back at Marcus is Wendy's favourite sport – and it's free. When he unveiled his cloud-cuckoo scheme for saving the Director of Public Prosecutions from very public prosecution, Wendy laughed mercilessly.

'And who is this new bird of yours, anyway?'

'Her name', he replied with gravity, 'is Heather Stuart. She is Angela Loftus's trusted assistant.'

'Yeah?'

'Yeah. And she frequents the Riverview. She works out like you do.'

'And she's better looking than Angela, eh?'

'Kindly remember the purpose of this exercise, Wendy.'

'Haw haw.'

'I'm serious.'

'Haw haw haw. I may have seen her around. Honey-blonde?'

'Possibly.'

'Built like an egg-timer?'

'Well, she's—'

'Looks like the actress Teresa Kent?'

'I didn't notice any resemblance, frankly, but—'

'Haw haw.'

Coaxing the Director of Public Prosecutions to the Riverview this Friday evening has been a feat of logistical ingenuity fraught with the risk of a last-minute defection by Lionel Lacey to Wardour Street's Les Enfants du Paradis.

Negotiations have been by telephone.

'Lionel, you will dine with the two young ladies and myself after they have worked out.'

'"Worked out", Byron?'

'It's a modern term for exercise, Lionel – for pumping iron.'

'For what?'

'After dinner we will move on to the floor show at the Tropicana Club. The new Egyptian belly-dancer could make the pyramids shake, and they have a stripper called Kerta – she's Icelandic and would bring a frozen cod to the boil. In fact you could call her a female microwave.'

'This is all very gallant of you, Byron – you want to keep me out of trouble.'

'Lionel, there are better bets than baby-snatching.'

'I've never enjoyed laying a bet on a horse with four legs.'

'Lionel! You owe this to all of us!'

Marcus heard a giggle. 'Very well.'

'I'll be waiting for you at the entrance to the Riverview Club on Friday at seven p.m. sharp.'

Lionel Lacey has dutifully turned up in his old Daimler. Now, seated in the futuristic visitors' (or voyeurs') gallery overlooking Gym 2, Marcus glances nervously at his haggard guest, whose frayed collar remains one size too large and whose blue suit would grace a scarecrow.

Lionel Lacey gazes down from the acrylic thermoplastic viewing gallery at the colourful choreography below with the earnest gaze of a pallid schoolboy trying to be good. What he sees is a group of sleek, well-made young women in harlequin leotards being put through an increasingly strenuous routine to the strains of Mozart's piano concerto No. 21 and Jimi Hendrix.

'They make a fine pair, don't you think, Wendy and Heather?' Marcus asks his companion.

'Oh, very fine.'

Wendy's graceful limbs have been poured into a satin-sheened white leotard, with black tights. A black orchid. Heather Stuart has opted for bright reds and yellows, her honey-blonde hair tied in a black bow: a Dutch tulip.

'As you can see, the women perform surrounded by mirrors; if they lose a pound from their rear end, they can see it fall off.'

'Narcissism is the fashion, I suppose.'

'If you're not in love with yourself, who else is going to be?' Marcus laughs heartily but there is no laughter in his heart. Arriving home from the Crown Court he had found a message on his answer-machine: Lucy had been arrested, charged with possessing Class A drugs and released on unconditional police bail.

The message was from Doug McIntyre. It ended: 'I'm truly sorry about this.' There was no message from Jill. Gripped by anxiety, Marcus had been tempted to call off this evening's journey into Dali-land, this surreal adventure which Wendy had warned him was bound to end in farce, but he remained convinced that the public disgrace of Lionel Lacey would deal a fatal blow to the criminal justice system.

To the Lemons. Same thing.

Marcus studies sidelong the man's racked features. A lost soul.

Brilliant at his job. Total integrity. And now longing to unbutton his weekly flies in a squalid back room. (Marcus divines that Lionel is still in the era of buttons; two of them are undone.) How do you divert another man's obscure sexual drives? You don't. You don't even succeed with your own.

'At phase eight,' he explains, 'the pairings in this workout group become competitive.'

'Really?' Clearly Lionel Lacey couldn't care less.

It is Marcus who is switched on by the floor-show. And Wendy had spotted that, too. 'Marco, how many balls did God give you? Three?' The women on the gymnasium floor are now abandoning their precious limbs to complex contraptions of gleaming chrome and shimmering plastic. Marcus leans into his guest's ear, explaining that during phases eight, nine and ten spinning meters and racing digital clocks will measure the women's performances, their battle against weights, pulleys, coiled springs, tractions, gravity.

Lionel Lacey's thin mouth twitches, twists, rather unpleasantly.

'Known her long, have you – the blonde one?'

'Just over a year.'

'We all have our little secrets.' A tongue comes out like a lizard from a hole, runs over the DPP's lips, then withdraws. A smile Marcus hasn't seen before is now in permanent residence.

'I'd call Heather a big secret,' Marcus says.

'You'd hate to be found out?'

'It would be ruin, frankly.'

'I hadn't suspected you were such a complicated person, Byron.'

'We may ultimately be in the same boat, Lionel. Ah, they're now on to the twenty-kilogram weights. When the anvil hits the top of the scale it strikes a bell. The one who gets most bells in three minutes wins!'

Lionel Lacey nods politely. 'All very ingenious.'

'Now they're into the rowing machine. The aim is to cover three hundred metres of "river" first. It's all down to arms, pelvis and leg-thrust.'

'You obviously find health and fitness attractive, Byron. I go for sickly specimens, myself.'

The women are towelling themselves down now. Fending off total despair and self-contempt, Marcus grips his guest by the elbow.

'We're going down to meet the girls.'

His thin mouth twitching, Lionel Lacey follows Marcus to the lower-ground floor. At the check-in to the women's dressing rooms, Wendy is waiting to escort them past the security guards.

The visitors must sign in. The DPP hesitates.

'You're right,' Marcus murmurs in his ear, 'it's dangerous, it's risky for men in our position to visit the women's dressing rooms. If the Press got hold of it . . .'

'Risky, eh? Shouldn't be here, eh?' Lionel Lacey's eyes have widened with excitement.

Marcus signs the visitors' register with a flourish. Lacey does likewise with a vibrating hand. Marcus notices that he adds 'DPP' after his name.

Wendy swaggers ahead of them down a cheery, brightly lit corridor decorated with murals and paper flowers. The DPP is suddenly beginning to enjoy himself.

'*Schadenfreude*,' he whispers to Marcus.

When Marcus Byron had spent a postgraduate year studying German criminal law at Heidelberg under Geoffrey Villiers's friend Heinrich Hof, *Schadenfreude* had meant, roughly, 'joy-in-grief' (or humiliation). It probably still does.

Wendy leads them into a small, scented dressing cubicle – highly mirrored and humming with electro-static – where Heather Stuart is found prostrate on a divan, her blonde hair now unpinned and flowing over her bare shoulders and heaving bosom.

Her greenish cat's eyes swivel up at both men.

'Oh, Marcus . . . I can hardly move.'

Wendy laughs. 'We had a wager,' she tells Lionel Lacey. 'Can you guess?' The DPP's 1,000-watt eyes are glazed by excitement. 'If I won,' Wendy tells him, 'Marcus would have to confess to his wife.'

'Ah! And Mrs Byron will exact vengeance! Byron will be ruined!'

Heather laughs provocatively. 'And you will be ruined next, Mr Lacey. I mean, coming in here.'

He giggles. 'Yes! I am the Director of Public Prosecutions of England and Wales. I ought not to be here.'

'But you cannot escape,' Heather murmurs, running her hand round his scrawny neck. 'Can you? You will be exposed! You will be disgraced!'

Lacey nods happily. 'Lionel Lacey will be nothing but detritus!'

'OK, OK,' Marcus says with a glance at Wendy. 'Lionel, we'll leave the ladies to have their showers and meet them in the bar.'

Lionel Lacey is wearing his oddball smile. 'No.'

'No?'

'I wish to be alone with your young dominatrix, Byron.'

Marcus and Wendy wear expressions of alarmed concern but Heather evidently does not share it. Her pretty mouth is tucked into a pert smile of complete confidence. She winks at them: Go.

Wendy's brow furrows in consternation but Marcus throws her white-satin robe over her leotard and pulls her out into the corridor, closing the door behind them.

'You bastard!' she hisses. 'You're crazy!'

'Just keep cool, sister.'

'Idiot! Blow-jobs are not in a probation officer's job description!'

'Ssh.'

'What are you asking her to do?'

'God knows!'

They both remain in the hot, neon-lit corridor with their ears anxiously pressed to the door, waiting for a cry for help. But none comes. What they hear is murmured conversation. Lionel Lacey is telling Heather something, his voice tremulous and confessional, but Marcus Byron and his sister cannot catch what he's saying.

Fifteen minutes later Marcus gloomily receives the two ladies in the Riverview brasserie. Both have changed for dinner – but Marcus has lost Lacey. Making hasty excuses, Lionel Lacey has fled into the night in his Daimler.

'We did our best,' Marcus breaks the silence.

'We!' Wendy explodes. 'Congratulations on your heroic role!'

He sighs. 'He just went! What happened in there, Heather?'

'You've no right to ask!' Wendy intervenes, still simmering.

Heather smiles. 'He said I was very lucky to have such a splendid and honourable "lover" as his friend "Byron".'

Wendy looks at Marcus nastily. 'Haw haw.'

'Then he said he was not worthy of me,' Heather continues. 'He said I was a lady. He said I was "too clean" for him.'

Heather is clearly enjoying the deep discomfort of Marcus and Wendy. Marcus groans and buries his head in his hands.

'Did Lionel say anything about urchins and *misérables*?'

'Not a thing.'

'Nothing about his baby prostitutes?'

'No! I thought he was going to dine with us. I really did. I was astonished when Wendy and I found you alone.'

Marcus sighs deeply. 'Lionel is sick.'

Heather rises. 'Excuse me a moment, I need to visit the powder room. You can order me the scampi, Marcus – and a large daiquiri.'

Marcus's gaze lingers sullenly on her supple body in its little black dress as she leaves the brasserie on silver-shimmering feet.

'Stop looking,' Wendy says.

'OK, OK, OK.'

'Why don't you ask this bimbo to marry you here and now?'

Marcus glowers at his sister. 'I'm married.'

'Did anyone tell your wife?'

'What happened in there – when they were alone together?'

'Marco, this whole madhatter idea of yours was never on!'

'Lucy was arrested and charged today. How about a truce, sister?'

'Oh, Marco. Oh God.' She takes his hand and squeezes it.

'Why should Heather need to visit the powder room?' he says.

'I wondered, too. We've only just left the powder room.'

'What will you drink? Bloody mary, as usual?'

'I'm driving. I don't want you to put me inside for four years like Liz Hargreaves.'

'I'd give you eight. Why don't you and Patrick have a child?'

'What is the charge against Lucy?'

'Possession of Class A. Whether crack or heroin I don't yet know. Apparently McIntyre picked her up right outside Benson Street Court while you were in there.'

'The Trish Richardson case. Lucy was waiting outside for Trish, you say?'

'She and Daniel Richardson.'

'Marcus, this is serious. The police are sure Lucy and Trish did over the old pensioner, Mrs Ramsden, in Century Park.'

Heather Stuart is gliding towards their table. Instinctively Marcus and Wendy cease to speak of Lucy.

'Let's pray that tomorrow's headlines never happen,' Marcus sighs.

# *Ten*

MARCUS RISES EARLY THE following morning, expecting the worst. Fortunately Louise is away, addressing Criminal Bar Association meetings in the Midlands. Marcus would rather wrestle with the demons of defamation alone.

At eight he walks to the corner shop, takes one glance at the headlines and buys a copy of every newspaper in the rack.

DIRECTOR OF PUBLIC PROSECUTIONS ARRESTED
LACEY CHARGED WITH UNDER-AGE SEX
IN SOHO CLUB

All the Saturday papers carry the scandal front-page, though it's the *Sun* which has scooped the exclusive stories of the two young rent-boys, Lionel Lacey's 'urchins', in whose company the nation's Director of Public Prosecutions had been arrested at 11.15 p.m. the previous night.

It's the name of the club which puzzles Marcus: not Les Enfants du Paradis in Wardour Street but the Monkey Tree in Denmark Street. Lacey had never mentioned the Monkey Tree to Marcus.

One of the rent-boys, 'Martin', told the *Sun* he had serviced this 'quiet gentleman' on several previous occasions. 'It's usually mid-week not Fridays.' The 'quiet gentleman' had paid above the going rate.

Why had Lionel avoided his normal Friday-haunt, Les Enfants du Paradis, last night? And how had they known where to pick him up? Whom had he confided in? Why should he confide in anyone?

Word also leaked that the DPP, when the police raided the Monkey Tree and burst into the back room, had haughtily rebuked them: 'You don't know who I am! You will regret this!' But in the police station he had broken down, made a full confession and wept.

Lionel Lacey is a 'lonely man', so the newspapers report. And who are his secret associates within the criminal justice system?

Marcus opens a centre-page spread of photographs under a blazing title: 'THE LEMONS!' Below it appears a remarkable gallery of pictures, each taken from a different vantage point with a wide-angled lens, of the now disgraced DPP enjoying a drink in the Bow Street Tavern with one or other of the following:

Max Venables, MP
Judge Marcus Byron
Patrick Berry, JP and Mrs Wendy Berry
Ms Louise Pointer, QC, 'otherwise Mrs Marcus Byron'
Detective Sergeant Doug McIntyre, CID
Inspector Herbert Knowles, British Transport Police
Miss Angela Loftus, Probation Service
Clive Wellings, Home Office Forensic Investigation Service
Brigid Kyle, journalist

'Christ!' yells Marcus in the empty room. 'At least they didn't get Ken Crabbe or Hector Coombe.'

Marcus had never met Lionel Lacey for a drink in the Bow Street Tavern, or any public house. Nor had Wendy or Patrick. Nor had any of them – Lionel never went near a pub. The pictures were fakes.

Another tabloid's Chief Crime Reporter explained that the Lemons were engaged in a 'conspiracy to crack down on crime under a new government'. The conspiracy was 'totally ruthless' and 'the brainchild of Marcus Byron'. Then a joke. 'It is understood that the Lord Chief Justice is anxious to interview Judge Byron.'

Quotes from members of the Congress follow – their instant availability, in the few hours between the late-night arrest of Lionel Lacey and the printing of the final, London editions was truly remarkable.

Lady Harsent: 'I shall not be surprised if we are in for

other painful revelations. I anticipate more than one prominent resignation.'

Sandra Golding QC: 'Those who proclaim themselves "tough on crime" should perhaps desist from special pleading. I know for a fact that the Lemon conspiracy exists and must be exposed.'

Jill Hull: 'We are slowly learning where the backlash is coming from and who has been misleading the public.'

Geoffrey Villiers: 'Let the righteous judge themselves by their own standards.'

Edgar Averling: 'All of us who believe in justice must hope that the CPS will henceforward adopt policies more in harmony with humane, modern practices.'

Nick Paisley: 'A number of prominent figures within the criminal justice system must urgently consider their positions. In my view Max Venables should ponder the company he has been keeping.'

Marcus desperately scans the pages for any reference to Lucy. She could not legally be named, of course, but he knows the slick formula – and there it is, on page 4 of the *Sentinel*:

> A sixteen year-old-girl was arrested yesterday and charged with possession of Class A drugs at Eden Manor police station. It is understood that Judge Marcus Byron telephoned the station to make inquiries later in the day.

Brigid does not normally work Saturdays. Raging, he tries her home number. There is no reply and the answer-machine is switched off – for which he's grateful. He would only have made a fool of himself.

The phone rings. Marcus expects the Press but it's Wendy.

'Oh, Marco,' she sighs. 'Patrick's right here beside me. Come and have breakfast with us, Marco. Please do. Please don't be unhappy all alone.'

'OK.'

'Don't cry, Marco.'

'Yeah.'

Patrick seizes the phone. 'Marcus! Come right over. On your bike, man! Wendy's doing your favourite pancakes.'

'OK.'

Wendy again. 'Marco?'

'Yes, Wendy?'

'A lot of people love you. I know one guy who'd give his life for you.'

'Tell him I'll hold him to that.'

He replaces the receiver. The phone rings immediately. It's Louise.

'Marcus, darling . . .'

'Where are you, Louise?'

'Birmingham. I'm coming straight back. I'm catching the 10.20. How are you, darling?'

'Not so good – you read about Lucy?'

'Does she have legal representation?'

'That's the problem. Eden Manor police – even Doug McIntyre – insist that they're not authorised to deal with me, only with Jill so long as she has custody.'

'Have you called her?'

'Yeah. She said, "The virus cannot call the doctor." Then she slammed the phone down.'

'Oh God.'

'Louise, I'm sorry your name was in the paper this morning. You're no Lemon.'

'Maybe I'll become one, darling. If they want a fight, they can have one.'

'You're wonderful.'

'I love you. Ciao.'

Marcus has fastened his bicycle clips and reached the door when the phone sounds again. It's Brigid.

'Marcus, I knew nothing about that odious item on page four. I telephoned the editor five minutes ago and demanded an explanation. I said to him, "How can this paper of ours stoop so low?" Of course he hadn't seen it either. Apparently Joe O'Neill had left the item on my answerphone – somebody just whipped it into the London edition.'

'Then you know what to do with Mr O'Neill.'

'No, Marcus, he thought he was coding a private message for me. He's horrified by what has happened!'

'Yeah? Maybe he can demand a royalty from every paper that picks it up for tomorrow's editions.'

'Can we meet, Marcus? I'm free all day. I'm always free for you.'

'Later, maybe. Louise is coming straight back from Brum.'

'A lot of people love you, Marcus.'

He chuckles. 'And a lot don't.'

He spends an hour with the Berrys, wolfing Wendy's pancakes, coffee and a gallon of orange juice.

'Hey, Marco, did you notice that all the papers say Lacey was arrested in a club called the Monkey Tree?'

'Hm.'

'Isn't his usual Friday-night haunt the club with the name of a movie?'

'Hm.'

'So how did they nab him? Who tipped them off?'

'It may have been a routine raid.'

'Oh yeah? And you tell me, Marco, why your bimbo Heather Stuart doesn't figure in the Press as a Lemon alongside her mentor, Angela Loftus.'

'Ken Crabbe's name is missing, too. And Hector Coombe's. Scores of names are missing. It's clear that most Lemons remain undetected.'

'All the ones you know well are listed,' Patrick points out. 'You are the main target.'

Marcus is again browsing and brooding through a pile of newspapers. As usual, public life quickly despatches private pains from the epicentre of his attention.

'I see Max Venables delivered a strong speech to the Police Federation's Annual Conference. Want to hear it?'

'Anything to cheer us up,' Wendy drawls.

> 'The CPS is losing the confidence of the public,' Mr Venables declared. 'Police officers now regard the Crown Prosecutors as wimps forever anxious to discontinue cases, or to downgrade the charge on a safety-first basis. Our party intends to take action.' (Applause.) 'Crime has more than doubled during the past 15 years,' Mr Venables continued, 'yet total convictions have slumped by 7 per cent. Last year the CPS abandoned 161,429 cases – twice as many as when it was founded in 1986. I regard it as a scandal that last year the CPS itself instigated more than 38 per cent of Crown Court dismissals by offering no evidence at the last minute. This must stop. When we come to power we will stop it.'

'Powerful stuff,' Patrick says. 'But the police, of course, have a healthy suspicion of all politicians. You're the man they wanted to hear.'

'I had to decline their invitation. I was a coward. I was scared by that note from the Chief, fuck him.'

Wendy has taken the paper from his hand. 'You didn't finish,' she says. 'Listen to this.'

> 'Nick Paisley, spokesman for the CPS section of the Association of First Division Civil Servants, responded immediately to Max Venables's speech. "Mr Venables is being badly advised," he said. "The CPS is being scapegoated by the police. The Police Federation may grumble about the number of cases dropped, but in 91 per cent of cases the CPS consults with the police before dropping a case."'

'Bilge. The police have simply given up,' Marcus says, glancing anxiously at his watch. 'Lovely pancakes, Wendy, just like old times. I must now go and meet my loving wife, who does not cook pancakes like yours.'

Wendy folds her arms round his neck. 'You should have married me, Marco. These white folk are over-priced.'

'I do the washing up,' Patrick protests.

Marcus takes hold of them, one in each hand. 'When are you guys going to give me a little nephew to play with?'

Normally Wendy would say, 'Girls no good?' but the phrase freezes on her tongue. 'Go easy,' she murmurs and kisses him.

Simon Galloway is learning about the youth courts the hard way. He no longer needs the *A to Z* to find Benson Street.

When Paul and Daniel Richardson had first appeared before the Benson Street Court on a charge of robbing Simon of a mobile phone and his wallet, Simon himself had not been officially notified – though Doug McIntyre tipped him off. As the victim he enjoyed no status during a 'first appearance'; he would not be granted access to the proceedings unless they came to trial.

Now they have. As usual, the Richardson boys are pleading Not Guilty to theft.

Theft! The charge has been downgraded by the CPS from robbery. 'On Nick Paisley's instructions,' McIntyre had warned Simon the previous day.

It's not so bad as his day in court with the Griffins. Paul and Daniel don't have a single relative on display and there is no heckling, no intimidation, merely a sullen silence which, oddly, he finds equally disturbing. The Richardsons are quiet in their knowledge but that knowledge – as Doug McIntyre has warned – can be deadly.

All the time Simon is thinking with utter dread of the day when Susie will have to face Amos Richardson in court.

For the first time since that grim afternoon on Hilton Avenue, Simon sets eyes on the boy who had offered to clean his car window, Lucy Byron's friend, Daniel. Simon sees only a baffled pain and a stifled intelligence. Beside him slouches a much larger youth, Paul Richardson, whom Simon marks down as an ugly customer; his demeanour in court is insolent, truculent.

The prosecutor, Derek Jardine, is claiming that Paul had snatched Simon's mobile telephone through the passenger door.

Simon is the second prosecution witness, after Detective Sergeant McIntyre, the motorcycle cop who'd bagged Paul Richardson with Simon's mobile phone still in his paws. (Simon's wallet, on the other hand, has never been recovered; he'd had to drag himself through the tedium of cancelling his credit cards while Susie was in hospital and Tom clung to his legs.)

Derek Jardine puts very few questions to Simon but the defence solicitor, whose name is Simmonds, becomes abrasive during cross-examination. Simon feels the sweat surfacing on his palms, which he clenches and unclenches almost involuntarily.

'You never saw Daniel take your wallet from your jacket, did you?'

'No, but—'

'You never saw Daniel running away with your wallet, did you?'

'No, but I—'

'When did you discover your wallet was missing?'

'I think it was some time after it happened.'

'You "think"?'

'It was almost immediately.'

'How can you be sure your wallet was in your jacket pocket at the time of the incident? You could have mislaid it earlier.'

'I was stalled in traffic. I was driving to a job interview. I remember checking the telephone number which was on a business card in my wallet. I then telephoned them to say I would be late.'

'Do you remember putting your wallet back in your jacket?'

'Yes.' (Simon lies, as he had lied once during the Griffin trial – he does not remember putting his wallet back in his jacket. The most routine motions pass unrecorded.)

'How long did you get a good view of Daniel Richardson before he covered your windscreen in soap and obscured himself?'

'Hard to say.'

'Your memory of these events is understandably uncertain? Your recollection is perhaps eroded by time?'

'My description of him to the police fits the boy in court today.'

'That is not for you to decide.'

Derek Jardine jumps up. 'Objection, madam. The witness is being asked his opinion and should be allowed to express it.'

'Objection sustained,' Lady Harsent rules magnanimously. (Simon remembers her lacquered beehive hair with a strange sense of loathing.)

'Do black boys all tend to look alike to you?' Simmonds asks him.

'Not at all.'

'How do you tell them apart?'

'By looking at them.'

'Thank you. No more questions.'

By some extraordinary indulgence, Lady Harsent grants Simon's request to be allowed to sit at the back of the court, beside Doug McIntyre, until the case is concluded.

'We try to be understanding,' she tells him.

Neither of the Richardson boys is called to give evidence. In Simon's view innocent people speak up for themselves. He would.

The magistrates don't retire for long: Guilty. Doug McIntyre's evidence (which Simon had, quite correctly, not been allowed to hear) had sewn it all up. If Simon had said, 'I can't remember a thing!' it wouldn't have made much difference.

Simon naively expects sentence to be passed there and then. But not a bit of it! Lady Harsent wants a pre-sentence report.

'Is a month long enough, Mr Haley-White?'

'Yes, madam.'

Simon would never hear Paul Richardson's list of previous convictions, nor would he be allowed back in the Youth Court for the sentencing – by that stage he, the victim, became just another member of the excluded public.

'That's the system,' McIntyre wryly tells him as they leave the court. 'How's your wife?'

'She's expecting.'

'Congratulations.'

'Actually, I need your advice, Doug. Jill Hull has been urging Susie to go back to part-time work for her.'

'Aha?'

'I'm dead against it myself. I just thought . . . well, that you might have a view.'

'I do. Steer clear. That girl Lucy is now up to her neck in trouble. She's in with Daniel, she's in with Trish, she's robbing old ladies in the park, she's drug-crazy, she's supplying and she's defended by Edgar Averling. But what makes Lucy Byron the most dangerous girl in my precinct is something else.'

McIntyre pauses and studies the decent young man standing, with his smart briefcase and innocent, bespectacled eyes, before him.

'Did you ever read *A Clockwork Orange*, Simon?'

'Long ago.'

'Lucy knows that book by heart. For her, the worse, the better. Her one aim is to get even with her dad. And she's succeeding. Believe me, Marcus Byron won't last long.'

But Marcus Byron continues to enjoy the esteem of the wider public. Although he has heard nothing from Max Venables or his boss, the Boy, since the Lionel Lacey scandal broke, messages of support flood into his chambers – only the racists urge him to 'get lost' or 'come clean' or 'go back to the banana trees where you came from'.

During a half-hour interval between trials in Crown Court 3, Marcus receives in his chambers a delegation of five women and three men, each of them bringing a face perfectly normal yet disfigured by intense suffering. But more than suffering: by a crazed hunger for justice. It is this quest which has brought them together in Justice for Victims.

They are inviting Judge Marcus Byron to accept the post of Honorary President.

'I am indeed honoured,' he tells them, 'and I'm deeply touched by your trust.'

'You're our man, your Honour,' insists their spokeswoman, whose twenty-one-year-old son had been battered to death with an iron bar while trying to protect a stranger from a gang attack outside a pub near Eden Manor. Her name is Ruth Tanner. She had not divulged her personal tragedy to Brigid Kyle, and her husband Ron never mentions it to his customers even when, as with Simon Galloway, the discussion turns to crime and punishment.

Marcus draws deeply on his pipe, a gleaming Gucci shoe cocked on a fine pinstripe Bentley Bros knee.

'Now correct me if I'm wrong. What you people want is a Charter for Victims, yes?'

'Yes, your Honour,' Mrs Tanner replies.

'You are demanding automatic and adequate compensation, plus the right to be informed of all relevant criminal proceedings?'

'And the right to be represented in court at the State's expense,' Mrs Tanner adds firmly.

'Hm. Difficult – but I don't say utopian. Let's call it "visionary". Hm.'

He offers them coffee and sympathy. As their individual stories unfold, he keeps sighing.

A bus driver describes, in harrowing detail, how his wife had been raped at home by a man passing himself off as a gas-meter reader.

'And may I humbly add, your Honour, that the victim's views should be heard whenever a prisoner is under consideration for home-leave or parole.'

Marcus lays his Sherlock Holmes pipe down in a huge ashtray – a present from Sandra, yesteryear – and gently folds his large hands on his desk.

'Sir, our present Government is unlikely to be responsive to that, I'm afraid. Anything which costs money is a non-starter with the Rt Hon. Jeremy Darling.'

'But we believe your Honour could force the Government to think again,' Ruth Tanner says.

(At Marcus's suggestion, he and Mrs Tanner had met together for ten minutes before the other members of the delegation arrived. They recalled their meeting at the Mason Lodge Attendance Centre in the company of Brigid Kyle – though Ruth remained unforgiving about Brigid's 'worse than animals'. Both had steered clear of the most painful topic: Lucy.)

'I'll tell you what I'll do on your behalf,' Marcus informs his visitors. 'First, I will publicly demand an audience with Darling. Secondly, my summer vacation is coming up. My wife and I had planned a trip to Rome but I'll cancel it.'

Marcus's guests display polite consternation. 'Oh no, please don't consider—'

'Yes! I will. Perhaps you would kindly send my wife Louise a large bunch of white roses expressing your appreciation of her sacrifice?'

He chuckles silently, his face a model of solemnity. He'd been wondering how he could wriggle out of Rome with Louise. Or anywhere with Louise. His thoughts dart to Brigid Kyle and Heather Stuart as he refocuses on the sad faces confronting him.

'My friend Patrick Berry and I will devote those two weeks to a sponsored bike ride in the Pyrenees. In that heat it will be a physical ordeal but the cameramen will be happy.'

'Please do not jeopardise your health, Judge Byron—'

He laughs. 'I've always wanted to be buried in the mountains. I shall solicit sponsorship from the Probation Officers' Association, the Police Federation, the Bar Association, the Law Society, the Home Office – and the Leader of the Opposition.'

Wonderful, wonderful, they murmur.

'The least I can do. I shall invite the various media covering the journey to make a handsome contribution. The money we raise will be used to publicise your demands.'

Judge Byron is pacing his chambers thoughtfully.

'Let's not forget that every year over 30,000 victims of crime fail to receive any compensation despite court orders against their attackers. More than 112,000 Compensation Orders are made each year – but one in three awards remains unpaid a year after the court order. That is, frankly, a scandal.'

'But what is the solution, your Honour?'

'Once a Compensation Order is made, it should be paid immediately out of public funds. It will then be up to the courts to recover the money. They will certainly do so with a great deal more urgency than now prevails. Agreed?'

Agreed.

The judge is now gazing out of his window with an air of intense concentration.

'Victims of crime deserve a statutory charter of rights,' he announces.

'Or a new government,' the bus driver suggests.

Marcus Byron lifts his eyebrows. 'Of course I cannot meddle in politics.'

He smiles. They smile too. These are people who believed they would never smile again. He poses with the victims on the steps of the Crown Court, then persuades Ruth Tanner to shake hands with Brigid Kyle, who is waiting to interview them.

'I'm sorry, Ruth,' Brigid says with her most winning smile.

At this moment, almost precisely, Marcus's kinsman Herbert Knowles is receiving an alarm call four miles away. Marcus is the posh end of the family but Herbert does not resent it – he's proud of Marcia's brother, and they talk as equals while ploughing furrows through Marcia's spectacular meals. But there may be limits to the pleasures of kinship.

British Transport Police Inspector Herbert Knowles had certainly said as much to his wife when he found his own name and face in the *Sun*, along with other Lemons. He was baffled. He had never heard of Lionel Lacey, let alone met him, and was pleased not to have done so, on the evidence.

'Why is our Marcus associating with unChristian perverts like this?' he had roared at Marcus's stricken sister. 'Child prostitutes! What is he thinking of?'

'It's all some mistake, Herb, some plot against Marcus,' Marcia murmured.

'And is all this Lucy business a "mistake"?'

'Herb! She's my niece!'

Two days earlier Herbert and a colleague had been on duty at Broadway Station when they observed two young people, a lad and a girl, leap the turnstile and ignore shouts from London Transport staff. Herbert had pursued them down to the Central Line platform.

'Hi, Herb.' It was Lucy with one of the Richardson boys, Daniel. 'Dan,' she continued cheerily, 'this is my Uncle Herb.'

'Now, Lucy,' he said sternly, 'you never bought a ticket.'

'Gotta travel card, Herb.'

'Kindly come back and show it at the gate.'

'Sorry, Herb, no time. Me and Dan, we're on our way to help orphans in Romania.' She giggled.

'Now, Lucy—'

He could see she was stoned. His heart ached with grief

and embarrassment. Her little wrists were now extended to him.

'Cuff me, Herb. You're a real juicy Lemon, ain't ya?'

Why did she have to speak in that uneducated way, after all the advantages she had enjoyed? Although shamed in front of his colleague, Inspector Herbert Knowles had allowed the couple to board the train. It stuck in his throat.

'I was sore tempted by the devil to toss my lemon straight under that train!' he reported to Marcia. 'What next, eh?'

And now, as Marcus Byron poses on the steps of the Crown Court with 'his' victims, Herbert is alerted by car radio to yet another case of 'mob vandalism' at Broadway Station.

Griffins again.

He reaches the station within three minutes. Walls, kiosks and ticket machines have again been defaced with aerosol sprays. The usual orgy of destruction. What can you do if the courts don't punish? The passenger pays, in the end. Herbert always says that: the passengers pay.

He recognises the Griffin boys at once. They scatter as the BTP move in, scything through passengers, leaping turnstiles, overturning flower stalls and newspaper stands.

Herbert sets off in pursuit, alone. Ahead of him, two elderly passengers are knocked to the ground. He follows Mark, Joseph and Darren out of the station and down among the defaced walls and pools of urine which grace the pedestrian underpass. On the last flight of steps he stumbles, recovers – and is flung back against a wall.

They are waiting for him, waiting for the f— nig who'd given evidence against them on one charge after another.

Herbert sees a hammer, a tyre iron, a switch blade. He turns to retreat but he is hemmed in. He activates his radio alarm, linked to the local police station, as the first blows strike.

'Fuckin' black bastard! Nigger scum!'

In attempting to defend himself, Herbert is battered, punched and smashed in the arm with the tyre iron – three fractures. Lying on the ground he is kicked in the stomach, the head, the scrotum. The Griffins are telling Herbert something. He has never known such pain, such agony, such fear. I am going to die. Good Baptist, he prays for his wife Marcia and his children. God help them. God is good.

The Griffins are out of the underpass seconds before McIntyre and Jenkins reach the scene.

'Ambulance!' Jenkins yells into his radio. 'Emergency!'

McIntyre has stretched Herbert Knowles out on his back and is pumping his lungs and heart.

'Griffins,' Herbert murmurs.

'Griffins!' Jenkins shouts into his radio. 'Go for them!'

Thirty minutes later Herbert Knowles is on a life-support machine and – St Luke's Hospital tells Marcia – in a 'critical condition'. Instinctively Marcia reaches out to the wider family: Wendy, Marcus, they will all be at her side by nightfall to join her in prayer.

But Marcus does not stay long. He has a prior engagement. And the news from the hospital is reassuring. Herb is pulling through.

Marcus picks up Brigid Kyle under the grand colonnade of the British Library in Great Russell Street and takes her to a late dinner at his favourite Knightsbridge bistro. On the days when the library remains open late, Brigid normally puts in a few precious hours of research on her new book, which promises to blow the lay magistrate system apart.

In the taxi he tells her about Herbert Knowles.

'Oh my God, Marcus, how awful. You should have stood me up.'

'Herb is strong as an ox.'

Settling into a corner table at the Knightsbridge bistro – at least half the clientele turn to look at him as he strides in – he unburdens himself about Lucy. She listens. A wonderful listener, Brigid, and all the while elfins dancing in her eyes, shamrocks in her hair and—

'You're a good woman, Brigid.'

'I'm not sure Ruth Tanner thinks so. And your wife certainly doesn't.'

'I feel like a kipper which has overshot its sell-by date.'

'Did you ever hear the joke about the Irishman who loved golf but thought his time might be coming?'

He smiles. 'What should I know about Mr Kyle?'

'Oh, him! What a coincidence – he was asking precisely the same question about you.'

'Yeah?'

'Trevor is great. Tall, handsome, intelligent, rich.'

'So what's in his favour?'

'He's working in Canada – an oil man.'

'I congratulate him for putting so much water between himself and so desirable a wife.'

'Thank you. Did Louise mention my interview with her?'

'She did. It took her about five seconds.'

'She even asked me whether I practise birth control. Maybe she wants a baby?'

'I shouldn't be talking about my wife. She came straight back from Birmingham, cancelling two speaking engagements. She spent the rest of the Saturday telephoning experts in drug law as it affects juveniles. It's a pity I don't love Louise. The tongue is the great Judas, you know. A man who commits adultery but speaks well of his wife goes to Heaven.'

'Have you told the Archbishop of Canterbury?'

'He said he'd think about it.'

'It's time we were heading for the Galloways, Captain.'

Brigid is happy to take him to 16 Oundle Square, more than happy. Having contacted Susan Galloway, then called on her and Simon, Brigid had negotiated the visit.

'But they're apprehensive, Marcus. They're afraid you'll want to talk about Lucy.'

'They're hostile to Lucy?'

'Simon Galloway is.'

Susan had expressed another fear to Brigid. 'I want Tom to be asleep. Please don't tell Judge Byron, but the sight of a black man inside the house would throw Tom into hysterics.'

Brigid had not told Marcus.

Late in the evening, after the summer sun has set, suits Marcus well. He does not want his visit observed from Jill's windows. Brigid's arm is tucked into his as they walk up Brancaster Road (Marcus having instructed the taxi to let them down in the High Street).

'I wouldn't want to be walking here alone,' she says. 'Your famous presence is comforting, your Honour.'

'Yeah, we Byrons are built large. And nasty. There are times when I'd let a fellow off a five-year sentence if I could just have five minutes alone with him in a very small room.'

They turn the corner. Visiting Oundle Square is painful for Marcus; he can see the light in Lucy's bedroom.

'So near yet so far,' Brigid says, reading his thoughts.

Simon Galloway opens the door. He adjusts his glasses – Marcus can tell they are new. Worry lines are surfacing not on, but beneath, this young man's smooth skin. Marcus reads his life at a glance: heavy mortgage, wife not working, victim of violent crime. Feels motivated but fears he doesn't know how to sell himself. Has recently caught himself running when he thought he was walking. Used to enjoy Sunday-morning football with an *ad hoc* bunch of casuals, but now has that early-thirties sensation of life becoming serious.

'Please come in,' he says, offering a rather shy handshake.

His wife greets Marcus and Brigid in the hall and leads them into the drawing room. Susan wears a loose Indian cotton smock and what Marcus recognises as Jaipur jewellery. Her left arm is still bandaged.

'Did you get that gorgeous brooch in India, Susan?' Brigid asks.

Marcus likes Susan's self-deprecating smile. He observes her husband's gaze resting on her with pure adoration.

'Oh no, dreams, dreams. Kipling is about as close to India as I've ever got. This brooch comes from a little place Simon knows – but he keeps it a secret.'

'Simon, I order you to disclose your little shop,' Brigid says, conscious that Simon remains ill at ease with his tall, powerfully built visitor, whose confident expression and operatic voice he recognises from television.

'Susie's expecting,' Simon announces. He tells everyone. Perhaps he wishes she wasn't.

'Brilliant!' Brigid exclaims, going Irish. 'It's the best remedy for everything!'

'Tea or coffee?' Susan asks.

'We have beer,' Simon adds. 'And wine.'

'Beer for me.' Marcus immediately feels at home in this cheerfully decorated room with its profusion of brightly coloured cushions, vases of flowers, picture books for the child. He picks one of them up.

'Your son is three, Mrs Galloway?'

'Tom is two.'

'I never had a son.'

'Heavens, Marcus,' Brigid says quickly, fearing he's leading the conversation towards Lucy, 'you're not on your deathbed yet.'

He picks up her signal. 'I've been forty for some years.' He winks at Simon.

Susie brings the coffee then tells Marcus about her bafflement when she attended the identity parade. Marcus listens attentively, drawing the details of her ordeal out of her.

'The Inspector's name was Crabbe, you say. Ken Crabbe?'

'I didn't catch his first name. He sounded as if he might have come from Yorkshire.'

'That's Ken. And you tell me all the boys wore sticking plasters on their cheeks to cover any scar? I can understand the rest but not that.'

'He told me that was the procedure.'

'I'm afraid the Police and Criminal Evidence Act leaves wide scope for interpretation,' Marcus says diplomatically. 'May I tell you what leads me to trespass on your hospitality? Would you like to help bring the Richardsons to justice? And those behind them.'

The Galloways glance at one another. 'We have Tom,' Susie says.

'We all have somebody, Mrs Galloway, somebody very precious to us. *They* capitalise on our fear, our vulnerability. I have someone, too.'

Simon is bridling. 'We have also had a brick through this window. I have so far made two court appearances as a witness, and Susie's ordeal in court is yet to come. Frankly, that's enough.'

'I think we should hear what the judge is proposing, Simon.'

Marcus nods. 'What I am proposing, Mrs Galloway – may I call you Susan? – is that you should go back to work for Jill.'

Simon shakes his head. 'Susan is never setting foot in that house again.'

A constrained silence descends. Susan looks to Brigid for sympathy but receives only a sweet smile.

'It's a lot to ask,' Susan says, 'given what we now know.'

'You don't dispose of criminals by lighting candles,' Marcus says.

The Galloways cannot bring themselves to disclose the truth: how can they explain their feelings about Lucy without seeming to accuse Judge Byron of being a bad father? Simon has put his foot down – no more baby-sitting for Lucy. Never again. The shy, gentle Nigel Thompson, who lives the other side of the square, and whose father Eric is always on the verge of making his fortune an an inventor, has been asked to stay with Tom on the rare evenings when Simon and Susie go out.

Young Nigel harbours a secret from the Galloways – and from everyone, even his parents. It was he who had picked Tom off the pavement and called the police. Nigel had told Detective Sergeant McIntyre that he hadn't really seen the attack on Susie Galloway – just caught a glimpse of 'a black boy running away'.

But Doug McIntyre had not believed him. Acutely aware that Nigel was scared stiff, he had interviewed him gently, at home, in the presence of his parents.

'May I explain the law, Nigel? There are "informants" and there are "witnesses". A witness makes a formal signed statement and is prepared, normally, to appear in court. An "informant" can remain anonymous – he signs nothing.'

There had been a painful silence in the Thompson living room, the other side of Oundle Square from the Galloways.

'Wait a minute,' Eric Thompson had said. 'Nigel's name would be on record somewhere, and I've heard that defence counsel go on fishing expeditions.'

McIntyre nodded. Private to his thoughts was the danger of depositing Nigel's name with the CPS – Paisley might see it.

Nigel, a very bright boy, grabbed a piece of paper, scribbled a few words and handed them to McIntyre. 'ARithmetic is my favourite subject.'

AR – McIntyre was convinced that Nigel had seen everything. Amos Richardson – all the boys of Chaucer School knew and feared him. McIntyre was right. For a split second Nigel had anticipated what was going to happen and could have shouted a warning to Susan. But his tongue stuck to the roof of his mouth. He knew what had befallen Chaucer boys who saw too much and gave evidence against the Richardsons.

The worst thing was that Amos had not 'run *away*'. He had run straight past Nigel and given him a look. Nigel would never forget that look: it was like being eaten by a shark.

The atmosphere in the Galloways' sitting room is tense. Marcus looks miserable and embarrassed. Brigid feels she must intervene.

'Marcus understands your ambivalent feelings about Lucy. But he knows, we all know, that Lucy is a complicated, distressed child who needs help. What she's getting in Jill's house, under the same roof as Nick Paisley, is the opposite of help.'

'So we should regard your daughter as a victim?' Simon says caustically, remembering his recent conversation with Doug McIntyre.

'Young people are always—' Brigid checks herself. 'God, I'm beginning to sound like Lady Harsent.'

Simon nods. 'Yes, Mrs Kyle. I thought, from your columns, that your outlook differed somewhat from that of the Congress for Justice.'

Susan is finding all this extremely painful. Simon's ferocity shocks her. Their visitor, the distinguished judge, looks as if he wished the earth would swallow him up.

'Judge Byron,' she says, 'please tell me about these Lemons we were reading about in the papers the other day.'

'Oh, that's just a fantasy of the Congress for Justice,' Marcus chuckles. 'The Press was full of faked photographs.'

'So it was all news to you and Mrs Kyle?' Simon asks.

'These absurd rumours fly around at a time of political tension. I've heard them before.'

'Why do you want me to go back to work for Jill Hull?' Susan asks.

'I'll explain. But first may I ask what time of day you normally finished work?'

'About twelve, depending on the workload.'

'Jill provided you with a house key?'

'Yes.'

'Fine. One day a man will call at Jill's door about noon to read the electricity meter. He will show you his London Electricity identity card. It will be in order. He will then say, "Marcus sent me." You will give him the house keys and immediately leave with Tom. About half an hour later he will return those same keys through your own letter box, here at No. 16. That's all. Nothing will be taken from No. 23 and nothing visibly disturbed. You will know nothing.'

Simon is wearing an intense frown. 'I really think that Susie has been through enough.'

'There is no risk.'

'But what you're proposing is that she joins the ranks of criminals. Or should I say Lemons?'

'Simon,' Susie says gently.

And then Simon's anger possesses him. 'Shall I tell you what a Lemon is, Susie? He's a man who holds the highest office of trust while secretly indulging in under-age sex.'

'Simon!'

'Oh yes. Or he's a man whose daughter robs old ladies in parks and gets away with it because the victim is suffering from trachoma. Excuse me, I'm going to bed.'

He leaves the room. Marcus is on his feet.

'We should go,' he murmurs.

'I'll do it,' Susie says. 'I think I understand. That Nick Paisley reminds us of a ferret. I believe he's rotten.'

'We don't want this to be a cause of friction between you,' Brigid says, waiting for Marcus to endorse the sentiment and call it off. But he doesn't. A large parcel has been resting on the floor beside his highly polished shoes.

'This is something for Tom,' he says. 'Building bricks designed for safety – with a tractor which can pick them up and build a stairway to the stars.'

Susie smiles bravely. 'I daresay Tom will have a hard time getting the tractor away from his father.'

Walking back along Brancaster Road, Brigid's arm tucked into his, Marcus suddenly releases himself, pulls his mobile phone from the pocket of his windcheater and puts a pre-set call through to the home of Ken Crabbe.

'Ken? What's all this shit I hear about sticking plaster over Amos Richardson's scar?'

Brigid Kyle, who could play the Dublin washerwoman at the drop of a hat, had never guessed that a Crown Court judge could utter such a stream of obscenities.

Then he remembers to telephone St Luke's Hospital.

# *Eleven*

MARCUS BYRON HAILS A taxi, gripping a clutch of morning newspapers.

'Hillhouse Probation Centre – do you know it?'

The driver doesn't. But he knows who his passenger is. The passenger groans as he is subjected to a tirade against one-parent families, young thugs who don't know what their fathers look like, and more.

'I mean your father is your father, isn't he? And I don't mean the mother's latest fancy man, which we're all supposed to call "partners", as if family life was ballroom dancing.'

Marcus assumes that the driver's wife has run off with the postman.

He buries himself behind broadsheet newspapers. *The Times* reports that the Lord Chief Justice is poised to invite Judge Marcus Byron to stand down 'in view of legal proceedings affecting a juvenile'. Prominent on page 6 is Sandra Golding's successful appeal against Judge Byron's four-year sentence on the young mother Liz Hargreaves. Custody has been commuted to Community Service. The tone is sardonic:

> This is another blow to Judge Byron's prestige. Like other sunbathers, the politically ambitious judge is learning that it never rains but it pours.

In The *Sentinel*, Brigid Kyle takes the opposite view:

> The Hargreaves decision looks remarkably like the Court of Appeal's white flag to political correctness and the now fashionable invasion of courtrooms by screaming viragos who scavenge for cases like pygmies hunt caterpillars. The message to all young mothers in search of some fun is clear: get plastered, climb in a car with your boyfriend, knock somebody down, don't stop, and deny any involvement when questioned.

All the papers report that Mr Nick Paisley has been appointed Acting Director of Public Prosecutions pending an appointment to replace the disgraced Lionel Lacey. Paisley's role in Lacey's arrest is hinted at but not spelled out. Some writers tip Paisley for the permanent post.

The *Guardian*'s report goes furthest. Although Paisley, a prominent member of the Congress for Justice, and a parliamentary candidate for the Opposition, might be an unlikely appointment for the present Attorney General to make, 'things are moving behind the scenes'. The war against the Lemons has created 'an unholy alliance of wets and boneheads'.

The taxi driver's oration continues. Marcus grunts politely at regular intervals while his mind is far away.

'I mean, it's hard enough keeping your kids in line even if you give them a short, sharp smack when they need one. And now these Europeans, Frogs mainly, are telling us we can't smack our own kids.'

Marcus tells himself that he had never once smacked Lucy.

'Now don't get me wrong, Guv, but things went downhill from the moment they abolished the birch – it was just about the time they made poofters legal.'

Marcus turns back to the comforts of Brigid's column.

> Isn't it odd that we are, quite rightly, not permitted to name juvenile defendants, yet we can wriggle and wangle round it by naming their parents? Who is fooled? No one. But what takes the biscuit, so far as the present whispering campaign is concerned, is this: the child's alleged and as yet unproven offences are being used as a stick to beat the father out of office. And this is a father who has been denied custody of his child, despite two applications, and who stands helpless while the web of treachery is woven round him. Who by?

'This is Hillhouse Probation Centre on your left, the big

Victorian building,' Marcus informs the driver. 'Many thanks for the ride.'

'It was my pleasure, sir. Keep it up, sir. Hit 'em where it hurts.'

Marcus is among the last to arrive for what he calls Display Day. Jill Hull is to address a distinguished group of invited judges, magistrates and media correspondents at Hillhouse. A few tame offenders will be on show, waving woven wastepaper baskets. Marcus has come girded for war.

'Take it easy,' Louise had warned him. 'Don't make it too personal.'

But Louise has cooled since her gallant return from Birmingham. Brigid Kyle is again the minefield between them.

Marcus is a member of the City Probation Committee, which consists of four judges, eight stipendiary magistrates and eleven lay magistrates, plus some co-opted members. The Committee meets only four times a year. As usual, the full-time professionals run the show. Jill runs it.

Marcus notices Lady Harsent in place, beaming in the front row. As Marcus finds a spare seat Jill is explaining, in her flat, worthy monotone, that Hillhouse receives selected offenders for a full-time, Monday-to-Saturday, ten-week course.

'It's optional, of course, but the alternative may be custody. All our clients sign an initial contract pledging themselves to abide by the rules of Hillhouse.'

Yeah!

– No dope or stolen goods on the premises, please . . .

– Be kind enough not to park this morning's stolen cars outside the main entrance to Hillhouse . . .

– And when Hillhouse's video cameras or computers are stolen, call the police.

Marcus nods to Jill across a crowded room but not a flicker of recognition comes back.

Jill is describing the value of teaching 'lateral thinking' to offenders. She speaks inexpressively, as if the colour of virtue is grey. She wraps herself in jargon. She drags her audience through statistics, apologises – 'I know how difficult it is to take all this in' – but ploughs on.

She must know what Paisley's game is. And lover-boy Jimmy's.

Marcus believes that most social workers, social psychologists and psychotherapists haven't a clue how to present a subject. They are without art and distrust art – unless it's an educational course called Art.

'During lateral-thinking sessions,' Jill is explaining, 'the clients are presented with questions printed on yellow cards.'

She distributes several specimen yellow cards to her audience. The one that lands in Marcus's hand reads: '"All seats should be taken out of buses." Do you agree? Please give your reasons.'

Jill introduces an ex-offender called Henry. Henry speaks from the lungs of a heavy smoker. He had successfully constructed a rabbit hutch during the Craft Programme and is now making rabbit hutches for the RSPCA. 'It opened my eyes', Henry tells the judges, magistrates and journalists, 'to the causes of my own offending. I definitely lacked self-esteem. I was weak-minded and easily led. I needed empowerment.'

Jill Hull nods solemnly. 'If Henry had been sent to prison, we would have lost another useful citizen.'

'Absolutely right, Jill!' Cecilia Harsent declares.

Marcus Byron is wondering what offences Henry had committed. No one likes to ask. He vaguely recognises the man.

'Henry, what brought you into the probation programme?' Marcus asks.

Jill is immediately up on her feet. 'May I remind visitors that all the offenders and ex-offenders you are meeting today are volunteers at this session.'

Henry ignores her. Clearly he recognises Marcus Byron.

'I was done for handling stolen goods once too often, your Honour. My fifteenth bust. I was twice in front of your Honour, but you were merciful. Frankly, I got off light.'

Marcus's eye has settled on Jimmy Haley-White, whose latest Rasta locks emerge from an otherwise shaven head. Heather Stuart sits beside him, dressed in the kind of clothes Marcus had told her not to wear. Lust and jealousy engulf him.

Jill calls on the willowy Jimmy to introduce the course on Black Empowerment. Marcus remembers that Jimmy was born into a distinguished Ghanaian family – his father was Chief Justice of the Ashanti. Jimmy charmingly admits that the white 'clients' of Hillhouse are not happy when the black 'clients' are separated out for sessions on Black Empowerment, but—

'But the whites are in no position to understand the impact of their own latent racism,' he adds.

Marcus is studying Heather Stuart. Her greenish cat's eyes are avoiding his. Her honey-blonde hair falls forward as she studiously notes down every pearl which falls from Jimmy's lips.

Poor Lionel Lacey.

None of the white judges and magistrates in the audience will venture a question on the super-sensitive subject of Black Empowerment until Marcus does.

'Yeah,' muses Judge Byron loudly. 'A question to you, Jimmy.'

You could hear a pin drop. But still Jill won't look at him. Jimmy's fine nostrils are dilating in anticipation of an outrageous attack. A ring dangles from one cocked ear. Marcus has turned silences into a fine art. Jill adjusts her glasses.

'Yeah . . . For whites "Black Empowerment" may carry disturbing echoes of the old sixties-seventies "Black Power",' Marcus drawls from the pit of his throat. 'Maybe the white offenders fear there is some plotting going on!'

Jimmy Haley-White nobly struggles to hold his temper. Probation officers learn patience.

'Judge, you should know that blacks have been marked down in our society, stereotyped on TV as criminals, street robbers, muggers.'

'That's the party line, Jimmy.' Marcus Byron is playing with his empty pipe – you can't smoke here, of course. 'But what does "stereotyped" really mean? Do we "stereotype" foxes when we erect wire round our chicken runs?'

'Judge,' declares Jimmy, 'our blacks are told they have no history of their own, schools regularly expel them, they are disproportionately imprisoned.'

'Maybe they disproportionately offend. If we don't trust our own observations in court, we can turn to Home Office statistics.'

'Oh, statistics!' Lady Harsent declares loudly. 'Statistics can prove anything.'

Marcus is struggling not to shout: You're the ones who coddle the Richardsons and Griffins while they terrorise the streets and parks around Eden Manor! You're the ones who massage the egos of the young thugs who almost killed my brother-in-law!

'And we all know', continues Jimmy, 'that the criminal justice system is biased against black people and ethnic minorities. That is what we are trying to remedy at Hillhouse.'

Marcus nods soberly. 'The real danger is that young black people have begun to stereotype themselves as outcasts. Crime isn't the beginning of this super-egoism, it's the end product. A fellow buys a Sony and the whole neighbourhood has to listen to *his* music. A fellow gets a girl pregnant and he walks away, swinging his shoulders, a real buck. Crime may be the next step. How do you people here cope with that?'

Jill Hull is tapping a pencil, pale and tight-lipped.

A white magistrate nervously points out that the majority of victims of black crime are blacks.

Jimmy Haley-White is fast on his feet, even when seated: 'That's because white society has brainwashed black people to dislike and despise black skins. If white society treats blacks collectively as criminals, black boys will conclude this society has nothing for us.'

'What about the high crime rates in the West Indies?' Marcus says.

'That whole system over there is a colonial importation.'

Marcus nods. 'True. I am descended from slaves myself. But I am not a slave now, you see: I am a free man, I make choices, I take responsibility for my actions. I don't shelter behind my skin. I don't always blame someone else – them over there – for what I do. Listening to you, Jimmy, I get the impression that *someone else* is always to blame. Never us.'

They break for coffee. The journalists present immediately crowd round him – Marcus Byron is always the news, now more than ever. Publicity feeds off itself; fame is its own parasite. Politely detaching himself, he insistently pushes his bulk through the throng towards the small figure of his ex-wife.

A jewelled hand clutches at his sleeve.

'Marcus, I'm so terribly sorry about Lucy,' Lady Harsent says. 'Amelia and Lucy were once such very good friends. I've always been fond of her – despite everything.'

He nods silently, moves on, pushing into Jill's circle of acolytes and journalists.

'Can we talk privately afterwards?'

'I won't have time.'

'When will you have time?'

'Communicate through your solicitor.'

Marcus decides not to stay for the second half of the Display Day, during which Jill and Jimmy will explain the fat package of documents and statistics now being distributed. As he makes for door he feels a scented presence at his side.

'I have something for you,' Heather murmurs. 'Can you come and see me this evening?'

'Aha.'

One document commands Marcus's attention as he is driven to the Crown Court by a young taxi driver who miraculously doesn't recognise him. 'A COGNITIVE MODEL OF DELINQUENCY PREVENTION AND OFFENDER REHABILITATION.'

The key (apparently) is something called 'cognition'. Marcus guesses this might mean 'thinking'. Offenders (Marcus is informed) tend to have 'cognitive deficits'. They suffer from 'conceptual rigidity', 'egocentricity' and 'impulsivity'.

Marcus chuckles grimly. In other words, they leap before they look.

Jill Hull arrives at the solution – 'a multi-faceted programme for fostering socio-cognitive skills'. This includes 'meta-cognition': 'We teach offenders thinking strategies as a means of self-regulating their behaviour.' Also on order are 'values enhancement' and 'emotional management'.

I need a bit of that, Marcus tells himself. Then it hits him in the pit of stomach: what he most urgently needs is Heather Stuart.

Angela Loftus has heaved herself up the emergency stairs of Probation House to Jill Hull's fifth-floor office. She can't face the claustrophobia in the over-crowded lift. Jill has granted her an interview. 'I can give you five minutes.'

Red in the face, Angela flops down into the appointed chair, then carefully places her handbag on the floor – no rolling lemons this time.

'What can I do for you, Angela?' Jill glances at her watch.

'Right-oh, then. You remember the PSR we prepared for Judge Byron in the Liz Hargreaves case?'

Jill's glasses glint. 'We prepared it for the Crown Court.'

'Leela Desai was in two minds, as usual. I wrote in a recommendation for custody. A man had been killed by reckless, drunken driving.'

'I remember.'

'You then reversed my recommendation. Your usual "gatekeeping". You went for the social damage to a child when separated from its mother. Prison would be entirely inappropriate.'

'Do we wish to breed a new generation of criminals?'

Angela is chewing her nails. 'That's not the main issue. A Community Sentence does not deter this kind of crime.'

'Angela, I refer you to the decision of the Court of Appeal. They specifically agreed with our PSR when overturning Judge Byron's sentence. Why are you raking all this up now?'

'Because I really feel that—'

'Angela, you are aware of my position. Of policy here. Save in the rarest cases, no woman or girl should be in prison.'

'You mean all those women languishing in Holloway – because caught importing commercial quantities of heroin, crack, you name it – they should be released and deported?'

'Yes. We are in effect orphaning the innocent children of the Third World.'

'Who will write the PSR on Lucy?'

Jill Hull removes her glasses, as if searching for a speck of dirt, then replaces them.

'On Lucy, did you say? Has she been convicted of anything?'

'It's none of my business but I think you should speak to Marcus. Two parents are better than one in a crisis.'

'As you say, it's none of your business.'

Angela loses it. She'd known she would. She'd known this would be the last time she ascended to the fifth floor of Probation House.

'You're destroying Lucy – deliberately. And lots of people know it! You won't get away with it, you bloodless little bitch!'

Jill rises, trembling. 'Consider yourself suspended from duty, Miss Loftus. You will be hearing from the Disciplinary Panel.'

Angela heaves herself up. 'How's the drugs baron?' she asks.

'The what?' Behind her granny glasses Jill Hull retains her neat, efficient, next-business look.

'The drugs baron. Your Nick. The one who's been supplying your own daughter with cocaine and ecstasy while you turn a blind eye – or do you?'

'Wait one moment, Angela.' Jill presses a buzzer under her desk – they all have them in case a 'client' turns nasty. Even a Deputy Chief Probation Officer sometimes receives a PO's client in her office. Five seconds later a security guard arrives.

'Now,' Jill addresses him. 'Miss Loftus here is suspended. Escort her out of the building. Remove her office key and ID pass. Make absolutely sure she takes nothing with her except personal belongings. Right?'

'Yes, Ms Hull. Understood.'

'Ha!' snorts Angela. 'I have fewer rights than a con!'

The Congress for Justice has cornered Max Venables. Shaken by the rumours concerning Marcus, and by Nick Paisley's impending elevation to Acting DPP, the Shadow Home Secretary has agreed to meet them. The Boy said he should. 'Don't put all your eggs in one basket, Max.' So now Venables is confronted by Paisley, Cecilia Harsent, Jill Hull, Jimmy Haley-White, Edgar Averling, Geoffrey Villiers – and by his own wife, Sandra Golding.

Her triumph in the Liz Hargreaves case has dazzled the Bar and brought Sandra a giant step towards the chairmanship of the Criminal Bar Association. Louise – or anyone temporarily married to Marcus – is finished.

'Byron is now calling himself Justice for Victims,' Paisley is saying. 'Don't be taken in, Max.'

Averling nods vigorously. 'They want courts to be informed of the impact of the crime on the victim before passing sentence. This is completly hostile to the interests of justice.'

'Quite so,' murmurs Villiers. 'Very good.'

Nick Paisley bores in: 'Victim Impact Statements, as they are called in America, will inevitably lead to grotesquely inconsistent sentences.'

Max shrugs, unconvinced. 'You snatch money from a young man and he chases you. You do the same thing to an old lady and she may die of shock.' Apologetically Max rises to switch on his TV set. 'I'm told Marcus gave an interview today. I expect we'd all be interested to hear what he has to say.'

'We know what he has to say,' Paisley snaps – but all eyes are fixed on the television screen. Marcus is seen leaving the Crown Court in a sparkling white shirt and flash Liberty tie.

'Nice tie,' Sandra says.

*Question*: Judge Byron, are we facing a general breakdown of public confidence in the law?

*Byron*: In aspects of the law – but most seriously in the criminal justice system.

*Question*: Is the public right?

*Byron*: Of course. No one within our criminal justice system is elected. The practitioners distrust the people as a monster, a

Leviathan, a mob which believes whatever it reads in the Press. But the public is right and the professionals are wrong.

*Question*: The Congress for Justice has denounced you as a reactionary.

*Byron*: Probably I should be deported to the time of the Old Testament. No camels were stolen while Moses preached.

In Max Venables's office, Jill Hull is seething. 'Frankly, *this* Moses is nothing but a cheap demagogue.'

'He'd thrive in America,' Sandra says, 'where trials are televised.'

'I've never known a man', Paisley declares, 'so despised by his own daughter.'

Max shakes his head, bewildered by so much animosity. 'You sound like a lynch mob,' he says.

'Oh, shut up, Max!' Sandra snaps. 'You're just a dupe.'

'Well, at least I didn't sleep with the man!'

Jill tries to calm things down. 'Much as we sympathise with all victims of crime, Max, they cannot be expected to form a rational view of whether a defendant should be granted bail.'

'But they might have an informative view,' Max suggests. 'A victim may be in an excellent position to spell out exactly why he or she fears intimidation from the accused pending trial.'

'That's the Crown's job,' Paisley says. 'A victim is incapable of forming a rational opinion whether an offender should be granted bail or parole.'

'I'm not so sure,' Max says.

Up Whitehall from the House of Commons, the Home Secretary Jeremy Darling also has his television turned on. On hand to steady his nerves are his Parliamentary Private Secretary, Hector Coombe, MP, and the Chairman of the Commons Home Affairs Committee, Sir Lawton Stanhope, MP.

*Question*: Judge Byron, do you see yourself at war with the criminal justice system?

*Byron*: Well, I'm part of it. The system is dominated by vested interests. By professionals, practitioners and experts. I mean the Bar. I mean the Law Society. I mean the Probation Service. I mean the Youth Justice Teams. And the criminologists who tell us what to think and how to think.

*Question*: Are you referring to your former tutor Geoffrey Villiers – who only yesterday described you as the greatest disappointment of his life?

*Byron*: When Villiers founded the Congress for Justice, we were still fighting capital punishment, corporal punishment and a medieval attitude to homosexuality. In those days magistrates' courts were popularly known as 'police courts' – the justices always believed what the police said. So did juries. All that has changed. Sixty per cent of trials in the Crown Court result in acquittals.

*Question*: Too many acquittals?

*Byron*: Of course. As usual this Government stabbed itself in the foot by allowing the self-employed and the professionals to wriggle out of jury service. Juries are now largely filled by the unemployed and others who wouldn't believe a policeman if he told them it was Monday. My point about Geoffrey Villiers is that he's a grand old man trapped in a time-warp.

*Question*: And what is happening now?

*Byron*: Too many criminals are being handed travel passes back to the scene of their crimes.

The Home Secretary has in his hand Marcus Byron's first public statement as President of Justice for Victims.

'It's outrageous,' Darling declares. 'Spend spend spend!'

Coombe smiles thinly. 'Perhaps you should contribute a fiver to Byron's scheduled bike ride to the Pyrenees, Jeremy. After all, he might have a useful accident up in the mountains – or just get lost.'

'Whatever I gave, Venables would give more. People would accuse me of parsimony. Tell the French and Spaniards to refuse Byron a visa.'

'We are members of the European Union, Jeremy. No visas.'

Sir Lawton has been reading the latest utterance by the Boy, as reported in the *Sentinel* by 'that bitch' Brigid Kyle.

'Listen to this nonsense, Jeremy. The Boy has been flashing his teeth again, like a piranha. "The Home Secretary", he declares, "has utterly failed the victims of crime. I am personally contributing one hundred pounds to Judge Byron's admirable and inspired initiative."'

Coombe takes the *Sentinel* from Sir Lawton. 'The Boy was addressing a businessmen's lunch in the City. Apparently he raised ten thousand for these bloody "victims" on the spot.'

'What's our rating in the latest opinion polls?' Darling sulks.

'Still forty per cent behind.'

'What's my personal rating?'

'Three per cent of the public think you're doing a good job, Jeremy. That's one per cent down on last month.'

Reluctantly Darling turns back to the television screen.

*Question*: You have been critical of pre-sentence reports?

*Byron*: Would you ask the bus company whether it's better to travel by bus or train? We don't want prison officers to write PSRs, so why probation officers? The Press never sees the claptrap jargon of sixties sociology which confronts magistrates every day of the year.

In the House of Commons, Max Venables tugs at his beard. The meeting with the Congress is not going well – he hadn't expected it to. Every word Marcus utters generates an electric storm of hatred. But Max is determined to go on biting the bullet.

'Marcus also wants new judicial powers to force victims to testify under oath. What do you say to that?' he asks.

'And if they refuse they will be locked up – victims twice over,' Jill Hull comments scornfully.

'That's a very good point, Jill,' Cecilia Harsent says.

'Spot on,' Jimmy Haley-White says. 'Victims twice over.'

Max Venables sips nervously at his mineral water. 'Marcus recently cited to me seven horrific cases of grievous bodily harm. On each occasion the victim was the main witness, arrests followed – then the victim subsequently withdrew the evidence, too frightened to testify.'

'Who knows?' Sandra says. 'There may have been a reconciliation. A woman might not want to send the family breadwinner, the father of her children, to prison.'

'Too many victims of domestic violence are intimidated into silence,' Max insists.

'The courts are rarely the right place to deal with domestic violence,' Jill Hull says. 'What estranged couples need is mediation: a social worker, a teacher, a psychiatrist, family and friends. Reparations and future good conduct should be negotiated.'

'In other words, more of the same,' Max snaps. 'More pie in the sky.'

A shocked silence falls across the room. But Marcus Byron's voice is insistent.

*Question*: Sandra Golding has accused you of 'playing to the gallery'.

*Byron*: Well, I expect she can afford seats in the stalls. QCs usually can.

*Question*: You have been strongly critical of the Home Secretary on many occasions. Should a judge meddle in politics?

*Byron*: I talk about crime and punishment to anyone who will listen. The public interest comes first.

*Question*: It's widely reported that you have angered both the Lord Chancellor and the Lord Chief Justice.

*Byron*: The Lord Chancellor is a politician. If and when the Lord Chief Justice wishes to speak to me, I shall listen with the respect due to his office.

*Question*: Has he in fact summoned you?

*Byron*: No. [Smiles.] Maybe it's a warrant instead.

*Question*: Has the Leader of the Opposition offered you the post of Lord Chancellor in a future government headed by himself?

*Byron*: No.

*Question*: Would you accept if he did?

*Byron*: No.

*Question*: Why?

*Byron*: I wouldn't want to be kicked upstairs.

Nick Paisley explodes. 'Oh yes, ha ha!'

'Marcus would grab at anything,' Sandra says, 'so long as he was allowed to dress up.'

The expressions around Max Venables's office table are grim. At this juncture old Geoffrey Villiers appears to come out of a personal trance, smiling sweetly.

'My dear Max, my own pressure group, Freedom, is supporting a demand by transvestites for dual identity cards, one male, one female, when travelling on British Rail and London Underground. This facility has already been granted to transsexuals on the ground that they carry a medical certificate attesting that they are preparing for a sex change.'

Max Venables sighs. 'I'm afraid we don't yet have a policy on that, Geoffrey.'

Villiers beams benevolently. 'I'm sure, Max, you will offer us transvestites your public support.'

'Shut up, Geoffrey,' Paisley snaps. 'Stop talking nonsense.'

'My dear Nick, we in Freedom are taking the case to the Commission of Human Rights in Strasbourg. I'm sure the Congress wouldn't wish to be seen dragging its feet.'

Brows darken further. Is the old man senile? Or is this sabotage? Villiers can be difficult. Of late, increasingly so. The Congress is no longer sure about its founding member.

Up Whitehall, prowling his office, the Home Secretary gloomily confronts the portrait of Disraeli.

'Don't they understand that my new, tariff-based criminal injuries compensation scheme is the result of long consultation?'

Coombe shakes his head. 'They only know that you're trying to save money by flat-rate payments, regardless of the victim's loss of earnings and medical costs.'

'No! I mean yes! I am not Scrooge! It will save us £85 million. By the beginning of the next century, £250 million. Isn't the public demanding lower taxation?'

'Byron rang again this morning,' Coombe says. 'He wants to see you, Jeremy.'

'Fix Sambo up with a prostitute like they fixed up Lionel Lacey,' Sir Lawton guffaws.

'They say that Byron takes his brains to bed with him,' Coombe smiles, glancing at the man himself on the screen.

*Question*: Various questions have been asked about your family life, Judge Byron.

*Byron*: Have they? Who by?

*Question*: Might you feel compelled to step down from the Bench for personal or family reasons?

*Byron*: No. Now you must excuse me, I have work to do.

The meeting in Max Venables's office is breaking up. It's clear that the Shadow Home Secretary will remain perversely hooked on Marcus Byron's primitive recipe for law enforcement until Byron is publicly disgraced.

Outside, in Parliament Square, Edgar Averling leads Nick Paisley and Jill Hull aside.

'We have to get rid of Villiers. He's gaga.'

'No, he's not,' Paisley snaps back. 'Villiers was the brightest person in the room.'

'Whatever can you mean?' asks Cecilia Harsent, who has attached herself to the group.

'Villiers', says Paisley, 'deliberately reduced our agenda to farce. Villiers has always been a Lemon. Lemons are for squeezing. Geoffrey Villiers is about to run out of luck.'

As they confer outside the Palace of Westminster, inside it Max Venables sneaks back to his empty office. Thank God Sandra has gone. Max has been taking notes on the meeting for the Boy, who's out of the country in Germany, selling himself to the Frankfurt stock exchange. After some difficulty Max gets through to the Hessischer Hof Hotel.

'He's in bed,' the Boy's Chief Deputy Assistant Press Officer says. 'Fax us a memo, Max, and keep it short, will you, old man?'

'Congratulations on your TV performance. You were formidable – as usual.'

Heather Stuart occupies a pleasant garden flat in Earl's Court. The garden is a small patio paved in coloured stones, adorned by potted plants and fringed by a narrow border of soil in which a surprisingly varied array of flowers thrives, despite the easterly aspect.

'I get very little sunlight. These Victorian mansion blocks were built tall.'

Marcus pretends to inspect her flowers while inspecting Heather and sipping the subtly subversive Spanish white wine he has picked up on the way, together with a fuchsia for her garden.

Desire makes him nervous. She's wearing a little red dress over black stockings and very high heels. One button seems to hold the whole thing together. He gobbles the salted nuts she offers him, then fills his pipe, to keep his hands busy.

'You know the Jewish joke about a seafood diet? Every time I see food I eat it.'

She raises finely pencilled eyebrows and simultaneously dips eyelids treated with Clinique's Ivory Bisque touched discreetly by Lancôme Maquicils mascara.

She reads his pleasured gaze. 'What does your wife use?'

'Use?'

'For make-up.'

'I am not invited to know.'

'Marcus I'm . . . I'm very sorry about Lucy. It must be harrowing for you.'

'She spotted you at the St Hilda's playing field. She said you reminded her of Teresa Kent.'

'I'm flattered!'

'I met the actress once. Long ago. Lucy found us together. In retrospect it was a fatal moment between Lucy and myself.'

Marcus had hoped – or had he? – that the fireball of lust

for Heather Stuart would subside. He ought to have known better: desire becomes its own aphrodisiac. The sight of Heather working out with Wendy at Riverview had wrought havoc with his libido. Since that bizarre evening he had tried to focus his imagination on the sweet love offered by Brigid Kyle but the fierce electric charges scorching his terminals were all generated by Heather.

'You said you have some information for me.'

'Yes.'

'Shall we go inside?'

'You don't like the garden?'

'I see a dozen windows overlooking this garden. At one of them I imagine a pro handling an F2AS Photomic Nikon, equipped with silicone photo diodes, A-1 Automatic Indexing and a DS-12EE aperture control unit. He's racing through a score of Kodak Tri-X frames at 1/500th of a second, using a 135mm lens. He's probably the same photographer who faked the photos at the Bow Street Tavern.'

'How would anyone know you were coming here?'

'They might, they might not. Your house and garden are under surveillance. I noticed an Alfa Romeo 2.5 Veloce parked outside.'

'So?'

'Its registration number is familiar to me. It was parked outside the Riverview Sports Club beside your Ford Punto when I arrived with Lionel Lacey. It belongs to Jimmy Haley-White. Top speed 120 m.p.h.'

'Perhaps I ought to tell you that Jimmy has been in pursuit of me for the past year. He has asked me to marry him.'

'Which flowerpot is he hiding in?'

'I am quite fond of Jimmy – though I don't approve of his permissive attitude to young criminals.'

Marcus smiles but you could wipe the smile away with a damp cloth, like chalk from a blackboard. 'Jimmy is a wanker.'

She leads him through the garden door into the sitting room. He knocks his pipe on his heel before stepping inside.

'Please sit wherever you find comfortable.'

He takes an upright chair. 'What have you got for me?'

'Jill and Jimmy have issued new instructions to the Youth Justice Team. The aim is to funnel even more young recidivists, habitual criminals, into diversion.'

'Ah, our old friend, "diversion". How many youngsters do you have on Supervision Orders in this patch?'

'Currently, sixty-eight.'

'How many actions were brought for breach of Supervision Orders in the past year?'

'Three.'

'Three! How many should have been brought – in your opinion?'

'At least thirty.'

'That's thirty lads sticking their fingers up the Youth Justice Team's arsehole?'

'The new tactic is to blame the parents for the boys' non-attendance – if the magistrates bother to ask.'

'Yeah.'

'The most sinister development is within the Youth Justice Community Options Team. What Jill and Jimmy call "effective intervention" simply means diverting every serious offender away from the courts. That is the long-term agenda.'

'What are the police doing about it?'

'The Police Youth and Community Section are now drowning within the new Multi Agency Juvenile Offenders Panel.'

'All this bloody jargon! All this bureaucracy.'

'The police are still allowed to charge a dozen super-offenders but the rest are simply cautioned. Jimmy has introduced a new Art Therapy programme for intensely disturbed offenders.'

'Like Mark Griffin? – if they catch him. The kind who cut the old lady up before taking her purse?'

'Well – yes.'

'Perhaps Jimmy should introduce them to Van Gogh. Then they could cut off their own ears.'

Heather is standing very close to Marcus's chair, as if daring him to reach out.

'Does Patrick Berry stand any chance in his contest with Lady Harsent?' she asks.

'Yes.'

'I don't think Wendy likes me.'

'She said you were a brilliant actress – a compliment, I assumed, given your Thespian task that Friday night.'

'"Thespian?" I'm afraid I don't know the word.'

'Ask Jimmy – he's a Thespian, too.'

'You really do hate Jimmy, don't you?'

He bites on the stem of his extinguished pipe. 'What else are you going to tell me, Heather?'

'I hear a rumour that the Congress for Justice has set aside a modest £200 per head for every MP prepared to put down a question in the House of Commons concerning certain topics.'

'Such as?'

'Such as the apparent conflict of interest between Marcus Byron's position as a Crown Court judge and his role as unofficial adviser to Max Venables. Such as the apparent conflict of interest between Patrick Berry's work as a magistrate and his commercial involvement in curfew-tagging. Such as the covert links between Judge Marcus Byron and the disgraced DPP, Lionel Lacey. And . . . one more too awful to mention.'

'Go on.'

'Marcus, they are putting it about that Lucy would have faced criminal charges long ago but for . . . your interventions.'

Marcus leaps up, incensed. 'My interventions! Who with, pray?'

'With Lionel Lacey, now the most despised figure in English public life.'

Marcus subsides into his chair. 'I see. I get it. Do you know something, Heather?'

'Marcus, you don't have to convince me! I belong to your legion of admirers.'

'Just hear me out, I have to get this off my chest. I have great difficulty finding out what is happening to Lucy. Jill has custody, you know. Jill appointed Averling as Lucy's lawyer. They won't tell me anything!'

'Shall I tell you, then?'

'Is this from Jimmy?'

'Yes. He's close to Jill. Averling is claiming that Lucy has "instructed" him that she is going to plead guilty to possession of Class A drugs. She intends to denounce the existing law in court. Drugs should be decriminalised, period.'

Marcus's head is in his hands. 'Jesus.' He sighs, straightens up, paces the room. 'What does Jill make of that?'

'According to Jimmy, Jill takes the view that Lucy was caught red-handed by a policeman of unimpeachable integrity, Doug McIntyre, so there is no defence against the facts.'

'Oh yeah? Bollocks! Lucy was with Daniel Richardson at the time. A Richardson! The stuff was planted on her – that's a defence! Just get her a proper lawyer! Just get Louise on to this case!'

'I gather that Lucy would never nark on Daniel.'

'Jesus.'

'And worse yet, Marcus.'

'Go on. Lucy's going to ask for ten other offences to be taken into consideration, including theft of the Crown Jewels?'

'Including the violent robbery of an old lady called Mrs Ramsden in Century Park.'

'But they have no identification evidence on that!'

'It's Lucy's voluntary confession. Averling will present it to the Crown Court on the rollmop principle.'

'Yeah. Yeah. I can just imagine it coming before my "colleague", Sir Henry Harsent.'

'But he won't be your "colleague", Marcus, if they have their way. The Congress is preparing a petition to the Lord Chancellor and the Lord Chief Justice. For justice to be seen to be done, you must be stood down from the Bench for the duration of the proceedings.'

'Bollocks. Bowers is no fool. How can the defence fear excessive clemency?'

'Averling and Sandra Golding will argue the reverse: the Crown Court might be tempted to prove its integrity by making an example of Lucy.'

'Look, I'm sorry, but do you have any whisky?'

'Not normally.' She smiles. 'But Angela warned me, "Don't forget the great man's love of Scotch." So I didn't forget.'

Heather plucks a bottle of Black & White out of a cupboard and hands him a tumbler. 'Say when.'

'Just count to ten.'

She smiles. 'Are you in love with Brigid Kyle?'

'None for you? I'm drinking alone?'

'I'll have a drop more of your nice white wine.'

'Cheers again, Heather. I'm very grateful to you for telling me so much.'

'But you didn't tell me whether you are in love with Brigid Kyle.'

'I'll have to pass on that, Heather.'

The little red dress bridles. 'Then you are in love with her.'

'Heather, as I grow older – and I've grown ten years older

during the past ten minutes – I grow increasingly wary of attaching words to emotions.'

She imitates his accent and tone of voice. 'Yeah?'

'Heather, I—'

'Don't you think I went well beyond the call of duty for you at the Riverview?'

'You did, you certainly did.'

'Do you know why?'

Marcus gestures agnostically. 'I assumed you thought Lionel Lacey was a good man worth saving.'

The cat's eyes dance. 'I couldn't care less about that ridiculous cadaver of a half-man. I fell for you on sight. I hated you as well, of course, but that's all part of the Marcus Byron charm, isn't it?'

'Is it?'

Heather Stuart stands over him with the self-assurance of a woman who can have any man any place any time. The flat of her palms move up his chest, across his face, then fold round the back of his head.

'This may be contempt of court,' he says, gripping her by the waist.

'Does your Honour wish to hold the trial in bed?'

'I'm almost old enough to be your father.'

'You don't feel like my father.'

'That's a nice perfume you use – Dior?'

'Come and find out.'

He follows her into the bedroom. The furnishing is Scandinavian, the prevailing colour brilliant white. An Andy Warhol silkscreen hangs above the bed; a long-haired cat lies on it. He knows – as he has so often known in his life – that he should not be doing this.

Heather unfastens the single large button which holds her dress across her breasts. She is wearing nothing underneath. He has never been so aroused by nothing. A casual motion of her hand sends the long-haired cat lazily to the floor. Her dress slides up her thighs as she falls back across the bed.

'I thought you were a man who knows what he wants.'

'Yeah.' He drops his shirt and trousers to the floor. 'I go for it even when the bottle is marked "Poison".'

'Poison, Marcus? Me?'

She throws off the duvet, pulls him down, slides her tongue into his mouth, locks her thighs round him.

'You like stockings on or off?'

'Are they insured?'

She almost smiles.

'Lovely hair you have, Heather – do you use L'Oréal or Clairol?'

'And the great public believes you're a gentleman.' Her hand expertly coaxes him.

'Is this a one-way street?'

'You'll never come out.'

'Just another Sambo in drag.' He penetrates her. Their loins lock. Her fast, supple motions stake a claim to power.

'Your Riverview workouts leave you some spare energy for the domestic chores, eh?'

'Do you like my invisible muscles?'

'I'm already listening for the bell.'

'Angela says the sight of *your* thighs in tight Lycra bicycling shorts gives her "the quivers-shivers".'

'Dear Angela.'

'Jill will sack her. She's in a bad state. She wants to see you. She has a big haul of documents for you.'

Heather's supple hips twist and thrust, goading him.

'Tell her I'm going cycling in the Pyrenees. I'll contact her when I get back.'

'Yes, master.'

'That sounds more like it.'

'Does Brigid Kyle call you master?'

'Let's leave her out of it.'

'We're certainly doing that! Is it true that your wife is pulling out of the contest with Sandra Golding?'

'What do you mean?' Marcus's hands are massive as they grip Heather's gently curving shoulders.

'Want to strangle me?' Heather half smiles. 'With one of my own stockings? It's traditional in *crimes passionnels.*'

Her thigh teases his leg. There are degrees of desire: this is the *summa cum laude*. He looks down into the sly face of perdition.

'How does it feel, hm, down there?' she asks.

'Like a gossamer-skinned *wurst* about to split its sides.'

She licks his mouth. 'What do you want to know about Nick Paisley?'

'Nice bedside telephone you've got. Schellen-Hahn GmbH do a fine line in miniaturised microphone transmitters. They occupy as much space as a large walnut.'

'The mike's hidden in my cunt. Behind my coil. Unreachable without a breach of the law "so serious, your Honour, as to justify a custodial sentence".'

Abruptly her pelvis and thighs lock. 'I expect Patrick Berry knows all about hidden microphones, hm? Who has he planted them on recently?'

'Make me tell you.'

'Is that a challenge? I'm prepared to pretend to lose contests with your sister but not with you.'

'Pretend? We niggers may be short of brains but we know how to lift something off the ground. Centuries of practice.'

He begins to thrust into the lovely woman beneath him. She moans. He takes her face in his hands.

'Did you betray Lionel Lacey?'

'Of course. Of course not. Which excites you more?'

'He confided to you he was heading for the Monkey Tree not his usual Enfants du Paradis. Lionel giggled, didn't he, as he told you how he would fool Paisley. So you made the phone call to Paisley. You and Jimmy. And they got him.'

'Do you enjoy being screwed by the Enemy? Maybe I did betray whatshisname, your moth-eaten pal, to spare you the absurdity of trying to save his soul every Friday night to the end of time. So go on, go on, pull out of me in disgust. Show me your high principles.'

She arches her back, thrusting her breasts up at him. 'Beg me to tell you about Jimmy's criminal record – and Nick Paisley's.'

'I never beg.'

'You will. Say, "I the famous Judge Marcus Byron, pillar of rectitude, man of honour, upholder of the law, torch of justice, defender of victims . . . am enslaved by a woman young enough to be my daughter." Say it.'

Marcus groans.

'Say you'll never see Brigid Kyle again. Or talk to her. Or listen to her. Come on, come on . . . say it!'

Marcus's breath is being dragged from him.

'Nothing to say, your Honour? Hmmm.' Her fingernails rake painfully down the smooth black skin of his broad back. 'I'm going to make you swear allegiance to the Congress for Justice. Because I am their champion.'

He groans. He can no longer hold it in. This has never happened to him before.

# *Twelve*

TODAY IS THE DAY – Susan Galloway must finally confront the ordeal of the Benson Street Youth Court. A mild sleeping pill has got her through a dream-plagued night. Rising at seven, she deposits Tom with her mother at eight-thirty: Susan has been told to report to the court at 9.45 and is desperately anxious not to be late.

Simon had 'insisted' on coming with her, to hold her hand, but he would lose most of a day's work and she wanted to face it alone.

'They won't let you into the court, anyway.'

'It's that bloody waiting room. I know it. You'll be suffering from nicotine poisoning by the time you give evidence.'

Dear Simon – it was he who hadn't slept a wink. She hopes he has forgiven her for going back to work for Jill, as Marcus Byron – a nice, sincere man, and very handsome – had urged her to do. Susie's heart bled for him whenever she read all these scurrilous articles in the Press. Simon has never asked whether the 'electricity man' had called at Jill's house to collect the key off Susie. They don't discuss it. Recently Simon and Tom have been enjoying Marcus Byron's building bricks. As the judge had predicted, Susie has caught Simon playing with the toy tractor after Tom had gone to bed.

'The child is father to the child,' Susie teased him.

On arrival she edges nervously through a crowd of loud, jostling youths at the entrance, whispers her name to the Burns

Security guard, and is shown to a small room reserved for witnesses.

At eleven-fifteen she's still sitting there. It's rather like a hospital waiting room, though in a hospital you don't suffer the constant shouting and obscenities and scuffles in the corridor outside. Simon was right: every time the list-caller pokes her head through the door, a thick stench of cigarette smoke follows. Susie always looks up hopefully – though she dreads it, she wants the trial called off, cancelled! – but the list-caller simply smiles sympathetically, like a harried hospital nurse.

At eleven-thirty the list-caller flashes Jill her 'the doctor-will-see-you-now' smile that nurses accord to patients.

'You should be called in ten minutes, Mrs Galloway. The trial's just beginning.'

Desperately Susie rehearses what she's going to say. The truth, of course. But what does she remember? Brigid Kyle had telephoned her the previous evening with a bit of advice from 'a certain new friend of yours' – understood. 'When the defence cross-examines you, Susan, don't take it personally. Don't be affronted. Just keep your mind on the facts. The facts are your best friends.'

'Thanks, Brigid. You wouldn't like to stand in for me, would you?'

'Susan, I'd give my right eye.'

The list-caller conducts her into the court room. She recognises Detective Sergeant Doug McIntyre, who has just given evidence. He's looking grim – Susan doesn't know why. The usher leads her straight to the raised witness stand.

'Religion?'

'None.'

Susie chooses to affirm rather than swear on the Bible. You may as well begin on an honest note. Now she glances shyly to her left, towards the three magistrates. My God! (though she has none). The man sitting in the middle! She recognises him! Those bright blue eyes! He was the fellow who—

The young prosecutor asks her whether she was attacked and robbed on her own doorstep.

'Yes, I was.'

'And what was taken from you?'

'My watch, my necklace and my handbag containing money, credit cards and other things.'

The prosecutor then removes each of the stolen objects from a plastic bag and shows them to defence counsel – who nods. The prosecutor crosses the floor and shows them to Susan.

'Are these yours, Mrs Galloway?'

'Yes.'

'Were they stolen from you?'

'Yes.'

'Are you sure?'

'I am absolutely sure. The watch has my initials engraved on the back. The necklace has one missing stone. Look, the credit cards bear my name.'

'Thank you, Mrs Galloway. No more questions.'

Susie is flabbergasted. No more questions! Nothing about the attack itself and the youth who did it! There he is – she has finally picked him out – the tall rag-doll boy with the scar on his cheek who had asked her for the time – 'Got the time?' – outside Century Park and then come upon her in Oundle Square, on her own doorstep, and—

'No questions,' says the defence solicitor, Mr Simmonds.

Susie is stunned. She'd braced herself for the ordeal of cross-examination. There is to be none!

'Thank you, Mrs Galloway,' the chairman of the magistrates says gently. 'That will be all. You are free to go but you may sit at the back of the court for the remainder of the proceedings, if you wish.'

She stares at him, a blond fellow with sharp, very blue eyes. Yes, that's the man who—

McIntyre makes room for her in the chair next to his own. At least it's nice to sit beside someone you know. But he doesn't look at her. She absorbs his expression of grim fury.

Mr Simmonds is up now. He doesn't call Amos Richardson to testify – that's his right. Simmonds is telling the court that someone else, a friend of a friend, had given Amos the stolen goods (which Amos had no idea were stolen, of course) in part-payment for 'a debt'. That's all.

'The court will stand!' bellows the usher. Everyone rises as the magistrates retire. Susie now has a view of the back of the head of the boy who had slashed her arm: no dreadlocks. And he's got away with it! Just look at him! He's even wearing the same red baseball cap, back to front! When he turns, grinning, to his social worker, you can see the scar.

McIntyre leans into her ear.

'They dropped the robbery and GBH charges before they began. Derek Jardine, that's the prosecutor over there, believed they should have had a go, but Nick Paisley over-ruled him.'

'Because I failed the identification thing and there were no other witnesses?'

'You didn't "fail" anything, Susie. It was fixed.'

'Fixed!'

'Ssh.' He lays a hand briefly on her still-bandaged arm to quieten her. 'Aye. We think it was fixed. There should never have been sticking-plaster on those boys' faces. It's damned odd because the Inspector who conducted the parade is a good man.'

'Crabbe?'

'Aye. Ken. He's one of us.'

'"One of us"?'

'Never mind. By the way, news is just in. Nick Paisley has been appointed Acting DPP. Lacey resigned, of course.'

A few days after she had gone back to part-time work for Jill Hull, the electricity man had called on the dot of noon. He was blond, with very blue eyes. 'Marcus sent me,' he said with a reassuring smile. He carried a large metal toolbag. Handing him the housekeys, she and Tom had fled into the street. Cooking Tom's lunch, she had suffered agonies: Lucy often came home from school at odd hours, claiming (Jill said) that she had a 'reading week' for her GCSEs.

An hour later Susie had heard the keys to No. 23 come through the door and land on the mat.

'Who is the chairman of the magistrates today?' Susie whispers to McIntyre.

'Patrick Berry. He's also one of us.'

'Does he know Marcus Byron?'

'You see the black court clerk over there? She's Berry's wife – and Byron's sister.' McIntyre throws Susie a penetrating glance. 'Why did you ask?'

Susie longs to tell McIntyre what she knows but she checks herself. Doug, after all, is a policeman and—

'The court will stand!'

The magistrates resume their seats.

'Stand up, Amos,' Patrick Berry says. 'We find you guilty of handling stolen goods. All other charges have been withdrawn.

Sit down, Amos.' Berry casts an eye further down the court. 'Do we have Amos's previous?'

Jimmy Haley-White rises. He shows a print-out to Simmonds. Simmonds shows it to Amos. Finally it's passed up to the Bench.

'In view of this,' Patrick Berry says, 'we cannot sentence today. Four weeks for a PSR?'

'Yes, sir,' Jimmy Haley-White says.

'Given Amos's record,' Berry says, 'we give notice that we regard this as "so serious" that a custodial sentence must be considered.'

'Good for you, lad,' McIntyre mutters.

'What is the bail situation?' Berry asks.

Jimmy Haley-White is up again. 'Sir, Amos was remanded into the care of the Local Authority six weeks ago. He was placed at the Magnet Hotel. However, this seems not to have worked out well. I should explain, sir, that after Amos was released from Downton he was sent to live with his granny. His granny could not cope so the court put him in the care of the Local Authority. The staff of the Magnet Hotel now report that Amos refuses to obey the rules of the hostel. No charity or voluntary association will receive Amos in view of past experiences.'

'Secure Accommodation?' Berry snaps.

'Sir, the National Bed-Bank has failed to find a secure place for Amos.'

Berry turns to the clerk of the court. 'Am I right,' he asks Wendy, 'that Amos currently faces five other charges, three of them involving robbery?'

'Actually, six other cases, sir. A new one was filed this morning.'

'So does he go home to Eden Manor or back to Granny?' Berry asks Jimmy Haley-White.

Simmonds is up. 'Frankly, sir, I recommend that he be returned home under a curfew, reporting conditions and restrictions on his movements . . .'

Susan slips out of the court by the back door. She has no wish to find herself in the street face to face with Amos Richardson.

Six days later the morning papers inform Susan that Marcus Byron and Patrick Berry are riding high in the Pyrenees, national heroes of the 'silly season'. The judge had been photographed outside the Royal Courts of Justice in the Strand, astride his mountain bike and wearing Lycra shorts under a King of the Mountains polka-dot jersey. A white helmet, a huge money belt and a broad smile completed the picture.

'GET ON YOUR BIKE, YOUR HONOUR!' roared the tabloids.

Marcus contrives to be on television almost every evening – the BBC has hired a Spanish helicopter crew. Money pours in for Justice for Victims.

Wendy instantly recognises the voice on the telephone but she cannot identify it. High pitched with tension, precise and pedantic, it crackles like stiff parchment.

'Mrs Berry, is it? I'm trying to reach Marcus Byron.'

'Who's calling, please?'

'Never mind that. I can't get anything on his phone except a recorded message. Where's his wife?'

'I'm sorry, but I do have a right to ask who you are.'

'We met. Twice. Once at Byron's place and once at that . . . other place.'

Wendy now knows who it is.

'Marcus is abroad – don't you read the papers?'

'I try not to. I find too much about myself in the papers. When will Byron return?'

'In a week.'

'There's something I must tell him. He ought to know.'

'I can pass a message.' She is about to add that her husband is with Marcus in the Pyrenees – but thinks better of it.

'Ah. But can I trust you? I trust Byron. Known him for years. We used to be fellow-members of the Oxford and Cambridge before he resigned.'

'The club in Pall Mall?'

'He's too trusting of women. He resigned because the club wouldn't admit women members.'

'And you didn't resign, Mr Lacey?'

'I'd have resigned if they had admitted women. You were in on it, weren't you?'

'On what?'

'The plot to ruin my life. With that other . . . that other creature in a leotard . . . What was her name? Where does she live?'

A woman's instinct surfaces protectively. 'What is your grievance against her, Mr Lacey?'

'Grievance! I liked her! I trusted her! I confided to her where I was going that Friday night. And they were waiting for me! I had told no one else, not even Byron!'

'I'll pass that on to Marcus.'

'Women!'

'Evidently they have their uses for you, Mr Lacey.'

'I'll find her, that . . . that . . . I'll catch up with her, don't worry.'

The phone goes down.

Wendy hesitates whether to call Heather Stuart at home. She is inclined to believe the demented Lacey – why had Heather slipped away to 'the powder room' only minutes after leaving it to join Marcus and Wendy for dinner in the Riverview brasserie? But duty drives Wendy to warn Heather Stuart. She scans her Lemons address book and dials.

No one answers. Heather's purring voice invites her to record a message.

Like her father, Lucy has taken to the road.

She always joins the New Age Travellers during August – at least she did last year. She has left London without a word to her mother – let Jill imagine that an incensed Marcus has abducted his daughter. Let writs (or whatever they're called) fly between their lawyers! When her GCSE results come through, no one will know where to find her.

If not writs, warrants certainly. Appearing before the Benson Street Youth Court, charged with possession of crack cocaine and ecstasy tablets, Lucy had expected to toss the 'up yours' two fingers at Auntie Wendy, but Auntie's chum-clerks had come to the rescue and spared her the horror-show. It was just a first appearance, no pleas taken, to settle bail conditions. Lady H., dah-ling Amelia's mother, had been in the chair looking like a melting ice-cream cornet.

The prosecutor-chap, Jardine, had asked for one condition to be imposed on Lucy's bail: residence, every night, at home. Ha ha. His reason was Lucy might 'abscond' and 'fail to appear' on the next occasion.

Averling's hack, Simmonds, objected. 'Lucy has appeared on time today, madam, and she has no previous convictions. To restrict a young person's movements during the summer vacation is, I submit, unnecessary.'

Lady H. had beamed at Jill, who was seated beside Lucy.

'Any views, Ms Hull?'

'I don't think the bail condition is necessary but I have no great objection.'

'Very well. Now stand up, Lucy, you have heard what has been said. You will sleep at home every night. And you will be back in this court in two weeks' time at 9.45. Failure to attend is an offence – you do understand that, don't you?'

'Yeah.'

Yeah! So Lucy has taken off for Wiltshire in flagrant breach of bail and failed to turn up at Benson Street for her second appearance. She can imagine Jill trying to explain to Lady H. or, worse, Miss Swearwell. A warrant not backed for bail! The pigs and their doggies are out, sniffing, hounding, slobbering. Bye.

This year the Travellers are set on thwarting the new motorway which is due to cut a swathe through a hundred acres of open parkland and precious trees in west Wiltshire. Their tree village is constantly harassed by bailiffs and the private hirelings of the road contractors. The more athletic resisters are living in tree huts and growing lovely dreadlocks – Lucy can climb a rope without spilling a cup of tea.

No one eats meat here and everyone gets dragged through the mud by meat-eating security guards, most of them building workers laid off by the recession. Lucy keeps dropping her contact lenses in the mud. She writes poems for the Druidic ceremonies honouring the pioneers who fought for access to Stonehenge, taking on the National Trust, English Heritage, the landowners, the pigs.

Lucy does quite a lot of serious writing during the long summer evenings. It's a novel about a black-white girl whose father can't keep his hands off women. She posts the first chapter to one of them, with an invitation to visit, and a beautifully drawn map of the 'war zone'.

Lucy attaches a P.S. 'If you bring the pigs with you, or tell anyone where I am, including the Cyclist, I will slash my wrists and bleed to death.'

Brigid Kyle had returned from a weekend in the Pyrenees with Marcus when she received Lucy's chapter and the accompanying note. Unaware that Lucy is in breach of bail conditions, Brigid cannot imagine why she should bring 'the pigs'; she packs a bag and climbs into her Saab with a pair of heavy boots.

The weekend with Marcus has been the happiest of her life. Getting rid of his brother-in-law for forty-eight hours had been awkward, but Marcus had persuaded a somewhat bemused Patrick to trace his ancestors in some distant caves.

Abandoning her Saab in the local market town, Brigid takes to the road and cuts across country with the help of an ordnance-survey map and Lucy's. She is wearing what Lucy may regard as ludicrous, up-market Travellers' trousers. For the last quarter-mile she aims for the wood smoke drifting pleasantly above the tree-tops. Mongrel dogs are scavenging among battered vans and converted buses, most of which sport TV aerials; some even run to satellite dishes.

Brigid's first inquiries – 'I'm looking for Lucy Byron' – are met with suspicion and guarded agnosticism. Brigid is not conducted to Lucy; Lucy is brought to Brigid.

'So you came alone?' Lucy greets her.

'Hullo, Lucy. Of course. Why wouldn't I?'

'Don't you know?'

'Know what?'

Lucy is wearing a ring through her nose and something – is it a sign of the zodiac? – daubed in wode on her forehead.

'I bet Louise knows,' Lucy says sulkily. 'Is Louise wetting herself in case I don't savvy emergency contraception? She's fanatical about birth control, that poor, childless bitch. Am I "at risk"? Have you brought a supply of pills?'

'Lucy, you invited me to come and see you. Are you going to brew me a cuppa? I'm dead thirsty.'

'I'd advise you to speak normally. People here hate phonies. Where's your packet of teabags then?'

Brigid offers Lucy the gift-hamper of delicacies which she'd brought from London in the unseen Saab. Lucy plonks an old tin kettle on a Calor gas burner.

'I liked the chapter you sent me,' Brigid says cheerfully.

'No, you didn't. You thought it was juvenile and pretentious.'

'I think you have real talent. Your father always says so.'

'I bet you told him where I'm living.'

'He's still abroad on his bike. So tell me all about it.'

'About what?'

Brigid shrugs. 'Your life here.'

'You want the usual rubbish? We love our countryside. It's our space, our environment, our planet, our heritage. We are demanding freedom.'

'What kind of freedom?'

'Actual freedom and metaphysical freedom, you see. We remember the Diggers of the seventeenth century – "True Levellers" they called themselves. We remember the poor people who were dispossessed by the Enclosure Acts. They became pariahs, you know – and we are pariahs. We roam in packs.'

'But most of the people here come from towns and return to the towns with the bad weather.'

'And it's in the towns that we gain experience of consumerism and capitalism and materialism. What it really is. We're mainly urban youngsters exploding into space. In the city you're totally trapped and going nowhere.'

'You're not afraid of the bailiffs?'

'Group Four Security, you mean? Privatised insecurity. Tomorrow we tree-defenders are holding a squat at the local courthouse to protest against the new Criminal Justice Bill. We're all expecting to be charged under Section 68 or 69, like the Manchester Nine.'

'What are you protesting against – apart from the new motorway?'

'The removal of benefit from sixteen- and seventeen-year-olds, that was diabolical. Paying farmers not to produce while the Third World goes hungry. And they transport veal calves like they took the Jews to Auschwitz, don't they?'

'I agree!'

Lucy doesn't want this woman to agree.

'But if you concentrate too much on baby seals and calves, toy animals, you're in danger of forgetting the whole factory-farming thing. So what are they doing? They're feeding the population on systematic cruelty, they're stuffing us with hormone-infested meat packed into dyed, fibreless bread.'

'That's a lot of issues, Lucy.'

'That's right, it is. Here's your tea. Everything's related, you see. Sorry about the powdered milk, the local farmers are unfriendly. This is a culture here, you see, a whole new culture. They thought they could pick us off one by one. Now we're all together. We won't go away.'

A stout woman whose face is lightly caked in mud, as if she was planning to bake it, and whose hair straggles unwashed, joins them. She is puffing a joint which keeps dying on her.

'This campaign is run by women,' she tells Brigid from a smoker's hoarse lungs. 'There's some really strong women here. And who may you be?'

'I may be Brigid Kyle, a journalist. How do you do?'

'This is Ellie,' Lucy says. 'She led a party of ethical shoplifters into a store in St Ives and walked off with mahogany planks illegally stolen from the indigenous people of Brazil. Ellie's mob handed the planks in to the local police station but the magistrates fined them all twenty quid. That's justice for you.'

'Justice!' Ellie laughs and relights her blackened joint from the flame-thrower she keeps digging out of her quilted anorak.

Lucy introduces Brigid to Ted. He's elegant, heretically clean and carries a video camera like a gun. Ted and Lucy are helping out for Small Planet, a company which teaches protesters how to use camcorders. Ted knows Brigid's columns in the *Sentinel.*

'I never go along with a word you write but I enjoy not going along.'

'Tell me about your camcorders.'

'Every skirmish with the police or security guards is documented,' Ted explains. 'Our videos demonstrate hands-on DIY activism.'

'Ted works for the Beeb,' Lucy says, 'though he doesn't like to admit it.' She suddenly smiles through her habitual scowl. 'One of our videos shows people leading geese on to common land which has been bought by a Japanese multi-national to build a golf course.'

'Do you support Friends of the Earth?' Brigid asks.

Lucy and Ellie laugh contemptuously. Ted looks uncertain.

'It's easy to sit at home in your panda T-shirt,' Lucy says, 'with your copy of *New Internationalist,* sending off a donation to save some faraway rainforest or whale. We believe in protesting right here.'

'This is parish-pump politics,' Ellie adds. 'We are the faces of refusal.'

'Right on,' Lucy says.

'What about the hunt saboteurs?' Brigid asks Lucy.

'The sabs? They're right on! They're getting Sections 68

and 69 of Jeremy Darling's new Hitler-law right in the neck! Aggravated trespass!'

'Using horns, whistles and spray cans to disrupt the Hunt doesn't bother you?' Brigid asks.

'No way!'

Lucy takes Brigid on a short tour of the Tree Camp.

'Do you favour the legalisation of hard drugs, Lucy?' Brigid asks, as soon as they are alone.

'"Decriminalisation" is the word. We don't need state-controlled drug dens like they have in Holland. I've been there, you know. They're littered along the border like those petrol stations in Luxembourg. Diabolical.'

'What does your father think?'

'Ask him. I expect you're wired up to those disgusting Lycra shorts of his as he displays his bulging calf-muscles to bemused peasants in the Pyrenees. I expect you adore him – they all do.'

Brigid studies Lucy's expression of elfin impertinence. Is there another Lucy lurking beneath these bright, perky, light-brown features?

'They all fancy Marcus,' Lucy goes on. 'Shall I tell you the name of his latest cracker? Don't pretend not to be interested!'

Brigid attempts a smile but it comes unwrapped before securely in place.

'It's Heather Stuart of the Probation Service. She works for Mum since Mum disposed of the cream cake.'

'The cream cake, Lucy?'

'Angela Loftus, fourteen stone at the last weigh-in and every ounce of it owes allegiance to his Honour Marcus Byron. Heather looks like Teresa Kent, know what I mean?'

Brigid's eyes are stinging.

'Heather and Jimmy are going to be married after Heather has ruined the great man. Mum says she won't stand in their way.'

'How does your mother come into it, Lucy?'

'Jimmy's her fancy man.'

They are approaching a new encampment. Smoke spirals up from a big communal fire. Brigid notices a black boy idly poking the sticks and looking unhappy. Lucy is searching Brigid's eyes for tears but evidently more torture is needed.

'Heather Stuart told me Marcus likes the woman on top,' Lucy says. 'Can you confirm that?'

'She *told* you?' Brigid is miserably aware of having lost ten points by yielding a response: Lucy's eyes are positively dancing now.

'Hm. Yes, she did. Heather pretends to Dad that she's a Lemon but she's just setting him up. It's such very enjoyable work when the dupe has a cock as big as Judge Byron's.'

Brigid's tears are arriving now. 'Lucy, you're speaking of your own father!'

'You're crying,' Lucy says.

'Yes. I am. I only wish you loved your father half as much as he loves you.'

'This is Dan,' Lucy says, proudly indicating the black boy. 'Dan's my boyfriend.'

'Hullo, Dan,' Brigid says.

He nods, almost, but keeps his eyes averted.

'Dan finds the sky in the countryside threatening. Too much of it, he says. Don't ask him any schoolmarmish questions about his family or he'll kill you. Won't you, Dan? Dan doesn't have a father either.'

'Your father loves you, Lucy.'

'Oh yeah?'

'You won't go near him!'

'Is that his story?'

Brigid's temper is snapping. 'Tell me why you telephone local journalists and accuse your father of being a drug addict?'

If this is intended to throw Lucy, it doesn't. 'Spotty Joe O'Neill told you, did he? Your sidekick when you go slumming in Eden Manor among the "animals" – sorry, the "worse than animals".'

'Why are you so aggressive, Lucy?'

Lucy is furiously twisting a coil of wiry hair between two wiry fingers. 'Dunno what you mean, frankly.'

'You're friendly with one of the Richardson boys, aren't you? Is Dan here the one?'

'And whose business is that?'

'They're ruthless criminals.'

'Dan isn't. Anyway, criminals are the heroes of society. Ever read *A Clockwork Orange*?'

Dan is no longer poking the fire. He's examing the hot, smouldering, sharpened end of his stick.

'Shall I do her?' he says. If it's a question, it seems to be directed more towards himself than to Lucy – an inward question.

'Do who?' Brigid addresses Daniel.

'Don't mess with him,' Lucy warns.

'Lucy, it's not you who's set on ruining your father, it's someone far cleverer and more worldly than you. Someone who's exploiting your pain and anger.'

'Piss off.'

'Lucy, how does it feel to be supplied with Class A drugs by the Acting Director of Public Prosecutions? And where does he get the stuff from? I'll tell you. From the thug who put to death Daniel's younger brother, Wesley.'

Daniel Richardson flies at the woman, aiming his red-hot stick at her eyes, but the men round the communal fire have been waiting for it, and wrestle him down.

'Now go!' a tall man yells at her.

'You'd better go,' Ted says quietly. 'It's amazing how much aggro you people bring with you.'

Lucy accompanies Brigid back across country to the B road. She seems very polite and courteous all of a sudden.

'Would you post this note to my mum without telling her where I am?'

'Yes.'

'But you'll tell Dad?'

'Yes. Of course. Send me some more chapters, Lucy.'

'Yeah.'

Sweeping towards London in her Saab, Brigid recognises Daniel Richardson by the roadside, gesturing for a lift with the lazy, derisive gesture of a black youth stranded in alien white countryside. In that split second she is tempted; her journalistic training tells her to stop but her right foot presses the accelerator rather than the brake.

Two days later Marcus Byron and Patrick Berry return in triumph.

According to newspaper reports, Geoffrey Villiers has been picked up by the police, wearing women's clothes, near a public toilet in Oxford's Carfax. Villiers had evidently chained himself to some railings and claimed he was Mrs Pankhurst.

FOUNDER OF CONGRESS FOR JUSTICE DEMANDS<br>VOTES FOR WOMEN<br>SUFFRAGETTE GEOFFREY CLAIMS SANDRA GOLDMAN<br>WILL DEFEND HIM/HER

'DAME' VILLIERS OFFERS ROUGED LIPS TO OXFORD CONSTABULARY
DOTTY DON CLAIMS KNICKERS IN A TWIST FOR ACTING DPP PAISLEY

Brigid Kyle's report in the *Sentinel* carries a short interview with Villiers.

> 'I have been framed,' claims the elderly criminologist Geoffrey Villiers, author of *Morality and the Criminal Law*. 'I can prove that Lemon elements in the police are conducting a campaign against Transvestites. Happily, my colleagues in the Congress for Justice have rallied to my support. Human rights for Transsexuals and Transvestites is high on the Congress's agenda.'

Pushing away the remains of a boiled egg, Marcus Byron begins to laugh.

'The Dame has pulled it off! Good old Geoffrey!'

Louise's mouth tightens. She can barely bring herself to speak to the husband who had cancelled their long-planned vacation in Rome without even consulting her. Worse, a plain brown envelope had arrived choc-a-bloc with colour photos of Marcus sipping Spanish wine – you could read the bloody label on the bottle! – in the company of a strikingly beautiful blonde and a fuchsia.

'Good old Geoffrey!'

Marcus is about to light his disgusting pipe. Louise's temper snaps. She couldn't care less about 'good old Geoffrey': what gets her is her unfaithful husband's unbridled laughter as he reads Brigid Kyle.

'I really can't fathom you, Marcus. Why do you so admire this vindictive old crackpot? He never says a good word about you in public.'

'Geoffrey was my tutor.'

'You carry loyalty too far – your wife excepted.'

'A peculiar feature of a tutorial with Villiers was to be invited to select an apple, orange or – when in season – plum from a large bowl piled with fruit. A gleaming lemon always topped the colourful display. Naturally one never chose the lemon – it was purely decorative. But it was always there.'

'So what!'

Marcus takes a Sunday train to Oxford.

'I had to do something,' Villiers greets him in his College rooms, 'to redress the balance. Oh why – oh why! – did Lionel Lacey have to let us all down! Long lists of Lemons on every front page! Faked photos!'

Geoffrey Villiers paces the floor of his study, threading delicately between disorderly piles of books, essays, eccentric items of discarded clothing.

'Villiers's days are numbered, Marcus. Old Dame Villiers is at long last suspected of sabotage and treachery by the Congress she herself founded.'

Marcus lights his pipe. 'By Nick Paisley?'

'Paisley has more brains than the rest of them put together. I heard of his appointment as Acting Director of Public Prosecutions with horror, Marcus. Horror! Why did Jeremy Darling allow it?'

'We all know why. How many members does the Congress currently claim?'

'Two or three hundred. Most of them are desperately sincere hypocrites – clones of F. Alexander in *A Clockwork Orange*. They call the police when *they* are robbed or burgled – then hurry off to well-funded conferences to denounce the police. The leading figures, whom you and I know so well, are ruthless in pursuit of their own ambitions. They protect their vested interests tooth and claw; the criminal justice system is their bailiwick and their adventure playground. Paisley is probably the only one to have embraced heavy crime. His close colleagues wink and study the stars.'

'Oh, they know what he's up to, Geoffrey, they know.'

'Have a brandy, Marcus. I've got something rather special – the grape is grown in only one *domaine* near Cognac.'

'If you twist my arm.'

Villiers pours two balloons of the dark, rich fluid, sniffs, smiles sadly. They clink glasses.

'Here's to Lucy,' Villiers says.

'She has absconded. Broken bail. There's a warrant for her arrest.'

'Oh mercy. Do you know where she is?'

'Yes. Brigid told me. She went to see Lucy. She thought that Lucy was indirectly asking to see me, when I got back to England. So I went down to Wiltshire. I walked into the trap.'

'Oh heavens – you mean . . .'

'She seemed friendly – even glad to see me. She brewed me a cup of herbal tea. We chatted about ecology and the fate of the planet. I hadn't known her so civil for years. I noticed that she kept placing us in front of camp fires and groups of Tree People – a friend of hers, a chap called Ted, was recording our meeting on a camcorder.'

'Oh dear.'

'When I finally told her I was taking her back to London she ran away into the trees and was surrounded by a coven of hissing women.'

'Did you explain why?'

'I merely said that she would be late for the start of the school term.'

'Nothing about her breaking bail?'

'No.'

'How did you know that she had broken bail?'

'Oh, she told me! She insisted on disclosing every detail of her court appearance and her bail conditions. She'd set up the perfect headline: "BYRON CONCEALS DAUGHTER ON THE RUN."'

'You were damned if you notified the police and damned if you didn't?'

'Correct.'

'So you returned to London without Lucy?'

Marcus nods. 'I talked to the wise Louise – and followed her advice. My solicitor wrote to Jill's solicitor, reporting where I had last seen Lucy and expressing concern that she was not back at school. My solicitor also protested that Jill had kept me in the dark about Lucy's legal position.'

'Clever.'

'My dear Geoffrey, don't forget *A Clockwork Orange*. We can never be clever enough to outwit young anarchists who embrace crime for the joy of it.'

'Jill's attitude baffles me, Marcus. She's a decent woman and a loving mother.'

'No, she isn't.'

Villiers flinches at the fury in his former pupil's voice.

'Oh poor Lucy, poor child, and to think I'm her godfather – and what have I ever done for her? She loves you, Marcus, I'm sure she does. These pathetic crimes of hers are nothing but a cry for help!'

'Hm.'

The smooth lemon from the top of the fruit bowl is dancing restlessly in Villiers's thin, vibrating hand. He is still wearing scuffed suede shoes – surely not the same pair as when Marcus first arrived as an undergraduate? – as they amble through the front quadrangle beneath the celebrated gargoyles.

'Yes,' he sighs, 'I'm afraid my fate will be not unlike Anthony Blunt's.'

'You're hardly a Soviet spy. You are a rebel not a deceiver.'

'Anthony would have said the same on his own behalf. We used to meet. He knew more about Poussin and the Queen's pictures than I shall ever know about English law.'

'I doubt it.'

'Anthony and I never discussed painting or the criminal justice system – I suspect that neither of us wanted to penetrate the hollow space in which each of us resided in the other. Both of us spies, both of us pederasts, both of us men who could shut off our valves and achieve zero temperature when lying. I think we both knew that they always get you in the end.'

Villiers is cut off. A vast pantechnicon is reversing outside the College gate, insistently emitting a recorded warning: 'Attention! This vehicle is reversing. Attention! This—'

'It's lucky we don't believe in omens.' Villiers smiles faintly.

'I'd better hurry or I'll miss my train.'

The old criminologist embraces his favourite former pupil passionately. 'Dear, dear Marcus . . .'

Fifteen minutes later, as he sinks into the window seat of an empty first-class compartment, Marcus has a presentiment: he will never embrace Geoffrey Villiers again.

Through the window, out of the Oxfordshire mists drifting off the meandering Thames, Marcus sees a silent funeral procession approaching him, yet never drawing closer. There are three coffins, each bearing a name he knows.

# *Thirteen*

LUCY KNOWS WHAT TO do, how to handle it. So she keeps telling herself, curled in the back of Ellie's battered van, but she's biting her nails to the quick, butterflies in her stomach. Dan has told her what a night in a police cell is like – the ones at Eden Manor stink of urine and carbolic, you could get Aids off the blankets. But what she dreads most is the clang of the metal gate, the turn of the key, the not being able to get out.

Yeah, scared. She could present herself at Jimmy Haley-White's office in Charles Street, headquarters of the Youth Justice Team. Jimmy would give her a hot drink and a hug, then call in her mum and that lump of lard, Averling.

She can imagine them all huddled together in anxious conference. If they took her straight to Eden Manor police station, with maybe a couple of nice social workers, they might be able to resist overnight custody in a police cell. They couldn't just take her home because Averling was an 'officer of the court' and – he would explain pompously – 'under an absolute obligation' to surrender her.

Once the pigs have you . . . Yeah. She can imagine McIntyre and Jenkins setting one of those shithead WPCs to body-search her, taking away her dope and her Mogadons and the bottle of coarse rum. Leaving her body screaming. One of their 'short, sharp shocks'. Yeah.

They imprisoned Oscar Wilde. And all those South African writers she can't remember.

Ellie drops her off near Victoria coach terminal, lots of hugs, shouts, clenched fists. But now you're on your own. Friendship is seasonal, goodbye. Lucy's thin, wasted body trembles as she buys herself a disgusting wrapped vegetarian sandwich. 'Got any bagels?' No, of course not. She puts a call through to Marcus's chambers. Old Henderson answers creakily.

'Is Dad in court? He is? Till when? Right, tell him to meet me on the front steps of the Crown Court in two hours' time. No, not in his chambers. I said the front steps, didn't I? Pass the message, you old fart.'

Next she phones Joe O'Neill at the *Post*. She has his number in her head.

'It's Lucy Byron. I'm on the run. Want to earn yourself a hundred quid and lasting fame?'

'Where are you, Lucy?'

'You always were a wanker, Joe. Got any contacts at the *Sun* or the *Mirror*? No? You're lying! I'll get my pals to do you over! What? Why should I stop screaming? God, you're thick.'

She slams down the phone. She searches the cubicle – not a fucking phone book in sight! Too many thieves in this world. She spends twenty-five pence on extracting the *Sun* and *Mirror* numbers from Directory Enquiries, wrestling with a blunt pencil stub and the label from the veg sandwich.

'Don't talk so fast!' she screams at the computerised operator.

She dials 141, to mask her own number, then the *Sun*'s. Just in case some wanker . . . you never know. She keeps telling a whole succession of dumbheads that she wants ten thousand quid for the scoop; she is passed from one desk editor to the other, her coins disappearing down the machine. Lucy *who* did you say? For Christ's sake, B-Y-R-O-N, like the judge. Yeah. Yeah, I am.

Finally some bastard offers her a hundred.

'OK, I'll ring the *Mirror*. Bye.'

'Five hundred,' he says.

'Bye.'

'A thousand's the limit,' he says.

Ninety minutes later a wild-looking girl, her hair matted in Wiltshire mud, her clothes filthy and plastered in stickers, breaks cover, dodges through the traffic lugging a huge rucksack, and runs up the front steps of the Crown Court to embrace her beautifully turned-out father, observed by a reporter and two photographers.

'It's OK, it's OK,' she smilingly tells them. 'My Dad will protect me. He won't let them fling me inside just because I believe it's criminal to punish people who find a little happiness in ecstasy and crack.'

'Tell us where you've been, Lucy.'

'How long have you been on the run, Lucy?'

'Are you pregnant, Lucy?'

'Who's your boyfriend, Lucy?'

'Did your dad know where you were hiding, Lucy?'

'Yeah, yeah, he never let on to the pigs, why should he, he's my dad.'

Doug McIntyre and Cliff Jenkins have been waiting tactfully under the shadowed portals of the Crown Court – and Lucy knows it. In the endangered rainforests of Wilts you grow eyes in the back of your nut. One big arm firmly round his daughter, Judge Marcus Byron finally gestures to the two CID men from Eden Manor.

Marcus's face is a death mask, carved from black ebony.

Horror crushes Lucy's little features. She cries out. She struggles to free herself from her father's grip. 'Help me, help me!' she screams to passers-by. 'No, no! Daddy don't let them! No! No!'

An hour later, all down Fleet Street and out to Wapping and the Isle of Dogs, editors are resetting their pages. The great protection on such occasions is the inverted comma. The inverted comma is a legal hedge. The inverted comma means you aren't saying it's true, you're merely reporting an allegation. But the reading public strips inverted commas from headlines and captions like grey squirrels strip bark from trees.

'MY FATHER THE JUDGE HID ME' CLAIMS LUCY
'HE NEVER LET ON TO THE POLICE' BYRON'S DAUGHTER ALLEGES
JUDGE BYRON HANDS DISTRAUGHT DAUGHTER TO POLICE OUTSIDE CROWN COURT
GIRL SCREAMS AS FAMOUS FATHER HANDS HER OVER TO COPS

Stills from Ted's camcorder, showing Marcus and Lucy laughing and hugging among the Tree People of Wiltshire, have miraculously surfaced on the inside pages.

* * *

Charged with the attempted murder of BTP Inspector Herbert Knowles, Joseph Griffin has been remanded in custody to Downton. Darren Griffin, still fourteen, is in Secure Accommodation at Nelson House. Mark Griffin remains at large.

The remands had been ordered by a Bench chaired by Miss Swearwell, despite vigorous objections from Edgar Averling and an outright declaration – later withdrawn – from Jimmy Haley-White that no Secure Accommodation was available for Darren.

'Darren does not leave this court until you find Secure Accommodation within a hundred-mile radius,' Miss Swearwell had warned Jimmy. An hour later a bed miraculously surfaced at Nelson House, a mile down the road.

Back from the Pyrenees, a bronzed Patrick Berry is chairing the Bench today. Ashen-pale, skinheaded, tattooed, Joseph has been vanned in from Downton. Darren's freckled face still wears its permanent smirk; he sits slouched, daring the world to hate him. Providing the Griffin lads with suitable pillows is costing the public £7,000 a week.

The issue before the court is jurisdiction.

Each boy is separately represented – an indication to Patrick of Averling's probable tactics on behalf of Darren. Joseph's solicitor has little room for manoeuvre: attempted murder must go up to the Crown Court.

Averling duly springs his anticipated coup. In the jargon, he offers to 'vacate a trial date' – in plain language Darren will plead guilty to a lesser charge, grievous bodily harm, here and now if the Youth Court will accept jurisdiction.

'Sir, my client's case is that Darren Griffin did not attempt murder, though his Dark Shadow may have done so.'

'His what?' Patrick asks.

'Darren maintains that his Dark Shadow surfaces at certain moments and takes control of his actions. Afterwards, Darren can remember nothing about this sinister *alter ego*.'

'He used the phrase *alter ego*?'

'No, sir, words to that effect.'

'Latin is not the language of this court, Mr Averling. It's Greek to us.'

Averling insists that Darren's age at the moment of this plea, still a month short of fifteen, determines his sentence. Since his age rules out custody, the Youth Court cannot logically decline jurisdiction on account of its limited sentencing powers.

Patrick Berry asks his wife for a professional opinion. She requests time to consult further and wider. Joseph is vanned away, remanded back to Downton, while Darren kicks up hell in the cells downstairs during an hour's tortuous legal arguments.

Finally Patrick delivers the Bench's ruling:

'We have here a charge of conspiracy to assault Mr Knowles with the aim of taking his life. At least three Griffin boys may have been involved. Only when the Crown Court has heard the full case can the appropriate verdict for each of the participants be determined. This court cannot determine Darren's role in the event without hearing the case for the other defendants. Jurisdiction is therefore declined in the case of Darren Griffin.'

Two days later the legal world is shaken by another Averling 'coup'. Appealing against Berry's committal of Darren to the Crown Court, he claims 'prejudice': Patrick Berry is related by marriage to the victim, Herbert Knowles. To be precise, both men are married to sisters.

Sitting in chambers, Judge Sir Henry Harsent refers the case of Darren Griffin back for a rehearing by a new Bench.

It duly comes before Lady Harsent. Nick Paisley has intervened to downgrade the charge against Darren from attempted murder to grievous bodily harm.

Supported by the sleeping Mr Dickenson, Lady Harsent accepts jurisdiction in view of Darren's age, despite a minority vote by Rodney Parker.

'Pleas may be entered today,' Averling informs the court.

Sick at heart, Wendy reads out the reduced charge to Darren.

'Do you plead Guilty or Not Guilty?'

'Gty.'

'Guilty?'

'Yeah.'

Rat Boy is three days short of fifteen. Derek Jardine has sent an assistant to check the Register of Births in St Catherine's House – but Darren's stated date of birth is correct.

For the prosecution, Derek Jardine outlines the horrendous nature of the attack on the innocent Herbert Knowles in the Broadway pedestrian underpass. Jardine passes photographs of Knowles's injuries to the Bench.

'Darren's plea of guilt, madam, is a plea of guilt to having committed these injuries.'

The pre-sentence report prepared by Jimmy Haley-White's

Youth Justice Team stresses the extraordinary improvement in Darren's 'attitude'. This PSR has been prepared at forty-eight hours' notice instead of the usual four weeks. In her long experience, Wendy has never before seen a PSR presented on the same day as a Guilty plea is entered.

Jimmy addresses the Bench with grace and courtesy, his dreadlocks bonded by a broad mujaheddin bandanna.

'Darren, madam, has recently begun to confront his own lack of self-esteem. He has shown real willingness to return to school and to resume his long-ago-abandoned education. Darren is for the first time beginning to accept personal responsibility for his own actions within the community. He enormously regrets what he has done.'

No mention is made of Darren's Dark Shadow.

Lady H. beams at Darren. Rodney Parker forces her to ask whether a school willing to have Darren has been found.

'We are still pursuing that, madam,' Jimmy replies.

Lady H. nods indulgently.

Wendy stares fixedly at her papers. She knows what's coming from Edgar Averling – a long argument insisting that Darren, as the youngest of the three Griffin boys, acted under their influence, indeed under duress, and was not responsible for Mr Knowles's 'more deplorable injuries' – though some of these may have been inflicted by Dark Shadow.

Wendy seethes in her chair. Of course this was precisely why Patrick had insisted that Darren should be sentenced by the Crown Court, after the full case was heard. The Youth Court was being asked to absolve Darren without hearing the full facts, arguments and cross-examinations.

Poor Herb. He is still off work, sick. Marcia fears he will never fully recover. He has emerged from hospital with a dreadful speech impediment.

Derek Jardine is up. 'Madam, I submit that this is basically a situation for a Newton Hearing.'

'Why?' snaps Lady H.

'Madam, where several people are charged with the same offence, and one pleads guilty, but then pleads in mitigation lack of full involvement or responsibility, only a Newton Hearing can resolve his degree of responsibility.'

'That is correct, madam,' Wendy says.

Lady Harsent has the awful Rodney Parker on one side of her

and old Mr Dickenson, half asleep, on the other. There will be no Newton Hearing.

'You are an extremely fortunate young man,' Lady H. tells Darren as he stands before her for sentence. 'We are giving you a Supervision Order to last eighteen months. Now make sure you cooperate with your social workers, Darren.'

'Yeah.'

Deputy Senior Clerk Wendy Berry is seized by a rage so all-consuming that her copy of Archbold flies across the court and strikes Lady H. full in the face, knocking her clean out of her chair. The beehive wig lies on the floor beside its bald *prima donna*. Oddly, no one else in the court notices this attack – not even Lady H., who serenely instructs the list-caller to bring in the next naughty boy.

Bitter internal correspondence ensues. Patrick takes the case to the Chairman of the Youth Panel, to the Magistrates' Courts Committee and to the Magistrates' Association. Lady Harsent hits back:

> It is highly regrettable that Mr Berry did not declare his interest in advance. We do not sit when a relative is involved. A more experienced magistrate would have known that.

Marcus leaks the correspondence to Brigid Kyle, although their relationship has cooled since she came back from Spain and visited Lucy in Wiltshire – he does not know why and she won't say. But she remains loyal to his cause:

> The battle for the chairmanship of the new Magistrates' Courts Committee is one of the bitterest ever to have hit the criminal justice system. Two strong personalities are in contention but far more is at stake: the fate of justice itself. The campaign against Patrick Berry is in essence the same campaign as the one against Marcus Byron.

Lucy is living at home again. She's back at school. After a night in the cells she has been granted bail, on the same conditions as before, by Lady Harsent, who fined her £50 for a breach of bail.

On the Sunday after her return, Daniel Richardson takes a bus to an afternoon jazz gig. A talented saxophonist, with a keen interest in music theory, he boards the bus, tells the conductor his destination, and is asked for thirty pence, the half-fare. The conductor has mistaken him for fourteen. Daniel believes in keeping out of trouble but there are limits. Paying sixty pence if you can get away with thirty is definitely one of them. A few moments later a bus inspector surfaces beside him. Daniel claims he's only fourteen. The inspector asks him his date of birth, his name and address. Out of habit, he falsifies all three. The inspector calls the police. They know Daniel and search him for drugs. They find none but that – as Jenkins puts it – is 'provisional'.

Daniel Richardson finds himself in the cosy interrogation room of Eden Manor police station he knows only too well. Goodbye, jazz gig.

Cliff Jenkins is not interested in an unpaid bus fare of thirty pence, but he is seriously interested in pressuring Daniel to inform.

'What do you want out of life, Dan? You're bright, aren't you? You want GCSEs, A levels, a college degree, a good job, a house of your own, a car. You want to make something out of your life, don't you?'

Daniel says he'll think about it.

Jenkins advises him to think about it now.

Daniel says he wants to talk to a lawyer, specifically to Edgar Averling. 'I have a right to telephone him,' he murmurs, eyes lowered, afraid of the sudden slap which leaves no mark, this Welshman's trade mark.

'No, you haven't, son. I'm not arresting you, am I? I'm not charging you with anything, am I? It's just a chat.'

'Yer 'oldin' me.'

'That's it, I'm holding you. Dan, did you ever hear of a bloke called Nick Paisley?'

Daniel nods. 'He's Lucy's mum's bloke.'

'Go on, son.'

Daniel shrugs. 'I met him once at Lucy's place.'

'You take drugs to Paisley, don't you? You're Paul's carrier, aren't you? And Paul gets them from Livingstone Lord, doesn't he?'

Daniel has nothing to say.

Lucy walks into the police station and asks to speak to 'Mr Jenkins'. The word has reached her through Trish Richardson: 'Dan's been done.' In these clans and gangs the bush telegraph works fast.

'And how can I help you, young lady?' The duty officer studies her fast-masticating jaw and firefly eyes. Lucy is working on a hunch but has the confidence to bluff – she's not her father's daughter for nothing.

'Yeah, it's about Dan,' she says. 'I hear Jenkins wants to turn a thirty-pee bus fare into some narking. I've put a call through to Mr Averling.'

She hasn't, but the duty officer disappears down the corridor. Dan surfaces almost immediately and slopes straight past her and out of Eden Manor police station, clutching his saxophone. There's shame in being rescued by a cunt. They amble down the High Street together, Dan and his girl, who has failed all her GCSEs in every subject except English. Mrs Nearcliffe, Headmistress of St Hilda's, has written to Jill to say that no girl from St Hilda's had ever performed so badly. She would keep Lucy in the school only 'on sufferance', conditional on a successful retake of the GCSEs.

Yeah.

'The Galloways are going out Monday night,' Lucy says.

'I thought you wasn't baby-sitting for them no more. After Amos . . .'

'I'm not. They rely on that drip Nigel Thompson.'

'Who's that, then?'

'Lives across the square. Goes to Chaucer School. A swot.'

'Paul and Amos always kill a Chaucer boy if they see one.'

'Anyway, the Galloways are going out to the theah-tar. Big deal. I heard Susan Galloway mention it to my mum.'

He tucks his spare, non-saxophone arm round her slender waist and squeezes. 'I missed that fuckin' gig.'

'That Susan Galloway's a bitch. She gave evidence against Amos, didn't she?'

'Amos cut her. He shouldn't have done that.'

'Yeah. The bitch. And that wanker Simon Galloway got you and Paul into trouble, remember?'

'Nah.'

'You know what I reckon, Dan? One day I came home and found things had been tampered with, things in my room, stuff and the like. My camcorder had definitely been moved. I reckon that bitch Susan Galloway did it.'

'Nah.'

'Or she let somebody into the house.'

'Nah.'

'Nick told my mum he doesn't trust Susan Galloway. He thinks Patrick Berry has been inside the house.'

'What, the beak?'

'Yeah. He's married to my Auntie Wendy, isn't he? It figures, doesn't it?'

'You reckon?'

'Yes, Dan, I do reckon. Anyway, I don't like the way Simon Galloway looks at me. As if I was dirt. It's him who won't let me baby-sit Tom, I know it is. I reckon he's a racist.'

'Yeah?'

'Hey, Dan, the Galloways are leaving for the theah-tar at six-fifteen Monday and taking the train. They'll be loaded. You could tell Paul.'

'Nah.'

'Yes, Dan. They'll be loaded with night-out-on-the-town dosh and credit cards. Simon gave her a new Rolex watch, too – out of the insurance, I bet.'

'Nah.'

'You can skip it, Dan. Tell Paul I'll meet him on the station platform at six. Eastbound, mind – he's thick, that big brother of yours.'

'You got enough trouble already. Crown Court stuff.'

'You think? My dad sent two blokes inside yesterday. I heard Nick say to my mum he can't understand why they haven't given "bloody Marcus" the boot yet.'

'What's that got to do with doin' the Galloways?'

'Plenty. Hey, Dan, why don't we TDA Simon Galloway's BMW to Knightsbridge and cut up Teresa Kent?'

'You're kiddin'.'

'I caught her in bed with my dad. Now he's bonking her lookalike sister. Jimmy told me – well, I heard him talking about it to Mum.'

'He gets around, your dad.'

'I wrote to Ms Kent asking for an interview. I got a shitheaded answer from her secretary. It's time someone spoiled that complexion of hers.'

Daniel is not responsive. Cutting up famous actresses is beyond his normal line of business. He'd like to play the sax professionally, in pubs and Covent Garden clubs. He'd like to get away from Eden Manor for ever. Returning home, he decides he may not say anything to Paul about the Galloways. Lucy's in too much trouble already.

But, if he doesn't, Lucy will fly off the handle again, and Paul, if he finds out that Dan has failed to report a likely job, will dish out another beating.

A white-helmeted cyclist, dressed in tight Lycra shorts and a yellow vest, swings into the forecourt of the King's Arms, a quiet pub situated on a B road near the village of Tyndale in Surrey.

Beneath the gleaming helmet the cyclist's broad features are strikingly black. Patrons leaving the pub register a surprise which, in some cases, spills over into faintly indignant suspicion. No black has been seen round here since an eighteenth-century squire of Tyndale fell in with the fashion and purchased a slave boy from the Gold Coast, dressing him in a wig and silk breeches. Miraculously the boy had soon mastered not only English but also Latin.

Or is it something else which arrests the attention of the locals leaving the King's Arms? Something specific about that face? And the bicycle! The newspapers have been full of Judge Marcus Byron's highly publicised 1,400-mile bike ride to the Pyrenees. A delegation from Justice for Victims had welcomed the judge and his brother-in-law like returning war heroes outside the Royal Courts of Justice in the Strand.

And then came that business about his daughter, front-page photos of the hysterical girl kicking and screaming as her father handed her over to the police. Every columnist in every newspaper, tabloid and broadsheet, had posed the question: what should a parent do? what would you do? Most of the writers reached the same conclusion: keep her out of trouble, teach her right and wrong, instil Christian values in the young.

Marcus does not venture into the King's Arms. He slakes his thirst from a plastic water bottle which clips on to the bike. Presently a black Fiat Punto pulls in and parks. Marcus leans through the driver's open window:

'Were you followed?'

The green eyes flash. 'We gave them the slip south of Staines.'

'So you *were* followed?'

'Not a thing. Isn't that right, Angela?'

Huge in the front passenger seat, Angela Loftus is finishing off a ham roll. Her mouth full, she flutters a friendly hand at Marcus.

'Unfasten this damned seat belt for me, Heather.'

Marcus helps her out of the car. She doesn't look well, her breathing is even more laboured than usual, and she leans on his arm for a moment to steady herself.

'Shorts like that, Marcus, offend a gel's modesty.'

'A gel isn't wearing them. Walk by the river?'

'You know how I hate walking,' Angela says. 'But you always insist so I brought my shoes.'

'We could head east along the towpath towards Amberly, or west towards Chilton.'

'There are some swans' nests near Chilton,' Heather says. 'They can be bad-tempered during the breeding season.'

Marcus appears to be examining his bike with a fatherly eye.

'Really? We didn't see many swans in the East End.' He knows this isn't the breeding season. 'What do you think, Angela?'

'It's easier under foot towards Amberly,' Heather says.

'I'm in your hands, your Honour,' Angela says. 'Now what about all these documents I've brought you? We can't leave this bulging briefcase in the car.'

Marcus takes the case. 'I'll carry it. Amberly it is, then.' He wheels his bike along the towpath, Angela moving in stately fashion at his side, her big cheeks gleaming like Worcester apples, flushed by the country air and all this exertion. Heather follows a few yards behind, lithe and graceful in jeans, her honey-blonde hair falling free to her shoulders. A long chiffon scarf is wound round her slender neck.

'Nice of you to waste your Saturday on me, Marcus,' Angela puffs.

'Nonsense. You're my girl.'

'I am not! And don't slap my behind, you know I can't abide it. Does he slap your behind, Heather?'

No answer. Marcus's pearly teeth flash. He adores Angela, she's a brick.

'So Jill suspended you, Angela?'

'I was frog-marched out of Probation House. They let me take my coat and umbrella, very decent. Luckily I'd already photocopied the documents and had them out of the building.'

'Is that why she suspended you?'

'Oh no, she didn't know anything about that.'

'What had you done then?'

'I had a bit of a dust-up with Jill about Leela's PSR on

the Liz Hargreaves case – which your Honour may remember.'

'His Honour does.'

'That Sandra Golding woman should be run over by a drunken single mother!

'Angela!'

'Sorry. The countryside makes me bad-tempered. Anyway, we had words, Jill and I. I spoke out of rank. I may have been indiscreet, actually.'

The pain of memory has brought Angela to a halt.

'What did you actually say to Jill?'

'I was a damned fool, Marcus. I can't bring myself to utter what I said.'

'OK. But what did you say?'

'Hm. Stuff about Lucy. I may have called Nick Paisley "the drug baron", it's all rather confused in my memory.'

They are progressing at snail's pace. Heather now walks ahead of them. Marcus strives to keep his eyes off her.

'What's the position with your disciplinary proceedings?' he asks.

'I haven't heard a damn thing! I've made a storm of phone calls but it's always "we'll call you back".'

'But what about the Association – your union?'

'They're "extremely concerned" and "looking into it". Ha! They'd have been fast off the mark if I'd been kept waiting five minutes at the prison gate when visiting an erring client! You bet! They know who their wars are with, that lot!'

'So I've lost my Deep Throat within the empire of Ms Hull?'

'You know I've never been happy with your flippant sexism, Marcus.'

'I prefer misses to ms's. You're a miss, Angela, and your staff know it.'

'I no longer have a staff.'

'Heather tells me that a muted rebuke from your trombone throat could ruin her week.'

Angela guffaws then drops her voice. 'Splendid gel. Jill took her from me before taking me as well. The best assistant I ever had. She knows the meaning of loyalty.'

'Aha. But she may not be out of earshot.'

Angela glances at her tall black companion mischievously.

'I daresay you've been seeing more of Heather lately than I have.'

'I've been abroad on my bike.'

'Oh, come off it, Marcus, everyone knows about your dangerous appetite for a bit on the side.'

'Me? A bit?'

Angela chortles, poking Marcus in the ribs. 'Who's the most beautiful woman in the criminal justice system?' she teases.

'My wife.'

'Jolly well spoken, Marcus. And when did you last take your wife a fuchsia?'

Marcus stops dead in his tracks. 'Who told you that?'

'Heather has never kept anything from me. Shall we change the subject?' she chuckles. 'Down to business. You haven't brought me all the way here merely to reward me with a cream tea in Amberly – though I'm not discouraging you.'

'It's a promise,' Marcus says. 'If they'll let me in.'

Spying a comfy bench, relatively free of bird shit, Angela promptly sits down. It creaks, groans, but holds up. Heather has rejoined them.

'Anyway, to business. I followed your instructions and—'

'Ah, swans,' Marcus cuts in. 'They don't look bad-tempered, Heather.'

She flashes him a gorgeous smile. 'Maybe the Amberly swans are nicer than the Chilton swans. If it's all the same to you two, I'll take a walk up the river while you conspire. I'm only Angela's chauffeuse when it comes down to it.'

'Don't do anything I wouldn't do,' Angela calls after her. 'Now, Marcus, let's look at this stuff. How's Lucy, by the way?'

'She's out on bail again.'

Quick to spot that he has no more to say on that subject, Angela snaps open the briefcase, breathing heavily, eyes gleaming. She does not seem to notice that Heather is in fact heading down-river, back towards the King's Arms.

'I followed your instructions and dug deep into Jill Hull's data base after office hours – no fun at all for a lady of nervous disposition – until I unearthed the true figures on reoffending. They're all here.' She slaps a file neatly tied in red ribbon. 'One thing is clear: Jill has been suppressing the real statistics.'

'She runs two data bases – the real one and the propaganda?'

'Clever boy. How many of the Probation Service's clients breach their orders while on probation? You know the official figure – his Honour always knows. But what is a "breach", hm? Hm? It isn't a "breach" until *they* decide to bring it back to court . . .'

'And if they bring too many cases back to court it begins to look to evil-minded judges and magistrates as if Probation is a less effective sentence than the PS claims?'

'Oh dear, it's like risking life and limb to offer the scriptures to the Almighty.'

'Dear Angela, the Almighty may still be in need of the real numbers. He may need the assistance of angels.'

Angela is beaming.

'Tell me, Angela: is Jill a law unto herself or do other devils also dance?'

Angela looks shocked. 'I have only worked under one person whose integrity I have reason to doubt. And here are the minutes of an off-the-record briefing by Jill to a meeting of senior staff. She actually came out in support of the potty-pinko Boroughs which are still refusing to disclose previous convictions to the courts. Anyone who has served a sentence, Jill announced, has discharged his debt to society. He couldn't be expected to pay it again and again, every time he stumbled into a new crime, could he?'

'I thought they'd dropped that nonsense.'

'*They* never drop anything, Marcus.'

'I suppose Jill regards herself as sincere.'

'Oh, very! She couldn't function otherwise. But what is crime to these do-gooders if not salaries? Crime means jobs. It means vociferous trade unions defending those jobs with every argument, and every lie, they can think up.'

'Angela, don't forget I am one of the few judges in this country who belongs to a trade union. I believe in unions. It's time *your* union did more for you.'

'You're such a tremendously progressive fellow, Marcus.'

'What we need in the Probation Service is more people with experience of the world – and fewer degrees or diplomas in Social Compassion.'

'You can say that again! Jill and her ilk despise policemen and prison officers as reactionary know-nothings. They are working class. Some of them are ex-soldiers and ex-policemen, the wrong types altogether.'

'Do you have any financial documents in here?'

'Jill's domain, public relations, nominally runs on a modest budget. But the real propaganda budget is concealed behind a plethora of apparently independent "voluntary agencies".'

'It's all in this briefcase?'

'All here. And now "wonderful Angela" is feeling knackered. She'll chew her nails and take a short nap while you and Heather decide what shape the world will be tomorrow.'

'We must fight your suspension, Angela.'

'Ha! We're all in it, we Lemons. Look what happened to Lionel Lacey! And you're next, make no mistake!'

Heather is coming back. 'Tired, Angela?' she calls.

'Tramping through the hateful countryside in the company of a lunatic judge in obscene Lycra shorts isn't my thing. You two take a walk while I take a snooze. But I'm holding you to that cream tea, Marcus.'

Rapidly he transfers the documents from Angela's briefcase to his own backpack. Angela watches bemused and faintly miffed – men never trust a female.

'Snooze well, then, Angela.'

'You can leave your bike with me.'

'We never part company.'

Heather takes his bike-free arm as they walk away, up-river. Twenty yards on, he glances back: Angela's eyes are already closed. Her ample bosom has begun to rise and fall with the added emphasis of sleep. A moment later Angela Loftus, daughter of the late Rt Reverend Charles Loftus, is lost to sight.

'Poor Angela,' Heather says. 'Her world has collapsed.'

'That's a nice scarf. Who gave it to you? Jimmy?'

A gentleman in shabbily formal attire, haggard and wild-eyed, blasts his old Rover into the forecourt of the King's Arms on smoking tyres, circles Heather Stuart's Fiat Punto like a dog sniffing a leg-up, enters the saloon bar and begins to examine each and every female customer with such intensity that their male companions are soon rocking on their feet and easing their shoulders. The stranger darts towards the publican behind the bar. 'I'm looking for a woman.'

The visitor has a thin, reedy voice. The accent is educated, posh even, but the publican knows that maniacs come in varying boxes.

'Any woman, sir, or a particular woman?'

'She's . . . she's from London. The black Fiat Punto outside is hers.'

'Any description, sir?'

'She's . . . young. Blonde hair. Extremely . . . she's young. She may be with a black chap wearing bicycling shorts.'

The publican laughs. 'It's caught on, has it?'

'What?'

'All imitating Judge Byron, are they? Up and away over the mountains. Best way to get rid of them, if you ask me.'

The visitor leans across the bar, his maddened eyes blazing 1,000 watts.

'You'd recognise Judge Byron? Has he been in here today?'

'No, sir. I haven't seen Paul Robeson or Muhammad Ali either.'

Outside, in the car park, Lionel Lacey gloomily scrutinises the black Fiat Punto. He peers inside. An ordnance-survey map is spread out on the back seat. An 'X' appears to have been inked in, by the river, towards the village of Amberly. The map is displayed in a prominent manner.

The voice had indeed said Amberly. The voice on the telephone. She – that slut – had called him only two hours ago, inviting him to meet Byron and herself at the King's Arms, Tyndale. Marcus and she wanted to explain, she said – to 'explain everything'.

'Ha! You ruin a man, destroy his life, then you "explain everything"!'

'I know how you feel, Mr Lacey. Marcus and I want to talk to you.'

'Are you the . . . the woman who—'

'My car is a black Fiat Punto,' she said. 'If you don't find us in the King's Arms, we'll be on the towpath, returning from Amberly. Yes, Amberly. But look at the spread-out map in the back of my car, just in case we have a change of route.'

'I want to speak to Byron,' he declared. 'Now.'

'Marcus has already left for Tyndale by bike,' she said. Then she hung up.

Lacey takes note that he cannot drive down the towpath towards Amberly. For one thing, a prominent notice says so. For another, a concrete bollard blocks entry to vehicles. The nation's Director of Public Prosecutions does not break the law.

Lionel Lacey believes that he is still the DPP. They will give him back his office tomorrow – if only he can prove that he was framed. For that he needs a signed confession from the slut herself. If she doesn't sign, if she imagines she can play fast and loose with him a second time, he will kill her. Then resume as DPP on Monday. It's all perfectly simple.

The publican's daughter, emerging from the rear of the King's Arms to empty the kitchen swill, observes a remarkable sight. A gentleman in a crumpled suit is wrestling with one of the bollards at the entrance to the Amberly towpath.

At that moment her boyfriend roars into the yard on his Norton 500 under a huge helmet. They engage in one of these disgusting public embraces the young go in for nowadays.

'Oh Ron,' she moans.

Lionel Lacey glowers at the bollard, then at the kissing couple, then at the bollard, striving to collect his scattered thoughts: a double first in Mods & Greats (not to be confused with Mods and Rockers) at Oxford, where he first met the remarkable East End boy, M. Byron, helps. Yes, helps: in Latin your verb can hide in the undergrowth before surfacing at the end of the sentence. Both the Latin and the Greek of the situation are crystal-clear to Lionel Lacey: he is the victim of a massive conspiracy.

Marcus and Heather have paused to admire the mallards.

'Marcus, I hate to say this but I don't hold out much hope for Angela.'

'So long as Jill and Paisley retain their power.'

'Angela and I believe the only way to get the dirt on Paisley is to penetrate 23 Oundle Square then really do it over.'

Marcus is tapping out his pipe. 'My daughter lives at 23 Oundle Square.'

'Can't you get her out, Marcus?'

'Ha! I've tried for years. Two custody battles in the High Court. Fathers don't stand a chance, you know.'

She presses his hand. 'Poor Marcus. So many enemies. I have one too.'

'Lionel Lacey? Wendy told me about his phone call. I've had a few myself. Don't worry about Lionel, he's harmless.'

'They say he's gone mad since his dismissal. I mean right off his rocker.'

'Life must be very difficult for Lionel.'

A swan lifts suddenly from the bankside rushes and swoops low over the water, as if hurrying to catch the post. Observing this season's ducklings doing their thing in their mother's wake, Marcus remembers the colour-in picture books Uncle Jeremiah used to bring him in the days before he'd ever seen a duck. His mum wouldn't let the smaller kids anywhere near the Thames.

Marcus wants to make love to Heather, here and now, observed only by the ducks.

'Nice pair of crested mallards there,' he comments. 'What do you have in mind for Nick Paisley?'

'Get into No. 23 and bug his phone for a start.'

'Two months ago I put a pair of businessmen inside for bugging a rival company's phone system.'

'Paisley's handling Class A drugs in large quantities. You know that – but to get the evidence we need access to the house.'

'So?'

'Patrick Berry used to be an expert burglar, didn't he?'

'He has retired. I told him he'd never marry my sister if he didn't.'

'There may be another way.'

'Yeah?'

'Doug McIntyre told me that Susan Galloway has gone back to work part-time for Jill Hull.'

'Who's Susan Galloway?'

'You don't know her?'

'Why should I know her?'

'Jill gives her the keys to the house. The Galloway woman could let someone in – preferably an electronics expert like Patrick Berry.'

'Why should she do that?'

'Oh God,' Heather says suddenly. 'Marcus, I've got the most dreadful period I've ever suffered and I've left my tampons in the car. I need to use the King's Arms loo in a hurry. Can I take your bike?'

Rapidly he lowers the saddle. 'Go. And lock it!' he shouts after her. 'The combination is 1950, the year of my birth.'

'OK!' she calls, speeding away, her sensitive area lifted from the saddle, her chiffon scarf streaming behind her. The fate of the dancer Isadora Duncan floats through his consciousness – her scarf had caught in the wheels of her car while travelling at speed.

He sits down, lights his Sherlock Holmes pipe and checks his watch. Perhaps he should amble back to Angela. No, have a smoke first. The sun is warm on his back and the slow-running river beguiling. He smiles at the passing ducks. He wishes Lucy was here to share the idyll.

Oh Lucy, Lucy . . .

Lionel Lacey has decided that he will wait for Marcus and the slut to return to the King's Arms. Then he has decided that he cannot wait. He is stumbling in crazed circles of indecision when a female figure swings into the carpark, a young woman with blonde hair and a long, flowing chiffon scarf, riding a large mountain bike. She circles him provocatively.

'Hi, Lionel!'

Lionel! Such impudence! That's her! The slut from the Riverview Club! Byron's whore! He recognises her voice, too.

She smiles. 'Marcus is expecting you.'

His eyes are at 1000 watts. He remembers her in a leotard, gracefully wrestling with chrome levers and pulleys. He stumbles forward to grab at her but she glides away on her purring wheels.

'Follow me,' she calls, still smiling. 'Come on, then, it's not far.'

And then she is gone, up the towpath towards Amberly.

The kissing couple – the lad with the Norton 500, Ron, and the publican's daughter – have stopped kissing to listen to the dialogue between the posh people.

Lionel Lacey scampers across to them – to Ron.

'Excuse me, young man, excuse me, it's imperative that you give me a lift along the towpath. I can't get my car past the bollard.'

The couple look him over. A nutter.

'I'm trying to commit a crime,' Lacey says. 'I mean – to prevent one. It's . . . desperately urgent.' On an inspiration he fishes out of his pocket a tatty old laminated Home Office pass issued to regular, top-level visitors to C3. Ron peers at it.

'You will be absolutely in the clear, young man, as far as any legal action is concerned.'

Should he offer the young fellow money? Probably not. Anyway, they have illegally stopped his salary cheques as DPP – he has written to the Ombudsman about it, and the Queen.

'How far do you want to go, mate?'

Lionel Lacey doesn't feel 'mate' appropriately applies to himself, just as he becomes distempered when young people say 'Cheers!' to him instead of 'Thank you' or 'Goodbye'.

'It might be as far as Amberly, it might be round the next bend.'

'Round the bend?' Ron laughs loudly. 'Did they let you out of a padded cell?' Then he relents. 'Hop on then.' He guns the engine. 'But don't blame me if you're done for no helmet.'

The girl trots back into the still-crowded saloon bar.

'Hey, Dad, Ron's just been abducted by some old fart from the Home Guard.'

'There she is!' Lionel Lacey yells in the motorcycle lad's ear. 'Stop!'

Lacey climbs off the pillion of the Norton, or tumbles off, and stumbles towards a bench where the beautiful young woman is sitting with the mountain bike and a very fat lady.

The motorcycle engine chugs gently. Something's up with this lot. The young woman has stood up, smiling, and taken a pace or two towards the nutter from the Home Guard.

'Ah,' the man gasps, wild-eyed. 'Ah! You! At last! Now you will confess!'

'Angela,' the young lady says serenely, 'may I introduce you to Marcus's good friend, Mr Lionel Lacey.'

But Lionel Lacey ignores the fat woman. He's not interested in fat women, never has been.

'Where's Byron? Where is he?'

'Oh, he's gone for a walk up the river.' Heather dips her long lashes. 'Was he expecting you, Lionel?'

'Was he . . . was he . . . What! Bitch!'

Ron can't believe it – the beautiful young bird has come right up to the nutter and is practically rubbing herself against him.

'Bitch! Slut!' Lionel Lacey reaches out to grab Heather Stuart, but she easily eludes him. Angela screams.

Ron watches, fascinated. He knows he should intervene, do the gallant bit, but the young lady is still smiling, as if it's all a game and she doesn't even accord Ron a glance. He turns his Norton and guns away in disgust. Toffs!

Unable to catch hold of Heather, or her flowing chiffon scarf, Lionel Lacey grabs Angela instead. She screams again, wriggles tremulously, tries to rise from her bench and her crossword puzzle, can't, topples sideways.

'Unhand me, sir!'

Lacey is shaking the fat lady violently. 'Make the slut confess! It was all a plot!'

Angela's blood pressure is bursting the airbag. Her face has turned crimson, sweat is pouring from her, her heart flutters madly, jerks, thumps . . .

Heather's greenish cat's eyes swivel beneath their long lashes as Angela rolls off the bench on to the footpath.

Marcus's broad back straightens. Is that a motorbike he hears in the distance, approaching from Tyndale? Some bloody fool riding along the towpath?

The distant engine abruptly cuts to a low growl. Marcus studies his watch. Give Heather another ten minutes . . . Is that the cry of a duck or a swan? It comes again.

He hears the motorcycle accelerating away, in the opposite direction, back towards Tyndale.

Marcus makes to mount his bike then realises that he has broken the golden rule and parted company with it. He begins to walk fast, then breaks into a run. The screaming draws closer – and it's human. Marcus rounds the last bend.

A man is attacking Heather. He has her by her long scarf, he's trying to strangle her. The bench is empty. Angela is slumped on the towpath, hugely sprawled in the dirt, all 196 pounds of her, the victim – at first sight – of a heart attack. *The Times* lies open at the crossword page beside her gnawed fingernails.

Marcus throws off Heather's assailant with a single motion of his shoulders. His breath rasping in his lungs, Lionel Lacey stares at him, stricken and demented, saliva drooling down his chin, half his flies undone.

'Ah, Byron,' he shouts, 'ah!'

'Who brought you here, Lionel?'

'She did! Your slut! Your whore! Make her confess!'

Heather is bending low over Angela and cradling her head. 'Oh God,' she moans, 'oh God.' Marcus gently pulls her off, stretches Angela out, kneels and presses his lips to hers in the kiss of life. It is the first kiss Angela Loftus has had from a man, and the last.

# *Fourteen*

TOWPATH MYSTERY DEATH
WOMAN FOUND DEAD BY SURREY TOWPATH WITH BYRON, LACEY
CONTROVERSIAL JUDGE AND DISGRACED EX-DPP QUESTIONED BY POLICE
RENT-A-BOY LACEY AND BYRON HOLD KEY TO MYSTERY DEATH
CONTROVERSIAL JUDGE WHO GOT ON HIS BIKE ONCE TOO OFTEN
PLEA OF NOT GUILTY, YOUR HONOUR?
NEW SCANDAL SEEN AS FURTHER BLOW TO LEMONS
CONTROVERSIAL JUDGE SUMMONED BY LORD CHIEF JUSTICE
BLACK JUDGE MAY BE SUSPENDED PENDING DAUGHTER'S TRIAL

On the Monday morning, less than twenty-four hours after the 'TOWPATH SCANDAL', an anonymous document surfaces in Brigid Kyle's fax machine. A few rapid inquiries confirm that the same text has already landed on the news and features desks of every other major media outlet.

The *Sentinel*'s lawyers confirm Brigid's guess: the document is a flagrant violation of the *sub judice* rules. Brigid remembers something Marcus had said over a paella and a bottle of Rioja during their happy weekend in the Pyrenees. 'In the media world, contrary to the physical laws of the universe, fire is born out of smoke.'

But Marcus spending his Saturdays in the company of Heather Stuart is both fire and smoke to Brigid. So Lucy had not been lying to her in Wiltshire. Brigid re-reads the document.

> Well-placed sources have confirmed that Marcus Byron met Lionel Lacey only an hour before the DPP's arrest for paedophile sex in a Soho club. Now it transpires that Byron, who has been resisting calls for his resignation as a Crown Court judge, and whose daughter faces serious charges, has been secretly maintaining contact with the disgraced Lacey. According to the same sources, a young female probation officer who knows both men was the intended target of Lacey's vengeance on the Surrey towpath.
>
> The dead woman, Angela Loftus, was recently suspended by the Probation Service for leaking confidential documents to Judge Byron. Like Byron and Lacey, Miss Loftus is believed to have been a Lemon. It is understood that more documents were handed to Judge Byron yesterday, shortly before Ms Loftus met her death.
>
> When will this scandalous conspiracy be brought to justice? Not only the prosecuting authorities, but also Byron's close chum Max Venables, MP, must face one fact: Judge Marcus Byron is a liability and a disgrace to the criminal justice system.

Simon and Susie Galloway are on their way to the theatre. They prefer to take the train from Century Park Station into the centre of town: no rush-hour traffic, no parking problems. Simon is happy. During the lunch hour he has drawn a marker pen round a job advertisement in *The Times*. Every detail is up his street – the ad only stops short of naming the successful candidate as Simon Galloway.

At the far end of the station platform, Paul Richardson sits with his young sister Trish and her friend Lucy Byron, swinging his legs over the edge. Occasionally he glances round at the white couple who are waiting, this late summer evening, between 6.15 and 6.20, for a Central Line train.

The Galloways scarcely notice them. Then they do. 'That's Lucy, isn't it,' Simon says. 'Oh yes it is, Susie.' But their attention is immediately diverted by three black youths ambling past them, in single file, sporting unfastened white trainers. Their eyes roll slowly over the Galloways; Susie sees nothing in those young, broad-nosed faces except the degraded calculations of the big city.

The three youths turn and come back, their body language somewhere between an innocent saunter and the predator's swagger. Simon and Susie both choke on their own tension. The boys jiggle on their trainers.

One of the boys asks Simon the time.

'Six-fifteen,' Simon says, without showing his watch. He remains seated. He knows he should immediately stand up and start shouting – but how can you shout before something happens? Don't panic.

'Show us your watch,' the first youth says.

'It's six-fifteen,' Simon repeats. 'I told you.'

The explosion of rage from all three is instantaneous:

'Don't provoke me, man!'

'You're a fucking shithead!'

'You address us respectfully, man, or I'll teach you respect.'

'You're a motherfucking white arsehole.'

One of the boys is now brandishing a switchblade. Susie can smell his hot breath as he bends over her, pointing the blade at her neck.

'Give us your bag. Now! Now! Cunt!'

She stares at the blade. 'Go away,' she whispers, her whole body shaking, vibrating. 'Go away! Leave us alone!'

When Simon tries to rise the first youth strikes him in the face – whapp! – sending his new glasses to the platform, where they smash. The youth rams his heel into them.

'Help!' Susie cries. 'Help! Robbery!'

She hears smashing glass, the habitual what-now? sound of the inner city. A broken bottle is thrust against her face. The jagged edges are pushing up into her skin. Her hand is up to protect her face, the same reflexive gesture of defence she had made when Amos Richardson robbed her. Someone – which one? – wrenches her bag from her shoulder and drags out her damaged arm to pull her new Rolex from her wrist.

'Arsehole! Cunt! Shithead!'

Attempting to rise again, his nose bleeding, Simon is knocked to the ground. Fast, lithe, rubbery black boys reach in for his wallet, tear off his watch.

They kick him in the head. They take it in turns. The thuds, and Simon's groans, turn Susie's stomach over – she screams.

Now they are running, whooping, the heels of their white trainers kicking high. They whoop with animal joy but also to intimidate any shitheads who might want to play the have-a-go-hero. No one does. The few other passengers on the platform shrink back into the walls. They know that anyone who intervenes is far more at risk than the victim.

Simon and Susan Galloway will not be going to the theatre tonight.

Paul Richardson is still sitting at the far end of the platform, beside his little sister and her friend Lucy Byron, idly dangling his big legs, keeping himself to himself.

It's only later, in the comforting presence of McIntyre and Jenkins, that Simon arrives at a 'fit' of Paul Richardson. He remembers seeing him in Benson Street Youth Court the day Paul was convicted of robbing him. Evidently the subconscious can serve as a delayed-action camera.

'Lucy Byron was with him,' Simon says.

'You're sure?'

'I'm sure.'

McIntyre and Jenkins listen attentively, solicitously, while a police doctor takes note of Simon's facial contusions and the slight nick on Susie's chin.

'You'll have a headache,' the doctor tells Simon, writing out a prescription. 'Take tomorrow off work. Do you have a spare pair of glasses?'

Simon can't bear the man's matter-of-fact tone. Evil thoughts collide in his aching head. He seethes with rage, humiliation.

'That fucking ape nigger sitting at the end of the platform was Paul Richardson! And Lucy Byron was with him!'

'But I don't think they ever moved,' Susie whispers.

'So what, Susan, so what!' Simon yells. 'Don't be so bloody naive!'

'That can be Paul's style,' Jenkins says, carefully writing down both Simon's and Susie's descriptions of Paul Richardson before an identification is attempted. McIntyre and Jenkins are up with the latest Home Office directives – and up with the clever-stuff to be expected from Averling and Simmonds.

'Paul', muses Jenkins, 'likes to play Mr Big.'

McIntyre watches the nonstop clenching and unclenching of Simon Galloway's hands.

'It was a mistake ever to let those illiterate apes come here!'

Simon shouts. 'I hate them, I hate them all! They should deport the lot, tomorrow! Dump them in the sea! They're scum! They're animals!'

The Galloways are offered a ride in a panda car to Eden Manor – not the ideal substitute for a night at the theatre, but the Galloways are seriously angry. They've had enough! Only this morning they have read in the papers about the secondary-school headmaster who had been struggling to impose some discipline on his pupils – forty expulsions in a year and exam results up by 15 per cent. He'd run out of the school to protect a boy who was being attacked on the street by a 'Triad' gang. The headmaster was now dead.

Susie has never before been in Eden Manor, not right inside. She feels as if she has surrendered herself to a slaughterhouse dripping with bats and vultures. She shrinks, praying for invisibility, plucking at anger to sustain her courage.

McIntyre stops at a familiar stairwell. Susie's empty handbag is lying there like an exhibit in a police museum.

'Yes, it's mine,' she says.

They drive to a derelict building called St Luke's House. McIntyre and Jenkins seem to know what they are doing and why. The noise they make as they thump on Paul Richardson's door could wake the whole estate.

Paul finally slouches to the door, looking all of twenty-five. He casts a slow, venomous, you'll-be-sorry glance over the Galloways.

'That's the one,' Susie says.

Simon peers, half-sighted. 'Yes. Yes!'

'Just a few inquiries,' McIntyre says while Jenkins plants a foot against the door jamb.

'I ain't interested,' Paul says. 'So fuck off.'

McIntyre and Jenkins take him and take him hard. Handcuffs on and then – to Susie's amazement – a gratuitous head-butt from Jenkins. She has heard about head-butting but she has never seen it actually done.

Spotting her consternation, McIntyre speaks gently.

'That's the worst thing that will happen to Paul, madam, until Lady Harsent sentences him to a five-course dinner at the Ritz.'

Madam? The policemen no longer address them by name in the presence of Paul Richardson.

A slip of paper carrying Susie's banking details is found in Paul's pocket. A search of the living room reveals Susie's NatWest Bank card and driving licence lying on the table. No sign of the precious new Rolex watch with her initials engraved on the back.

'How do you explain this?' Jenkins asks.

'Fuck you.' Paul is still nursing his head-butt.

Taken to Eden Manor police station, Paul is charged with conspiracy to rob and handling stolen goods. He is interrogated in the presence of Edgar Averling's underling, Simmonds.

'I was assaulted by this motherfucking shithead!' Paul yells.

Simmonds isn't interested. There are no marks and no court would believe Paul's word against a trusted local policeman's. Simmonds has often enough seen Jenkins, Honest Cliff, on the witness stand, solemnly denying the minor acts of invisible violence for which he is notorious. Jenkins always turns to look the magistrates in the eye when telling lies. Even Lady Harsent is taken in. 'No, your Worships, I did not.'

Simmonds advises Paul that silence is no longer the best policy after the change in the law. Paul grudgingly admits to having been on the station platform at the time of the robbery.

'What were you doing there?'

'I was waiting for a train, man, wasn't I?'

'Did you take the train?'

'Nah.'

'Why?'

Paul shrugs. 'Things began happening.'

'Who were you with?'

'Nobody.'

'You were with two young females.'

'Nah.'

'Did you witness the robbery?'

'I might 'ave.'

'Do you know the boys involved?'

'I might 'ave recognised one or two of 'em. I'd seen 'em around a few times.'

'So how do the contents of the handbag, minus the money, end up in your room?'

'This boy came up to my house and emptied some woman's bag out after I'd gone out. He took the bag and money with 'im.'

'Which boy?'

'Don't know 'is name.'

'How did he get into your room?'

'I might have left the door open. Ask 'im. Maybe 'e's a coke head or takes heroin or something.'

'So how did the slip of paper with the woman's banking details get into your pocket?'

'No idea. This bloke must have put it there to fix me up.'

'You ran this robbery from start to finish, didn't you, Paul?'

'You're just trying to fix me up.'

Paul is thrown back in a cell. Simmonds and Social Services will get him out on police bail in the end but there is a tacit understanding with the police – Paul is easier to handle when released after some hours in a cell.

The Galloways are driven home by Jenkins. 'Who's baby-sitting for you tonight, then?'

'Nigel Thompson,' Susie says.

'Not Lucy?'

'We don't use her,' Simon says.

'Is there any way she could have known your movements this evening?'

'I told her mother,' Susie says. 'Lucy may have overheard.'

'Brilliant,' Simon says bitterly. 'I warned you never to go back into that house. If that damned black—' He dries up abruptly, aware of Jenkins. Simon was about to say 'that damned black judge'.

Jenkins remembers Lucy coming into the police station only last week to fetch Daniel Richardson. But he keeps his thoughts to himself: with characters like Averling and Simmonds, you can never be too careful. Jenkins can already hear Averling in court, defending Paul:

'Madam, Paul now realises that, if he ever offends again, custody will be inevitable.'

For Lady Harsent, custody is always one step into the future, never now. Jenkins could name a dozen magistrates who regularly warn serious offenders that 'next time it will be straight into Downton'. But next time is never this time. The Richardsons and the Griffins just laugh. You no sooner nab them than they begin telling you the limits to your powers, how domestic burglary carries a 'max' of fourteen years whereas for commercial burglary ten years is the limit, and how they'll be out on bail because of the 'Croydon ruling' on what constitutes a 'serious threat to the public'.

'These boys can hardly write their own names,' Ken Crabbe had once remarked, 'but they'd all pass the bloody Law Society exams with flying colours!'

Ken! Jenkins and McIntyre have never understood what went wrong when Susan Galloway was called to identify Amos Richardson.

'Take care,' Jenkins calls to the Galloways before driving out of Oundle Square. The panda car circles the area for a couple of minutes before parking in Brancaster Road.

'Any point in talking to Lucy?' Jenkins asks.

'None.'

'At least she'd know we are on to her.'

'That's what she wants, isn't it?'

'You'd like a new sax, wouldn't you, Dan?'

'No money.'

'I can get you the money. A certain person wants you to do a job for him.'

'Who?'

'You know who.'

'What kind of a job?'

'You'd get a thousand when you've done it.'

'A thousand? You're kidding.'

'Did your Lucy ever do you a bad turn, Dan?'

He grins affectionately. 'Nah. What's the job?'

'It's in another part of town. Randall Road. You'll get caught.'

'What – nabbed? Stuck? By the pigs?'

'You break into this geezer's house in mid-afternoon when him and his missus is at work. He has more security and alarms than the Bank of England but you get in. Right?'

'Hm.'

'Then you mess the place up real nasty. You know, what they call "vindictive". Empty out the freezer. Bugger the dishwasher. Smash vases. Rip paintings. Empty out the drawers in their bedroom. Smash up the computers. If you can spare any shit, use it. When you've done that you put your feet up and watch television.'

'Who is this bugger then?'

'He's someone. So then he walks in and he sees you with your feet up and a broad grin and his house proper tolchocked. You tell him you're staying to watch the end of the TV programme and then you'd like a kiss from his missus when she comes home – I mean stoke him up real good. Watch him catch fire. He's a big strong bloke, he'll go for you. You don't leave a scratch on him. That's important, Dan – he mustn't have nothing to show for it. If he's not hitting you hard enough, round the head, you taunt him till he does – you've got to be in good hospital condition by the time the cops come.'

'Thanks a lot. No way.'

'A thousand quid, Dan. You could have the best sax in town.'

'Yeah, when I come out of Downton. A job like that counts as "aggravated".'

'Not with your record. And you'd probably get Lady Harsent on the Bench.'

'It might be Berry.'

'Definitely not.'

'How d'yer know?'

'I'm sure.'

'When's this job?'

'Wednesday.'

'And suppose his missus comes home first, this bloke of yours, suppose I've got a cunt on my hands. What do I then?'

'His missus always goes straight from the— I mean straight from work to her sports club Wednesday evenings.'

'Yeah. Who says?'

'I make it my business to know things, Dan.' Lucy squeezes his hand. 'You'll do it for me. I wouldn't want to give myself to a bloke if I knew he was chicken.'

Lucy has been undressing as she speaks.

Mark Griffin remains at large.

Doug McIntyre is studying the boy's file in search of clues, patterns of movement. A year ago Mark had been placed in a secure unit. Two psychiatrists had diagnosed him as unfit to stand trial for the several grave offences charged against him, including sexual assault of a child and rape. According to the psychiatrists, whenever Mark's 'sense of reality' was impaired by his latent schizophrenia, he was incapable of telling right from wrong. (Though he knew all about running away, which they ascribed to 'conditioned reflex'.) The psychiatrists also concluded that Mark now lacked 'aggressive potential', though he might pose 'a danger to himself'. He should be returned 'to the community under strict care'.

He had been released. But into whose care? The Youth Justice Team is in the dark; Social Services do not wish to know where Mark Griffin is.

McIntyre is thinking about Herbert Knowles. Herb has recovered from the physical injuries inflicted by the Griffin brothers in the Broadway underpass, but his inner landscape will never be the same again. In the kindest possible way the British Transport Police are talking of transferring him to 'less stressful duties' – Herb can recognise an exit door at any distance. His working life is over.

McIntyre and Jenkins are convinced that the Griffin family are sheltering Mark whenever he surfaces – but never at home. The CID have targeted five likely addresses but they need a warrant. Normally they would apply to Patrick Berry or Miss Swearwell, but Berry is out of town on business and Miss Swearwell has not yet returned from her favourite health farm in Sussex.

It has to be Lady Harsent.

A sensor light comes on as the two policemen approach the front door of the Harsent mansion. The Harsents had become security conscious after two burglaries.

Amelia Harsent answers the door, pert, pretty and plumpish. She looks McIntyre and Jenkins up and down as if they were weeds in a rose garden, then leaves them standing on the doorstep.

'I'll see if Mama will receive you,' Amelia says.

'A chip off the old block,' McIntyre mutters.

'I won't quote you.'

'I'm not giving you a quote not to quote.'

Lady H. eventually appears with a faintly distracted air. She too keeps them on the doorstep – with Miss Swearwell you'd be into ham and eggs by now, and pouring milk for her cats, and fixing a light-bulb, and trying to remember why you'd come.

Lady Harsent bridles. 'A warrant, you say? Whatever for? Disturbed boys like Mark suffer terrible traumas when seized in the middle of the night and left to languish in police cells.'

'Madam, Mark was remanded in a secure hospital as unfit to stand trial. He has been released and no one knows where he is. We have to bring him back to court. That lad is dangerous.'

'When they released him I'm sure they knew what they were doing.'

'It's called "resource-based diagnosis", madam: the patient has the illness you have the budget to treat. You first remove the bed, then you discover he can stand up and walk.'

'I quite agree,' Lady H. says. 'This Government has shown a callous indifference to the interests of the mentally sick. Poor Mark, how the boy must be suffering. I might consider a warrant backed for bail.'

'Madam, he would merely abscond again. He will not appear before any court unless in police custody. We believe he may strike again at any time. Women and girls are at risk.'

'I shall have to take advice. Good day to you.'

McIntyre and Jenkins drive back to the police station.

'It may be bad news for girls and women crossing Century Park at dusk,' McIntyre remarks. 'But I suppose the girls and their parents should know better.'

'In fact, they're asking for it, aren't they?'

'I'd go further, Cliff. The victims should be charged with provoking poor chaps like Mark Griffin who are suffering from blurred reality, blurred morality and abandonment by society.'

Lady Harsent sends a message to Eden Manor police station two hours later. 'There is no case for a warrant.'

Wednesday: Wendy feels dead tired, emotionally drained by the ongoing newspaper headlines. She dutifully takes a grip packed with workout kit to the office, although tempted not to bother.

Lady Harsent is in exceptionally cheerful mood all morning. She keeps tossing compassionate smiles at Marcus Byron's sister. Those who live by the headline die by the headline. Lady H. is sporting a new, tangerine outfit and a dazzling diamond brooch to celebrate.

'The Archbishop will be my dinner guest tonight,' she confides to anyone and everyone. 'Such a nice man. Henry has known him since they were at school together.'

Towards mid-morning, the court is forced to adjourn. All listed defendants are still in bed or drifting hours behind schedule through the London transport system. The little list-caller, who announces that each new case is 'ready' as proudly as if she'd just laid an egg, looks forlorn.

Wendy feels exhausted, drained. The Tyndale towpath business has eaten her up. Marcus won't talk about it, not even to Patrick.

'It's *sub judice*, period.'

Yeah. It's painfully clear to both of them that Marcus has been sleeping with Heather Stuart as well as Brigid Kyle – and Louise knows it.

'How could he *do* that, Patrick?'

'He may be driven to women by unhappiness about Lucy.'

'Oh yeah? You men always stick together.'

Patrick had not revelled in being suddenly shunted aside, and sent off to explore mountain caves, while Marcus enjoyed a lovers' weekend with Brigid in the Pyrenees. But Patrick remains fiercely loyal to Marcus.

Wendy glowers at her sportsbag. She is rigorous about working out on Wednesdays. If you break the routine you may break the habit. Patrick has warned that he may be home late tonight.

'We're having difficulties with one of our clients on remand. He claims that our electronic tab is malfunctioning. The police grabbed him for breaking his curfew but he swears he never left the house. I may have to go down to Ramsgate tomorrow. The entire Home Office contract is at stake.'

'And the Probation Service is protesting vehemently against curfew tagging.'

'So we have to get it right.'

'Well, don't go kerb-crawling along the front at Ramsgate. It's notorious for hookers.'

He kisses her: 'My hooker lives right here.'

Lady H. has taken the afternoon off to prepare her dinner for the Archbishop. Miss Swearwell bustles in shortly before two, to take over. The court stands.

'Good afternoon!'

'Number one on the afternoon list, madam. Paul Richardson.'

Paul is brought in, big and sullen. He knows where to sit and spreads his legs.

Handling stolen goods. The victim had been a Mrs Susan Galloway. This is Paul's 'first appearance' before Benson Street Youth Court. The issue is bail.

To the fury of Detective Sergeant Doug McIntyre, Nick Paisley has vetoed a 'conspiracy to rob' charge. 'Insufficient evidence,' he told Derek Jardine dismissively. 'It wouldn't stick.'

Miss Swearwell is chairing the Bench, uncannily resembling the late actress Dame Margaret Rutherford in her thick tweeds, and claiming to be a stone lighter after her health farm. The task is to consider an application for bail from Simmonds. She, Rodney Parker and the new black magistrate, Conde Jackson, take a long look at Paul's record, which extends to several typed pages.

Derek Jardine asks for a remand in custody on the grounds that Paul is likely to reoffend and to intimidate witnesses (the Galloways). But Jardine's heart is no longer in it; he has been applying for work in private practice since Paisley took over as Acting DPP. 'There used to be two sides in a court,' he told Wendy over a gloomy lunch, 'now there's only the defence. If so, I may as well be part of it.'

Miss Swearwell asks the Youth Justice Team whether Paul had been keeping to the conditions of his current Supervision Order.

Jimmy Haley-White jumps up. 'Unfortunately Paul's case worker is not available today, madam.'

'Why?'

'He's leading an outing of young offenders to Ostend.'

'Isn't that rather hard on the Belgians? We will put the case back until we have information on the Supervision Order.'

A chap called Barry Webster shows up two hours later. His lank hair is tied in a pony tail under a beret, a ring dangles from one ear, and he wears an expression of vexation, as if called from his real, useful work.

'As far as I know, Paul has more or less been abiding by his Supervision Order. But I'm not his case worker.'

'More or less?' Miss Swearwell snaps.

'There may have been a few lapses.'

'How many "lapses"?'

'That I don't know.'

'Kindly find out.'

She would like to say, 'No more prevarication!' but after twenty years on the Bench she knows better than to challenge the integrity of any member of the court. 'They always know when you think they're lying,' she has privately confided to Wendy, whom she adores. The expressions of the YJT are frosty – if the abrasive Patrick Berry is the magistrate they loathe, Miss Swearwell is one they most fear. Patrick tends to lunge at solutions prematurely, and then to beat a retreat under his wife's admonishing eye. Miss Swearwell bides her time: she knows that races are won at the end.

Eventually Jimmy Haley-White returns holding a fax. Sullenly he hands it to Miss Swearwell. She reads.

'I see here that you have made thirty appointments to meet Paul, only eight of which have succeeded.'

'Correct.'

'He didn't show up on twenty-two occasions?'

'Paul has told us that he didn't want to come because he was bored.'

Miss Swearwell regards the slouching Paul.

'Downton is quite boring, too. Perhaps we should remind Paul that the Supervision Order was imposed as an alternative to custody. Why have breach proceedings not been brought?'

'Madam, in Paul's case we need to find a menu—'

'A what!'

'A menu, madam. We need to find a menu which will capture Paul's interest, something which will prove attractive to Paul and address his disadvantaged background, his alienation, his lack of self-esteem and his troubled relations with the community.'

Miss Swearwell cannot order the Youth Justice Team to bring breach proceedings (which could send Paul to Downton).

'That's no good at all,' she tells Jimmy.

'I will pass on your comments, madam, to Paul's case worker.'

'When he gets back from protecting the British public in Ostend.'

The Bench refuses bail and – to Derek Jardine's astonishment – remands Paul into custody.

Stowing her briefcase and her sports grip in the car boot, Wendy drives straight home through the rush-hour traffic from Benson Street to Randall Road.

She has decided to skip the Riverview workout even though Patrick is due home late. She wonders how the curfew-tagging tests are holding up: Patrick's company has invested a lot of money in the project and Wendy is convinced that the experiment is justified in human terms. Marcus agrees. But Jill Hull had delivered a stinging public attack in the propaganda sheet called *Probation*: 'Must we treat offenders like animals?'

Yeah. Sounds like a good idea when you've had a few drinks. But Patrick is always in danger of getting carried away by technical wizardry. After gaining access to the Hull–Paisley household, he had linked the phone system to three walnut-sized miniature transmitters manufactured by Schellen-Hahn GmbH and marketed in the UK by a company part-owned by Patrick Berry, JP.

The resulting evidence had been delivered to Scotland Yard via Clive Wellings.

Wendy would always remember when Susan Galloway came into court, to face her ordeal in the Amos Richardson case, and caught sight of the blond, blue-eyed chairman of the Bench. Her face! She couldn't believe her eyes! Yeah. But the Paul Richardson case this afternoon led Wendy to wonder. The Galloways had been violently robbed on a station platform by young thugs beholden to Paul – and Doug McIntyre had tipped Wendy off that Lucy had been seen with Paul at the time of the robbery.

Threading through the traffic, Wendy sees the connection with painful clarity. Marco, you have that on your conscience, too. Yeah, what conscience?

She arrives in Randall Road shortly after 6.30 p.m. Reaching into her bag for her house keys, she runs a practised eye over the doors and windows – Patrick has trained her to do that whenever she arrives home to an empty house. 'Just look,' he says.

She looks. It's fine. A hot bath beckons.

There's no way of examining the rear of the house.

The Archbishop is Lady Harsent's guest for dinner. Sir Henry, her husband, sits at the other end of the table flirting with Sandra Golding – which she could do without. His Grace is seated at his hostess's right hand. It's a splendid affair, with silver candelabra and Dresden tableware. The Archbishop listens attentively, gravely, as Lady H. brings one guest after another into the conversation. He isn't quite sure who they are, these dozen good, earnest men and women, and he has no inkling that he is dining with the Congress for Justice.

Marcus Byron once described the Archbishop as a 'professional dupe'. The Archbishop has not forgotten it.

Cecilia Harsent is set to strengthen her power base by taking over the chairmanship of the Magistrates' Courts Committee. The MCC employs 1,200 people, with a budget of £47 million, and is vested with complete responsibility for training lay magistrates, for employment and for the upkeep of premises. Its twelve members include three stipendiaries and nine others, either 'stipes' or lay, chosen by a selection panel.

It is the members of this panel who have recently been blitzed by campaign calls on behalf of Lady Harsent or Patrick Berry.

Lady H. has invited all of them to her dinner party to meet the Archbishop . . . and other guests. All but three have made their excuses. Lady H. is inwardly fuming at the affront.

'The right training for magistrates,' she is telling the Archbishop, 'is so very very important. Many of my colleagues, I regret to tell your Grace, are dismally ignorant of the good work done by probation officers and the social workers of the Youth Justice Teams.'

'Ah,' says the Archbishop. 'We are all on probation to the Almighty.'

'Of course,' says Sandra Golding, 'we had hoped that Cecilia would be elected unopposed. But Marcus Byron's gang, the Lemons, have been fighting her all the way.'

'Lemons, you say?'

'Yes, your Grace,' Nick Paisley chips in. 'It's not simply a loose-knit group of like-minded people – like ourselves. It's a ruthless conspiracy to subvert the criminal justice system.'

'They are all stooges and acolytes of Marcus Byron,' Jimmy Haley-White adds.

'Byron?' The Archbishop wraps a slice of smoked salmon round his fork. 'Hasn't he been in a spot of difficulty recently?'

'More than "difficulty", your Grace,' Paisley says. 'I'm afraid we are facing a major scandal.'

'Well, of course, major scandals are always more fun than minor ones,' the Archbishop says. 'The Church, alas, seems doomed to stagger along through the minor ones.'

They all laugh.

As soon as the front door closes behind Wendy she hears a click in the sitting-room and sees an opaque, blueish light cast in the hallway through the open door.

Obviously Patrick had got home unusually early and turned on the television.

Obviously?

Then she begins to notice things. All the coats from the stand lie in a heap on the floor – and the linings have been ripped! The hallway mirror has been shattered. For fun. The house has been trashed!

She considers retreating straight back into the street but she's not a retreater. Byrons have learned to stand their ground from earliest years. 'Never back off,' Uncle Jeremiah used to say.

She lays her briefcase and sports bag down.

She steps into the sitting room. The television is indeed on. The days are drawing shorter now and dusk is descending beyond the large, Georgian windows. The normal, accustomed shapes and silhouettes of the room seem crazily disturbed, destroyed – for a moment she actually believes she has stepped into the wrong house.

Her gaze fixes on a pair of white trainers. They are up in the air, resting on the back of something. Of what? Nothing looks right.

'Patrick?' she says softly.

'Shit!' A figure bounds out of an armchair in front of the television.

She gasps and stands frozen in the doorway.

The young man's face is masked by a stocking. He hesitates. 'OK, missus,' he says, 'I'm on my way, just clear a path.'

She reaches sideways and turns on all the sitting-room lights, 100 watt bulbs and halogen spots. The room has been wrecked! Torn apart! Devastated! The bookcase has been gutted! Every ornament has been smashed! The lithographs ripped in their frames! Something brown and disgusting has been smeared across the new velvet covering of the antique sofa.

'Just back off and take it easy,' he says. 'I don't want no trouble.'

It's a young voice, only recently broken, still uncertain of its status on the ladder of manhood. She understands: one of Patrick's 'victims' has come seeking vengeance. All magistrates fear it will happen. Thank God Patrick isn't here – though she wishes he was.

'I don't want no trouble, missus. Just back off! Clear a path and I'm off!' He takes a stride towards her.

'And who is Cecilia's opponent for the job?' the Archbishop is asking Jill Hull.

'A Youth Court magistrate by the name of Patrick Berry,' Jill says. 'A hanger and flogger.'

'Of course, he's merely Byron's surrogate,' Lady H. adds.

'We have surrogate bishops,' smiles the Archbishop, 'but we call them suffragans. It sounds better.'

'Berry is Byron's stooge and acolyte,' Paisley says. 'His directorship of the curfew-tagging company creates a clear conflict of interest with the essential impartiality of the magistracy.'

'I'm afraid you have lost me there,' the Archbishop says.

'Magistrates should not have a personal financial interest in the sentences they hand down,' Jill Hull explains.

'Oh, quite so,' the Archbishop says.

'I shouldn't say this,' Lady H. wears her saddest expression, 'but Patrick Berry's people have been campaigning in the most blatant way – quite out of keeping with our traditions.'

'Ah.' The Archbishop nods to his hostess. 'Democracy.'

'Frankly, your Grace, that's the last thing we want. What one needs is pedigree.'

'As in Pedigree Chum,' Geoffrey Villiers adds solemnly. The doyen of the Congress is only marginally less outrageously dressed than usual. Eschewing gaiters and silk stockings, which might seem to pose a challenge to the Archbishop's, he has confined himself to a satin suit and a shocking-pink cravat. Paisley throws him a venomous look. He'd urged Lady H. not to invite Villiers but she had insisted. 'Geoffrey has class, Nick.'

'Did you know,' Sandra Golding asks the Archbishop, 'that Marcus Byron is on record as opposing all conditional discharges?'

Lady H. beams. 'A CD wonderfully focuses an offender's mind on the consequences if he errs again.'

This strikes a clear bell in the Archbishop. 'I always feel that God and our Lord Jesus Christ has put us all on a conditional discharge. He shows mercy but does not forget our past sins if we reoffend.'

'Right on!' says Jimmy Haley-White. 'Show us the way, O Lord.'

'Now, Sandra,' Lady H. beams down the table, 'do tell his Grace, and all of us, how Louise Pointer has been coping with her husband's downfall.'

Sandra flutters her hands dismissively. 'Oh, it's all very sad for Louise. I rang her today, as an act of mercy, and suggested that she could honourably withdraw as my opponent, but her response was hardly friendly.'

'Your "opponent"?' the Archbishop asks Sandra. 'Forgive my ignorance, is this another contest?'

'For the chairmanship of the Criminal Bar Association, your Grace,' Averling explains. 'Frankly, Sandra will walk home. Louise Pointer is hopelessly compromised by her marriage to Marcus Byron.'

'Not to mention his current adulteries,' Sandra says.

Lady H. emits a little shriek. 'Heavens! Don't tell me there's more than one! I knew about the Kyle woman but—'

'Her name is Heather Stuart,' Jimmy Haley-White says softly. 'Sad to relate, she works for the Probation Service. I have tried to warn Heather but Judge Byron, like Don Giovanni, has the devil on his side.'

'I'm surprised the devil has time,' the Archbishop smiles. 'I thought he was currently employed full-time in drafting the new divorce laws.'

Laughter.

'We have a great tradition of timely resignation in this country,' Lady H. says. 'It's the cornerstone of good government. Someone should tell Marcus Byron.' She turns to Villiers. 'Don't you agree, Geoffrey?'

'I pass,' old Villiers sighs.

'Someone has to explain Angela Loftus's death,' Nick presses Villiers.

'It won't be me, dear boy. Poor Angela.'

The corpulent Edgar Averling eases his belt as the main course is cleared away by Lady H.'s Filipina maid.

'My own view is that Marcus Byron's involvement in his daughter's breach of bail renders Patrick Berry's position as a Youth Court magistrate untenable.' Averling smiles affably towards Lucy's mother. 'No offence to you, Jill.'

'None taken, Edgar. I quite agree. Marcus knew where Lucy was and told no one.'

'Ha!' cries Sandra. 'A Crown Court judge. What do you make of that, your Grace?'

'I am listening,' the Archbishop says.

'I really think Patrick's wife should consider her position as our Deputy Chief Clerk,' Lady H. says. 'A transfer seems to me imperative – at the very least.'

Geoffrey Villiers has reached the end of the road. After years of self-disciplined duplicity, he can take it no more. And much is at stake: the Archbishop dines in the same club, the Fitzroy, as Lord Chief Justice Bowers and the Lord Chancellor. And the Archbishop is, as he says, 'listening'.

'Well, your Grace,' Villiers says, 'I can tell you something which may shed light on the moral level of your fellow-guests tonight. It was Mr Averling, over there, who chose, a moment ago, to cast aspersions on Judge Byron's integrity. Yet Mr Averling knows perfectly well that Judge Byron's solicitors lost no time in informing Ms Hull's solicitors exactly where Lucy Byron was hiding in Wiltshire. It was Ms Hull who, enjoying full custody of Lucy, had refused to discuss Lucy's legal difficulties with the man who is her father. Now, I am a lawyer and I know that Mr Averling's immediate duty, on receiving that letter, was to inform the police. But Mr Averling did not do so. And when Lucy was finally brought before Lady Harsent's Bench, for breach of bail, no disclosure was made.'

A dreadful silence lies across Lady Harsent's dining room.

Geoffrey Villiers rises. 'Cecilia, you must forgive me, but I have a train to catch. So very kind of you to invite me. So very kind.'

'I don't want no trouble!' The youth takes another step towards her. She's still blocking his exit. If she moves to the telephone, at the other end of the room, he'll escape. She can't identify him beneath that stocking mask; as for his clothes, they're standard. She's thinking about the filthy shit-smear across the sofa: can they do a DNA test, a genetic fingerprinting, from excrement? She's not sure. Patrick would know.

How fit is she, how strong? All those hours of exercise and weightlifting at Riverview, do they count for anything? The intruder is slightly built, not heavily muscled, but suppose he carries a knife? They often do, especially the smaller boys. The smaller boys are very dangerous when cornered.

His left hand goes deep into his donkey-jacket pocket.

'I've got a blade,' he says. 'I'll use it!'

'Show me your blade,' she says.

'Now look, missus, you're asking for it!'

The front door slams behind her. She gasps from the shock of it.

'Patrick?' she calls.

'What the hell is going on here?' she hears his voice from the hall.

'Patrick, be careful, we're not alone!'

Patrick walks into the room. Slowly he takes in the scene.

'He says he's carrying a knife, Patrick.'

'Jesus Christ!' Patrick snarls, surverying the devastated room.

'I just found him here,' she says.

Patrick hands her his mobile. 'Dial 999.'

'Yeah,' says the youth, 'this fuckin' shithead sent me down. Six months in Downton. Very nice thank you. Want a conducted tour of your premises, arsehole? Yeah, I reckon you and your missus will be eating off the fuckin' floor tonight. You won't want to sleep in your posh bed tonight, no way. You wouldn't put a dog in it tonight, arsehole. It's bye-bye to all that lovely computer equipment upstairs. As for your fuckin' discs, you wouldn't want to wipe your stinkhole with them – motherfucker.'

The television is still on. 'Now the London regional news,' says the presenter. 'Judge Marcus Byron declined to speak to reporters today when he arrived at the Crown Court . . .'

As Wendy gets through to the police on Patrick's mobile, the masked youth makes a dash for the door. Patrick moves as if to step aside, then swings his clenched fist. The boy dodges, anticipating it; the blow glances off his shoulder.

'I don't want no trouble, mister!'

The next blow strikes his upraised arm. He's prancing and skipping round Patrick, jeering and leering behind his stocking mask. Then Patrick really goes for him. Not a single blow comes back. No knife either.

The youth seems helpless before Patrick's furious onslaught. To Wendy his inability to defend himself is unreal. Patrick's fists keep thudding into the face. The boy is whimpering now.

'Stop, Patrick, that's enough.'

'Nothing's enough for this bastard!'

'Patrick!'

A red police light is swivelling in Randall Road. Wendy runs to open the front door, stepping over the battered youth. Patrick has ripped off the stocking mask and is staring at a very young black face he has almost pulped.

# *Fifteen*

MAGISTRATE BATTERS INTRUDER
QUESTION AGAIN RAISED IN COMMONS: WHAT IS 'REASONABLE FORCE'?
BYRON'S BROTHER-IN-LAW SUSPENDED AS MAGISTRATE AFTER POLICE BRING CHARGES
MESSAGES OF PUBLIC SYMPATHY FOR MAGISTRATE AND WIFE
EDEN MANOR RIOTS SPREAD

A night of rioting followed news of Daniel Richardson's arrest. The trouble started in Eden Manor when a police patrol car was overturned and set on fire, then rapidly engulfed the High Street. A mob of youths, mainly black, ran amok, smashing shop windows, overturning cars and beating passers-by. The local sports shop was the focus of looting – indignation about police brutality had an uncanny way of translating itself into an appetite for trainers, tracksuits and rollerblades.

Lucy herself had spread the word through her friend Trish Richardson: Dan had been done over in a police van after being assaulted by a magistrate. When she had visited St Luke's Hospital, the pigs wouldn't let her near Dan.

Trish's all-girl gang is out on the streets fanning the riot and loading up. Frightened shoppers give the rampaging girls a wide berth as they scream and swear their way up the High Street. They blow into newsagents' shops, starting with the Patels, demanding free cigarettes, chocolate and cokes as 'compensation'. Storming the local 'Paki' off-licence, they raid the shelves and lift enough Aussie lager to fuel their rage until the pigs pay proper compensation to Dan and his family.

It is Lucy who has coined the slogan: COMPENSATION!

Through the post comes a letter from Mrs Nearcliffe, Headmistress of St Hilda's, summoning Marcus 'most urgently' to meet her.

Lucy!

'Don't forget the opera tonight,' he calls to Louise as he climbs into his smart new autumn coat.

'What? Oh yes.' (Perhaps he should wear a coat at home, given the temperature.)

He departs for the Crown Court – probably his last morning in wig and purple gown. He is due to meet the Chief in his chambers at 1.30: they will not be sharing a club meal this time. On arrival Marcus's clerk, Arthur Henderson, squirming with embarrassment, confirms that Sir Henry Harsent has been put on stand-by to cover Marcus's afternoon list.

'I'm so sorry, your Honour. Working for you has been a most remarkable privilege.'

'Thank you, Arthur. I've no doubt we will get together again.'

'I hope so, Marcus.'

Arthur Henderson has never used his first name before. The human gesture feels like the thrust of a gravedigger's spade.

The only case of the morning, a trial, is over by noon. Marcus has noticed the jurors staring at him with such curiosity that they barely listened to the evidence. It didn't matter; Marcus threw the whole case out when the prosecution admitted that the key police witness had not cautioned the defendant before 'interviewing' him handcuffed in the back seat of a police car.

'Quite disgraceful.' He dismissed the jury.

'The court will stand!'

For the last time he strides to his retiring room. A correspondent from *The Times* comes on the line almost immediately.

'The Archbishop delivered a speech to a Church of England conference this morning. Would you please comment?'

'What did he say?'

'The Archbishop expressed "horror and deep concern" about the rapid rise in the prison population to 51,000. The Archbishop spoke of the "lynch-mob culture" of the tabloid press. He said he was appalled by the rising number of prisoners on remand. "What a way", said the Archbishop, "to usher in the millennium."'

'It sounds to me as if the Archbishop has been dining with Lady Harsent and the Congress. I hear he's partial to smoked salmon and grilled pheasant.'

'I'm afraid I can't quote that remark.'

'You must excuse me, I have work to do.'

'I quote the Archbishop: "Who can forget that when Pontius Pilate was about to release Jesus Christ on the grounds of justice, the mob bayed: 'Crucify him! Crucify him!'"'

'You want my personal reaction to that?'

'Yes, please.'

'Among the murderers, rapists, armed robbers, wife batterers and child abusers passing my way, I have yet to spot one resembling our Lord Jesus Christ. Of course it's entirely possible that Jesus has been appearing before the magistrates' courts, charged with less serious offences such as assault, theft, stealing cars or driving without insurance.'

This exchange is no sooner terminated than Brigid Kyle comes on the line.

'How are you, Marcus?'

'It's not going to be a wonderful day. The Chief is giving me ten minutes. Mrs Nearcliffe will give me five. And Lucy none. At the end of the day my wife will probably not turn up for the opera.'

'Why?'

'An anonymous caller informed her that you spent a weekend with me in a small village in the Pyrenees. I could hardly deny it.'

'She's taking it badly?'

'Louise said that the only sin I ever regretted was being found out. She called herself "the laughing-stock of London". She said the papers printed grim little photos of herself surrounded by pictures of my smiling mistresses and ex-mistresses.'

Marcus is conscious of not mentioning to Brigid the wad of photos, depicting Heather's patio-garden in Earl's Court, which Louise had thrust under his nose.

'Will they press charges against Patrick?' Brigid asks.

'They already have: assault and GBH. Patrick has had to stand down from the Bench, pending trial. He appeared before the magistrates' court this morning. No pleas were taken. He intends to fight it. He's been receiving floods of fan mail through his letterbox. "Pity you didn't kill the black bastard" – that sort of stuff. Wonderful for Wendy.'

'Patrick can hardly continue his contest with Cecilia Harsent for the chairmanship of the MCC?'

'He has thrown in the towel.'

'Have you heard from Max Venables?'

'Apparently the Boy told him to drop me – I'm now a liability.'

'They're all shits. When shall I see you?'

He glances at his fob-watch. Judges are sticklers for punctuality, so much of their time is wasted by late arrivals and non-attendance. As Patrick once put it, 'Waiting for the villains to honour us with their presence.' A summons from the Chief carries the force of a warrant not backed for bail.

'I must go.'

'Good luck, Marcus! Call me, won't you?'

The taxi driver recognises him.

'I reckon they've been setting you up, Guv,' he says, turning his meter. 'It's probably those Yardies from Jamaica, all drugged up. Drill a hole in you as soon as look at you.'

Marcus ponders this. White folk are usually eager to invert their natural racism; there must always be one 'good' black judge, one 'good' black TV newsreader, one 'very funny' black stand-up comedian. But what they give with one hand they take with the other. Their fevered imaginations despatch Jamaican Yardies down to butcher nice English spinsters beside the duck-waters of Surrey.

Poor Angela. Marcus's mind spins laterally to another victim, Susan Galloway. For weeks he had been puzzled by the identification parade Ken Crabbe set up for her. And then, one evening, Ken had come to see him, close to tears.

'I have to tell you, Marcus. As soon as I read about your friend Miss Loftus, and the trick they pulled on you, I said to myself, "Ken, you go and make a clean breast of it to Marcus or you'll never look yourself in the face again."'

'A whisky, Ken?'

Ken Crabbe had, many months ago, lost control of himself. He had been upstairs in the gymnasium of Mason Lodge Attendance

Centre when Darren Griffin began spray-painting the new toilets, then set about wrecking the new kitchen in an extended display of respect for the law. Downstairs old George had pretended not to notice until finally he pressed his alarm buzzer.

Infuriated by the insolent Darren's vandalism, Ken had dragged him out into the street and laid into him. Years of discipline training had flown out of the top of his head; years of frustration had packed into his steel-bonded fists.

A police inspector himself, Ken Crabbe had been obliged to call the police and incriminate himself. A charge of GBH against him lay on Derek Jardine's desk. Then Nick Paisley had taken the case over himself – and nothing happened.

Charges against Ken Crabbe were neither pressed nor withdrawn. Why? Paisley was no friend of the police.

All this had occurred some weeks before Inspector Ken Crabbe conducted Mrs Susan Galloway through an identification parade where Amos Richardson's facial scar was hidden by sticking-plaster. Challenged by Marcus, Ken had failed to provide a satisfactory explanation. He had merely cited 'new regulations' which either did not exist or were open to interpretation.

'Marcus, I've been sitting on Nick Paisley's desk like a half-bitten worm awaiting the mole's pleasure.'

Marcus listens, refills Ken's glass. Patrick's encounter with Daniel Richardson runs and re-runs though his head.

'Paisley ordered you to sabotage Amos Richardson's identification parade?'

'He doesn't risk direct contact, that bastard. I got a message, let's say.'

'So you were set up, Ken, like Patrick was set up.'

'Exactly, sir – Marcus. Both boys, Darren Griffin and Daniel Richardson, committed vandalism. In each case a Lemon was provoked to lose his cool. In my humble opinion, both boys were put up to it.'

'By Nick Paisley.'

'I have no doubt. And you were set up at Tyndale, if you'll forgive me – though I don't know how.'

'A woman forgot her tampons.'

'Sorry?'

The conversation with Ken Crabbe took place less than a week ago. The taxi is now setting Marcus down at the Gates of Justice.

* * *

Marcus Byron is conducted to the chambers of the Lord Chief Justice of England. Oil paintings of his predecessors, darkened by the grime of centuries, some fat and florid, the beefeaters, some hollowed out by learning, hang from heavy gilt frames. And there is the bust of Blackstone, the greatest of them all, his marble eyes sightless yet all-seeing.

Uncle Jeremiah's nephew almost bows to him as he passes.

The visitor cannot hear his own feet on the thick Kashmiri carpet. He walks through the silence of the final judgment.

Vast pillars rise beside him, each poised to dwarf him, each a testimony to the architect's passion for authority and doom. Elaborate cast-iron chandeliers threaten to fall from the high ceilings, ending his days in shame.

And the bookcases. That smell of musty leather and mildew. The accumulated wisdom in those yellowing pages! The whole history of the liberties of England, from the Conquest to Magna Carta and the Bill of Rights, all assembled, arrayed, stacked up in rebuke to this ignorant upstart blackamoor who thought he could combine the most dignified of vocations while fornicating with the media.

Men of breeding, men of class, men with a heritage slowly matured in the cask.

This vast hush, these long hanging curtains of rich purple velvet, this funereal twilight, this stranglehold of tradition, this irresistible sense of awe.

He is politely received by the Chief's senior secretary. Offered a seat in a high-ceilinged ante-room, Marcus studies the elaborate cornices, the brass mountings on the huge double doors, the Ionic and Doric scrolls decorating the pilasters.

A small, dumpy man in a slightly faded suit emerges through one of the double doors, takes Marcus by the arm – a very brief touch – and leads him into quite a cosy little room furnished in the most unpretentious way.

The Lord Chief Justice of England sits. Marcus sits.

'I don't have good news for you, Marcus.'

'I didn't expect any.'

'The Lord Chancellor and I are agreed: you must step down.'

'Not voluntarily, Chief.'

'Then involuntarily, Marcus. I won't beat about the bush. You've been a damned fool. You've not only made too many enemies, you've lost too many friends. You have forgotten the difference between a judge and a politician. Publicity, mail bags and opinion polls have gone to your head.'

'And I come from the wrong end of town.'

'I rather thought you would say that. Frankly, I would have respected you more if you hadn't. We are constantly battered for selecting our judges from a narrow social background – public school and Oxbridge. And what happens when we reach out wider?'

'You certainly don't get another Sir Henry Harsent.'

'Do you want me to run through the charge sheet? – I'd rather not.'

'Yes, do.'

'I have to begin with your daughter. I'm not the least bit interested whether you did or did not technically aid and abet her breach of bail. We are all fathers. To adapt a phrase, *honi soit qui mal y pense*. It's not so much what your Lucy has done or not done as why she is doing it. Any of us can have an errant child. But that scene on the steps of the Crown Court was, frankly, over the limit. Your Lucy is determined to involve you in scandal and nothing will stop her.'

'Nothing will stop the Congress for Justice.'

'Yes, I've heard those rumours. The Archbishop put in a good word for you. He was impressed by Villiers's peroration on your behalf.'

'His what?'

'You didn't know that Geoffrey threw off his many disguises at a Harsent dinner party?'

'No.'

'Marcus, I realise you are convinced that Lucy is being used, exploited, against you. If that is the case, I have to tell you that they have won and you have lost.'

'A provisional victory.'

'Life itself is somewhat provisional. Then I am obliged to mention the two incidents involving Lionel Lacey. You may have acted in good faith, I'm sure you did, but you were foolish in your method, too foolish for a Crown Court judge. And your folly caught up with you on that towpath near Tyndale.'

'Yes. I agree.'

'Receiving confidential documents may be more tempting than wise.'

'It depends who wins.'

'Yes, yes, I know. "Treason doth never prosper: what's the reason? For if it prosper, none dare call it treason." Marcus, it has not prospered.'

'Not yet.'

'Hm. Marcus, why not go back to the bar?'

'No.'

'As a barrister, a QC, your talents enjoy free rein and you can make four times as much money.'

'No.'

'It wouldn't harm your chances of preferment if the Boy sweeps the country.'

'I have no such ambitions.'

'There have been too many scandals, Marcus. Too many. And too many angry ladies in the frame. A man who takes on the Government is hardy; a man who takes on the entire female sex is foolhardy; a man who takes on both is a fool. We don't need judges who so fascinate juries that they are not listening to the evidence.'

'Who made that claim?'

'I was told. People tell me things.' The Chief rises. 'I am suspending you, Marcus, as of now.'

'Without hearing the case for the defence?'

'The genius of this country is never to practise what we preach. Go and enjoy a well-earned rest. Think it over, about returning to the bar. Your good wife might be glad, don't you think?'

Marcus smiles. 'Very.'

Entering a taxi, it strikes Marcus in the pit of his stomach that if he were to drive to the judges' entrance of the Crown Court he would be refused admission.

'St Hilda's School,' he tells the driver. 'Near the Broadway.'

Thirty minutes later he sits in Mrs Nearcliffe's 'study', feeling, as always, only ten years old. A neat, clean desk and a small vase of dried flowers lie between them.

'I am expelling Lucy from St Hilda's. I have told Ms Hull but I wanted the opportunity to express my regret to you.'

'Mrs Nearcliffe, I hope you will reconsider when I—'

'I should have done it some months ago. I no longer have any choice in the matter, Judge Byron.'

Mrs Nearcliffe shows him a brief statement approved by the School Governors which will be sent to every parent.

'You realise this will appear in the Press tomorrow, Mrs Nearcliffe?'

'Inevitably.'

'Perhaps St Hilda's was never the right school for Lucy.'

'A number of parents have come to see me. I have received more than a hundred letters. The Governors concluded that the situation was untenable.'

The Headmistress rises and extends her hand to him. The interview is over.

'Thank you, Mrs Nearcliffe, for everything you have done for Lucy over the years.'

'A very talented girl. I used to have high hopes for her. Such a pity.'

He leaves the school for the last time.

Lucy, oh Lucy!

He decides to walk to Oundle Square – what else is there to do? A man normally driven by the clock suddenly realises that he has time on his hands. He has been dispossessed. Since 1.30 p.m. he has been nobody.

He rings the bell. Neither Jill nor Nick will be at home at this hour, but Lucy might be. Light filters from Lucy's room through drawn curtains. He bangs on the door. Finally a beloved face is seen peeping at him through the curtains, then it's gone. His heart aches.

'Lucy!' he shouts. 'Lucy!'

He stands on the doorstep helpless.

A boy walks past him in a smart blazer, carrying a rucksack loaded with books. His name is Nigel Thompson.

Arriving at the opera – *The Marriage of Figaro* – he waits in vain for Louise. No, there is no message for him at the box office. He dials home on his mobile and is invited by his own recorded voice to leave a message. Which he does, before taking his seat in the stalls – latecomers are not admitted until the interval, and quite right too.

The empty seat beside him yawns like an open grave. Everyone seems to be looking at him and the seat his wife refuses to fill. Normally he would smile around him, nod and wave to friends, but now he encounters only frozen faces, averted glances. He sits as rigid as a man in a straitjacket. He soaks up Mozart but the marital machinations he witnesses on-stage amuse him less than usual.

During the interval he stands alone with his whisky, ostracised by people he knows well. The chattering classes look right through him. Sandra offers him a derisive glance of contemptuous pity. Jeremy Darling raises an eyebrow as he passes. Sir Henry and Lady Harsent bow ironically, then glide on.

Opening the front door of his South Kensington flat, he sees a light on in the sitting room. Louise is watching television. She doesn't even glance at him.

'You missed the opera,' he growls.

'Yes.'

'I sat next to an empty seat which had cost me one hundred and fifty pounds.'

'You should have invited Brigid Kyle. Or the honey-blonde with the patio-garden and a taste for fuchsias. Cheap at the price.'

Louise has folded her arms across her narrow chest, a sign in her of extreme tension.

Marcus raises his hands and then lets them flop against his flanks.

'Publicity is all you care about, Marcus. The only sin is being found out! I'm the laughing-stock of London! They publish grim little scowling photos of me, surrounded by pics of your smiling mistresses and ex-mistresses!'

'You said all that last night. Word for word.'

'I see. I'm allowed one protest, is that it? That's my ration.'

'A man comes home', he bellows, 'after being suspended by the Lord Chief Justice, and his wife doesn't even ask him what happened.'

'I know what happened. It's in the *Standard*.'

She tosses the evening paper at him. He sits down, sighs, stands again, pours himself a whisky.

'Lucy has been expelled from St Hilda's.'

'That's in the *Standard*, too. The phone hasn't stopped ringing. I gave up answering it. You'll find all the messages on your answerphone. Plenty from Brigid, of course, though none from Heather – she's very discreet, isn't she?'

'Louise, I really don't think you—'

'Marcus, I'm leaving you.'

'I'm sorry.'

Louise is crying. 'You're not sorry. You have never been truly sorry for anything you did. You are incapable of genuine contrition.'

Marcus Byron crawls into the spare bed. This has been the worst day of his life. Could any day be worse?

He will find out.

Brigid walks with Marcus in Hyde Park, her arm tucked through his. She picks a stray hair off his sleeve.

'Promise not to go bald, your Honour.'

'I wouldn't be surprised.'

'Such a gloomy boy I have with me today.'

'Yeah.' He kicks lifeless ashes from his pipe.

Three smartly dressed horse riders canter past them along Rotten Row, rising in their saddles as if brimming with *joie de vivre*. Marcus eyes them sourly, then stoops, picks up a small stone and throws it after them.

'Marcus! Hooligan!'

'Do you know what Louise said before she left?' he growls. 'She said there's no point in trying to domesticate a dog determined to leave hairs in other beds.'

'Nice hairs. Let's discuss my exposé of Paisley and the Congress. You did read the proofs, I suppose?'

'I read them.' Marcus abruptly halts his long stride and takes her by the lapels of her light coat. 'I'm not having you referring to Lucy as a "drug addict" in print. You're keeping Lucy right out of it.'

His furious face is close to hers.

'Are you about to head-butt me, Marcus? If so, kindly count to three so I can close my eyes and pray to Our Lady.'

'Nothing about Lucy!'

'But Lucy has been the centrepiece of Paisley's campaign to discredit you.'

'I intend to kidnap Lucy. Got it?'

He releases her.

'Well, I can't blame you, Marcus. Where will you take her? To Zanzibar?'

'That's my business.'

'Such trust.'

'Yeah. I never slept with a journalist before. Big mistake.'

'Thanks! God, you're odious!'

'Never trust women with flaming hair.'

'It might not be her own, you mean? When do we come to the bad news?'

'What you have to understand is that I am not having Lucy dragged through the mud.'

They pass the tall, isolated edifice of Knightsbridge Barracks. Uncle Jeremiah had once told Marcus they used to have vegetable allotments here during the war. Hard to imagine now.

'I hate all journalists! They're scum!'

'Is that why you talk to them more than any other judge in England?'

'And I don't trust any woman, either!'

'Well, you never told me.'

'Or anyone.'

'I'm not anyone.'

He chuckles. 'Really? What does it feel like to be no one? Who does that flamethrower on your head belong to? Whose are those pretty little feet?'

'No idea. I tie them in bandages to make them littler. Hey, you're smiling! Can this be the Marcus Byron who has been auditioning for the part of King Kong all afternoon?'

Casually he strokes her neck, plays with his pipe. 'That might be a racist remark. I shall report it to Jimmy Haley-White.'

'Marcus, just one question: that obscene cassette you received from Lucy – did Paisley have a hand in that? Did he do the filming?'

They reach the Serpentine and gaze at a few tourists out on the water, struggling with oars. The weather is rather chill for boats now.

'Yeah, he did.'

'Then give me the evidence. The *Sentinel*'s lawyers love evidence.'

'You're another victim of linear reasoning,' he says.

'I thought women were incapable of any kind of reason.'

'I never said that!'

'You say it in your sleep. I watch your beautiful big, wicked lips move.'

'Inadmissible evidence.'

'I'm waiting for some "non-linear reasoning" loaded with testosterone.'

'When Patrick did his job in Oundle Square he found a

Zeiss F726 camera, made in Jena. Paisley is known to have paid an official visit to Communist East Germany, where his admiring colleagues in the People's Probation Service showed their appreciation with the gift of a Zeiss–Jena F726 camcorder.'

They pass an exotically dressed black youth zooming and weaving on deluxe rollers. He wears mirrored shades and primrose-yellow leggings hooped like croquet posts. Huge earphones suggest a disc jockey on wheels. He lifts a hand to Marcus in passing:

'Hi, Judge.'

Marcus smiles back. 'How long did I give you inside?' he shouts.

'Marcus, will you kindly pay attention or go to the back of the class and stand in the corner with your face to the wall?'

'Where was I?'

'The Lucy tape and a German camera.'

'According to Clive Wellings, the tape of Lucy reading from *A Clockwork Orange* and baring her privates was shot on a Zeiss–Jena F726.'

'Paisley might now be anxious to retrieve the Lucy tape, don't you agree?'

'It's in a safe place.'

The rollerblading Puck returns, wheeling and pirouetting.

'Hi, Judge! You gave me ten years for picking a daisy but I got out! I'm on parole!'

Brigid shakes Marcus by the arm. 'Never mind the fan club! I'm trying to nail Paisley!'

'You're tunnelling up my arsehole.'

'I never heard that word in Dublin – unless you're quoting James Joyce, in which case it's OK.'

'When Patrick did over 23 Oundle Square he picked up heroin and crack cocaine with a street value of half a million. It's with Scotland Yard now, with Paisley's name and address attached. But they can't prosecute unless Patrick gives evidence and confesses to burglary.'

'Theft, surely – Susan Galloway let him in.'

'We can't say so.'

'No, you can't. What about the bugs he attached to Paisley's telephone system?'

'Clear evidence of criminal conspiracy with Livingstone Lord. Clear evidence that all charges against Lord are on ice while the drug supply continues. We can also prove that Paisley set up the burglary of Patrick's house, using Lucy and that boy, Daniel Richardson.'

'Can I hear the telephone taps, Marcus?'

'Same difficulty – how did we obtain them? How do we keep Susan Galloway out of it? How do we avoid criminal prosecution?'

'You must have anticipated these problems – so why did you do it?'

'We have passed the evidence to Scotland Yard through Clive Wellings. We are telling them something.'

'Do they want to know?'

'Not yet. Paisley is Acting DPP.'

'Did you mention any of this to the Lord Chief Justice?'

'Of course not. How could I? But I did have a word with Max Venables. Max got really interested when I told him we had taps of Paisley in conversation with Jeremy Darling.'

'Wow! Tell me!'

'A straight deal: Darling would persuade the Attorney General to confirm Paisley as permanent DPP, to replace Lionel Lacey, if Paisley could persuade Max and the Boy to denounce someone called Byron – in public – as a villain.'

'Nice.' She squeezes his arm. 'I mean nasty. Did you play those telephone taps to Venables?'

'Yeah. He wanted to listen to every word. So did the Boy. They went straight to the Attorney General.'

'Wow. Wow! Can I give you a hug, right here?'

'The only woman I hug is called Brigid Kyle.'

'Brigid who? Is she your latest?'

He chuckles. 'I reckon she's half of London's latest.'

'I'll ignore that on a conditional discharge.' She whirls her handbag and strikes him on the head. 'There's one person we haven't mentioned, your Honour.'

'Yeah?'

'Yeah! And what about Heather Stuart!' she yells.

The black roller boy glides gracefully between them.

'Lady, are you about to assault this old-age pensioner? Is this a racist attack, please, or just a robbery?'

'Sonny, who are you?' Marcus asks.

The roller boy smiles beautifully – Brigid is stunned by his beauty.

'Let's say, Judge, that I'm the son you never had. And it may be too late now, with all due respect to Mrs Kyle.'

The boy glides away in a riot of colour and muffled stereo sounds, perhaps destined to fall in love with his own reflection in the Serpentine.

'So what about Heather Stuart?' she repeats.

Marcus refills his pipe with elaborately ritual gestures. A flock of complaining gulls is circling above their heads.

'You haven't cautioned me,' he says.

'I award you the Nobel Prize for Eloquence and Candour.'

'Brigid, I—'

'You're not looking your best at this moment in time, Judge Byron.'

'Hm.'

'That bitch has you by the short hairs, if you'll pardon my French.'

'It's all over.'

'Marcus Byron, I am demanding an apology.'

'Brigid . . . it was only once.'

'Once, he says! Ha! Wait while I cross myself and say ten Hail Marys! Once!'

'How about a dash for the Coliseum in St Martin's Lane? They might have two spare seats for *Rigoletto* tonight.'

'Wouldn't *Don Giovanni* be more appropriate?'

'Mario Barletto is singing the title role.'

'I don't care if it's Marcus Byronetto.'

'OK, I'll sing the part. Right here.'

'You voice has gone – if you ever had one. And you're overweight. Too much flab and flatulence. I don't want to be sitting in the stalls with a black blancmange, do I?'

'It was only once!'

'She says six times. She counted your orgasms, too.'

'She "says"? She . . . You mean . . . I mean . . . hey—'

'She came to see me. She brought her cat's eyes along. She wanted to set her side of the story straight. Don't avert your fine head, Marcus. Did you know that Heather is Teresa Kent's sister?'

His eyes roll. 'Jesus!'

'She's the spitting image, isn't she? She reminded you of some unfinished business, eh?

'This is the Inquisition.'

'Your floozie wanted me to know exactly what happened at the Riverview Club and later on the Tyndale towpath.'

'Oh yeah? What did happen?'

'You asked her to do a kneeling blow-job on Lacey to keep him quiet. She refused. There was a scene. Angela Loftus keeled over.'

'And you believe that!'

'That's what you wanted her to do at the Riverview Club, wasn't it, when you left her alone with that madman in the dressing room?'

'No. No! Wendy and I were right outside the door.'

'So what did you want Heather Stuart to do to Lacey?'

'God knows, Brigid . . . Dinner, a floor show, a belly-dancer, anything to divert him from rent-boys, urchins and *misérables.*' Marcus strides away a few paces. 'I'm going to the Coliseum alone! Is that understood?'

'Yep. Go.'

'I said, is that understood?'

'Bye.'

'Brigid, I swear I'll never touch another woman.'

'Never? You mean till next time?'

'Never!'

She smiles. 'Well, I'm only coming with you to make sure you go alone.'

The roller boy passes them at a safe distance, shaking his head, shocked to see they haven't moved in twenty minutes, two middle-aged people brawling in public and now embracing like kids.

# *Sixteen*

LUCY SITS ON A bench in Century Park, smoking and brooding. The world is at school. She is used to bunking off, sabotaging the Establishment's private timetable, but now no one in authority demands her presence; no one requires her to be anywhere at any time of day. And they have remanded Dan to Downton. Dan is inside.

'That's aggravated,' he'd objected when she first put the plan to him without telling him whose house he was going to rubbish and soil. She knows 'soiling' is a legal term; to the propertied classes it's the ultimate outrage, a form of 'mindless vandalism', and therefore a stark declaration of class war, of envy, of hatred. *They* can understand the thieving aspect of burglary because they're all thieves and crooks themselves, but what they can't stomach is hatred. Hatred forces them to feel guilty and to question their own privileges.

Yeah. Lucy's head is fuzzed by dope. Should she feel guilty about Dan? After the riots and the raids on shops for 'compensation', Trish had aggro-ed her about Dan's promised payment, the one thousand pounds. The Richardson 'family' were claiming it on Dan's behalf but Lucy knows he'll never see a penny of it if she hands it over.

Besides, she doesn't have the money. Nick just looked through her when she mentioned it.

Sitting cross-legged on her bench in Century Park, Lucy placidly observes a youth she has not set eyes on for many months.

It's Mark Griffin – you couldn't mistake those cross-eyes and that loopy look. Lucy has never had anything to do with Griffins. They hate anything coloured. Besides, if you 'run' with the Richardsons, you're automatically a target for the Griffins. But she's not bothered.

Dressed like a tramp, totally disgusting, Mark is wandering along the railings bordering the One O'Clock Club. But it's empty, closed at this hour of the late afternoon. No toddlers to snatch.

Three smartly dressed girls from St Hilda's walk past Lucy's bench. She doesn't know them but she recognises them. They keep their eyes averted and giggle as they pass. What's so funny?

Mark Griffin is eyeing the three girls: cross-eyeing them. Lucy watches them quicken their step. She's not afraid of Mark herself, maybe it's the dope. One of the old Irish park wardens has emerged from his hutch beside the tennis courts. Lucy can see him sizing Mark up, then talking into one of the mobile telephones recently dished out by the Council's Leisure & Rec. Department after Councillor Ruth Tanner had raised a big fuss about security in the park. Lucy had overheard her mum talking to Nick about it. Nick and Jill wanted to boot Ruth Tanner off the Council because she was too cosy with the police and belonged to the wrong political party, or something.

Mark is ambling away now across the open expanses of grass, towards the filthy copse they call Dog Shit. The three giggling snobs from Saint Heeldah's have disappeared, safely delivered home to their mamas.

Yeah, she feels terrible about Dan. Jill told Lucy that he was brought before Miss Swearwell and that shit Rodney Parker, who Auntie Wendy is so chummy with. It didn't matter that Dan had been battered, his face still swollen and covered in plasters, all that mattered was that he'd trashed Auntie Wendy's posh house and sworn he was getting revenge for Patrick Berry sending him to Downton.

Lucy had never told Dan to say that. But Lucy hadn't warned him whose house he was doing over, so probably Dan just made it up on the spot when he recognised Berry. According to Jill, the court clerks had checked out that Berry had never sent Daniel to Downton, no one had, he'd never been inside, but Miss Swearwell convinced herself that Dan was acting on behalf of other Richardsons, his elder brothers Paul and Amos, in an act of 'revenge and intimidation' directed, can you believe it, 'against the Rule of Law' not to mention the 'Administration of Justice'.

Miss Swearwell would say 'loah', very posh. So they remanded Dan in custody and refused jurisdiction, which meant he was heading for the Crown Court.

Yeah. Poor Dan. Lucy wishes she could break into Downton and spend a night cuddling him in his locked cell. She'd take his sax along, and some dope.

'Nick told me to do it,' Lucy had confided to her mum, in tears. Jill's mouth had set. She never talked about Nick. That was the night the pigs came to the house in their hundreds, Drugs Squad, Special Branch, CID, all flashing warrants and shoving each other aside as they did the house over, top to toe, carting away loads of stuff in plastic sacks. They'd trashed the house like Dan trashed the Berrys', slitting open duvets and cushions, ripping up carpets, slicing into the linings of clothes and curtains. The only thing they didn't do was 'soil' the place – the shit was all in their heads.

Nick hadn't been at home. He'd rarely been seen lately, only occasional glimpses of that clamped ferret-face crippled by calculation. Jill and Lucy had 'received' their nocturnal visitors alone, Jill frantically phoning every lawyer in sight but no one, not Averling, not Simmonds, had wanted to come.

POLICE RAID ACTING DPP'S HOME

Yeah, that Brigid Kyle bitch launched her great 'exposé' of the Congress for Justice in the next day's *Sentinel*.

Hey ho! Who is this prancing smartly along? Who but posh Amelia Harsent, carrying her new flute in a smart case and hurrying home from her private music lesson to teeee with Mama. She's seen me. She's deciding whether to carry straight on past me or take the short cut across the grass, though that might spoil her pretty shoes. Yeah. The Harsents had led the parental pack demanding Lucy's expulsion from Saint Heeldah's – Amelia had gone to Mrs Nearcliffe and claimed that Lucy had been pooling money for cut-price drugs, then not delivering. What a fucking liar.

Yeah, she's thought better of it. She's diverting herself across the grass. Lazily Lucy swivels on her bench and scans the wide expanses towards the copse called Dog Shit. No sign of the dopey, lumbering figure of Mark Griffin. But Lucy knows where he is. He's flashing his dick to the squirrels over in Dog Shit.

Perhaps she should warn Amelia. Perhaps she shouldn't. You wouldn't get thanked, would you?

Amelia is dwindling into the horizon, her step brisk and confident, buttocks bouncing, as befits a young lady inheriting the earth.

Eden Manor police station is alerted by a park warden to a youth resembling Mark Griffin who has been spotted, drunk, filthy and in rags, heading across Century Park. Howling siren and rotating beacon, McIntyre and Jenkins leap lights and bring traffic to a halt as they race for the Brancaster Road gate to the park. This time they don't need a warrant.

The park is vast, the silence also. Old Sam Caughey, one of the Irish park wardens, seems to be gesturing, from a considerable distance, towards the dense, ugly copse known to the kids as Dog Shit. The two cops run, caps off. Jenkins's long stride, which has earned him a place in the London Welsh Second XV, carries him ahead. Is that a scream they hear? A pitiful cry of fear and pain?

A group of young children are running towards them from the direction of the copse, screaming hysterically and babbling wildly. The CID men accelerate from a canter into a gallop. Mark Griffin may be a menace to the entire female sex but they haven't forgotten that he led his brothers' murderous assault in the Broadway underpass on Herb Knowles (now forced into early retirement from the BTP), before vanishing down his sewer.

Lucy sits on her bench watching the two pigs hoofing it across the long expanse of open ground towards the copse. She unwraps a stick of chewing gum, spearmint, and lays it on the tip of her extended tongue.

Half a mile away, in the offices of the *Post*, Joe O'Neill is sifting through the day's stories when he takes a call from Detective Constable Cliff Jenkins.

'Put this statement into the paper, Joe.'

'All systems go, Cliff.'

> The police are now looking for a youth they wish to interview about the rape of a 16-year-old girl. She was crossing Century Park at about 5 p.m., when she was threatened with a knife by a teenager wearing a balaclava. He forced the girl to undress,

ripping off some of her clothing, then blindfolded her and tied her wrists to a tree with her own shoelaces. After the rape he ambled away, taking her clothes with him. The victim described her attacker as white, aged 15 to 17, of medium build with a chubby face, a thick growth on his chin, and 'crossed eyes'. He was wearing a black jacket, a grey T-shirt with a picture on the front, blue-grey jogging shorts, and white trainers. All his clothes looked 'filthy'.

Members of the public are advised to exercise extreme caution and to notify the police if they observe any youth of similar appearance whose behaviour arouses suspicion. He should not be approached as he is known to be dangerous.

'Mark Griffin, Cliff?'

'We have no doubt. But', adds Jenkins bitterly, 'we cannot name a juvenile.'

'Who was the victim, Cliff?'

'She's female and a juvenile. You know the rules, Joe.'

'Give us a break, Cliff!'

'Joe, you wouldn't spot a break if it ran from the top of your skull to whatever you carry between your legs – and no offence. However, I could go right off the record, boyo.'

This surprises Joe; he'd asked his question without hope of an answer but remembering one of Brigid Kyle's casually dropped pearls of journalistic wisdom. 'Always ask, Joe, never make their rules your own. The most dangerous form of censorship is self-censorship.'

Even by Jenkins's standards of sarcasm his tone of scorn is striking: 'Let's just say that the shattered mother of the victim is a prominent Justice on our Youth Court who had refused us a warrant for the arrest of the suspected rapist.'

'Holy smoke! It wasn't the Harsent girl?'

'Draw your own conclusions.'

'And you say Lady Harsent had refused to sign a warrant?'

'She bloody told us there was no bloody case for one.'

Joe begins to rearrange his reports, captions and headlines. Items headed 'Join Our Loyal Supporters' and 'Senior Citizens Can Celebrate in Comfort' must go. Mark Griffin deserves the front page. Typing furiously on his computer keyboard, Joe transcribes his copy into the 'yesterday' idiom – the story will run in tomorrow's *Post*.

He picks up the phone – this will be the hardest call of his life.

He can imagine the scene within the Harsent home – no, he can't do it. He loses his nerve and calls Brigid Kyle instead.

Nick Paisley had been shown the proofs of Brigid Kyle's exposé (part one) by the *Sentinel*'s lawyers the day before scheduled publication. The day, as it turned out, that 23 Oundle Square was raided by the police. Cancelling a routine meeting with Area Prosecutors, he had urgently contacted Edgar Averling and Sandra Golding: could they secure a High Court injunction preventing publication? Both lawyers immediately declined their services on the ground that they themselves were accused by Brigid Kyle of conspiracy and collusion.

'So it's cut and run?' Nick had snarled down the phone at Averling.

Nick Paisley had then attempted to contact the Home Secretary and the Attorney General. Neither was 'available'. News came through that Max Venables was due to put a 'personal question' to Jeremy Darling in the Commons concerning private telephone conversations he had held with Paisley.

What happened next became public knowledge only when Derek Jardine decided to leak the story to Brigid Kyle. Himself set on leaving the CPS – he already had two offers from legal-aid firms – Jardine had happened to be in the CPS's Travel Bureau, applying for a rail ticket to a conference in Leeds, when Paisley burst in, pushed him aside and instructed old Mr Yardley to attend to him first.

Paisley then demanded a Business Class flight voucher to Buenos Aires 'on urgent official business'.

'When, sir?'

'Tonight. First available flight.'

Mr Yardley was flustered. This was the Acting DPP, the Boss. He mildly pointed out that such an outlay required two authorised signatures. No official, not even the highest, could draw funds merely on his own say-so.

'Sign this, Derek.' Nick had thrust the form in front of Jardine.

Jardine had looked at Paisley's narrowing eyes and seen a frightened ferret. 'Why Buenos Aires? Why the hurry?'

'Just sign.'

Derek had leaned across the counter to Mr Yardley.

'Shall I tell you something interesting, Sid? There is no extradition treaty between Britain and Argentina.'

'Really, sir?'

'Hm. It's because of the Falklands or Malvinas or call them what you like.'

'Frankly, sir, I prefer the Falklands.'

'It sounds as if our Acting Director here prefers the Malvinas.'

But the Acting Director was no longer 'here': Nick Paisley had taken to the emergency stairs marked 'Fire Exit'. He would pay for his own ticket to Argentina before Brigid Kyle's story went to press. Reaching Heathrow airport he had time to put through one call. It wasn't to anyone within the CPS. It wasn't to Jill Hull. It was to Livingstone Lord.

'I'll be away forty-eight hours,' he said.

It was an agreed code. Lord knew what he must do. He had no idea that the man authorising the killing could do nothing further for him.

McIntyre and Jenkins are expecting further trouble round Eden Manor. Reading the *Post* during a tea break, Jenkins laughs grimly.

'I see Joe O'Neill has got it right again.'

'You mean he copied down everything you told him.'

Jenkins insists on reading a passage aloud – he's always happy to see himself nestling anonymously between the lines of Joe's crisp prose:

> It's open season. The prominent individuals who have taken a stand on crime have been publicly smeared. That message gets across – even to youngsters who couldn't spell their own names.
>
> The morale of Benson Street Youth Court staff is today at an all-time low. The criminal fraternity of Eden Manor is cock-a-hoop. The suspension of Crown Court Judge Marcus Byron has been interpreted by the nation's criminals and delinquents as the green light for a free run.
>
> In addition, the recent indictment of the hard-line Benson Street magistrate, Patrick Berry, on charges of assault and causing grievous bodily harm, has provoked riotous celebrations and a new outbreak of looting and vandalism. The walls of Eden Manor estate have been crudely spray-painted: 'Kill a cop, eat pork.'

Mark Griffin has finally been bagged while threatening an off-licence proprietor with a broken beer bottle. When seized by four officers Mark had displayed a deeply moving attachment to Amelia Harsent's underwear – the DNA tests would hopefully nail him (the testimony of the victim herself never being entirely 'safe' once a skilled defence barrister got to work on her).

But Amos Richardson is again at large – this is what preoccupies Doug McIntyre. Granted bail on appeal by Sir Henry Harsent in chambers, Amos has returned to Eden Manor from Downton. The hard information reaches McIntyre from Ruth Tanner. Firing himself up on a day-and-night cocktail of drink and drugs, Amos has been wandering around threatening vengeance for what happened to Daniel. Tooled up and out of his head, he is vowing to teach someone what he calls 'respect'.

It could be anyone who crosses his path at the wrong moment. On the other hand, McIntyre reasons, the victim is more likely to be an individual against whom Amos has concocted a grievance.

Who?

Trawling through Amos's long criminal record, McIntyre keeps coming back to the same two youngsters most at risk.

One is Lucy Byron herself. McIntyre's sources in the juvenile underworld of Eden Manor report that the Richardsons believe themselves to have been betrayed and cheated by Lucy. They are convinced that she had offered Daniel a large sum of money to do over the Berry household and to get himself beaten up by Patrick Berry, JP. Various figures are floating around, from five hundred to an improbable ten thousand. Whatever the sum, the money (according to rumour) has not been paid. McIntyre reckons it never will be, now that Nick Paisley has done a bunk and declared himself Governor of the Malvinas (which is the local joke in Eden Manor police station).

McIntyre is in little doubt that one thousand pounds paid into Amos's hand on Daniel Richardson's 'behalf' would instantly divert Amos's quest for justice – and therefore vengeance. But there is nothing he can do or say about that since Lucy's involvement in the Berry burglary is hypothetical, unproven and not admitted. How can he go to Marcus Byron with the advice, 'Find the money and fast,' without seeming to invite the judge to admit his daughter's involvement?

McIntyre feels less convinced about Amos's other potential target. McIntyre had managed to bury his interview with young Nigel Thompson after Amos robbed Susan Galloway. Nigel's bright formula for indicating what he had seen without admitting it – 'ARithmetic' – had never reached other eyes. Amos had merely been convicted of handling stolen goods. If Amos has not pursued Nigel, why should he do so now?

It all depends. McIntyre remembers an occasion, about one year ago, when a party of a dozen Chaucer School choristers wearing their neat blue crested blazers and grey flannels had been set upon by a gang of black youths while crossing Century Park.

Boys from Chaucer School and Eden Manor Comprehensive had been at war around Century Park for years, but the big movers and shakers were youths who had long since been expelled from the Comprehensive or had lapsed into permanent absconding. The senior teachers of both schools anxiously conferred with the Borough Education Committee. The Headmaster of Chaucer instructed his pupils to avoid Century Park and keep to the High Street – but some of them, being proud and spirited, ignored the advice. Anxious Chaucer parents forbade their sons to take Walkmans and even wristwatches to school. Mothers began turning up in nice cars at 4 p.m. to collect boys from the school gates.

McIntyre has Joe O'Neill's yellowing report of the attack in Century Park on file:

> Two Chaucer School pupils were recovering from serious injuries yesterday after their choir was attacked in Century Park by four black youths armed with knives and hammers. The Chaucer boys were on their way home after a rehearsal for a school centenary celebration. Police are treating the attacks as racially motivated after statements from the choristers.

Interviewing the Chaucer boys, McIntyre had been convinced of Amos's involvement. But none of the boys would sign a witness statement. They were terrified.

Marcus receives a call from Oxford CID. Geoffrey Villiers has been found dead in his garage. The engine of his car was still running and a hosepipe had been attached to the exhaust.

'On the face of it a clear case of suicide, sir.'

'Suicide? Geoffrey was a member of the Voluntary Euthanasia Society. He once showed me what he called his "Exit Kit". Highly sophisticated and nothing to do with toxic exhaust fumes.'

'There's no sign of a struggle, sir.'

'Anything taken?'

'Nothing obvious. But we thought you might be able to help.'

'In what way?'

'We're at a loss to trace his next of kin, sir. The College knows only of an elderly sister, but she's living in New Zealand if still alive. Evidently Mr Villiers told the College Bursar some time ago that, in the event of his death, you were the person to contact.'

'I'll take the 11.20 from Paddington.'

'Thank you, sir, much obliged. We'll send a car to meet you at the station.'

Villiers had occupied the same modest, semi-detached, red-brick home in North Oxford, between the Woodstock and Banbury Roads, ever since Marcus could remember. He cherishes memories of Geoffrey's summer barbecues for law students (and any pretty boy who caught his eye). At a certain stage in the revels Geoffrey would begin to sing an old English revolutionary song, 'Stand up, stand up, you Diggers, stand up, you Diggers all'.

Geoffrey Villiers was a man you always stood up for.

An inspector from Oxford CID conducts Marcus round the house. If intruders had broken in, there is no sign of it – an expert job, no traces. And absolutely no hint of a struggle.

'We found the Exit Kit you mentioned, sir, in the bathroom cabinet. Quite sophisticated – but elaborate. Sometimes, when despair comes, people take the shortest route.'

'Yeah.' Marcus lights his pipe and wanders out through the french windows into the pleasant garden where Geoffrey used to stage his barbecues.

'Is there anything you can tell us, sir?'

At the bottom of the garden stands an ancient tool shed, its timbers rotted by the years, its ugly corrugated-tin roof coated in moss and rust. Marcus notices that the door of the shed is swinging lightly in the breeze. The padlock has been prised off – one rusty screw lies in the long, uncut grass. Marcus bends to retrieve it.

'They broke in.'

The smell inside the shed is a pleasant blend of compost, the remains of some chemical fertiliser, charcoal cinders and plain wood-damp.

'Got a flashlight?'

'Yes, sir.'

He runs the beam round the interior of the shed: immediately visible are a very old hand-push mower, a few spades and the rusting barbecue. Handing his jacket to the Inspector, Marcus rolls up the sleeves of his shirt and thrusts his arm deep into a 5kg brown-paper sack half-filled with charcoal. Then he empties the contents out on to the grass.

Nothing. The Lucy tape has gone.

'They found what they were looking for. Poor Geoffrey.'

'"They", sir?'

An hour later he visits the city mortuary to pay his last respects. Bending to kiss the great man, he does not dare lift the closed lids, perhaps fearing to discover a last look of anguished accusation. He places a fresh lemon in Villiers's rigid, resisting, hand.

'Poor, bleeding England,' he murmurs.

Two of Marcus's imagined graves have been filled – two out of the three he had seen from the train, shrouded in mist, the last time he travelled back from Oxford.

Nigel Thompson has been walking home from school, crossing Century Park, for years. It's a short, convenient route from Chaucer, across the park, along Brancaster Road (passing Ron Tanner's repair shop) to Oundle Square. After the Susan Galloway robbery, Nigel had been haunted by the livid scar on Amos's cheek. In his dreams he was constantly followed by this tall black, loose-limbed youth, with his dreadlocks and his red baseball cap worn in reverse. But time has assuaged Nigel's fears. Things which don't happen aren't going to happen.

Loaded with three hours' homework, he leaves Chaucer at 4.00 p.m. He notices some black youths lounging half-way up the alleyway used by Chaucer boys heading for the High Street. Instantly recognising the unmistakable Amos Richardson among them, Nigel turns back, his heart thumping, his stomach knotted. Seeing Mrs Webster-Brown's Audi parked outside the school gates, he considers asking her for a lift home. He knows her quite well; she always chats to his parents at school 'report' days, and Nigel has more than once been home to tea with his friend Charlie Webster-Brown.

He hesitates, though. It would sound flappy, windy, to explain. He might lose face in front of Charlie. Too much embarrassment.

Amos has seen the boy turn back. Smelling fear, he suddenly remembers who that white prat is, a wanker with the placid look of an overturned milk bowl. Amos knows the boy's name: Nigel Thompson. A moment ago Amos and Trish had been planning a visit to Lucy Byron's house, to get the money or else, but now his drug-blasted brain is totally diverted by that piglet Nigel Thompson, who'd seen him attack the Galloway woman. And isn't that trial coming up? Amos can't remember which trial is coming up and which isn't. Yeah, that Thompson boy will be the sole witness, he's sure of it, apart from maybe the Galloway woman herself.

Too much knowledge in his insolent head. Too much knowledge! Disrespect!

Nigel makes tracks for Century Park. It seems quiet enough – just the usual mix of old men snoozing on benches, mums with children, a couple of joggers, a lone black boy on rollers, dogs . . . He passes the One O'Clock Club for toddlers, closed for the afternoon.

He sees a girl sitting on a park bench, smoking something and looking phased-out all round. In recent days he has more than once passed Lucy Byron on his way home; she always sits curled up on the same bench, with that possessive knack tramps have. He has heard about her expulsion from St Hilda's and would like to say a word, but she always stares right through him, stoned out, and he walks on. There had been a time when he'd secretly rather fancied Lucy, and plotted excuses to waylay her in Oundle Square, just casually, as if by chance, but he never did and in recent times he hasn't fancied her at all.

Actually, there are two black boys on rollers, wheeling and leaping and executing spectacular turns. One sweeps past him . . . then the other. Very close. He has to dodge them. His heart thumps sickeningly. He feels sick.

'Hi, Nigel,' Lucy calls. 'Can you lend me twenty pee?'

'Yes, yes, of course.' He puts the money into a rather grimy little hand covered in iron finger-rings and tattoos.

'Want a smoke?' she says.

'No, thanks.'

'Been baby-sitting for the Galloways, have you?'

The black roller boys are coming back. He begins to move away from Lucy.

'Friendly, aren't you?' she calls.

'Yes, sorry, I—'

Nigel quickens his stride as he takes the short route across the grass.

Amos Richardson passes the girl on the bench without a glance.

Five minutes ago she had been his target for the afternoon but now he is compulsively driven by the need to silence the posh little wanker who's going to give evidence against him.

Nigel would like to steer clear of the small copse known as Dog Shit. Things can happen very suddenly near the copse. A St Hilda's girl had been raped there a few days ago. Nigel's mind goes blank on the word 'rape' – he has never kissed a girl. Chaucer and St Hilda's have a joint orchestra. Nigel plays the clarinet. He thinks he remembers the raped girl, Amelia Harsent, in the flute section, a rather posh, haughty individual, but he isn't sure.

To avoid the copse he would have to cut across back to the Tarmac path bordering the sandpit area, and he notices that the two black boys on rollers are now cruising parallel with him along that path.

His heart is hammering. He wants to vomit.

The adult world, which he has always trusted, the world of his parents, has evaporated.

A hundred yards behind him, the park bench where Lucy had borrowed 20p from him is empty. She has picked up the ugly vibes from Amos Richardson and fled in the opposite direction. Mark Griffin hadn't scared her but Amos does.

Nigel glances back – and all the dreams, the nightmares, open their gates. They are closing on him from behind, the black youths who had been lounging in the alleyway leading to the High Street. He sees Amos Richardson's scar.

He looks for help, one of those old Irish park keepers, perhaps, Paddy or Sean. Nothing. And then they're on him. He raises both arms in a pathetic gesture of self-defence and howls for mercy.

One minute later Nigel Thompson lies half-dead on the grass in the middle of Century Park, his skull fractured, one eye dangling from its socket, arms and legs broken by iron bars, urine flooding his clothes.

Manically excited, high on crack, eyes burning, Amos yells, 'Stand back, brothers, and watch this!'

Yeah . . . this is the prat who had seen him rob the Galloway woman on her own doorstep in Oundle Square, the posh wanker whose fear-paralysed dial betrayed his insolent knowledge.

No respect!

Kneeling on the sobbing Nigel Thompson, Amos raises his right arm high and stabs the boy three times, with all his weight and power and venom, through the heart.

A Latin dictionary lies on the grass.

Lucy is alone in the house when she hears the front door close. She would like to talk to her mother about what happened to Nigel Thompson but Jill has been disintegrating, falling apart, ever since Nick took off for Argentina without a word. You can't really talk to her. Lucy knows that her mother has been suspended by the Probation Service, following the police raid and the publication of Brigid Kyle's articles, but Jill merely weeps in helpless anger – is it anger? – if you try to show sympathy.

Lucy has read Brigid Kyle's three-part series, 'The Byron Affair'. Her eye kept settling on one passage:

> If Jill Hull has been unaware that her partner, Nick Paisley, was systematically supplying drugs to her daughter, right within her own home, she must be the most myopic mother in Britain. Marcus Byron's two anguished attempts to recover control of his daughter, his applications for custody, were successfully resisted by Ms Hull. In the most recent, she submitted to the court an affidavit signed by Lucy Byron herself: 'I would not touch that man with a bargepole.'

Yeah. Lucy remembers flashing her signature across the document drafted by Edgar Averling.

Lucy would like to talk to Jill about her interview at Eden Manor police station today. She would and she wouldn't. She hasn't sorted it out in her own mind yet. Ever since she saw Amos pursuing Nigel across the park, and knew what was going to happen, and ran away, but still couldn't help hearing Nigel's cries, Lucy has suffered attacks of nausea and giddiness and rushes of menstrual blood.

McIntyre had called at the house when Jill was out; her mum was still desperately trying to persuade the Association of Chief Officers of Probation to contest her suspension, despite the hailstorm of phoney statistics and propaganda slushfunds hurled at her by Brigid Kyle.

'Hullo, Lucy.' The haggis was standing on the doorstep of No. 23, wearing his 'honest Doug, your neighbourhood friend' look.

'Yeah?' Lucy was sure he wanted to question her about Nigel's death because she had been in the park at the time. She still had Nigel's 20p. She hadn't needed 20p, she'd just wanted to chat him up, pass the time.

'Is your mother at home?'

Lucy shook her head. You don't waste words on pigs.

'We'd like to have a word with you at the police station.'

Lucy immediately held out her skinny arms. 'Where's the cuffs, then?'

'Just a chat, Lucy, entirely voluntary.'

'What about?'

'Mainly about you, Lucy.'

'Yeah?' In fact Lucy desperately needed a bit of action, a bit of excitement, a bit of something-happening, in her life, so she sullenly accepted a back seat in McIntyre's panda. When they got to the police station she was taken into a back office and offered a cup of tea, all very cosy. There was another bloke there, who she vaguely recognised.

'Derek Jardine of the CPS,' he introduced himself.

'Now, Lucy,' McIntyre began, 'it's my belief that you may be at risk from the Richardsons.'

'Oh yeah?'

'Rightly or wrongly, Lucy, the Richardsons believe you owe them the money you promised to Daniel.'

'Oh yeah. What money? And where's my lawyer? Where's my parent? What kind of a fix-up d'yer think you can get away with?'

McIntyre nodded. 'Quite right. We'll have to wait until your mother is available.'

But Lucy didn't want that. She wanted some fun. When Jill was around you got squeezed out of the picture, they talked over your head as if you weren't there. She'd happily confess to putting Dan up to the job on the Berrys, but it might let that bastard Patrick Berry and that superior, disapproving bitch Auntie Wendy off the hook for the assault and 'grievous' inflicted on Dan. They'd want to nail it all on Nick because Nick was now the devil incarnate.

At this juncture Derek Jardine entered the conversation.

'Lucy, we intend to withdraw the drugs charge agaisnt you.'

'Yeah? Why? Doug here and his sow WPC found the stuff on me, didn't they?'

'Lucy, we don't think think it's safe to prosecute these charges. Where an adult can be shown to have systematically corrupted a minor, the defence of duress applies.'

'Duress? What bloody duress? Nick never made me do anything I didn't want to do!'

'It is not in the public interest to proceed,' Jardine said quietly.

'It's a bloody cover-up! You're in collusion with my dad! Shall I spell "collusion" for you? You're a fucking Lemon, aren't you, Jardine? Nick always said you were. Nick always said you had long cosy chats with my Auntie Wendy, the sow. So now's your big chance, eh?'

'Lucy, I have not spoken to your father about this.'

'Yeah? Oh yeah! I bet!'

'Lucy,' McIntyre asked gently, 'why are you so anxious to be prosecuted?'

Lucy bit her nails and sulked. 'Who says I am? And what about me doing over old Mrs Ramsden in the park – that was vicious, wasn't it?'

Jardine and McIntyre exchanged glances.

'Lucy,' Jardine said, 'if you're not charged, you cannot ask for other offences to be taken into consideration.'

'Anyway,' McIntyre said, 'you couldn't confess to robbing Mrs Ramsden without implicating Trish Richardson and Debbie O'Grady.'

'They had nothing to do with it!'

'Mrs Ramsden was robbed by three girls, she's sure of it.'

'Maybe she saw double or triple with those rotten eyes of hers!'

McIntyre sighed. 'Shall I drive you home, Lucy?'

'I can walk.'

For the past few hours Lucy has been watching boring daytime television and biting her nails. Now she can hear her mother moving about downstairs in a distracted kind of way. Poor Mum. In the old days Jill would have called her down as soon as she came in, laden with shopping bags, to ask whether Lucy had eaten and generally to fuss over her. But Jill hasn't cooked a proper meal since Nick left. The fridge is empty. Lucy's dirty clothes just pile up in the basket.

Lucy beats back rising fear. The world, her world, is falling apart.

The phone rings. When Dan was free and Nick was living with them, the telephone rang all the time. Now it's a rarity in a silent house. Lucy waits for Jill to take the call, then softly lifts the upstairs extension and listens. She recognises the caller at once. It's an hysterical Cecilia Harsent.

'Jill! Where have you been? I've been trying to find you everywhere. Have you seen today's *Sentinel*?'

'Yes.' Jill sounds half-dead to Lucy.

'I am accused by that Brigid Kyle woman! How dare she! And I hear that she's Marcus Byron's mistress! And I've had a letter from the MCC. They're rubbing my name off the list of candidates for the chairmanship.'

'I see,' Jill murmurs.

'Is that all you can say, Jill? I have also had word from the Lord Chancellor's office that I may have to stand down from the Bench. I'm accused of refusing to issue a warrant for the arrest of Mark Griffin.'

'Did you refuse?'

'The police utterly failed to present me with the relevant facts!'

Jill is silent. Lucy holds her breath to suppress any sound down the line from her extension.

'Jill, I need your support. I need everyone's support. I thought you were my friend. You and Jimmy Haley-White must do something—'

'Jimmy has left the country.' Lucy hears Jill's voice break. 'He has gone home to Ghana.' Lucy's mother is crying. She'd loved Jimmy, Lucy is sure of it.

'Has he? How typical! No consideration or loyalty. Frankly, I never trusted that young man. Now, Jill, I'm counting on the support of the Probation Service.'

'I have been suspended . . .'

Lady Harsent offers not a word of commiseration. She doesn't hear, or want to hear, Jill's tears.

'I've spoken to Sandra and Edgar and I'm at my wits' end. They're no help at all. Patrick Berry's allies – people like Sally Swearwell and that dreadful Rodney Parker – are threatening to reveal whole files of complaints against me – what complaints, I ask you? – stretching back over "years", they say, from fellow magistrates and clerks, are you listening, Jill?'

'I'm listening, Cecilia,' Lucy hears her mother murmur. 'How's Amelia?' she asks politely.

'What?'

'I said: "How is your poor daughter?"' To Lucy's ear each word seems dragged out by thumb-screw.

'Please stick to the point. What are you going to do for me, Jill?'

'I am not in a position . . . to do anything . . . for anybody.'

'I warn you, Jill, I know things about you and Nick and—'

'Goodbye.'

Ten minutes later Lucy creeps to the head of the stairs. She can hear her mother weeping in the kitchen. Lucy closes her bedroom door and curls up in bed with her best photo of Dan. She tries to imagine him in his cell in Downton. Then she ponders what McIntyre said about the money due to the Richardsons.

Her mind begins to skim and somersault with invention. Yeah! She will go straight to Marcus to ask him to hand over the thousand quid – 'For my protection!' That will land him in it. That will put an end to the cosy love-in between his Honour and the Berrys. Brilliant!

Lucy falls asleep but wakes up shortly before midnight, she's not sure why. She creeps out on to the landing. The house is in darkness. Jill's bedroom door is closed.

Something – one of those uncertain street sounds – takes Lucy to the window. Cautiously she draws back the curtain. She is not sure what she sees. It seems fast, shadowy, then it's gone. Oundle Square is now haunted, a nocturnal playground for poltergeists.

Simon Galloway is also working late. Susan is already asleep upstairs on sedatives. The murder of their neighbour and occasional babysitter, young Nigel Thompson, has shattered her.

Such a nice boy, so friendly to Tom. Such a bright future. His poor parents, Eric and Jane. Oundle Square is in shock and mourning. The curtains remain drawn at No. 36.

They say that the boy arrested is the Amos Richardson who had robbed Susan – though he was never convicted of that, only of handling goods stolen from her. They say that the magistrate, a Miss Swearwell, has remanded him straight into custody but his lawyers plan to lodge an appeal, asking for a secure psychiatric unit on the ground that Amos lacked the resources to control his emotions at the time of the killing, and was therefore not responsible for his actions.

But boys emerge from 'secure' psychiatric units in strange ways. It had happened with that Mark Griffin who raped that poor girl from St Hilda's School.

They say this, they say that. Simon and Susie have discussed every rumour with each other, and with neighbours, until they are exhausted by speculation, uncertainty, fear . . .

Everyone is agreed that the 'system' does not work. But no one agrees why. Some blame the shark-lawyers but others, anxious to be fair – the British are always fair – argue that you cannot blame lawyers for exploiting every available loophole in 'the law'.

So it comes back to the law and the politicians. No two Londoners risk a quarrel if they slag off the 'politicians' while steering clear of declaring their own party allegiance. Politicians are like the weather – never good.

Simon works late, Susan sleeps upstairs on a doctor's sedative. At some stage during the night she will wake up, sobbing hysterically that she wants to move from Oundle Square. Three FOR SALE notices have already gone up during the past few days.

Simon brews himself another cup of decaff. His back aches. Mortgage interest rates have gone up and mortgage tax relief has been slashed. (Never vote for that lot again!) Simon feels obligated to set aside a substantial sum each month to cover Tom's future schooling. Simon and Susan believe in state schools but . . . but Tom is a very nervous, timid child . . . And the two local primary schools, one hears, have recently taken a dramatic turn for the worse: rampant bullying by kids from Eden Manor, academic standards in decline. Children are emerging at the age of eleven barely able to tackle simple arithmetic.

Simon allows himself one lump of sugar in his decaff. His waistline is a reproach. But there you go – no time for squash or the gym lately. Work, work.

He tries to settle at his desk. The students who occupy the flat next door – nice enough when you talk to them individually – have begun to blast away with their rock music and their infernal drum machine. Must he ring their doorbell again?

I'm getting stuffy in my old age. I used to be just like them, up all night, sleep all morning.

Sometimes, tossing sleepless under their bombardment, he contemplates a special revenge: to ring their doorbell every fifteen minutes from the time he gets up at seven to the moment of his departure at eight.

How do you like that? And yet, and yet: it's curious how, in the mellow light of morning, the pains of the night are washed away: the world – Oundle Square – is at peace and everything is forgiven. The idea of tormenting nice students seems impossible.

They don't attack your wife on her doorstep with knives. They don't murder schoolboys.

Simon hears a loud report outside, as of splintering glass, followed immediately by a car alarm which sounds like his own. He is out of the house and down the steps when he sees the front nearside door of the car hanging open; a skinny leg protrudes, capped by a gleaming white trainer. Simon hesitates but instinct is more powerful than reason. Maybe his subconscious has been waiting for the moment of revenge, waiting for the moment of Gotcha.

Lucy sees a man run out from his house and up the street. It looks like Simon Galloway. She hears him shouting.

'What the hell do you think you're doing?'

Simon reaches into his L-registration BMW to grab the youth who is working the audio cassette and graphic equalizer free of their mounting. The youth curses, kicks, twists and tries to force his way out of the car. But Simon is heavier, stronger and leaning down.

He recognises Darren Griffin, Rat Face.

'You're coming with me, sonny. Let's take a good look at you.'

Lucy's warm breath is steaming up the cool night windowpane in her bedroom. She wipes the glass . . . difficult to see what's happening in the street below.

The knife goes straight up between Simon Galloway's ribs. In the split second which is both timeless and an eternity, Simon thinks a fist has struck his chest. He wants to say, 'For God's sake,' but something soft and viscous is welling up his throat. The world turns over as he is kicked back on to the pavement.

Lucy sees Simon Galloway lying on the pavement. Amazed at herself, she dials 999.

The front door of the Galloway house still stands wide open when the police cars arrive. Hearing the crackling radios, the residents of Oundle Square come to their doors and windows. An ambulance turns into the square, wailing, searching. Neighbours are beginning to congregate on the pavement.

Susan Galloway remains fast asleep upstairs in No. 16. Even when they ring the bell, she doesn't stir.

McIntyre climbs the stairs. 'Mrs Galloway,' he calls.

Tom begins to scream from his cot. The black men have come.

Susan emerges on to the landing, clutching at a dressing-gown, her eyes glazed by sleep. McIntyre retreats a step or two by way of reassurance; his training teaches him to keep repeating her name, Mrs Galloway, Mrs Galloway.

'Susie,' he says.

Gradually, patiently, McIntyre explains to Susan that there has been an 'incident' involving her husband. They have taken Simon to the Emergency Unit of St Luke's Hospital.

McIntyre cannot bring himself to extinguish the desperate hope written into her stricken features as she cradles Tom.

Lucy is standing on her own doorstep, shivering in her nightdress. She is trembling violently and her eyes are glazed. She has seen the body on the pavement. First Nigel, now Simon Galloway.

'Where's your mum?' Jenkins asks her gently.

'Asleep,' she whispers.

'So you called the police, Lucy?'

'Yeah.'

'You look cold, Lucy.' He moves to place his own jacket round her shoulders but she recoils.

'What did you see, Lucy?'

'I heard a noise. Like breaking glass, I'm not sure. I was asleep. I saw the bloke . . . Mr Galloway . . . lying on the pavement.'

'Anyone else?'

'No.' Lucy is crying.

'Did you see anyone running away?'

'No. Yeah, maybe.'

Jenkins regards her sceptically as she stands shivering and shifty, eyes lowered. Oddly, he believes her. But he can't exclude from his mind the possibility that she'd had some part in this and was suffering from shock because it had gone wrong.

In No. 16, Susan sits huddled in her dressing-gown, her eyes glazed by sedative-induced sleep. Little Tom is asleep in her lap, his rosebud lips lightly parted, his brow warm – the brow Simon kisses when he arrives home late from the City.

Susan slowly refocuses on the man standing hesitantly in the doorway, his cap twisting in his hand.

'Doug?'

'Aye, it's me.'

'Why are you here?'

Doug McIntyre braces himself for the pain of explaining all over again.

'Well, Susan, I'm sorry to tell you that—'

'Doug,' she cuts in.

'Yes, Susan?'

'Where's Simon?'

# *Seventeen*

LUCY BYRON HAS BEEN living with her father and her father's wife. Flat 4 is not the ideal habitat for a hot-wired teenager, a posh, one-floor apartment where it's almost a crime to spill things, or leave a Coke can on the floor, or lose your front-door key, or play loud music. The Byrons' well-ordered apartment, polished and scrubbed twice weekly by a Mexican lady, is a stark contrast to the sprawling, friendly, upstairs-downstairs home Jill had created at 23 Oundle Square.

Marcus knows it. He is both relieved and worried that Lucy is now isolated from friends of her own generation, from street life, boyfriends, pubs, £12 tablets and liquid dynamite. And the telephone, which rang for Lucy nonstop in Oundle Square, is now monopolised by efficient, businesslike voices bearing urgent messages for Louise Pointer, QC. There are fewer, now, for Marcus Byron.

And yet Lucy seems to thrive on her drastic change of life-style. Her attitude towards her new school, where she is resitting her GCSEs, is entirely positive. When she comes home she works solidly in her room for hours at a time. She eats regularly, indeed she cooks delicious 'Chinese' meals for Marcus and Louise in the new wok she'd wanted for her seventeenth birthday. Lucy throws garlic around rather too liberally for Louise's taste but Louise, having reluctantly decided to return to Marcus, to 'make a go of it', or at least 'to make one last effort', religiously praises whatever Lucy serves up.

Louise is too perceptive to cuddle up to her stepdaughter. She has never said, 'Lucy, I'd like us to be friends.' Childless herself, and now doomed to remain so by Marcus's refusal to contemplate a baby, Louise is determined to confront the hot flushes and hormonal depletion of the menopause with dignity and good sense.

'You don't win over a hostile seventeen-year-old by pretending,' she has remarked to Marcus.

Or an indifferent husband in love with another woman.

'They can see right through one,' Marcus agreed, as they lay in bed, listening to the discreet tape – could it be Bach? – filtering through Lucy's door. 'Young people understand everything except themselves.'

'That doesn't only apply to teenagers, Marcus.'

He nodded, though nodding on a pillow is difficult. 'Yeah.'

'Having Lucy here sometimes feels like camping in the Dordogne all over again.'

'Without Amelia Harsent and the arson, I hope.'

'Poor Amelia. No girl deserves an experience like that. It's astonishing how Lucy has survived those two traumatic experiences in Century Park – the rape, then the murder of that boy.'

'She never talks about it.'

'Traumas often lie below the surface. Particularly where guilt is attached.'

'Guilt? Why guilt?' Marcus changes the subject. 'Lucy's new taste in music frankly astonishes me. Arias, sonatas, nocturnes, concertos, Purcell, Bach – I mean, is she pretending?'

'Perhaps Lucy is an all-or-nothing person. She has decided to embrace her father from his taste in music to his love of garlic.'

'Maybe.'

'She regularly attends the clinic. She's off methodone. Her teachers' reports are glowing. Her bed is piled with books.'

'Yeah. Too good to be true?'

'She's painfully aware of what she has done to you. Hardly a week passes but she whispers to me, "When will they give Dad his job back?"'

'A good question.'

Jill had moved out of Oundle Square soon after the deaths of Nigel Thompson and Simon Galloway. No. 23 became yet another FOR SALE sign. Jill now lives in a one-room flat consistent with her straitened circumstances following her dismissal by the Probation Service. When Marcus proposed that Lucy should come and live with himself and Louise, he had been astonished by Jill's rapid, listless acceptance. Clearly she no longer had the stomach for any kind of fight.

But Marcus and Jill can barely speak to one another. Every note, inflection and familiar phrase in the other's voice triggers an uncontrollable antipathy. Almost all practical negotiations concerning Lucy are conducted between Jill and Louise.

'Mum will talk to you because she believes Marcus doesn't love you,' Lucy innocently informed Louise while ironing her father's shirts. 'Of course, I tell her that he does love you, but she doesn't want to listen.'

Louise absorbed this thrust without reporting it to Marcus. She had developed her own ways of striking back.

'Does Jill ever hear from Nick Paisley, Lucy?'

'She only knows what she reads in the papers.'

What one read in the papers was diminishingly front-page news. Paisley was sitting tight in Buenos Aires. Despite an Interpol warrant for his arrest, Argentinian lawyers were confident of blocking his extradition. Nick had lost little time in denouncing Britain's 'imperialist seizure' of the Malvinas (Falklands) – indeed he filed papers for political asylum and refugee status.

Nick was only the most conspicuous casualty of Brigid Kyle's three-part series, 'The Byron Affair'. Jill, of course, was another. Lady Harsent stood down from the Bench under pressure. Jimmy Haley-White returned to Ghana to marry the daughter of a paramount chief. His role as manager of the Youth Justice Team was assumed by his former fiancée, Heather Stuart.

Brigid Kyle had not written a word about Heather Stuart.

Wendy and Patrick were embroiled in insurance claims, refurnishing and, worst of all, a lingering sense of defilement. In the end they decided to move house.

Brought to trial before the Crown Court on a charge of causing grievous bodily harm to Daniel Richardson, Patrick had been acquitted by a sympathetic jury and restored to the Youth Court Bench. However, it was considered wise to move him into an adult division and he concurred.

Wendy moved too. Unable to confront the prospect of Heather Stuart's daily presence in Benson Street Youth Court, as the new leader of the Youth Justice Team, Wendy applied for the post of

Senior Chief Clerk to an adult division. She got the job and settled into a less dramatic routine of unpaid TV licences and motoring offences.

What came between Marcus and Wendy was Lucy. Marcus wanted his sister to befriend his daughter and, as he put it, 'show her the way'. But Wendy could never forgive Lucy for masterminding the vandalisation of her home, and the attempt to ruin Patrick.

Marcus hotly defended Lucy. 'There is no evidence at all! She denies it!'

'Listen, Marco, Lucy would have been charged with conspiracy if Dan Richardson had not maintained a resolute silence from the time of his arrest. He didn't "grass", it was outside his code.'

Marcus knows Wendy is right but he doesn't want to know.

'Wendy hates me,' Lucy remarked to Louise. 'Everyone hates me.'

'I don't!'

'You should!'

'Why, Lucy?'

'But for me you would be Chairman of the Criminal Bar Association.'

'I lost that one because Marcus was embroiled.'

'By me!'

'The wise barristers decided it might be useful to elect the wife of the next Home Secretary.'

Lucy thought about this – Louise had a nasty habit of outwitting her.

'Isn't Max Venables great pals with Dad?'

'It's quite some time since Marcus heard from Max Venables.'

'Well, there's no gratitude in politics, is there?'

'Not much.'

'And Max Venables has been riding high since Darling's resignation. Which was all to do with Dad. So there you are – no gratitude.'

'I suppose you could argue that.'

'Anyway, the Boy did well out of it. The Boy always does well. Cleaner than clean, flashing his teeth at bankers and businessmen from Sydney to Singapore.'

'I'd have expected so young a leader to appeal to people of your generation, Lucy.'

'No way! He's a complete phoney with all his talk of "tiger

economies". Yeah. "Put a tiger in your tank, put the Boy in your bank."'

'That's rather good, Lucy. Have you told it to Marcus?'

'No way, sensitive area, steer clear.'

Now Marcus and Louise are due to take a long weekend in Paris. They have chosen dates to coincide with Lucy's half-term break, but Lucy politely declines the invitation.

'It would be lovely,' she says, 'but I really ought to spend some time with Mum. She's been very depressed, you know. I think she misses me.'

Marcus swallows hard. Jill still enjoys formal custody of Lucy and Marcus always fears that she will suddenly decide to reclaim her daughter, even though she is renting a one-bedroom flat far from Lucy's new school.

Louise telephones Jill to confirm that the arrangement suits her.

'Fine,' Jill says without a trace of enthusiasm.

'You're quite sure?'

'Yes, why not?'

Departing for Waterloo International to take the early-morning Eurostar train via the Tunnel, Marcus and Louise leave Lucy asleep. She will find her way to Jill's in her own sweet time. She has her door key and can return to Flat 4 whenever she wishes.

'You'll be a good girl?' Marcus has said to her the previous evening. 'No rave parties in here while we're gone?'

Lucy smiled. 'Don't put ideas into my head.'

'Now, Lucy—'

'Who would I invite? I used to have friends, you know.'

Passing under the English Channel, Marcus is still brooding on that disturbing flash of resentment.

'It's not an entirely natural life for a youngster,' he sighs.

'No, dear, but it does make a rather wholesome change from the previous "natural" life.'

'Yeah.'

Teresa Kent is happy.

The famous actress is walking along Florence Avenue, an exclusive street favoured by millionaires, heading home to the luxury flat she shares with the box-office actor, David Williams. According to the gossip writers, Kent and Williams are among Britain's Top Ten couples in the How Long Will They Last? category.

'The strain of leading separate working lives, often thousands of mile apart, is certainly not something that gives me that Day-Glo feeling,' Teresa has confided to *Vogue*.

Teresa receives a huge fan mail. Occasionally she is plagued by letters from sex maniacs, stalkers and nuts – but these are usually filtered out in her agent's Shaftesbury Avenue office, her private address being a well-guarded secret.

But not from 'Lucy'. 'Lucy', whoever she is, has been sending Teresa Kent poisonous letters for over a year. And 'Lucy' knows her address! Teresa has shown the letters to the police but there's nothing much they can do about it; the postmarks on the envelopes constantly change, there is no pattern.

'Lucy' evidently has her head screwed on, even if 'she' is mad. Some extracts:

> *Dear Bitch, I don't believe that pearly white-white skin of yours is natural. Whose is it? Shall I come and take a sample from your tender cheek, Teresa? Love, Lucy*

> *Dear Teresa, According to my calculations you and David spent only 32 nights under the same roof during the past calendar year. Did you know that David has been having it off with a very tall, very black, New York street girl called Mamba? She lives at 18 East 64th Street in case you are interested. Always anxious to be helpful. Love, Lucy*

> *Dear Teresa, How much did you make last week? I don't say 'earn' because you're not worth a penny and couldn't act to save your life. Which is what you are going to have to do soon enough! Love, Lucy*

> *Dear Bitch, If you or your lookalike sister ever lay a finger on my Daddy again I'll have my girl-gang turn you both into streaky bacon. You thought you could have his pants down, didn't you, and pick up some cheap PC cudos [sic] from bedding a famous Black Hero of the Nation. You have been warned! Love, Lucy*

Teresa Kent does not normally walk alone, or walk at all, but she had thought how nice it would be to feel like a normal person for half an hour, with no one watching. Alone with the trees, the birdsong, the sky. God, when did she last see the sky! When did she last catch a glimpse of her own feet by natural light!

She giggles to herself. The top executive of a satellite TV station has just propositioned her with a lucrative new contract, loads of lolly. He wants to experiment with 'a more aggressive image'. She skips and quickens her stride; she is due at a Leicester Square première at eight – her agent said 7.57 – and the limo will be waiting at 7.23.

Suddenly she is not alone with her thoughts. The trees, the birdsong, the sky are blotted out by terror.

'Your money! Quick! Your money or I'll cut yer!'

Teresa Kent drops her bag to the pavement.

'Take it,' she whispers.

A van driver, a hat seller called Sammy Chinn, catches sight of an elegant young woman backed up against a wall at knifepoint by three teenage girls. He can see the blade of the knife glinting within inches of the cringing victim's stomach.

The van stops on screeching tyres. Born of an English mother and a Chinese father, Sammy is a public-spirited fellow. He would cripple the Triad gangsters of Soho's Chinatown single-handed, given the opportunity.

He shouts. The girls run.

Sammy instructs the terrified woman – a fantastic looker with a where-have-I-seen-you-before? face – to stay with the van. He dials 999 on his mobile phone as he gives chase on foot. Twice he catches hold of one of the gang, a slender coloured girl whose frightened legs wobble under her, but the black girl with a broad nose and heavy lips threatens him with the knife – 'You're asking for it!' – and Sammy releases his captive. Maybe he won't tackle the Triads after all.

The gang run into Ashburton Road where they jump into a stationary taxi and yell at the driver to get going. The taxi doesn't move. Sammy catches up with it. The girls tumble out cursing and screaming just as four large cops disembark from a patrol car. The slender coloured girl capitulates immediately but the other two lash out furiously, kicking and screaming until restrained by handcuffs. It is fast-eyed Sammy who retrieves the knife from under the taxi.

Two hours later Marcus Byron returns from Paris, with Louise, to discover that his daughter is held in custody. The police have put a message through his door. Louise immediately contacts the best solicitor she knows, Derek Jardine, now back in private practice despite Nick Paisley's downfall. Her main task is to calm down her husband.

Raging, Marcus phones Jill before leaving for Denham Street police station.

'I wondered where she was,' Jill says apathetically. 'I haven't seen her at all.'

'I leave her in your charge and what happens?' Marcus roars. 'You put her up to this!'

Louise pulls him away from the telephone. 'We'll keep you informed,' she tells Jill.

The bail conditions granted to Lucy by the South Western Youth Court are stringent: (1) residence – she must unfailingly sleep the night at her father's address; (2) she must on no account approach or communicate with either Ms Teresa Kent, Mr Sammy Chinn or her two co-defendants, Trish Richardson and Debbie O'Grady; (3) she must not go within a one-mile radius of Eden Manor estate.

The last provision is for her own protection.

The newspapers are full of it.

JUDGE BYRON ACCOMPANIES DEFENDANT TO YOUTH COURT IN KENT ROBBERY CASE
BYRON ANGRILY PUSHES ASIDE PHOTOGRAPHERS
KEEPING IT IN THE FAMILY – LOUISE POINTER TO DEFEND GIRL CHARGED WITH ROBBING TERESA KENT

Life resumes in Flat 4. Lucy is contrite, apologetic and straight back into her school books. 'It was old demons catching up with me,' she tells Marcus. 'I wish I'd come to Paris with you.'

'Lucy, did you plan this in advance?'

'Yes, I think I did. It's rather like your friend Lionel Lacey going back to paedophile sex – he was arrested again while you were away. It's compulsive.'

Louise intervenes with a barrister's stern expression.

'Lucy, you did *not* plan anything in advance. The other girls led you into it. That's what you said in your signed statement. It's on that basis that Derek Jardine has instructed me. Understood?'

'Oh gosh, yes, exactly, Louise! What I meant was that I kind of planned in advance to go slumming around Eden Manor and pick up Trish and Debbie.'

To Marcus's distress, and despite Louise's eloquent pleas, the Youth Court declines jurisdiction and commits all three girls for trial in the Crown Court.

'Poor Dad.' Lucy holds Marcus's hand all the way home. 'I'm not much use to you, am I?'

Marcus and Lucy often venture out together at weekends, arm in arm. They talk about everything – except the past. The past is off-limits. Marcus has bought her a whole lot of smart clothes at Harrods – his taste, but she swears that it's hers, too. He takes her to watch West Ham United, he takes her down the Old Kent Road, he shows her where he and Wendy grew up, although the site is now occupied by a tower-block. Father and daughter walk together by the Thames, arguing about architecture, music, sex and astrology.

'Dad.' (They are crossing Waterloo Bridge in a strong wind rather than one of Claude Monet's pea-soup fogs.)

'Hm?'

'You're still seeing Brigid, aren't you?'

'From time to time,' he murmurs dismissively.

'I used the word "seeing" as a euphemism – rather like people saying "sleep with" when the sleeping is the last thing they have in mind.'

'I'm awarding you a place at Oxford.'

'No, Cambridge. Your footprints are too large at that other place.'

'But my old College now takes girls. Forty per cent of its undergraduates are female.'

'Let's get back to Brigid. You must tell me – why is she willing to share you with Louise? Or should I put the question the other way round?'

'Perhaps you shouldn't put it at all.'

He has not meant to sound brusque but her silence is a rebuke: has he blundered fatally back into the mistakes of the past?

If so, retribution is deferred. They wander happily together along the South Bank, dive into the National Film Theatre to see an old movie by Renoir or Chaplin, plunge into the Cottesloe to take on something taxing. Lucy visits the African art exhibition at the Royal Academy three times, though Marcus only once.

'Is this ancestor worship?' he teases her.

'Oh no,' she shoots back, fireflies in her eyes, 'I'm white.'

'Aha?'

'Each of us can be whatever we decide to be, don't you agree? That's existentialism.'

He smiles sadly. 'That may have been poor old Geoffrey Villiers's illusion when he dressed up as a woman.'

'Did you know that a distinctive feature of African woodcarving south of the Sahara is that it's almost inevitably worked out of a single block of wood? No carpentry, you see.'

'I never knew that.'

'You should try harder, Marcus, shouldn't you?' After a moment's reflection she says, 'I know why you never get the call from the Lord Chief Injustice. They're waiting to see what comes out when your daughter stands trial.'

'Yes, I think they probably are. But we know, you and I, the truth, don't we?'

'Oh absolutely. Louise has been kosher to defend me.'

'"Kosher"?' Marcus laughs. 'Are you sure that's the word?'

A few days after this conversation, and exactly one week before the Crown Court trial is due to take place, Lucy vanishes without warning. This time Marcus and Louise are not in Paris. Lucy leaves behind her a one-word message: 'Bye!'

'I haven't seen her,' Jill replies curtly when he telephones.

Lucy is now in breach of one of her bail conditions, to reside with her father.

'Do I report this or not?' he glowers at Louise.

'Marcus, we have been here before. It's ten-to-one she has gone back to the Wiltshire Tree Camp.'

'Not in mid-winter. I don't believe they live in trees at this time of year.'

'Why has she done it? Out of fear? A flight from judge and jury? Or to embarrass you?'

'"Embarrass" may be the understatement of the year. If I report her absence, they'll issue a warrant for her arrest, throw her in a cell overnight, and then bung her into Local Authority accommodation. If I do nothing, she may turn up here, smile sweetly, and no one will be the wiser.'

'Her note said "Bye".'

'Yes, but—'

'Would two "byes" have convinced you? She is bailed to reside in her father's house. You have to tell Derek Jardine.'

Sighing deeply, he telephones Derek.

Debbie O'Grady's mother – no one can pin down when she'd last seen her daughter – flies in from Dublin for the Crown Court trial. The malign forces of law and order have activated her maternal instincts. Justice is very dear to her – as she's prepared to tell any newspaper for cash in hand.

'Debbie was never in any trouble in Ireland.'

'And when was the girl last in Ireland, Mrs O'Grady?'

'I have no memory for dates, but I'll tell you this, what you have in England is downright racism, an Irish girl never gets a chance or the benefit of the doubt, isn't that right? She gets fixed up, that's what she gets. The film bosses spend how much flying that cow Teresa Kent back by Concorde from the United States – it's all good publicity for her, isn't it?'

Marcus Byron reads such reports gloomily. Enforced idleness does not suit him. He broods.

'I stink of mothballs,' he tells Louise.

The Congress for Justice is gradually regrouping for counter-attack. Sandra Golding, QC, has been engaged to represent Trish Richardson; Edgar Averling will represent Debbie O'Grady.

Louise Pointer, QC, will defend Lucy. The Crown Court judge hearing the case is Jonas Sawyer.

'Jonas is all right,' Marcus assures Louise. 'He's straight as a cricket stump. He'll prefer your style to Sandra's.'

'Oh? What *is* my style?'

Louise will defend Lucy but Lucy has vanished. The week preceding the trial is a nightmare of desperate phone calls to the police and the Crown Court clerks. Heavy rains and gale-force winds strike southern England. Day after day Marcus stands at his window, watching the scudding clouds in the turbulent sky, wondering about the young person who is more precious to him than anyone else in the world. Alone in the flat, he holds long conversations with her, tries to explain, observes her sweet little face as she bends intently over an African carving.

He cries often.

Marcus and Louise leave early for the Crown Court by taxi. Despite the blinding rain, the photographers are clustered at the entrance. They shout to him. He hurries inside behind dark glasses, head bowed.

Lucy turns up, unaccompanied, ten minutes before the trial is due to begin. She is soaking wet. Judge Jonas Sawyer sends word that Louise may have ten minutes with her client.

On Judge Sawyer's instructions, the proceedings are delayed while a breach-of-bail charge is put to Lucy. She stands before Judge Sawyer looking pale, hungry, sleepless, shabbily dressed in loose, patchwork-quilt clothing, unwashed. Her hair is once again in dreadlocks, matted with dirt.

She pleads guilty to breach of bail with a shrug.

Louise addresses Judge Sawyer. 'I have had a brief conversation with Lucy. Fear of these proceedings overcame her. She has never been in court before. She fled. But then, and this is immensely to her credit, she resolved to face the music. She surrendered voluntarily.'

Judge Sawyer looks at Lucy. 'Lucy, you have caused your parents a great deal of worry and heartache.'

'Mm.'

'Not to mention wasting public funds on the police search for you.'

'Mm.'

'Are you listening to me, Lucy?'

'Yeah.'

'Now, Lucy, do you think you will be tempted to run away again if I grant you bail on the same conditions – which I would like to do?'

'I don't like living with Hitler.'

'Hitler?'

'Him.' Lucy gestures to the man sitting beside her, Marcus Byron.

'Any comment on that, Judge Byron?'

'Lucy seemed very happy with us these past months. She and I . . . all my life I have dreamed of being so close to her.'

Marcus is weeping.

'I can confirm that, your Honour,' Louise adds. 'I myself witnessed the harmonious relationship between father and daughter. They were always rushing off, arm in arm, to do this or do that. Lucy's school reports have been wonderful. I would ask you to remand Lucy back on the same bail conditions.'

'No way,' Lucy says.

Sighing, Judge Sawyer raps out a short order remanding Lucy Byron into the care of the Local Authority for the duration of the trial.

He orders a fifteen-minute recess and sends word to the jury.

The court room fills up. Marcus and Jill have been allocated seats on the floor of the court, alongside the Richardsons and the O'Gradys. Debbie's mum chatters nonstop and stinks of gin. Having to sit next to each other for two days is a grim punishment for both Marcus and Jill. They have nothing to say to one another.

'To protect the identities of the juvenile defendants,' Judge Sawyer rules, 'none of the parents of the defendants may be named or photograped in the media. Is that clearly understood?'

But everyone knows.

The prosecution case is presented by the barrister Mark Ralston. He has often appeared before Marcus in Crown Court 3. Marcus knows him as factual, fair, unemotive.

'All three girls conspired to rob Ms Kent, your Honour, all three joined forces to rob her at knifepoint, and all three should be found guilty of robbery, as charged.'

Marcus and Louise have long been aware that the main threat to Lucy comes not from the prosecution but from her co-defendants, from Sandra Golding and Edgar Averling. Their line of defence is known in advance: indeed, it's obvious, any lawyer would have pursued it.

Lucy, they will allege, the oldest girl in the group, the best educated, the most sophisticated, had been supplying drugs to Trish and Debbie. It was Lucy who had put them up to the robbery. Lucy alone had knowledge of Teresa Kent's address – indeed Trish and Debbie had never before ventured so far from home territory into a smart, wealthy neighbourhood.

But Lucy will insist that she had been taking the girls on a legitimate shopping expedition to Knightsbridge when Trish and Debbie dragged her into trouble. She cannot deny that she knew Teresa Kent's address but she had no idea that the smart young woman accosted by Trish and Debbie was the actress.

She had not wanted to rob anyone.

And what were they doing in a quiet residential street if their intention was to go shopping? Here again Lucy would blame the others, who insisted on jumping off the bus, 'to do a job' on the smartest handbag they could find.

Teresa Kent excites admiring murmurs as she walks, hips swaying, hair gleaming, to the witness stand. Such beauty, such radiance, such poise! She speaks so softly that Judge Sawyer has to urge her to 'shout a bit, Ms Kent'.

'I'm so sorry,' she smiles modestly.

Mark Ralston, the prosecutor, briefly takes her through the facts – what happened.

'You suffered no injury?'

'No.'

'But you were thoroughly frightened?'

'I was terrified!'

'It didn't seem to you like a juvenile prank, a lark?'

'No.'

'Might you have been making a fuss about nothing?'

'I have thought about that. People have accused me of pursuing this for publicity. I believe this kind of thing is all too prevalent in London and women need to be protected.'

'Thank you, Ms Kent. My learned friends will no doubt have some questions for you.'

Sandra Golding is gentle with Teresa Kent in cross-examination. She understands how traumatic the experience must have been. Ms Kent's good faith is not in question, but:

'When something happens suddenly, and frighteningly, one's observations may be impressionistic rather than accurate – would you agree?'

'Oh certainly.'

'In your witness statement to the police, you said that the older girl, Lucy Byron, was not to the forefront of the attack?'

'That's correct. She didn't have a knife.'

'I put it to you that she was directing the operation. She was telling the younger girls what to do.'

'Oh no,' insists the glowing actress, 'the coloured girl didn't say anything. She seemed to be hanging back. I thought she was quite nervous about the whole thing.'

Sandra Golding is less tender with the second prosecution witness, Sammy Chinn. Had not Lucy Byron violently resisted his attempt to arrest her?

'Didn't she call to the other girls to come and "cut you up"?'

'No, no no,' says Sammy Chinn. 'She was just frightened. It

was the other girl I now know to be Trish Richardson who threatened me.'

'But Lucy Byron was calling for help?'

'She never threatened me. She just kicked and wriggled.'

Trish and Debbie are scowling at Sammy Chinn furiously from the dock. If looks could kill . . . Lucy sits apart, her gaze a blank, as if she was somewhere else.

The prosecution case is concluded by 11.30. It is the three separate defences which will soak up time.

Sandra Golding rises on behalf of Trish Richardson.

'Lucy Byron was clever enough not to carry the knife,' Sandra tells the jury. 'She had been manipulating these working-class girls for months. And why? Not for profit, just for kicks. Everything Lucy Byron did was calculated to get back at her famous father. The father who – she believes – deserted her mother and herself. The father who constantly calls for firm measures against crime, against juvenile delinquency – and yet smoked cannabis reefers in her presence while camping in France.'

Louise is up. 'Objection, your Honour. There has been no evidence during this trial to support the last statement. It is simply defamatory.'

'You must withdraw the last statement,' Judge Sawyer tells Sandra.

'I withdraw it, your Honour. I regret that a young witness who was to have confirmed the truth of it, from her own observation, was recently raped – and is unfit to give evidence.'

Louise is up again. 'Your Honour, that is not a withdrawal.'

Judge Sawyer nods. 'You cannot withdraw a statement and then claim it is true, can you, Ms Golding?'

'No, your Honour.'

'Thank you, Ms Golding.'

Sandra Golding stresses that her humble clients are victims of publicity. They should never have been committed to the Crown Court.

'Is this really so serious that it would attract a sentence of more than two years if the girls had been adults? Two years! No one hurt and ten pounds stolen! The victim suffered nothing more than shock and distress. Not a scratch on that famous face. But she is famous! She is headlines! If she had been the ordinary woman-in-the-street, the magistrates would have accepted jurisdiction.'

Sandra cites a similar case recently before the Youth Court.

'The victims on that occasion were not famous, your Honour. Nothing to attract the interest of the Press. The Youth Court magistrates let the offending girls off with a wigging and £40 each in compensation to the victims – whom they had thoroughly terrorised. You may think that the magistrates acted sensibly. We do not need a two-tier system of justice.'

Sandra does not mention that it was Lady Harsent who had chaired the Bench on that occasion. Lady H. has rapidly been relegated to the ranks of the unmentionables.

So far Sandra has produced nothing terribly damaging to Lucy. But Louise knows that her 'learned friend' has merely been warming up.

'I call Teresa Kent,' she says.

This is a sensational *démarche*: for the defence to call a prosecution witness is almost unheard of, but it had been arranged by bargaining. Sandra could have presented Lucy's anonymous letters to Kent during cross-examination, reading them out herself and merely asking Kent for verification. But Sandra wants Kent to read out the letters from Lucy herself, in her beautiful, soft, hurt, tremulous voice – and Kent has agreed to do so. Judge Sawyer had summoned all the lawyers to his chambers. Louise had strenuously, furiously objected to what she called 'a clear conflict of interests', but the judge over-ruled her.

'Justice is best served by all parties calling the witnesses they wish to call.'

Fingerprint and handwriting evidence has shown conclusively that the tormenting letters were written by Lucy – and Lucy has never denied it.

The court listens spellbound as Teresa Kent, close to tears, carries her audience through nine letters.

Lucy's face is a blank. She stares into space. Only yesterday she was happy and free – though soaking wet – among the Tree People of Wiltshire. The police had come looking for her, of course, but they never stood a chance.

'Were any of the accusations in these letters true?' Sandra asks Teresa Kent. 'Had you ever met Marcus Byron?'

'Once, at a charity party some time ago.'

'What happened?'

'I found him interesting and attractive. I think "charismatic" is the word. He gave me dinner. When he invited me back to his flat I accepted. He told me that his wife was away and his daughter was staying a few nights in the next bedroom.'

'Please go on.'

'We were in bed together when his daughter burst in screaming. I believe she tried to throw herself from a window but I am not sure, I was too busy getting dressed and out of there.'

'Do you recognise that girl as the one you see in court today?'

'No, it was all a bit traumatic and I have no clear recollection of the girl.'

'Did you know her first name?'

'No, he didn't mention it.'

'So when you subsequently received letters signed "Lucy" it didn't ring any bell?'

'No, none.'

'Have you ever seen Marcus Byron since that occasion?'

'Never.'

'And did you fear,' Sandra asks Kent, 'that the writer of these poisonous letters might one day physically attack you?'

Louise leaps up. 'Objection. Leading question.'

'Try again, Ms Golding,' says Judge Sawyer.

'What went through your mind when you read these poisonous letters?' Sandra asks Kent.

'I thought that she – always assuming that "Lucy" was a she, you never know, do you – was mentally unbalanced and might try to do me serious harm.'

'And do you now believe your fears were borne out?'

'Objection!' says Louise.

Judge Sawyer studies Sandra. 'I rule out "mentally unbalanced", Ms Golding. We have no evidence on that and the witness is not in a position to have a view beyond her fears.'

Teresa Kent stands down and leaves the court room. The scene on the pavement outside the Crown Court can be imagined.

Sandra Golding, QC, Chairman of the Criminal Bar Association, now pulls off her greatest coup.

Teresa Kent appears to be returning to the witness stand! Here she is again! Yet she has changed her clothes! And her jewellery! Even her shade of blonde has subtly altered! More remarkable still, she has changed her name.

'I will now call Heather Stuart,' Sandra announces.

Sandra runs through her new witness's biographical details.

'You are Teresa Kent's sister?'

'Yes, I am.'

'She is one year older than you?'

'Yes.'

'Have people remarked on the striking physical resemblance between you?'

'Yes, sometimes.'

'Have you ever been mistaken for your famous sister?'

'Sometimes, not often.'

'Have you ever spoken to Lucy Byron?'

'Yes. Once.'

'In what circumstances?'

'I was leaving Benson Street Youth Court. She seemed to be waiting for me in the street, at least that was my impression. She said, "You're my dad's latest bird."'

'What did you say?'

'Nothing.'

'Go on, please.'

'She said, "I saw my dad flirting with you while pretending to watch me plays tennis for St Hilda's" – actually Lucy said "Saint Heeldaah's" mockingly. I'd been a pupil there myself.'

'What did you say?'

'Nothing. She then asked me for my autograph – rather sarcastically.'

'What did you do?'

'I said, "Aren't you perhaps confusing me with someone else?"'

'And then?'

'Lucy said, "Your bitch sister, you mean. No, I'm not."'

'Did she put a name to your "bitch sister".'

'Yes. Teresa Kent.'

'Go on.'

'I excused myself and began to move away.'

'And then what happened?'

'I felt a hand grab my arm, my sleeve, in an obviously aggressive way. I turned. Lucy's face was . . . well . . . livid with animosity. I cannot recall her exact words because they came so fast, but she was accusing both of us, Teresa and myself, of being "cheap tarts".'

'That's one phrase you do remember?'

Heather Stuart smiles sadly. 'Yes.'

'Anything else?'

'She said she had "friends".'

'"Friends"?'

'Friends who would cut both me and my sister into small pieces.'

'Did you then walk away?'

'Yes.'

'Did you ever encounter Lucy again?'

'No.'

'Did you warn your sister?'

'Good heavens, no, I didn't take it seriously.'

'You knew Lucy's father?'

'Hardly. I had met him.'

'Did you report this conversation to him?'

'No.'

'Why not?'

'I knew his relationship with his daughter was a painful subject to him. We had both watched her attempting to play tennis while clearly incapable.'

'Incapable?'

'He and I both thought she was on drugs. So did her games mistress.'

'Thank you, Ms Stuart. If you will just wait there my learned friend may have some questions to put to you.'

Louise Pointer, QC, indeed does. 'You never met Lucy Byron outside Benson Street Court or anywhere else. Your story is a tissue of lies, isn't it?'

'It's true.'

'What was Lucy wearing that day?'

'I really can't remember.'

'What was the exact date of this "encounter"?'

'I can't remember – probably some time in July.'

'Someone threatens to "cut you up", yet you don't make a note of when?'

'I didn't see the point. Frankly, I felt sorry for her.'

'And you didn't tell anyone about it?'

'I told my then fiancé Jimmy Haley-White.'

'But he is now in Ghana?'

'Yes.'

'Were there any witnesses to this exchange?'

'Not that I'm aware of.'

'Do you feel slighted by Lucy's father, Marcus Byron?'

'Why ever should I?'

Judge Sawyer intervenes. 'Answer questions, please, don't ask them. Repeat the question if you wish, Ms Pointer.'

Louise repeats it.

'No, not at all,' Heather Stuart says.

'Did you ever invite Marcus Byron to sleep with you?'

'No.'

'Did you send his wife these photographs – the usher will pass them to you – of yourself and Judge Byron in your garden?'

Heather bridles. 'Send them to his wife? To *you*?'

'Answer the question,' Judge Sawyer says.

Heather Stuart looks at the photographs. 'No, I didn't.'

'Why was Judge Byron with you in your garden?'

'I believe he wanted to talk to me about Probation Service policy on juveniles. That is my field.'

'You invited him to go to bed with you, didn't you?'

'Certainly not. I was engaged to Mr Haley-White.'

'And Judge Byron refused politely, and you felt slighted?'

'That's utter rubbish.'

'Did you later conspire to inveigle Judge Byron into a scandal on the Tyndale towpath?'

'Certainly not – what a preposterous idea.'

'Did you invite Mr Lionel Lacey to meet you at Tyndale that Saturday, knowing that he had been angrily pursuing you and was likely to assault you?'

'Nonsense. I felt that it would be useful to clear the air by bringing Judge Byron, Mr Lacey and myself together.'

'So why did you not inform Judge Byron?'

'Of course I did.'

'He says you did not.'

Sandra is up. 'Objection, hearsay.' Sandra knows that Louise does not intend to call Marcus as a witness – by convention, a father's testimony can virtually be discounted.

'Yes, objection sustained,' Judge Sawyer murmurs.

Louise goes at Heather again. 'Your plan was to concoct a scene, a violent incident, which would bounce into the newspapers and discredit Judge Byron.'

Here Judge Sawyer intervenes. 'Ms Pointer, if this line of questions is relevant to the case before this court, which is the alleged robbery of Ms Kent, perhaps you could remind us why it is relevant.'

'Your Honour, Ms Stuart has described an alleged incident between herself and my client, Lucy Byron, which I believe to be fictitious. If true, your Honour, the incident might tend to show Lucy's animosity towards Ms Kent and prior intent to do her harm. I am seeking to show, your Honour, that Ms Stuart has fabricated her story because of her role in the plot to discredit Lucy's father, Judge Byron.'

'Yes, understood, but we are not here to write the history of England, Ms Pointer. Continue, please.'

Louise turns back to Heather Stuart. 'When walking along the Tyndale towpath with Judge Byron, you suddenly announced to him that you had a menstrual period, the worst in your life, and asked to borrow his bicycle so that you could make haste back to your car to find your spare tampons and use the ladies'. Correct?'

'Yes.'

'But when you reached the King's Arms car park, you found Mr Lacey there. You circled him on the bicycle, showing no interest in tampons or the ladies' facilities, and bade him follow you immediately back up the towpath. Correct?'

'I really cannot remember.'

'You told Judge Byron a lie because you were so anxious to make sure that Mr Lacey became embroiled in the scene you had pre-planned all along. Correct?'

'Not at all. I had no idea Mr Lacey would attack me. What woman would invite attack?'

'When you left Judge Byron you were riding high, keeping your backside off the saddle, as a woman might who was bleeding badly, but when you reached the King's Arms you were sitting very easily on the lowered saddle, no problem. Correct?'

'This is all complete nonsense.'

'I can call two witnesses from the King's Arms: Does that sharpen your memory, Ms Stuart?'

Heather Stuart's fine breasts heave with indignation. 'No,' she says.

'Don't you feel that you have the tragic death of Ms Angela Loftus on your conscience?'

'No!' Heather Stuart looks appealingly to Judge Sawyer. 'This is outrageous. It is not I who am on trial, your Honour.'

The judge wears the ghost of a smile. 'It's called cross-examination. Answer the questions.'

'Did you ever visit the journalist Brigid Kyle?' Louise asks Heather.

'I believe I may have done.'

'Ms Stuart, I assume a good memory is a quality needed in your work?'

'Yes, I remember a brief conversation with her.'

'You asked to see her, didn't you?'

'There were a lot of rumours flying around. I heard she was drafting a long article. I wanted to set the record straight.'

'What about?'

'Mainly about the tragic incident at Tyndale – which got into all the papers, along with my name.'

'Did you confess to Brigid Kyle that you had had an affair with Marcus Byron?'

'I . . . I don't remember doing so.'

'Did you ever tell the journalist Brigid Kyle that you had had an affair with the King of Albania?'

'No!'

'You seem more certain on the second question than the first, Ms Stuart?'

'No, I'm not. I was just surprised by your first question.'

'Ms Stuart, you hesitated. You said: "I don't remember doing so"? If you had never had sexual relations with Judge Byron, how could you hesitate?'

'I said nothing of the sort to her because it's not true.'

'Thank you, no more questions.'

Sandra Golding closes her case. She does not call Trish Richardson.

Averling, though lugubrious, is briefer. He does not call Debbie O'Grady.

Louise rises on behalf of Lucy Byron. She calls Brigid Kyle. Brigid bustles to the stand, hair aflame.

'Ms Kyle, did Heather Stuart ever visit you?'

'Yes, she did.'

'What did she tell you?'

'That she had had an affair with Marcus Byron.'

'Did she say whether this was a single occasion or—'

'More than once.'

'In your view what was her motive for telling you this, Ms Kyle?'

'I had been having an affair with him myself. She knew –

many people knew – that I was about to publish an exposé of the Congress for Justice. I construed that she wanted me to feel personally betrayed by Judge Byron.'

'Thank you, Ms Kyle. Please wait there as my learned friends may wish to ask you some questions.'

Sandra Golding rises. She looks at Brigid. She plays with a silver pencil.

'Are you Judge Byron's lover, Ms Kyle?'

'As I said, yes.'

'No, you said you "had been having an affair with him". That was some months ago. I am asking you something quite different. I am asking whether your affair continues – now. Today.'

'Yes, it does.'

'Does Lucy Byron know?'

'I . . . believe she may.'

'Does she approve?'

'That I don't know.'

'Might she not be furiously resentful, to find herself living with her father and stepmother, who is my learned friend here, while her father is carrying on with you?'

'That I don't know.'

'Might she not have decided to seek vengeance against her father by masterminding a violent robbery?'

Louise is up. 'Objection, your Honour.'

Judge Sawyer shakes his head. 'Objection over-ruled.'

Sandra's eyes are devouring Brigid. 'Shall I repeat my question?'

Brigid Kyle is trembling in the witness stand. 'I see no evidence of it,' she whispers.

'Do speak up, Ms Kyle,' Sandra harries her.

'We heard the reply,' Judge Sawyer says.

'Thank you, no further questions.'

By now the noise in the court is getting out of hand. Judge Sawyer's gavel is in constant use. Joe O'Neill, who has wangled a seat in the Press section, is into his second notebook:

> Holy smoke! What can the jurors be thinking? Their eyes are popping! They can't believe they got in here free, without having to buy tickets at Covent Garden prices. Have they reached the provisional conclusion, like your ace reporter, that every female over twenty years of age in this courtroom has slept with Marcus

> Byron? What a pity Golding and Pointer won't be appearing as witnesses, and cross-examining each other! The rules should be changed, it should all be settled with sharpened steel knitting needles. Is this a trial of three little girls for robbery or what?

Louise continues:

'Your Honour, no knife, no weapon, had been been used in the case of robbery cited by my learned friend. That is why the Youth Court retained jurisdiction. An offensive weapon makes all the difference, does it not? Lucy Byron also carried no knife. It is not in dispute that Trish Richardson held a kitchen knife with a six-inch blade within an inch of the victim's stomach.

'"She will use it, you know," Debbie O'Grady warned Ms Kent. That is Ms Kent's testimony. Later Trish Richardson threatened Sammy Chinn with the same knife after he had pursued the three girls. That is Mr Chinn's testimony. Neither Ms Kent nor Mr Chinn has claimed that the third girl, Lucy Byron, associated herself with these threats in any way. Not by word, not by deed.

'I quote Ms Kent: "I was aware of a third girl, a thin coloured girl, standing off. I wasn't sure whether she was with them or a passer-by."

'I quote Mr Chinn: "I twice caught the coloured girl whom I now know to be Lucy Byron by the arm. She wriggled and kicked, but it was Trish Richardson who threatened me with the knife."

'No one can dispute this evidence, your Honour, yet my learned friends ask you to believe that Lucy Byron masterminded the whole operation. But where is the evidence? My learned friends have not called their clients, Trish Richardson and Debbie O'Grady, as witnesses. That surely speaks for itself.'

Golding and Averling are on their feet, though Averling makes the ascent more slowly.

'Objection!'

After a brief discussion involving counsel, Judge Sawyer allows Sandra to address the court on 'a point of law':

'We now see, your Honour, why the recent curtailment of the ancient right to silence by a reactionary Government is a grave threat to justice. My learned friend can now draw inferences from a young girl's decision to exercise a hallowed, centuries-old English liberty: silence. Trish Richardson comes from a poor home. Her mother can barely read or write. Such people are terrified by grand, posh places like this Crown Court. Trish Richardson has neither the confidence nor the vocabulary to explain herself under the kind of cross-examination I advised her to expect from my learned friend. I said to her: "Even if your laces are tied in a double bow, she will make you confess they are untied."'

Louise is up. 'Objection.'

Judge Sawyer looks at Sandra Golding. He looks at the jury.

'Forget all the stuff about the shoe laces. Wipe it from your minds. Now, Ms Golding, play by the rules, please.'

'That is all, your Honour.'

Judge Sawyer turns to the jury. 'At the conclusion of evidence I will tell you what inferences you may or may not draw when defendants choose not to give evidence. But nothing "speaks for itself". Continue, Ms Pointer.'

'Thank you, your Honour. I will now call Lucy Byron, who is a girl of good character.'

Sandra Golding and Averling both leap up to object vehemently. Louise has pulled a trick which makes even Marcus wince. Her choice of words might suggest that Trish and Debbie are not of 'good character', which means they have previous criminal convictions. But that is something the jury must on no account be told.

Judge Sawyer immediately invites the jury and all spectators to retire.

'I may have to declare a mistrial,' he tells Louise. 'You may have fatally prejudiced the jury. I shall report your conduct, which was clearly calculated, to the Bar Council.'

Louise apologises for 'any error of judgment' but defends her right to insist on her client's good character – 'bearing in mind what has been alleged against Lucy Byron's character in the course of this trial'.

Judge Sawyer is not convinced. '"Good character" has a quite precise meaning in this place: it means "no previous convictions". You know that, Ms Pointer.'

Judge Sawyer sends a message to the jury in the form of a question: 'What do you believe you have been told about the three defendants?'

The jury is back in court within ten minutes. The foreman addresses Judge Sawyer:

'The jury has been told that the defendant Lucy Byron is of previous good character.'

'That's all?'

'Yes.'

Sawyer's expression is disbelieving. Jurors hate to be stood down from an interesting trial.

'The court will adjourn until ten a.m. tomorrow.' He rises.

'The court will stand!' cries the usher.

Marcus stands. He and Jill both send messages requesting to see Lucy, but an embarrassed woman from Social Services comes back to convey the girl's refusal to speak to her father.

'Please come this way, Ms Hull.'

Marcus does not sleep at all that night. Louise cradles his aching head and soaks the sweat from his large, muscular body with warm water and astringent witch-hazel. Methodically he works his way through a bottle of whisky, which Louise insists on diluting with warm water and Mexican honey. Smoking too much, he begins to cough; his lungs feel like sandpaper, phlegm clogs his throat. He wants to urinate but cannot.

'I know what's coming.'

'No, you don't, Marcus.'

The first witness the following morning is Lucy Byron. She looks tired and bored as she shuffles listlessly to the witness stand. Where has she spent the night? Where did they put her? In some bed and breakfast? Decked out in dreadlocks, she has shoved a large ring through her nose. When asked her religion before taking the oath, she shrugs her fragile shoulders:

'Anything you like,' she tells the usher insolently.

'Do you wish to affirm?'

'It's all the same voodoo to me.'

When Lucy reluctantly reads aloud the oath, the word 'truth', repeated three times, sounds like 'ha ha'.

'Are you now seventeen, Lucy?' Louise begins gently.

'Yeah.'

'Were you sixteen at the time of these events?'

'Yeah.'

'Do you have a clear memory of the events we are discussing?'

'Yeah. Very.'

'The three of you took a bus from the Broadway to Knightsbridge?'

'Yeah.'

'What did you personally have in mind when you took that bus? What was the purpose of your journey?'

'To rob this rich bitch.'

Marcus Byron feels his heart crack.

Uproar in the court. The Richardsons and O'Gradys are howling with joy only feet away from Marcus and Jill. The Richardsons now hate Lucy; they are convinced she deliberately landed Dan deep 'in it' by sending him to burgle the home of the magistrate, Patrick Berry. Two years in Downton. And Dan never got paid his money. And then this little bitch Lucy Byron deliberately landed Trish 'in it'.

Louise tries again. 'Lucy, did you that day set out on a shopping expedition?'

Golding is up. 'Objection. My friend is leading.'

Judge Sawyer nods. 'Ms Pointer, you know that in examination of your own witness you must not lead.'

'Yes, your Honour. Lucy, what was your original purpose when you set out from the Broadway by bus?'

Lucy Byron is mistress of the dramatic occasion.

'It was always my idea. I didn't hold the knife because I'm no good with knives and I wanted someone else to do the dirty work. I may have no previous convictions but that's only because the police have been protecting me. Because of my father. I've been into crime ever since my father walked out on my mother. It was then that I read *A Clockwork Orange*. Got it?'

Louise does not glance across at Marcus. She knows she is on her own. She asks Judge Sawyer to send the jury out.

He does so.

'Your Honour, Lucy has reneged on what she told the police in her signed statement, and she has reneged on her own instructions to myself. In view of what you have heard, I ask permission to treat Lucy as a hostile witness.'

Sandra Golding rises to object. She takes her time. She is enjoying herself. Louise is out for the count and Marcus Byron is at long last getting the punishment, the lynching, the crucifixion, she has dreamed of.

'Lucy is the defendant, your Honour,' Sandra addresses Judge Sawyer. 'She is not any old defence witness. She cannot in law be hostile to herself.'

Judge Sawyer ponders this. 'She's young, a juvenile. At a real human level she appears to be hostile to herself. I am going to question Lucy Byron in the absence of the jury.'

Fireflies have been dancing in Lucy's dark eyes during this

exchange. Her new Rasta locks seethe like snakes in a fire – or so it looks to Marcus. His heart aches. He should never have rebuked her, that beautiful, happy day, for asking whether Louise was jealous of Brigid, and Brigid of Louise.

'Now, Lucy,' Judge Sawyer asks her gently, 'why did you tell the police one story, and the same story to Ms Pointer, and now a quite different story to this court?'

'I was frustrated at the police station,' Lucy drawls. 'I was running short of a fix and I couldn't think straight. I needed my stuff. I'd say anything to get out of there.'

'But', Judge Sawyer probes, 'you have maintained a plea of Not Guilty since that time. You have instructed your counsel accordingly. Why?'

'No, she was instructing me. "Lucy, you did *not* plan anything in advance. The other girls led you into it."'

Lucy displays a band of sparkling white teeth, a grin of cruel joy. Her imitation of Louise is perfect.

Judge Sawyer adjusts his half-glasses. 'Are you showing off, Lucy?'

'I knew I'd do the bitch Kent the day I saw her lookalike sister flirting with my dad on the St Heeldaah's playing field.'

Jonas Sawyer nods slowly. He has never been in this situation before.

'Lucy, do you wish to change the lawyer representing you? You are a juvenile and Ms Pointer is your stepmother. I can see this might give rise to difficulties which are not helpful to the cause and course of justice.'

Lucy shakes her head. 'It's all bollocks. You can send me down for all I care. I'd like to say something – call it a personal manifesto.'

The judge nods. 'Very well.'

'Our pockets weren't full of deng that day, so we had to tolchok this pretty polly and viddy her swim in her sweat while we counted the takings and divided by three, then this Chinese loon shows up so we threatened this ptitsa with the ultra-violent and told him to smeck off or we'd have his guts for garters.'

Lucy pauses. She stares at her father, tears pouring down her face.

'Pity we didn't slice them both,' she sobs.

# *Eighteen*

THE BLOSSOM IS OUT in Oundle Square. There are always bunches of flowers resting at the foot of the two trees planted in the communal garden to commemorate Nigel Thompson and Simon Galloway. But beneath the pink and white blossom of spring is blight. Morale is low. The FOR SALE notices have multiplied. Selling is difficult; the housing market is depressed and the word seems to have got around that Oundle Square is no longer a good place to live.

A FOR SALE notice has been erected outside No. 16.

Susie Galloway no longer takes Tom to the One O'Clock Club. She never ventures near Century Park. When Ruth Tanner called, collecting signatures for a petition against dog mess in the park, so dangerous to children, Susie signed apathetically.

'I'm moving,' she told Ruth through blurred eyes. 'I don't mind what happens in the park.'

Her doctor has put her on Valium.

Susie has roused herself to do one positive thing: she has joined Justice for Victims, whose Chairman is Ruth Tanner and whose Honorary President is Judge Marcus Byron. More than once she has asked Marcus why the boy who killed Simon, Darren Griffin, had been convicted only of manslaughter, and given five years:

'He'll be out after two and a half. Is that justice?'

Susie would call it murder, not 'manslaughter'. She would put Rat Boy away 'for life' – though she would rather hang him.

She never thought she would believe in capital punishment, but she does.

Marcus does not attempt to explain because legal explanations are the last thing Susie wants, or needs. He could tell her that murder hinges on intention to kill. Simon had clearly flung himself on Darren and caught him unawares; in such circumstances intention is hard to prove beyond all reasonable doubt.

Susie is always pleased to see Marcus and Brigid – though she knows how painful it is for him to come near Oundle Square. For Marcus No. 23 is a haunted house; he gazes up at the window of the bedroom which had once belonged to Lucy. The house is now sub-divided into three flats: loud rock music blasts from the open window of Lucy's old room.

Susie's visitors carefully avoid occupying Simon's favourite armchair. Marcus plays with Tom and the gift he has brought while the women chat.

'This clockwork train set, Tom, was mine when I was a boy. Look at this LNER engine – you don't see these nowadays. Do you know what LNER means?'

Susie smiled faintly. 'I don't know either.'

'London and North-Eastern Railway. Perhaps you had better teach your mother about trains,' Marcus suggests to Tom.

Soon the boy is absorbed in fitting together the tracks, points and signals spread across the carpet.

'When is your baby due?' Brigid asks Susie.

'In six weeks. It's a girl.'

'Wonderful. Tom will enjoy having a sister to play with.'

'Yes, Simon wanted it to be a girl.'

Hearing his name, Tom looks up from the LNER.

'Engine not go,' he announces.

'Of course it goes,' Marcus chuckles, kneeling beside the boy. 'You must turn this key hard – look.' Marcus sighs. 'Maybe the key is a bit stiff for him.'

Susan says: 'I oughtn't to say this but I can never forgive. Never.'

Marcus nods. 'One of my ancestors was whipped to death on a slave ship sailing from Sierra Leone to Barbados. His pregnant wife survived the journey. According to family legend, she never forgave either.'

The doorbell sounds. Susie jumps up.

'I suggested to Eric Thompson that he might want to drop round. I hope you don't mind.'

'I'm always glad to see Eric.'

After Nigel Thompson's burial, attended by hundreds of friends, schoolmates and members of the public, his father Eric was finally persuaded to grant an interview to Brigid. What she wrote deeply moved thousands of readers of the *Sentinel*:

> 'Nigel's death changed my life. I had been about to start production of my own model £2,500 mountain bike. I had hundreds of orders. I haven't worked since my son died. Jane and I had never realised what Nigel meant to us, what happiness he brought us, until he was taken. The psychiatrists tell me I have a fifty–fifty chance of pulling through.'

Eric Thompson joined Justice for Victims on the same day as Susie. Marcus, himself a mountain-bike fanatic, invested in Eric's enterprise. Another prominent investor and two-wheel enthusiast is Patrick Berry. After Brigid Kyle's tribute appeared, five hundred readers wrote in, offering to back Eric Thompson's venture.

> Eric Thompson [Brigid reported in a subsequent issue] is both moved and upset by this display of human kindness – upset because, as he told me, he sometimes feels as if he is benefiting from Nigel's death. But then his wife Jane takes his hand and reminds him that Nigel would have wanted him to find a way out of his grief.

Amos Richardson's trial had been less frustrating for the Thompsons than Darren Griffin's for Susie. The psychiatric claptrap advanced by the defence, and the infuriating argument that no one sane could commit so motiveless a crime, had been destroyed by Louise Pointer, QC, prosecuting for the Crown. As soon as Detective Sergeant Doug McIntyre was called to testify, Amos was finished.

Out of Doug's pocket came a famous slip of paper – Exhibit 16 – on which a single word was written: 'ARithmetic'. The defence challenged its authenticity, of course, but to do so was to call Doug McIntyre a liar.

'You are convinced that Nigel Thompson witnessed an assault by Amos Richardson on Mrs Susan Galloway?' Louise asked him.

'Yes, I am.'

'And why would the boy not sign a statement?'

'He was terrified.'

'Why?'

'I think the manner of his death is the answer to that.'

Louise also called Ken Crabbe, now retired as an inspector of police, who told the court that he had been 'arm-twisted' to fix an ID parade.

'To what end, Mr Crabbe?'

'I was ordered to pull the wool over Mrs Susan Galloway's eyes.'

'Did you succeed?'

'She failed to identify Amos Richardson as her attacker. It's not an episode I'm proud of.'

'And who "twisted your arm", Mr Crabbe?'

'A senior figure in the Crown Prosecution Service, Mr Nick Paisley.'

'Was Mr Paisley engaged in any relevant activity at that time?'

'Drug-dealing with the Richardsons.'

Sentencing Amos at the Old Bailey, Mr Justice Dwyer had ruled that the offender's name could be published in the public interest.

'Amos Richardson, you have been found guilty of murder. There is only one sentence I am permitted by law to make. Because of your age, you will be detained during Her Majesty's pleasure.'

Amos's mother had cried out and wept in the arms of relatives. Her daughter Trish was serving three months; her son Daniel, two years; her son Paul was now remanded in custody; her son Amos was lost to the mists of time.

After the trial the Thompsons asked Susie whether she could forgive Nigel for not having given evidence against Amos. She said yes, but they came away from No. 16 unconvinced. Grief and rage had turned Susie into a difficult person. What none of them knew, not even McIntyre, was that Nigel could have shouted a warning to Susie as she wheeled Tom to her front steps. That was one secret Nigel took with him to the grave.

Eric Thompson enters Susie's sitting room shyly, smiles at Tom – 'Hey, that's some railway!' – and offers his hand to Brigid and Marcus.

'How are you, Eric?' Marcus asks.

'Some days are better than others.'

'One doesn't know what one has to lose until one loses it,' Brigid says.

Susie wears a strange smile. 'But actually, with Simon, I always knew.'

Eric Thompson hesitates. 'Marcus – is it presumptuous to say how sorry I am about Lucy?'

Brigid sees Susie freeze.

'Where did you say . . . she is?' Eric persists innocently.

Marcus shifts uncomfortably. 'May I smoke a pipe, Susie?'

'Please do,' Susie says frigidly.

Marcus lights up. 'Since you kindly ask, Eric, Lucy is now in Aston's Hall, a small prison for women and girls in Hampshire.'

'Have you been to see her?' Eric asks.

'Her mother has. Lucy declines to receive me. Lucy never had a father, you see. That's what she tells the staff at Aston's Hall: "How can my father visit me if he doesn't exist?"'

An awkward silence settles on the room. Everyone knows what Marcus has been through.

'But wasn't six months rather hard for a first offence?' Eric asks naively. 'I mean Lucy didn't lay a hand on anyone, did she? When you think of what—'

Susie claws her hair and screams. Tom, horribly startled, begins to cry.

'That girl was on the station platform when Simon and I were beaten up!' Susan yells. Sobbing hysterically, she runs from the room, pursued by Brigid.

Marcus blows his broad nose and shakes his head. Eric sits stricken dumb. Nowadays he can't take any kind of stress or conflict.

Tom is calming down now. 'Train,' he says to Marcus.

Marcus winks at him. 'Yeah, train.'

'Single,' the boy says, pointing.

'You mean signal, Tom.'

'Single.'

Marcus chuckles. 'Yeah. That's what I said.' He turns back to Eric. 'Mountain bikes, Eric, that's the thing, eh. Big orders in the pipeline?'

'Not bad. And how are things with you, Marcus? Do you expect to be back at work soon?'

Marcus chuckles. 'Any day! Isn't that right, Tom? Any day.'

'Day,' the boy murmurs, absorbed by the train set.

Eric hesitates. 'I mean . . . no word about your reinstatement?'

'None.'

'Everyone wants you back on the Bench, Marcus.'

'Everyone, Eric? I could name you a few distinguished persons who aren't "everyone".'

Pulling dreamily on his pipe, Marcus ambles to the big Victorian window and looks out across Oundle Square.

'Lovely blossom,' he murmurs. Then he takes a brilliant big lemon from his pocket and offers it to Tom.

'Lemon,' he says. 'There will always be Lemons, Tom.'

'Why?'

'Because they grow on little trees.'

Tom carefully examines the lemon then lays it down on the carpet, tucking it between his legs. Tom Galloway has already forgotten what his father looked like.